MW01698198

# Dedication

I dedicate *REUNION* to my brothers, Peter Lodian Fuller and Harold Deen Fuller, and to all the men and women who put their lives on hold and traveled to faraway places to fight and die to defend our great country, the United States of America.

## Acknowledgements

I have many friends and relatives to thank for their help in getting my book ready. My friend, Elouise Fort, my granddaughter-in-law, Tara Gardner, and my son, John, all helped me get started. Encouragement from my sons, Peter, James and John, my niece Deborah Van Brunt, and my daughter-in-law, Pat, who would not let me quit and kept me on track. My dear late husband, Charles, gave me much needed support and encouragement. But most of all, I am indebted to my editors, Dan and Mary Hubley, for their patience and hard work in getting *REUNION* prepared for publication. I thank you all.

# Reunion

Elizabeth Ann Scott

Bluefish Bay Publishing • St. Augustine, FL

Reunion

Elizabeth Ann Scott

Copyright © 2003 Elizabeth Ann Scott

All rights reserved. No part of this publication may be reproduced, stored in a retrieval system or transmitted in any form or by any means electronic, mechanical, photocopying, recording, or otherwise, without the prior written permission of the publisher.

For additional copies call 813-695-8633

Published through:
Bluefish Bay Publishing
1093 A1A Beach Blvd., Suite 148
St. Augustine, FL 32080

www.bluefishbay.com

First edition

Publisher's Cataloging-in-Publication Data
(Prepared by The Donohue Group, Inc.)

Scott, Elizabeth Ann.
Reunion / Elizabeth Ann Scott.— 1st ed.
p. cm.
ISBN: 0-9707267-4-0
1. United States. Navy—Fiction. 2. World War, 1939-1945—Fiction. 3. Class reunions—Fiction. 4. Man-woman relationships—Fiction. 5. Alabama—Fiction. 6. Love stories. I. Title.

PS3569.C620 R48 2003
813'.54—dc21

# Table of Contents

# Reunion

## REVELATIONS

Alex Presswood was sitting in the back seat of his new Lincoln Towncar as it moved slowly through the outskirts of the sleepy little town of Atmore, Alabama. The sun, rapidly sinking into the western sky, created a spectacular pinkish glow across the broad horizon. Streetlights came on up and down Main Street. The car moved quietly down the once familiar street, across the railroad tracks, stopped for a red light and then continued into a parking space in front of the Escambia Drug Store.

Alex remained in the car, looking around, as his son, Jules, a tall, handsome man in his late forties, got out and hurried into the store. Jules' ten-year-old son, David, sat silently in the front seat. Jules hesitated at the store entrance and looked around. There were various displays of cosmetics, stationery, candies, magazines and books, and several showcases filled with a multitude of items made to relieve pain and give comfort to patients suffering from every imaginable malady. Then his eyes traveled to the back of the store where he saw the PRESCRIPTION sign. He made his way to the counter behind which stood a white-coated pharmacist. There were no other customers in the store.

"Hello, Doc," said the pharmacist in a friendly voice.

"Good evening," Jules answered, not realizing that he had been mistaken for a local physician.

"How is your mother?" the pharmacist asked.

"My mother passed away," Jules said without emotion since her death had occurred over a year ago. The pharmacist looked shocked. He stepped closer and looked at the man who stood across the counter.

"I must have you confused with someone else," he said. "You are not Dr. Anderson, are you?"

"No, I am Jules Presswood." His voice was unfamiliar to the druggist.

"Spitting image of the doctor. Uncanny!" he mumbled. Then he asked what he could do for Jules.

"I need an aerosol inhaler for my son who had an asthma attack. Could you sell me one without a prescription? We are visiting here and don't have a doctor to give us one."

"I'm sorry. I can't sell them without a prescription. Actually, I am out of them just now. I called in an order to our supplier in Mobile a couple of hours ago, but they won't be here until tomorrow morning. Why don't you take your son to the emergency room at the hospital? They will take care of him there."

"Could you direct me to the hospital?" Jules asked.

"Sure," the pharmacist answered, still a bit disturbed. He walked around the counter and stood next to Jules. He observed that Jules was just a little taller than Dr. Anderson.

"Go south to the second red light. Then turn left, for, let me see, about four blocks to the next red light, and turn right. Go south for a block and a half. The hospital is on the left and there are signs for the emergency room. It's no more than two miles from here."

The pharmacist followed Jules to the front door and pointed south, repeating the directions. "You can't miss it," he said. Then he locked the front door and walked to the back of the store.

Jules slipped into the driver's seat and started the car. He repeated the directions to his father who said, "They've moved the hospital. The old hospital was to the left of the first traffic light."

"You remember a lot about this town," Jules said.

"It doesn't seem to have changed much in fifty years, at least not downtown. Some of the stores are different. I noticed Elmore's isn't on the corner now and the bank has been moved to the center of the block over there," he said, nodding toward the bank. "But these stores along here look almost the same and the theater is in the same spot. Jules backed the car into the street and headed south.

"The Baptist Church is in about the same spot, but the building is new," Alex observed as they turned left on Horner Street. "I didn't see the beautiful old Patterson home though, nor the Goldsmith home."

Jules looked at David on the front seat. "How long has he been asleep?"

"I'm not asleep," David said. "Did you get me an inhaler?" Talking made him cough.

"You were so quiet. No, the pharmacist wouldn't sell me one without a prescription. We are taking you to the emergency room at the hospital."

David was coughing hard and wheezing when they reached the emergency room. They were met by a nurse who summoned a doctor. David was quickly wheeled to a room in the pediatric ward. He was immediately hooked up to oxygen. The relaxed look on David's face and the smile that followed after a breath or two of air erased the anxious expressions from the faces of the two men who stood beside the bed.

"That's better," David said. "Man, what a difference!"

"We'll keep him overnight," the doctor who introduced himself as Dr. Simmons, said. "I'll give him a light sedative so he'll get a good night's sleep."

"Don't leave me," David said.

"We'll stay right here," Jules answered. David was soon sleeping quietly.

"Why don't you go on out to the motel, Dad? I'll stay here with David."

"I hate to leave you," Alex said. "Let's get something to eat here and I'll go to the motel later."

They found the cafeteria and went through the line. Alex was surprised at the friendliness of everyone they met. Several people asked Jules if Alex was his father.

Alex and Jules talked about their trip from California. After dinner, Alex admitted to being tired and ready to go to the motel for the night.

"I'll see about getting a cot so I can sleep in David's room. I'd like to be there when he wakes up."

"I'll be back early tomorrow morning. I'll call Agnes tonight and let her know that everything is under control."

"Thanks, Dad. Tell her I'll call her tomorrow when we get back to the motel." Then Jules went to check on his son and made arrangements for a place to sleep. He was tired also and wanted to lie down, although it was still early evening. They had driven from

Jackson, Mississippi that day, changing drivers every few hours, so he was anxious to stretch out. The trip had become more stressful after David's inhaler ran out and he had no help with his breathing. This had happened in Biloxi, about eighty miles from Atmore. They were traveling on U.S. Route 10, making good time, so Jules opted to continue to Atmore rather than search for a drug store in unfamiliar territory. When he was quiet, David seldom needed his inhaler.

David began coughing and wheezing soon after they reached the motel in Atmore, making it imperative that an inhaler or another device be secured at once to give him relief. Thus, they ended up in the Atmore Hospital.

A cot was brought in for Jules and he fell on it at once. Sleep came quickly and father and son passed the night together, resting peacefully.

The next morning, Jules met his father in the waiting room. He left David playing a computer game in the recreation area, completely recovered from the asthmatic attack he had experienced the day before.

A man entered the room and stopped at the desk. He asked for information about his mother, Jeannie Anderson.

"Dr. Simmons is with your mother now, but he would like to speak with you. I will call you when he comes out," the receptionist said.

Dr. Daniel Anderson absentmindedly picked up a magazine and sat down. Glancing around the small waiting room, he noticed that the man sitting across from him looked exactly like himself. Jules looked up and their eyes met. They stared at each other for a moment, and then they both smiled.

The newcomer extended his hand. "I am Dr. Daniel Anderson."

"Jules Presswood."

"You look familiar." Daniel said, "You must be the reason I have been asked such strange questions this morning. When I was in the drugstore, I was told that my inhaler had arrived from Mobile. I don't need an inhaler. I was asked how my son was getting along. I don't have a son."

"And I was asked how my mother was," Jules said. "My mother passed away over a year ago, and nobody here knew her anyway."

Then Jules introduced his father. Alex stood up and shook hands with Daniel Anderson.

"You certainly do favor my son," he said. "I was born and raised here in Atmore, Daniel. Perhaps you are a distant relative. Tell us something about yourself."

"My mother is Jeannie Carlson Anderson. My father was Walter Anderson. He died several years ago," Daniel said.

"Jeannie Carlson! Jeannie Carlson? I don't believe it. You are Jeannie Carlson's son?" Alex looked as if he had seen a ghost. He put his hand to his head as he began to swoon.

"Do you know my mother? Are you related to her?" Daniel asked.

"I think I knew her." He asked Daniel how old he was.

"Forty-nine," Daniel said. He was looking from one man to the other, trying to think of a reason for this query.

"Your mother is here, in this hospital?" Alex asked, his voice quivering anxiously. "Jeannie is here?"

"Yes, she was brought in last night. I had gone to Montgomery. Her doctor brought her in while I was away. He keeps a close check on her."

"Why is she here?" Alex asked anxiously.

"My mother has emphysema. She started smoking when she was in high school and just couldn't give up her cigarettes until she got the disease. She's admitted to the hospital when she has difficulty breathing. We hope to avoid an operation which would be painful and debilitating for her."

Alex exclaimed, "Jeannie has emphysema!" He couldn't believe what he was hearing. "Oh my God!" he sat down and put his head in his hands.

Jules stared at his father. "What happened?" he asked, looking from his father to the man who could have been his twin. "What is the matter, Pop?"

Daniel put his hand on the other man's shoulder. He, too, looked as if he had seen a ghost. "I think I know," he said. Daniel was about to tell Jules something his father had revealed to him a short time before his death when he heard someone call his name.

"I'll see you later," he said. "I have to talk to my mother's doctor now. Where are you staying?"

"We are at the Best Western, a few miles north of here," Jules had time to say. "Ask for Alex Presswood." Daniel leaned over and spoke in Alex's ear. "I think I know who you are. Do you know who I am?"

"I don't know," Alex had a confused look on his face.

"I'll see you later," Daniel said as he walked down the hall toward his mother's room. Dr. Simmons stood beside the door. The two doctors shook hands and Daniel asked about his mother's condition.

"Jeannie had some difficulty breathing yesterday, so we brought her in and gave her a little extra oxygen. She rested all night so I think it is safe to let her go home. She must rest more and take her time breathing. One thing she must overcome is becoming frightened when she can't catch her breath. She just needs to relax and concentrate on breathing normally. Fear is her worst enemy."

"Thank you, Bill," David said. " I will take care of getting her home."

Then he walked in and greeted his mother who apologized for the trouble she was causing.

"You did the right thing, Mother. Call the doctor anytime you feel upset. Just try not to panic because that aggravates your condition."

"I will try," Jeannie promised.

"Mother, do you know a man named Alex Presswood?"

Jeannie looked shocked. "Yes. I used to know someone by that name," she said. "Why do you ask?"

"Well, I met a man in the waiting room who looks exactly like me. He was with his father. His father's name is Alex Presswood".

"Oh, Daniel, I will have to tell you something that will be very upsetting for you." She looked at Daniel. Then she put her hands over her face. "No! I can't tell you. I can't tell you." She began to cry.

Daniel let her cry for a minute or two, and then he said softly, "I already know, Mother. Daddy told me before he died."

"You know about Alex?"

"Daddy didn't tell me the name of my biological father. He said that if you ever wanted me to know, you would tell me. But I am sure the man in the waiting room is my biological father."

"What is he doing here in the hospital?" Jeannie asked.

"I don't know. He must be here with someone. I have an idea it's an asthma patient."

"His wife?"

"No, I think his wife is dead. His son, Jules, mentioned that his mother passed away."

"Is he still here?" Jeannie asked.

"Yes, I left him in the lobby. Do you want to see him?"

"I would like to see Alex. We were good friends. More than that, we had planned to be married. It was during the war, World War II. He was in the Navy. I haven't seen or heard from him for fifty years. I married your daddy and completely broke off with Alex."

"Did you tell him that you were expecting a baby? Does he know about me?"

"No, I didn't want him to know."

"Are you sure you want to see him now?"

"Yes, I want to tell him what happened. He deserves to know," Jeannie said. Then she asked, "How do I look?"

"Changed, I am sure," Daniel said seriously. Daniel went to the waiting room to talk with Alex, but he was not there. He hurried across the empty waiting room to the desk.

"Mr. Presswood was in the waiting room a few minutes ago. Do you know where he is now?" Daniel asked the nurse.

"I believe they went down to the children's ward, Doctor," the nurse said. "The younger man certainly looks like you. Are you related?"

"Possibly," was the only thing Daniel could think to say. He felt nervous as he walked down the hall toward the pediatric ward. He had extremely mixed emotions about what had been revealed in the past fifteen minutes. It was as if his whole life was taking on new dimensions.

When Daniel reached the children's ward, he saw Alex and Jules talking to a young boy about ten years old. The boy was telling them about a new computer game that he had been playing. They were waiting for the doctor to come and release him.

"Oh, hello again," Jules said when he saw Daniel in the

doorway. "This is my son, David. He is the reason we are here today."

"How do you do?" Daniel said to the boy as they shook hands. Turning to Jules, he asked, "How is he doing?"

"He is fine now. These attacks leave him tired and weak, but usually after a good, long rest, he is up and going again."

Then he put his hand on Alex's shoulder and said, "Sir, my mother would like to speak to you. Would you come with me?"

Alex walked unsteadily beside Daniel, unable to comprehend what was happening. His greatest hopes and dreams for this vacation were about to be realized, and he felt anxious and excited. Yet, the realization that the man walking beside him, this man whom he had met only minutes ago could be his son, was totally beyond his grasp. In a flash, he understood what had happened fifty years ago, but he did not know why he had not been told. He and Daniel did not talk as they virtually ran down the corridor. Each man had a million questions, but they knew they must wait for the woman to answer them.

Daniel stopped outside the door, giving his mother and this man a few moments alone. Alex bent over and kissed Jeannie. They just looked at each other, trying to see some inkling of the person they had known fifty years ago. Both of them had changed over the years, actually beyond recognition. Both were well preserved. Jeannie was still so beautiful it took his breath away. Alex was more handsome than she remembered.

Jeannie said, "Hi! I am sorry we had to meet in the hospital." She smiled and reached her hand out to him. Alex paid no attention to the huge diamond she was wearing on her left hand. Suddenly Alex felt woozy. He looked at the oxygen tank that stood beside her bed. An enormous sense of guilt overcame him, remembering that it was he who had asked Jeannie to take that first smoke with him when they were in high school.

"Jeannie, this is entirely my fault," he said, wiping tears from his eyes. "I did this to you. I asked you to start smoking with me."

"Don't blame yourself, Alex," Jeannie said. "We didn't know the real danger then. We were so young. I should have quit smoking long ago, but I didn't want to."

## Reunion

Then Je nnie said, "Alex, you met your son?"

"You kept this from me all of these years. You gave me no hint in your last letter that you were having my baby. I hated you for what you did. Now, I know that was my fault too. What misery I have brought to your life, and I never knew. I loved you. I worshiped you. And I hurt you. I hurt you so badly. How could I have been so wrong?"

"When I found out that I was pregnant, you were in the Navy, about to leave the States. I didn't know where you were going or when you would come back. I did what I had to do Alex. I told no one what really happened, except your mother, and I made her promise not to tell you or anybody else, ever. I had to do it."

"I had hoped to see you when I came home for the reunion. I hoped you could explain to me why you had suddenly decided that you didn't love me." Alex was on his knees beside the bed. "But I did not expect this. I did not dream that I had caused you so much grief. I am so sorry." He dropped his head to the bed and sobbed.

"I am glad that you finally know the truth. I didn't want to hurt you, but I didn't know what to do," Jeannie whispered.

"How can I make it up to you?" Alex said. "I love you, Jeannie. I always have."

"It has been a long time, Alex. So much has happened to both of us."

"I want you to tell me all about it. I want to know what you did, how you managed and what your life has been like."

"My doctor said I could go home this afternoon. I am much better today. I just have to rest. Will you come by to see me? I am living in my parents' old home."

"I will be waiting for you when you get home."

"Are you going to the dinner tonight, Alex?" Jeannie asked.

"Yes, and I would like to take you. What time shall I pick you up?"

"Alex, I am sorry, but I already have a date," she said. "I didn't even know you were coming. An old friend, Bill Simmons, is taking me."

"You are going with me, Jeannie. Bill Simmons will have to find another girl."

"We'll talk about that when I see you this afternoon. We have so much to catch up on. I want you to become acquainted with Danny. Meeting you was a shock to him."

"I think I am still in shock myself."

"I am so excited about the reunion, Alex. It has been fifty years, can you believe it? Fifty years since we have all been together. I have been thinking about it for weeks, never dreaming that you would be here."

"I don't know how much more excitement I can stand," Alex said as he bent over and kissed her goodbye. "I'll see you this afternoon."

Daniel was still standing outside the door. "I will see you later," he said to his mother.

*This has to be the most wonderful day of my life. Not only have I found my precious Jeannie again, but I discovered that I have a son whom I never knew existed. How could something like this happen*? Alex thought.

Daniel grabbed Alex and hugged him. They stood holding each other in a manly embrace for a whole minute, tears flowing down their cheeks.

At last Daniel said, "We will get it all sifted out when we have time to talk. Mother will have to fill us in on the details, but I have learned the answers to questions that have bothered me for many years."

Daniel walked down the hall with Alex leaving his arm on Alex's shoulder. Then giving his father another quick hug, he said, "I am taking Mother home this afternoon. You may come over about two, after she has had time to rest."

Alex found Jules and David in the lobby, ready to leave. "I have a prescription for an inhaler. Could we stop at the drug store to pick one up?"

"Of course, but let's drive by the high school first," Alex said. "I'd like to see what condition the old building is in."

Alex drove past the school, trying to take it all in. He remembered the tall white columns, the windows, the trees, the flagpole, and the sidewalks leading to the front steps from three directions.

## Reunion

Amazingly, everything was just as he had remembered it, except some of the large trees in front of the school were gone. Alex slowed down and turned into a driveway. He turned the car around and drove back slowly. He parked in front of the building and opened the door. He got out of the car and put his feet carefully, almost reverently on ground he had not touched for fifty years. He walked thoughtfully up the sidewalk, observing every detail as he had done that first day at Escambia County High School over half a century ago. Jules and David waited in the car as he immersed himself in the memory of those long ago, almost forgotten years when he was growing up in the little town of Atmore, Alabama.

## *GROWING UP IN ATMORE*
## ALEX ENTERS E. C. H. S.

Alex Presswood stepped down from the bus and glanced around. The feeling of anticipation quickly turned to awe as he followed the group of students up the sidewalk toward the huge Greek columns that marked the entrance to Escambia County High School. It was 1938. Alex had just turned thirteen and was entering junior high school. He had looked forward to this moment for a long time and was excited that this day had finally come.

Alex walked through the door alone. Students who had arrived with him on the bus had dispersed into the crowd. They chatted with friends they had not seen since May. His friend, Jim, joined him. They made their way down the hall to the large auditorium.

Passing the principal's office, they got their first glimpse of Mr. Hodnette, who sat at his desk smoking a cigarette and reading the morning newspaper. They walked a little faster when he cleared his throat. "Ahem," they heard.

When the bell rang, students rushed into the auditorium. Nobody wanted to be late on the first day of school. All of the noise subsided when the next bell rang. The door opened and Mr. Hodnette walked to the front of the huge room. Nothing could be heard but his footsteps as he made his way up to the stage.

Mr. Hodnette had everyone's attention before he said a word. Before welcoming the students and introducing the teachers, he led The Lord's Prayer and the pledge to the flag. Everyone sang "The Star Spangled Banner" and the "Alma Mater." He talked about school rules and punishment for breaking them, made a few announcements, and dismissed the classes one at a time.

No one spoke as students left the auditorium. Talking at an assembly or in the halls was forbidden. Alex's class, the largest one in school, followed their teacher, Miss Wallace, to their classroom on the second floor.

Alex looked around the room, hoping to see faces he recognized.

He saw his friend, Jeannie, and waved to her. She waved back. He spotted Bill and Willie and several other boys and girls who were in his sixth grade class. Other students had come from different elementary schools in the vicinity.

The class of more than one hundred was divided into three sections- A, B, and C. Alex, Jeannie, Bill Simmons and thirty others were placed in Section A. After announcements and assignments, they were instructed to go to their first class. Student guides were on hand to accompany each section to their first classroom.

Alex studied his schedule. He discovered that the day was divided into eight periods. He had three classes, math, English, history, and two study halls in the morning; and science, and two study halls in the afternoon. He felt good about his schedule. He'd have plenty of time to do his homework assignments in study hall.

At noon everyone went outside to eat lunches they had brought from home. Alex joined a group of boys under a large oak tree and listened to Horace Bailey, an older, popular student, talking about Mr. Hodnette. He told about the time Mr. Hodnette was on the stage talking when he began to beat himself on the leg. He thrust his hand into his pocket and drew out his pipe, which was smoking. The audience all laughed. Mr. Hodnette's face turned red. "I nearly caught my britches on fire," he laughed and went on with his speech. All of the boys laughed.

The story reminded Alex of the cigarette he had found on the bus that morning. He got up slowly and walked away from the group. Nobody noticed him. He looked around for a place to hide. He spotted the incinerator and walked over to it. He crouched down, crept behind it, and sat on a cement slab. He slipped the cigarette out of his pocket, put it between his lips, and lit it with a match he had been carrying in his pocket. He sucked in hard like he had seen his dad do and blew the smoke out. Two puffs and he was reeling. He was snuffing the cigarette out on the cement when he heard a voice. His hair stood on end. His first thought was that it was Mr. Hodnette, but he realized that it was Bill Simmons. Almost as bad.

"I caught you, Presswood. I'm gonna tell Mr. Hodnette!"

"No! No! Don't tell him!" Alex exclaimed. "Don't tell on me. I won't do it again."

Bill stood over him with an evil look in his eye. "Give me five bucks and I won't."

"I don't have five bucks."

"Yes you do. I saw you counting it this morning."

"That's my book money." Alex's head was spinning. "I can't give you my book money!"

"Give me the money and I won't tell," Bill repeated.

"No!" Bill started walking toward the schoolhouse.

"All right." Alex threw the money at Bill's feet.

"Pick it up." Bill commanded.

Alex picked up the bills and handed them to him.

"That's more like it," Bill smirked.

Alex forced himself to get up. He stood for a few minutes, clinging to the incinerator for support. Finally, he felt strong enough to walk to the building. His head was still swimming, but he managed to make his way to the door where everybody was lining up. After standing for a few minutes, he began to feel better.

Later, in study hall, he thought about it. Alex needed that money for his books. He looked at the branches of a tall tree growing just outside the window. He placed his head in his hands. He got an idea. He jumped up, got a pass from the teacher, and ran to Mr. Hodnette's office.

"What can I do for you?" Mr. Hodnette asked without looking up.

"I've got to get my money back," Alex spoke barely above a whisper. He trembled with fright. He didn't realize that Mr. Hodnette was so big. His eyes were steel blue. His face was severe and unsmiling. He continued reading a letter in his shaky hand. Alex waited patiently.

At last Mr. Hodnette looked at Alex. "What money?"

"Bill Simmons made me give me him my book money."

"Why?"

"He caught me smoking and said he would tell you if I didn't give him five dollars."

"Smoking on the school grounds?"

Alex nodded.

"Speak up."

"Yes, Sir."

"I'll cut your conduct ten points for that," he said. "Now, go back to class."

Alex was stunned. Mr. Hodnette wasn't going to help. He wanted to scream out "What about my money?" but he was too scared to utter a word. He made his way back to study hall and sat down. He was in a daze for the rest of the day.

Just before the dismissal bell, Alex was summoned to Mr. Hodnette's office. Bill Simmons was standing there looking unhappy. Without a word, he handed Alex his money. Mr. Hodnette gave Bill a note for his parents to sign. Both boys were dismissed.

Alex met Jeannie in the hall. "What happened?"

"Nothing really," he said. "Nothing."

"You look like something is wrong." She had noticed the grim look on Alex's face in science class.

"I lost my book money and Bill found it. I got it back."

"I'm glad you got it back," she said as she walked ahead of him to the bus.

A line of students was waiting to board the bus. Girls lined up in front, boys behind them. It seemed strange to Alex that girls took the front seats and the boys had to stumble over their feet and knees to get to the back. *Girls always want to be first*, he thought.

Mr. Marshall finally drove up, opened the door, and everybody climbed on. Alex's sisters, Liz and Marge, were seated before he got on. Jeannie and Peggy sat together. He looked for Jed, his little brother, who was picked up at the elementary school along with Marge and others. He sat down beside Jim.

The five-mile ride to Canoe gave everybody a chance to unwind and talk with friends. The bus wasn't crowded because several of the larger boys stayed after school to practice football.

When the Presswood children got home, their mother had milk and cookies for them. They ate their snacks, changed their clothes, and headed for the cotton field. Daddy had instructed them to pick at least one row of cotton each before they did their other chores.

"Cotton picking is almost over," Alex said. They had already picked over the field two times, but they had to go over it once more. All of the bolls did not open at the same time, so they had to continue picking until every boll had opened. "We'll have it all done by the end of the week."

"I'm so tired of picking cotton," Liz said.

"Me too," Alex said. "But everything we do is a big help to Mom and Dad. We wouldn't have food to eat if we didn't raise it."

"We don't eat cotton," Marge said. Everybody laughed.

"You know Daddy sells the cotton to buy clothes and stuff."

"It's hard to make a living on a farm," Liz said. "I'm not going to be a farmer when I grow up."

"I'm not either," Alex said. "I'm going to be a doctor." He stopped and stood up. He noticed the pink glow in the western sky and the darkening light. "Let's pick one more row. Then we'll be done."

"I'm too tired," Jed said. He wiped a tear from his eye.

"We'll help you," Alex said, patting Jed on the back.

Mama walked down to the field to see what was taking the children so long. She found them by following their hats flying in the air and their happy shouts. "We're done, we're done, no more cotton! Not another boll! Hoorah! Hoorah!" They ran to the cotton house, tossed their sacks in the door, and slammed it shut. They ran to Mama, laughing and shouting.

Jed kept going up the path and opened the gate for the cows. One of the older cows let him ride her to the barn. Alex milked while Liz and Marge fed the chickens and gathered eggs. Jed brought in wood for the cook stove. Daddy drove up just as they were sitting down to eat.

Conversation at the table was lively. The other children talked about meeting their new teachers and seeing their old friends. All Alex could think about was his experience with the cigarette, but he had no intention of sharing that. Daddy was pleased that the last row of cotton had been picked.

"Tomorrow, you can start pulling the corn," he said. After a few moments of silence, Daddy said, "Actually, you need to buy your books tomorrow, don't you?" Everyone nodded. "Come over to my office after school and we'll go together. But tonight, take a look at the books we already have and see if there are some you can use." He added to Liz, "Maybe you can find some second-hand books. Alex and Marge should be able to use your old ones. We'll save a lot of money if you can find used ones."

"I don't have to buy any books," Jed announced. "The school has been getting them. They are up to the fourth grade this year, so I don't need any."

"That's wonderful," Daddy and Mama said together.

*TROUBLE ON THE SCHOOL BUS*

After football season was over, the older boys began riding the bus. They picked on the younger ones. They pulled their hair, thumped their ears, snapped them with rubber bands, pushed them to the floor, and worst of all, they grabbed them, dragged them to the back of the bus, and pulled their pants down. Then they called the girls to look. The younger boys kicked and screamed and lashed out with their fists, but it didn't stop them. Every day they picked on a different kid.

Bill Simmons thought that he wouldn't be bothered because he wore glasses, but one day he was "it". As he was dragged to the back, his glasses were knocked off. Alex, who tried to dodge his flailing arms and legs, lost his balance and stepped down hard on Bill's glasses, crushing them to bits.

Quiet fell over the bus like a blanket. The boys released Bill. When Bill realized what had happened and saw Alex's shoe on his shattered glasses, he went into a rage.

"Presswood, you have to buy me a new pair of glasses," he screamed. "They cost twelve dollars and fifty cents. I can't do my homework without them."

"It wasn't my fault," Alex cried. "I didn't knock them off."

"You stomped on them."

"I don't have twelve dollars and fifty cents," Alex said.

"You'll do it," Bill said, and sat down.

Willie Ray Peoples sat down beside Alex. "Do you have any money?"

"Only $1.78. It was for Christmas."

"I'll give you $1.85." Willie went to Buddy Rawles. "Alex ain't got that much money. It wasn't really his fault. Everybody ought to pitch in."

"You're right," Buddy said. Buddy had been the instigator. He reached in his pocket, pulled out a dollar, and handed it to Willie. Buddy turned to Steve who was sitting next to him and said, "Give him a dollar." All the boys pitched in. Willie handed Alex a handful of bills and change just as the bus reached his house.

Alex murmured, "Thanks." He made his way to the front of the bus as Mr. Marshall was closing the door.

"You'll have to move faster," Mr. Marshall said. "You take longer to get off the bus than anyone."

Alex ran straight to his room. He threw the money on the bed and counted it. He had $9.26. He added his Christmas savings of $1.78.

"Alex," Marge called from the kitchen. "We have to take some corn to the mill. Mama is out of meal and we have to go right now."

"Come here a minute," he called back. He told her what had happened.

"I have a quarter and a penny." She handed Alex twenty-six cents.

Alex now had $11.30. He'd have to owe Mr. Simmons the rest. "Let's get the corn and go before it gets dark." They hurried to the corncrib.

When they came out of the crib, a car was parked in the driveway. It was Jeannie. She called to Alex, "I left my math book at school. May I borrow yours so I can finish my homework?"

"Sure," Alex said. Jeannie followed him into the house. She handed Alex a handful of coins. "Willie told me what happened. I don't need the book. I just had to have an excuse for my brother to bring me over here."

"I can't take your money."

"You can pay me back when you get it." She dashed out of the house with Alex's book in her hand. "I'll give your book back tomorrow," she said loud enough for her brother to hear.

Alex and Marge ran to the gristmill. When they were out of sight of the house, they stopped and counted the money. "We have $13.20," Alex smiled. "Boy! I wish it was all mine."

# Reunion

They reached the mill and stumbled in the door. Mr. Simmons took their bag and poured the corn into the hopper. When he turned the switch on, the kernels hopped about as the grinders pulverized them. It took only a minute or two to grind a peck of meal.

"Is Bill here?" Alex asked.

"No, he went home after school."

Alex nervously told Mr. Simmons about the glasses. "I have $12.50 to pay for them." He offered the money to Mr. Simmons.

"Them glasses didn't cost but $6."

"Just six dollars?" Alex exclaimed.

"That's right."

Alex counted out the money and handed it to Mr. Simmons.

"Was you boys fightin'?"

"No, Sir. His glasses just fell off and I stepped on them."

"Thank you," Mr. Simmons said. "Lots of boys wouldn't have paid for them."

Alex and Marge hurried out of the door. Alex thought about the money in his pocket. "I'll be able to pay some people back," he said. "I don't know what everybody put in. I'll try to find out."

The next morning, Bill sat down beside Alex on the bus. Alex started to push him out of the seat, but Bill said, "Wait a minute. I have something to tell you." Alex stopped pushing.

"My daddy told me to 'pologize for asking for too much money. He made me tell him all that happened." He whispered in Alex's ear, "It ain't gonna happen again."

"What?" Alex looked surprised.

"My daddy is going to see Mr. Hodnette today. We won't have our pants pulled down any more." Bill grinned importantly.

"You'd better not let anybody else know you squealed," Alex warned.

Bill moved over and sat beside Jim. Jeannie was in the seat in front of Alex. She handed him his math book. "I can pay you back," he whispered. He put $1.90 in her hand.

"Thanks," she said.

Alex gave Willie $1.85. Then he gave Buddy and Steve a dollar each. "Who gets the rest?"

"Just keep it," Willie said. "I don't know who else put in money."

## *HONOR ROLL*

Alex was disappointed in his first semester grades. He had hoped to make honor roll, but his science and history grades were too low. He did pass, but that was not good enough. He'd have to study harder.

Jeannie was in line just ahead of Alex at the Coke machine. She dropped her nickel and Alex picked it up for her. "How were your grades this semester?" Alex asked her.

"I made honor roll. Just. My average was exactly 90. How did you do?"

"87," Alex admitted. She looked surprised. "You usually beat me. What happened?"

"I fell down in history and science," Alex said. "I like history, but I can't remember all of those dates. And I get so sleepy in science that I can't concentrate."

"I do too," Jeannie said. "Maybe if we took a little nap in study hall before science, we wouldn't get so sleepy." They both laughed.

"I don't think I can sleep sitting up. And I usually study for science that period."

"We'll think of something." They got their Cokes and left.

That afternoon, Jeannie sat down beside Alex on the bus. "I've thought of a way to help remember dates," she said. She had Alex's attention. "When you come to a date in your reading, write it down. When you finish reading, go back and write what happened beside each date. Start at the first of each chapter and continue to the end. We just started a new chapter, so start writing the dates tonight and do it every night. Maybe that will help you."

"Good idea," Alex said. "What do you think about science? Can you find the constellations?"

"Not really."

"Me either, but I can usually find the North Star."

"You'll have to show me sometime."

When Alex got home, his mother said, "Hitch the mule up to the cart. Daddy hired two men to cut down trees for firewood. He needs you and Jed to haul it to the house." Alex changed his clothes and put on his coat. Mama said, "The girls will help you unload and stack the wood. I'll help too."

Alex had the mule ready to go in a few minutes. Jed jumped on beside him.

"I want to go," Marge said. She had already changed her clothes.

"Go on, but be careful," Mama said.

The men helped them put a load of wood on the cart. When they got back to the house, Liz and Mama helped to unload. "You go back for another load while we stack," Mama said.

It took longer for the second load because everyone was tired. The woodcutters walked back with the boys and helped unload he cart. Mama paid them for the day's work, seventy-five cents each. "We'll be back tomorrow," they said.

"Get your chores done and then you can study," Mama said to the children. "I'll get supper ready."

Alex opened his history book first. Remembering what Jeannie had suggested, he took out a clean sheet of paper and wrote the first date, 1492, the year Columbus discovered America. He wrote the dates of and names of the people involved in the four voyages and the names of the ships and their cargo.

Alex checked his math and passed over his literature book because he had read his assignment already. He picked up his science book and read about the constellations. He went outside to see if he could find Orion. He lay down in the field and tried to locate stars that matched the ones described in his book. He recognized the Big and Little Dippers and he found the North Star. He studied the night's sky a little longer before he went to bed.

Alex's average for the fourth six-week period was 91. He had made Honor Roll, but he still did not beat Jeannie's average of 93. "You beat me again," Alex laughed. "Just wait till next time."

School got out in May, just in time to start planting the late corn. Daddy had already broken ground, run the harrow over it, and was ready to plow the rows.

Alex, Marge, and Liz dropped kernels of corn into the damp furrows. Daddy plowed dirt lightly over them. It took a whole day.

"We'll plant the peanuts next week," Daddy said. "We should have everything in the ground by the end of the week, except for sweet potatoes and the sugar cane.

*Then we can relax*, Alex thought, but Daddy went on. "Then we'll start chopping cotton and hoeing weeds. We can't let the weeds get ahead of us."

The summer was over before they realized it. There hadn't been much time for fun though they did get to go swimming and had a fishing trip. Then it was time to go back to school.

Alex was determined to make good grades, right from the start. He paid attention in class, did his homework and didn't let unruly kids distract him.

His friend, Horace Bailey, was the class clown. He tried to attract attention. He regularly visited Mr. Hodnette's office. He said he'd rather sit in the office and watch everything that went on than be bored in a classroom, even if it meant a few whacks on the butt by Mr. Hodnette's paddle. Alex told him what he had missed in class when Horace delivered papers in the evening. They often did their homework together before Horace completed his paper route. It helped both boys keep up. When grades came out at the end of the first marking period, Alex discovered that he had made the Honor Roll. He committed himself to doing as well all year.

## *THE SNIPE HUNT*

One cold day in late October, the students were dismissed at noon because the teachers had to attend a countywide meeting. They were thrilled when their fifth period teachers announced the early release. Students who lived in town walked home as usual. Alex's bus was not due to arrive at school until the usual time, so most of the girls walked home with friends in town or visited relatives for the afternoon. The boys just hung around to talk and pick at each other.

Buddy Rawles and Steve Dunn walked up and asked, "How would you boys like to go on a snipe hunt?" Steve was holding an old burlap bag. The younger boys were surprised that Buddy had spoken to them. They looked at the ground. Alex kicked a stone and Willie and Jim bumped shoulders. "What's a snipe hunt?" Bill finally asked.

"Well," Buddy said, "we go out into the woods and look for a snipe. We were studying about snipes in science and I thought maybe we'd like to go out and find one. We have plenty of time."

"What's a snipe?" Bill asked.

"It's a little animal that lives in the woods. It's a little bigger than a squirrel. You want to go?"

"I guess so." Bill looked at the others to see if they would go too. One by one they nodded their heads and followed Buddy and Steve into the woods.

Alex felt apprehensive when they reached an unfamiliar field. He paused. He sniffed the air. There was a faint, sweet odor coming from the woods. He saw a cloud of dark smoke. "I know where we are," he said to Willie. "There's a sugar cane mill over there. I've been there with my dad. Mr. Henshaw makes syrup for people who grow sugar cane."

They came to a clearing. The mill was just ahead. They watched a man drive two mules that were hitched to a shaft that turned two grinding wheels. As the mules pulled the shaft around in a circle, the wheels turned. Another man fed long purple stalks of cane between the grinders. Juice squeezed out and flowed into a five-gallon bucket on the ground.

They stood mesmerized watching the manufacture of the sweet stuff. They saw a bucket fill up, and the workers pour the juice into barrels. Two barrels were covered with a mesh cloth that kept yellow jackets out of the juice. Mr. Henshaw drained syrup from a large cooking vat into tin buckets. Helpers covered the buckets with lids and crimped them on tight. When Mr. Henshaw finished emptying the vat, the boys walked up.

"Why aren't you boys in school?" Mr. Henshaw asked.

"Early dismissal," Buddy explained.

"Where are you going?"

"Down by the creek to look for snipes."

Mr. Henshaw smiled. "Want a drink of cane juice?"

Buddy said, "Sure." Mr. Henshaw took a long-handled dipper from a nail on a tree. He filled it with juice and handed it to Buddy, who took a drink and passed it on. The dipper went around a couple of times, each boy taking a drink and smacking his lips when they tasted the cool, delicious juice. Then Buddy said he'd better be on his way. All of the boys smiled and thanked Mr. Henshaw.

"Help yourselves to a stalk of cane," Mr. Henshaw said.

"Thanks," Buddy said, and each boy pulled one out of the pile.

When they reached the creek bank, Buddy stopped. He told them to gather around and he would explain the plan.

"We'll spread out on this side of the creek and somebody will go over there and drive the snipe out. We'll catch him when he comes across the creek." He glanced around at the boys. "Bill, you take this stick and go across the creek. Yell and scream and beat the bushes and old dead logs and he'll come running out. We'll be waiting." Then he yelled, "Spread out, Boys."

Bill took the stick and headed for the creek. The boys soon lost sight of him because the trees and bushes grew thick along the bank. Bill glanced at the swimming hole, but skirted around it. He stepped on roots and stumps and jumped over puddles as he carefully made his way across. When he reached the other side, he beat bushes and stumps. He screamed and made a lot of noise.

When Buddy heard the shouts, he dropped the sack and motioned for the other boys to follow him. They raced through the woods back toward the school. At last he stopped and the others caught up with him.

"What's going on?" Alex asked. "Did we catch a snipe?"

Buddy laughed and laughed. "There is no snipe. It's a joke on Bill. He'll stay over there beating the bushes until he's tired. Then he'll come back across the creek, find the sack, and know it is all a joke." The boys thought it was hilarious. They fell on the ground laughing.

Bill took his part in the hunt seriously. He yelled and screamed, beat the bushes, and tried to scare the animal out. Then his stick hit an old hollow tree, which disturbed a colony of hornets. Within seconds, Bill was covered with angry, stinging hornets. They stung his face, hands, neck, and arms. They went down his shirt and stung his back. He slapped at them and tried to chase them away, but they stuck to him. Bill screamed. He called for help. He ran toward the creek, trying to find his way across, stumbling blindly over rocks and roots and bumping into trees as he tried to escape from the angry horde of insects.

# Reunion

Bill remembered the swimming hole he had passed on his way across the creek. He headed for the creek and plunged into the cold water. He stayed in the water just long enough to free himself from the flying monsters. Shivering violently, he climbed out of the water.

Bill was in agony. He called to his friends. No one answered. He stumbled over an old burlap sack lying on the ground and kicked it aside. He couldn't understand what had happened to Buddy and the other boys. He tried to remember where he was and how to get back to school.

A puff of wind carried the scent of boiling cane juice. Through half-closed eyes, Bill saw smoke in the distance. He knew he could find help at the mill. He wanted to fall down on the ground and cry, but he knew he had to make it to the mill. Not only was Bill throbbing with pain from stings all over his body, but he was trembling from the cold water. His clothes clung to his body and chilled him to the bone.

At the edge of the clearing, Bill fell to his knees and crawled to where Mr. Henshaw was stirring syrup. Mr. Henshaw heard Bill cry out and ran to him. One look and Mr. Henshaw knew what had happened. "You went to look for the snipe, didn't you?"

"Yes," Bill said.

Mr. Henshaw and his helpers carried Bill to his truck and put him in the cab. "Stay here and take care of things," he said to one of the men as he started the truck. "I'll take the boy to the hospital."

"What is your name?" Mr. Henshaw asked.

"Bill Simmons," was the faint reply. "My daddy works at the cotton gin in Canoe."

"I'm taking you to the hospital, Bill. I'll get word to your papa. You're in pretty bad shape, but we'll get you fixed up." Bill lay his head back and rested his already closed eyes. He ran his hand over his face and neck and felt the welts forming. It helped to know that he was being rushed to the hospital as fast as Mr. Henshaw's truck could go, but the excruciating pain was almost more than he could endure. Luckily, the hospital was close to the cane mill. Within twenty minutes of his reaching the mill site, Bill was being wheeled into the emergency room. Dr. Lisenby gave Bill an injection to calm him down and to help him go to sleep. He told the nurses how to remove the stingers from his body and how to reduce the swelling. Finally, Bill was wheeled to a private room and put in bed.

"Bill could develop pneumonia because of the exposure. I am glad he doesn't already have a cold, but one could easily develop. This is not the season for swimming, but jumping into that water hole may have saved his life," Dr. Lisenby said.

The group of snipe hunters had reached the bus stop at school long before the bus was to arrive. They sat and talked, but kept a watchful eye for Bill. They continued to laugh about the trick they had played on Bill and everyone agreed that he deserved it. Buddy, who had masterminded the plan, kept repeating the story to everyone and laughed hilariously each time he told it.

Alex felt a little uneasy as time passed and Bill had not made his way back to school. He thought that something may have happened to Bill. A snake could have bitten him. An escaped convict could have attacked him. He could have fallen and broken his leg. A hunter could have mistaken him for an animal and shot him. An angry bull could have attacked him. After an hour, they were all worried. The boys tried to reassure each other.

"Maybe someone he knew came along and picked him up," Willie suggested.

"What should we do?" Alex said.

"Don't be paranoid, Presswood," Buddy said. "He'll be back in a few minutes. He's just trying to scare us. He can take care of himself."

"I'm going to look for him anyway. If the bus gets here before I get back, I'll get a ride home." Alex darted off toward the woods where they had last seen Bill.

"I'm going with you." Willie dashed off in the same direction as Alex.

When Alex smelled the sweet fragrance of the cane mill and saw the smoke, he ran toward it. Willie was right on his heels.

The boys did not see Mr. Henshaw, but the workers were there. The boys jogged up to the mule driver and asked him if he had seen their classmate.

"Your friend got into a pack of trouble. He stumbled in here over an hour ago covered with hornet stings. Mr. Henshaw took him to the hospital."

"Hornets!" Alex cried. "Hornets! I never thought of hornets!"

"People have died of hornet stings," the man said.

"We didn't mean any harm. It was all in fun."

"It weren't much fun for the boy that got hurt." He turned back to the mules. "Y'all better think about that."

Alex and Willie ran back through the woods toward the schoolhouse. When they were a block away, they saw the yellow bus pull up and the students begin to board it. Someone saw Alex and Willie and yelled for the driver to wait. The two boys used their last bit of strength to get on.

Buddy slipped into the seat beside Alex. "Did you find him?" he asked anxiously.

Alex nodded his head. It was a while before he could catch his breath enough to talk. Finally, he told the others what had happened. Buddy stood up and rushed to the front of the bus and asked Mr. Marshall to let him off at the corner near the hospital.

"Where are you going?"

"I have to check on somebody in the hospital." Buddy stepped down and jumped through the door when it opened.

Just then, Mr. Henshaw's truck pulled up. He motioned for Mr. Marshall to roll down the window. "Can you get a message to Mr. Simmons?" Mr. Henshaw asked after establishing that the bus was going to Canoe.

"What happened?"

"Bill Simmons, his son, is in the hospital in serious condition. He was attacked by a swarm of hornets. Can you get a message to him?"

"I'll go as fast as I can." Mr. Marshall looked back at the students on board. Many of the regular riders had found other ways to get home. The students who were riding agreed to get off at a central location and walk home from there.

"I'll get a message to Mr. Simmons." The bus began to roll.

Buddy walked up to the desk in the waiting room and asked if he could see Bill. He was denied permission to see him, but he was invited to sit down and wait until someone could give him a report on Bill's condition. Buddy didn't know what to do or to say, but he knew that what had happened was his fault. What had started out as a practical joke had turned into a nightmare. Why was he so stupid?

Buddy sat with his eyes cast down and a worried look on his face. He was thankful that nothing worse had happened, but was afraid that the worst was yet to come. What if Bill died? Buddy still sat in the waiting room an hour later when he felt someone's presence. He looked up to see a tall man staring at him.

"Are you Buddy Rawles?" the man asked.

Panic seized Buddy. He had never met Bill's father before, though he had seen him at a distance. "Y-y-y yes."

"Do you know what happened to my son?"

"Not exactly. It was a sort of accident."

"I want you to tell me what happened, if you can. He's a very sick boy, in great pain. He's in danger of developing pneumonia," Mr. Simmons spoke quietly. "I want to know what happened this afternoon."

"I'm sorry, Mr. Simmons. I really am sorry." The look on Buddy's face conveyed sincere sympathy and fear for Bill. "It was all my fault."

Mr. Simmons lowered his large body into a chair just opposite Buddy. "I'm sorry, too. Why don't you start from the beginning?"

Buddy told Mr. Simmons the same story he had told everyone else, but without the guffaw and hilarity he had used before. "We didn't mean for anyone to get hurt."

"Why weren't you in school?"

"Our teachers went to a meeting in Brewton."

"So you boys went on a snipe hunt. Did Henshaw know what you were up to?"

"I think he knew."

Dr. Lisenby came out and sat beside Buddy. He looked at Mr. Simmons. "Bill is awake now, and the swelling is going down. We're lucky he got here when he did. We'd better keep him overnight because he'll be in a lot of pain. I think he'll be good enough to go home tomorrow or even to school if he wants to. You can go in and see him now."

"I'd like to see him, too," Buddy said.

"You go first," Mr. Simmons said. "Then wait for me. We can

walk home together."

Buddy nearly fainted when he saw Bill. "I am sorry. I didn't mean for this to happen. We were just playing a joke on you."

"I know. But it sure was scary."

"I'll never do a thing like that again."

The next morning Buddy, Steve, Alex, Willie, and all of the boys who went on the snipe hunt were called into the principal's office. Mr. Hodnette arranged the chairs in a circle to discuss the incident. Each boy had to tell about his part in the prank. They got a lecture. Mr. Hodnette told the younger boys that they were responsible for their own behavior even when someone older leads them. He kept the boys in his office the whole first period talking about responsibility and self-control.

The boys squirmed. They didn't dare look at each other. Before he finished, Mr. Hodnette spoke to each boy in the group.

"Alex, this isn't the first time you've been in my office. And I believe . . ." he pulled a card from a file on his desk, "that your last visit had something to do with Bill Simmons. Is that right?"

"Yes, Sir."

"Speak up," Mr. Hodnette snapped.

"Yes, Sir!"

"This is the last time." Mr. Hodnette looked long and hard over his glasses at Alex, who squirmed and nodded his head.

"Each of you will have your conduct cut 10 points. Buddy and Steve, yours will be cut 15 points and you are both off the football team for the rest of the season."

Buddy almost fell off his chair, but he didn't argue. Nobody argued with Mr. Hodnette.

"And by the way, you boys will get together the money to pay Bill's doctor and hospital bill. $1.50 each. Bring it to me by next Thursday."

Alex left the office both relieved and frustrated. Mr. Hodnette hadn't given him a whipping. He had cut his conduct only 10 points. But that meant he could not be on the honor roll this six weeks. He still could hope for first semester honors. The difficult task would be getting the money to pay Bill's doctor and hospital bill. He had a week. He'd work it out somehow.

Alex walked toward his second period class. He was about to sit down when his eyes fell on Bill Simmons. "Bill! My God!" Then he caught himself. It must have taken a lot of nerve for Bill to show up at school already. He looked like a monster; a freak with puffed cheeks, bumpy head, swollen eyes, enormous nose, and humongous lips.

"How do you feel?" Alex wasn't just being polite. He really wanted to know.

"I probably look worse than I feel. The doctor said I could come to school if I wanted to and my dad said I wanted to. My dad doesn't want me to miss a single day."

Alex explained that the boys had not intended to hurt him. "We didn't even know what was going on until we were halfway back to school. Buddy finally told us that we were playing a joke on you. Willie and I went back to look for you. I really am sorry."

## *HELPING MRS. WRIGHT*

Jeannie sat beside Alex on the bus that afternoon. She had seen Bill and was shocked by the way he looked. Alex told her he blamed himself.

"Mr. Hodnette took Bill home," Jeannie said. "I saw them leave."

"Having my conduct cut is the worst part for me," Alex admitted. "I don't know how I can come up with $1.50, but I will think of something." He saw Jeannie reach for her purse. He quickly added, "I have a whole week to work on this, so don't you worry."

When Alex got home, his mother said that Mr. Wright, their next-door neighbor, had asked if Alex would do him a favor while he was away on a business trip. He wanted Alex to stay overnight with his wife and young son. He would pay Alex twenty-five cents a night.

*Could life be better?* Alex thought. *What a break!*

"What time do I go?"

"You should go talk with Mr. Wright now. Don't forget that you have chores to do at home before you can go away for the night."

Alex and Mr. Wright agreed that Alex would begin sleeping at the Wright home Saturday night and continue every night through the next Saturday. Mr. Wright planned to return the following Sunday. He paid Alex in advanced and thanked him.

"My wife doesn't feel comfortable staying alone, especially with the baby. You can at least run for help if there is a problem."

"I can help with the chores, too," Alex said.

"Thank you. I will feel better having you here." He handed Alex $2.00.

*Perfect timing!* Alex chuckled to himself. *I can pay Mr. Hodnette tomorrow and I'll have half a dollar left. I can't believe my good luck.*

When Christmas came that year, Alex was prepared. He had worked for Mr. Wright for two months. Mr. Wright had been away from home five nights a week for nine weeks. Alex finished his chores as quickly as he could each day and then went to the Wright home to help gather the eggs, milk their cow, feed the pigs, and sometimes go to the store for Mrs. Wright. He had time to do his homework and listen to the radio. Alex had money to spend for Christmas presents and put some into his savings account.

Alex always spent the weekend at home with his family. As spring approached, many jobs had to be done. He and Jed knocked down the dead corn and cotton stalks so they could be raked into piles and burned. Chores took a lot of time on Saturdays, but when the jobs were finished, the boys could spend a little time exploring the woods and playing on the creek bank. At the creek, birds twittered as they devoured the last of the berries clinging to the highest branches of the tall trees. Frogs that had sunk deep down in the mud last fall to escape the winter cold emerged and basked in the warm afternoon sunshine on logs near the creek.

The boys heard the splashing sound of the frogs plunging to safety in the deep, dark water. Squirrels chattered in the trees, signaling the approach of strangers. Jed and Alex watched a pair of white cranes that had been standing in shallow water. They spread their broad wings and rose silently into the clear, blue sky, their long legs stretched straight behind them. Alex and Jed enjoyed their time together in the woods.

Alex had put a lot of effort into his studies during the weeks he had stayed with Mrs. Wright. He always studied while she fed and bathed the baby and put him to sleep. Mrs. Wright would look over Alex's work, point out errors and offer suggestions for improvement. She helped him learn his spelling words and listened to him read. When examinations were given, Alex was ready. He made high scores on all of his tests and he reached his scholastic goal. He made the highest average in the whole school for the semester and was recognized at an assembly on the first Friday in February. In addition to the recognition in school, he was given two passes to the movies. He decided that he would work for this honor every semester.

Jeannie stopped Alex in the hall. "I'm so proud of you. I was working for the same thing, but I fell down in math. Congratulations!"

"Thanks. I hope to do it every semester from now on."

"Quite an ambition. I intend to give you a lot of competition."

"Then I'll work even harder," Alex laughed. "By the way, I have two tickets to the movies. Would you like to go?"

"I'll ask my mother, but I am sure she'll say 'no.' She won't let me go anywhere alone, I mean without her."

"Ask her anyway." Alex blushed when he realized that he had asked a girl for a date.

Alex was disappointed but not surprised the next day when Jeannie told him that her mother wouldn't give her permission to go. He knew girls usually couldn't date until they were sixteen.

"Would you have gone if your mother had let you?"

"Of course I would," Jeannie smiled.

"Then will you be my girlfriend?" Alex's face turned a little pink.

Jeannie blushed too. "Yes."

They both smiled and he touched her hand. She squeezed it, and then nervously pulled it away.

Knowing that Jeannie was his girlfriend would make it easier to talk to her. It would be hard to wait two more years for a real date, but he knew there would be time for dating later. There were lots of things they could do together. They could sit together at football games. They could help each other with their homework. They could eat lunch together, and he could lie awake at night and think about her.

Mr. Wright came home one weekend in April and announced that he had decided to move his family to Mobile. Alex's services would no longer be needed. He said that moving day would be in two weeks and he asked Alex if he could stay with his family until then. He also said that he would pay Alex to help with the packing and other preparations.

"I'll do it – no charge. Mrs. Wright has helped me so much with my homework that I'll be glad to help you move."

Mr. Wright smiled. "Thank you, Alex."

When the Wrights moved, Alex knew that he would have to study even harder. Mrs. Wright had taught him to read over his homework carefully to look for mistakes. She taught him to pay close attention to what he was reading and to look up words that he did not know or understand. She taught him to study his spelling words instead of spelling them the way they sounded. She wished him success and said that she would miss him.

### *AMERICA GOES TO WAR*

As time went on, there was news about the war in Europe. Some of the older boys volunteered for the military, but nobody expected the United States to actually be involved in the war. The high school students who had never experienced war could not conceive that anyone, even Hitler, could provoke the United States into action. The United States was preparing for war, but most people believed it was just a pretense, a show of strength to make Hitler back down. Trainloads of military personnel traversed the country, being trained and prepared for a war that would never happen.

Several hundred troops were camped on the outskirts of Atmore for a short period of time, probably waiting for a permanent camp to be made available to them. Local boys rode their bicycles out to the camp, hoping to hear exciting stories about the life of a soldier. Alex asked his father to drive by and let him talk with some of them, but his father refused. He said he did not want his son to become interested in the military. People talked of war, but Alex and his friends did not expect their country to become involved.

But it did happen. Alex was in the tenth grade when Japan bombed Pearl Harbor. Fear and anger gripped everyone, but the reality of war had not yet begun to envelop their lives.

On December 8, 1941, the day after Pearl Harbor, Mr. Hodnette assembled the entire student body in the auditorium. On the stage was a radio tuned to the National Broadcasting Company, which transmitted the voice of President Franklin D. Roosevelt across the nation. Not a word was spoken as President Roosevelt told of the events that had led up to the attack on Pearl Harbor. He said there were hundreds of lives lost in the secret attack. It wiped out the entire fleet. He told of the outrage of every American citizen. He said he would ask Congress to declare war against Japan immediately.

War was declared against Japan that day and against Germany the next. Changes took place immediately. All military personnel who were on leave were ordered to report to their posts. Before the families who were left behind had recovered from the shock of seeing their men leave for distant assignments, they were informed that certain products would no longer be available in the stores and purchase of others would be rationed. They rationed coffee, sugar, canned milk, butter, cheese, and meat. Families were issued a book of stamps for each member of the family. Stamps had to be presented along with money for goods and products. Shoes were also rationed; two pairs of shoes per year, and gasoline could not be purchased without stamps. Only people doing government or defense-related work could purchase new tires. Many household goods and personal items, farm implements, farm machinery, and especially automobiles were no longer available. Factories that had been building automobiles and trucks were ordered to make military vehicles.

Families that had suffered through the long Depression entered into a different period of deprivation. They were denied modern conveniences even though they now had money to buy them.

As Alex grew older, the war began to impact his life. One by one the young men in the community volunteered to join up and fight for their country. Under-aged Horace Bailey was one of the first to join after the war began. He was discharged after a few months and told to wait until he reached seventeen. Others waited to be drafted.

# Reunion

Ships were being built in Mobile and airplanes were built in Pensacola and Mobile. Defense plant jobs paid high wages. Good-paying jobs and patriotism drew people in swarms away from Atmore and other towns in the area to those jobs available in shipyards, the Pensacola Naval Air Station and Brookley Field in Mobile.

Alex's dad wanted to continue selling insurance. He did not want to leave his business, which was thriving. However, Dave Presswood had depended upon his automobile to take him to the far corners of Escambia County where many of his customers lived. The Defense Council did not consider selling insurance an essential occupation, so he could not purchase tires or the gasoline he needed. He could not continue his business. Instead, he sought employment at the Mobile shipyard.

When Dave went to work in Mobile, Alex took on the responsibility of operating the farm. Besides doing his regular chores, he had to plant, cultivate, and harvest the crops with little assistance from his father. The other three children and their mother worked alongside him, but the burden of making it all work was on Alex's shoulders. All chores were done without electricity, running water, or a reliable automobile.

Alex found it harder to keep up his grades. The classes that he was taking were hard. He had difficulty with mathematical concepts for the first time and found that English, biology, and literature required a lot of study. History, a subject he enjoyed, had to be studied and facts and dates memorized. And running the farm, even with the help of his brother and sisters, took a great deal if time. Alex was concerned about his grades and was disappointed when they dropped. He was determined to work harder.

The family had to depend more on their horse cart as a means of transportation, but Sadie, the mule, was getting old and feeble. The old car was still running, but the shortage of gasoline curtailed its use. Dave used it on an occasional business trip. It was on one of his trips that he found a beautiful young mare for sale.

One morning, Dave woke Alex at daybreak. His father led him out to the barn. In a stall next to faithful old Sadie stood the most beautiful horse Alex had ever seen. She was sleek and smooth, black from head to toe, except for a white star on her forehead between her gorgeous big, brown eyes. Alex gasped. He had never imagined such a wonderful animal.

"Whose is it? Why is it here?"

"Do you like it?"

The look in Alex's eyes conveyed his admiration and delight, but he dared not dream that this wonderful creature was to be his own.

"I traded for her last night. Her name is Mamie. She hasn't been used for farm work or for riding in about a year. Her owner is in the Army and his wife can no longer care for her. I thought we could use her here on the farm. We can let her work along with old Sadie until she is ready to work alone. Do you suppose you can help to shape her up?"

"I'll certainly try."

"You'll need to walk her first and get her used to you for a while. Don't just jump on her back until you have become acquainted. She will respond to you better if she knows what to expect."

Alex took hold of the reins. He walked Mamie down the path through the orchard. The sun was just coming up in the east, sending its golden light across the woods and fields. The pear trees were in full bloom and their fragrance attracted bees that were already buzzing in their branches.

Alex led Mamie to the gate at the end of the orchard. He wanted to climb upon the gate so he could mount Mamie, but he heeded his father's advice to spend time letting her get used to him. He led her back to the barn, fed her and gave her water. He brushed and rubbed her. He smoothed her mane. Alex did not try to ride her or to hitch her to the cart that first day. There would be time for that when she became more familiar with her surroundings.

Mamie quickly responded to Alex's patience and gentle treatment. She worked for him, pulling the plow and the cart, but Alex was happiest when he climbed upon her back and rode through the fields and woods.

Soon after the acquisition of Mamie, old Sadie had to be let out to pasture. She was no longer able to pull the cart or plow and was of little use on the farm.

The old Chevrolet finally ground to a standstill. Dave spent many hours patching up her aging parts. He replaced wires with old pieces of wire from his workshop. He had the battery charged and recharged. He flushed out the radiator and put in gook to try to stop leaks. He patched inner tubes and eked a few more miles out of the tires. But finally, he gave up. He and the boys pushed it to the back of the garage and left it alone. Dave thought he might sell it for junk iron, but he couldn't bring himself to go that far. Perhaps one day he would find a way to repair it.

That left Mamie as the family's only means of transportation. She was used for errands in the neighborhood and for pulling the cart around the farm, but she could not take the place of the old car. A bicycle would have come in handy, but even bicycles were hard to find, and the family often relied on public transportation.

Another Christmas came and went. There were only a few gifts that year, not because there was no money, but because so little was available. Mama went to town on the train and bought new clothes for everyone, but other gifts that the family wanted were simply not to be found.

Dave Presswood tried to think of ways to make more money. It had been his ambition to be a doctor, but his father's untimely death prevented him from attending the University of Alabama like his older brother. He began working as soon as he finished high school, first running his mother's farm and later striking out on his own selling insurance.

Dave had always wanted to try raising cattle. Cows that grow up on a range from birth to maturity are ready for market in a year and a half. It was a fairly effortless way to make money as long as he kept tabs on his herd. There was enough open pasture around Atmore to accommodate a number of small herds. Dave started with three young heifers that he bought at the sale pen, marked them with a circle P brand and turned them loose on the range. When the heifers produced calves, these were marked and left to follow their mothers on the range. By the time Dave went to work in Mobile, he had twenty-four cows wandering in the pasture.

One Sunday afternoon, Alex rode through the pasture to check on the cows. He found three or four at a time eating grass and leaves. He counted twenty-one. He was anxious to spot the other three before he went home. While riding through a grove of oak trees a rabbit jumped out in front of Mamie. The frightened horse reared and ran. A branch struck Alex's forehead, cut a gash just above his hairline, and knocked him to the ground. Alex was knocked out cold.

Alex regained his senses, looked around, and blinked his eyes. He felt pain in his head and raised his hand to his forehead. He discovered the gash and felt the oozing blood. He nearly fainted. He took off his shirt and wiped the blood from his forehead. His eyes were unharmed, but his back ached. He didn't know if he would be able to get up, but he knew he had to try. He found a stick on the ground and used it to help raise him up.

Darkness was coming. His horse was gone and it was over two miles to the farm. He walked, using the stick for support. His back hurt, his legs hurt, but he felt sure that nothing was broken. He was more frightened than he had ever been in his life. Alex had not cried in a long time, but this situation was so desperate, he felt tears in his eyes.

Alex called for Mamie. He heard an animal walking. He stood beside a tree and watched. He hoped it was Mamie, but he wasn't sure. He recognized her as she walked closer. He called softly and stepped out into the open so Mamie could see him. With effort, Alex mounted his steed. Giving the horse her lead, he lay his head forward as she carried him, dodging branches that could have dragged him off again. It was an hour before they were out of he woods and heading home.

Mama helped Alex into the house, cleaned his face, and examined the wound. She sent Marge to a neighbor's house for help. The neighbor drove Alex and his mother to the hospital where the doctor stitched up the gash on Alex's head.

When they returned home, Alex got out his books and did his homework, even though his mother insisted that he go to bed. Alex had not missed a day of school so far and didn't want tomorrow to be his first time. He wore a huge bandage over his forehead for several days, but went ahead with his studies as if nothing had happened.

The population of the school was changing. Girls outnumbered the boys in every class. Girls filled positions that were formerly filled by boys. There were more girls in the band and in the chorus. Girls were chosen to help hoist the flag at flag drill each week. And girls filled more seats at assembly than boys did. As soon as a boy reached his eighteenth birthday, he was drafted. Many who were bored with school left to join the Navy when they were only seventeen.

*RESTORING THE OLD CAR*

The 1931 Chevrolet that was stored in the back of the garage was just twelve years old, but it had been gathering dust for a long time. The upholstery was rotting, the paint was peeling, and it was taking up space. The chickens that tried to roost on it were chased away at first, but eventually they were left alone. Their feathers and droppings added to the appearance of dilapidation. Sixteen-year-old Alex saw through the crusty filth. He wondered if it could ever run again.

Alex got a parts manual, but was disappointed to learn that no new parts were available. He looked for old 1931 Chevrolets that had been abandoned to see if they might have parts he could use. He talked to mechanics about restoration, but they gave little encouragement. Some said it would be impossible to remove rust and to separate parts that had frozen together during long months of neglect. One mechanic told him that if he soaked old parts in gasoline or kerosene, the stuck joints might loosen.

The more Alex learned, the more convinced he became that he really could do the job. He had stood by and watched his dad work on the car for years and helped him fix broken parts or hand him tools he needed. Alex spoke to his father about getting the old car started again. The ancient auto was pushed out of the dark garage. They began their appraisal of the project that would occupy Alex during the summer.

Liz and Marge helped. They scraped, washed, and chiseled the chicken droppings for days before they could stand to work on the car. At last the real work began. Alex had studied the manuals. He knew by heart the names of the parts and the function of each, how each part fit, and how it worked. He showed Jed how to clean them.

Every screw, nut, and bolt was put into the bucket to be cleaned and then laid out on the garage floor to dry. This arduous task tested every ounce of endurance Alex could muster. Jed was at Alex's elbow every step of the way, assisting, presenting ideas, and making funny remarks that cracked them both up.

Alex stopped by his mechanic friend's shop every few days to borrow tools and to ask advice. There was a spot in the garage next to his that was unoccupied.

"Is there any way you could haul your car down here and put it in that vacant spot while you're working on it?" His friend said. "You could use my tools here and I wouldn't have to wait for you to return the ones that you borrow."

Alex apologized for inconveniencing his friend. Then he said. "We'll find a way to get it down here."

After that, Alex and Jed went to the shop as regularly as the employees, often staying far into the night to complete a job. Other mechanics stopped by to see what the boys were doing, to give advice, and sometimes to shake their heads in disbelief.

At last every part was back in place. Every eye in the large garage was on Alex as he stepped on the starter. A whoop of joy resounded throughout the building when the motor turned and started. Men rushed over to pat their backs and shake their hands. Everyone laughed and the boys grinned from ear to ear. But the car could not yet be moved.

The car had been up on blocks while they worked on the engine. It still needed tires. All of Alex's uncles helped him look for tires in different areas where they lived or worked. One by one, four used tires were located. They locked up the tires in the garage until the farm work was finished.

School started before the car was ready to roll. Alex and Jed hurried to the garage every day after school to resume assembling the remaining parts. It was Halloween before the job was completed. The mechanics who worked late that night shook their hands, wished them good luck and waved as Alex drove the car slowly out the door, down the road, and into his own garage, which had been cleaned and swept by Liz and Marge. When Dad came home from his defense plant job in Mobile, he had nothing but praise for the job that the boys had done. They hopped in the car and had a ride all around town, attracting attention, friendly waves, and looks of admiration as they went along.

Alex applied for a driver's license and passed the test on the first try. He took the car on short trips. Gasoline was too scarce for long rides. Alex had a profound sense of pride for seeing the job through to completion. There had been many times when he had felt like quitting. Having Jed by his side gave him the support he needed to push ahead.

The entire family had joined in the final stage of restoration. The car was washed and cleaned. Dad was able to buy enough black paint and their friend, Willie Lee Gay, a painter by trade, helped them paint. Meanwhile, Mama measured, cut, and stitched seat covers to reupholster the interior. It was beautiful when all of the work was done.

### *MR. HODNETTE GIVES ALEX A LECTURE*

Alex's grades dropped. He passed all of his subjects, but he was far from reaching his goal of having the best grades in school. Jeannie had higher averages than he, but she was taking different subjects. When Alex failed to make the Honor Roll the first time, Mr. Hodnette called him into his office for a conference.

Alex told Mr. Hodnette about the work he was doing to keep the farm going and about the car he and Jed had restored. He explained that his father was working in Mobile and had little time to help with the farm.

He said, "I don't have time to study, but I will try to improve."

"I know your ambition is to be a doctor," Mr. Hodnette said. "I admire that. I have a son who is a doctor. But I wonder if you really know what you're facing. You've moved out of first place. That could be construed as lack of interest in your schoolwork or that you might not have what it takes to be a doctor. You might assume from your interest in mechanics and your ability to keep farm machinery in working order that your talent might lie in the automotive field or in farming. You are in the eleventh grade this year. You have only one more year to pull up your grades to be considered for a pre-med program."

Alex was shocked. He knew he had not been able to keep his grades up, but he always felt that he could get back on track when the pressure eased up. He was embarrassed and angry. "Mr. Hodnette, I have never considered being anything but a doctor. I have had to help my family because my father is working away from home. I like to think that we are doing our bit for the war effort. I do want to be a doctor and I will raise my grades."

"I'm glad to hear that. I certainly understand the sacrifices that we've all had to make. You won't be able to get into college if things continue as they are. I hope you're able to find more time to study. Keep your goal in perspective."

The next day when Alex received his report card, he saw his biology grade had dropped to 79. He stood for a long time looking at his grades. He was disappointed in himself. He went into the empty auditorium, sat on the back row and leaned his head on the back of the seat in front of him. He felt like crying, but he didn't cry. He just sat there a long time thinking and evaluating himself, his grades, and his family.

Alex had always been a good son. He had done everything he possibly could to help his family through whatever situation arose. His family accepted his contribution as a given. Alex would always be there. He didn't smoke. He didn't drink. He was truthful and fair.

Was he too easy going? Was he imposed upon and taken for granted? Was he living his life for his family and letting it slip away without having any time for himself? Perhaps he should stop being there every time they needed him. Perhaps he should go out at night and have some fun. Maybe he should take up smoking and drinking. Maybe he should forget about being a doctor.

Alex felt a gentle tap on his shoulder and a soft kiss on the back of his head. "Hi!" is something wrong?" Jeannie sat down beside him. She had a concerned look on her face.

"Yes. I didn't make Honor Roll. I got a 79 in biology."

"Oh, Alex, I'm so sorry. You've had a hard six weeks. But don't be discouraged. You can make it up. I know you can."

"I would have to make 100 next period and 90 on my final test to bring my average up to 90."

"Promise me one thing. Promise you'll try."

"O.K., Sweetheart."

"I'll help. We can study biology on the bus every day"

Alex looked at his grades again. He had an 88 in English, his lowest English grade ever. Jeannie looked at his grades.

"I'm so ashamed of this report card. I know my parents will be too." He asked, "May I see your grades?"

Jeannie hesitated. "I made Honor Roll." Alex looked at her report card and smiled. "Jeannie, your average is 96. What a beautiful report card!" He squeezed her hand.

"Thanks. I'm pretty proud of it."

"I'll be up there with you next time."

"That's what I like about you, Alex, you're not a quitter."

"Jeannie, I love you. You are so good for me. You're the one thing in my life that keeps me going. I sometimes feel like giving up. I could join the Navy and get away from all of this, but I don't want to leave you."

"Alex, don't ever mention dropping out of school. I know it's hard for you. It's hard for all of us. So many people have gone into the service and too many of them won't be coming back. My brother is over there. My mother is out of her mind with worry. I don't want to have to start worrying about you."

"You'd worry about me, Jeannie?"

"You know I would," she didn't look at him. "Your parents depend on you, too."

"Maybe too much." Alex put his arm around her shoulder and drew her close to him. He kissed her cheek. "Thanks for the pep talk. It'll help me face my mother. She'll be upset about my grades."

The door opened and Bill Simmons poked his head in. "So there you two are. The bus is waiting for you."

"Oh, no!" they both said. Jeannie jumped up and was out the door before Alex had gathered up his books. He dropped his notebook and had to scramble to pick up his papers.

"What's the matter with you, Presswood?" Bill asked in his usual sarcastic tone.

"Drop dead," Alex spoke under his breath as he rushed after

Jeannie who raced toward the bus. Bill followed, taking his time.

"Thanks for waiting," Alex said to the bus driver. "I wasn't watching the clock."

"Thank your pal, Bill. He noticed you weren't here."

"He would."

He forced himself to say "Thanks" to Bill when he got on the bus. Jeannie did too.

That night Alex showed his report card to his mother. "I'm sorry, Mama, but I didn't make Honor Roll this period."

"You didn't what?"

Alex held up his hand. "I feel bad enough about this. You don't need to say a word. You couldn't say a word that I haven't already said to myself. I just didn't study enough. I have promised myself and I will promise you that I'll do better next time."

"I know you will," Mama said quietly. "It isn't completely your fault. We tend to lay all of the blame on the war. We just have to work harder. At least we're all still together. We will all help. Right now, I'll milk the cows." In a loud voice so everyone could hear, she said, "Jed, go and get the cows from the pasture. Liz, come in here and start cooking supper. Marge, pump a bucket of water, then churn the milk. Let's get our chores finished early so everybody can study."

"Do we have to do this every day?" Liz asked.

"Yes. Every day."

Liz shrugged her shoulders. "My friends don't have to work like we do. They get to have fun."

"You'll get to have fun some day. Right now there's a war on and everybody has to do a little more. Your friends are probably doing more than you think they are."

Mama picked up the milk bucket and started to the barn. "I could use a little fun myself."

Alex worked harder. On his first weekly biology test, he made 100. This boosted his ego. He was determined to do the same thing next week. He was excited when his second, third, and fourth weekly grades were the same. "Miss Porter couldn't even find a misspelled word," he bragged.

"Don't get cocky. You still have two more weeks to go," said Mama.

"I know. But I think I have the hang of it now. My other grades are coming up too."

"Just keep it up." Mama was as elated as Alex, but she knew that absolute perfection is hard to attain. Alex was determined. He studied harder than ever.

When report cards came out, he had a grade of 100 in biology. He made 96 on his final test, earning him an average of 92. Alex was elated.

*SENIOR YEAR*

A dark cloud of despair fell over the classroom as the class of '44 entered and took their seats. Alex sat in a desk beside an open window, looking out. This should have been an exciting day. He and his friends should have been standing around laughing, joking, making plans, looking ahead. But they were not. They were not even talking. News had just reached the class that Willie Ray Coons had been killed in action. Willie had dropped out of school last January and joined the army. He had gone through basic training and was sent directly to Europe without a leave to visit his family. He should have been in this classroom today anticipating his last year of school.

Miss Hodnette, their homeroom teacher, walked into the room. She had been standing at the door watching her sad students file into the room, wiping tears from their eyes. She tried to decide what she would say to these seniors who faced such an ominous, uncertain future. She had prepared a speech a few days earlier. She had planned to tell her students to try to unburden themselves of the worries and conflicts of the world and to concentrate instead on the job at hand. She would tell them to think of themselves and try to make this year a glorious success for themselves and their families, their school, and their community. She could still use those thoughts, but she would have to begin by mentioning their sadness.

Miss Hodnette always felt grief when one of her former students had been injured or killed. Each of her students was, in a way, a reflection of herself. She hoped that she had given each of them something; an idea, a thought, an expression; that would enhance their appreciation of life and would help to guide them to a meaningful future. Many of her hopes for her students were shattered because of the war. She was sad, but she must not convey this message to the young students who sat before her, waiting for her guidance through this, their final year of high school.

When Miss Hodnette reached the front of the room, she wiped a tear from her eye. She cleared her throat and began the speech that she hoped would give some meaning to the sacrifices that they had been called upon to endure. She expressed her sympathy for their grief and loss. Miss Hodnette emphasized that this was not a useless war. It was one that had to be fought to bring down the forces that were threatening the survival of democracy and the freedom of all people throughout the world.

"I do not mean to minimize the tragedy of the injury or death of one single American who has gone across the seas to fight. We read of victory after victory being won because brave men from America are fighting to protect their homeland. We must keep this in our minds and in our hearts. Life must go on. This war that has been raging for three long years will come to an end. You have the responsibility to learn what you must to enable you to walk out those doors and take your place as a useful, contributing member of the community. Some of you will go to college and continue your quest for knowledge; some will find work and begin your careers. No matter what path you choose, or are forced to follow, what you learn this year will help you reach your goal.

"I do not want this year to be without joy and happiness. I hope that friendships that have developed in the past will grow and flourish and new friendships will begin." Alex looked at Jeannie. She glanced at him, but did not smile. They both had been close friends with Willie and both were on the verge of tears. They listened as Miss Hodnette continued.

"It is up to each one of you to build on the foundation that we, as a school, have tried to build for you. Part of that foundation is brotherhood, love, and consideration for each other. I challenge you to make strides in that direction."

She stopped and looked around the room. She made a few announcements about schedules and committees, and elections for class officers. At last students were dismissed from homeroom.

Alex caught up with Jeannie. She looked at him, and fell into his arms and wept. Alex cried too. Willie had been Alex's friend all of his life and he would miss him. Other students were also crying as they made their way to their first classes.

After school that day, Alex and Jeannie went together to Willie's home to offer condolence to his mother and father. Mrs. Coons cried and hugged them and thanked them for coming. She pleaded with them to come again and help her to make sense out of the whole awful situation. Alex and Jeannie promised to visit again. Alex walked quietly, holding Jeannie's hand. He thought about their future.

"I think we should try to make this as complete a year as we possibly can. I started to say 'perfect' but perfection is too much to hope for. When school is out, I'll have to go. I feel sure of it now. Let's make the most of every day. Miss Hodnette didn't mention a senior play, a senior trip, or a senior prom. I was hoping we would at least have a prom this year since we didn't have a junior prom. Let's talk with Miss Hodnette; maybe we can try to do something."

"I don't see how it could hurt. My sister said they used to get lots of donations from the townsfolk, but not now. Everybody is buying war bonds or giving to the Red Cross and the Salvation Army. There just isn't any money left for frivolous things. We may just miss out on everything," Jeannie said.

"I wish Mr. Crosby hadn't given up on the band. Football games just won't be the same," Alex said.

"At least Mr. Hodnette kept the football team. Most of the games will be played in the afternoon, though, because the lights use up so much electricity. I heard we're going to have pep rallies and we'll be marching downtown like we did last year to create interest in the game."

"I like going downtown together," Alex said. "You don't realize how many students we have until you see them all marching down the street. How will we march in time without the band?"

"I expect the drummers will play to keep us together."

When Alex got home, he sat down at the kitchen table and started his homework. He glanced through all of his books. He read the tables of contents to get an idea of what he would be studying.

He knew he had a rough road ahead.

Jed and Marge had already done their homework and were playing dominoes. Alex asked how the game was going. Jed was winning, for a change.

"I'm sorry about Willie," Jed said. "When did it happen?"

"I believe it happened Friday, but the family didn't get word until this morning. They said he had stepped on a mine. I feel so sorry for his family."

Their mother came into the kitchen. "I just finished the ironing. Everybody has a freshly starched and ironed outfit for the rest of the week. I'm sorry you didn't get new clothes to start the year off, but I couldn't find clothes or material to make them."

"Thanks, Mama. We'll be O.K., as long as we have something to wear," Marge said.

Everybody was weary of war. They wanted to taste the food they had been denied for so long. They wanted enough sugar for their coffee and coffee for a second cup. They wanted real leather shoes, enough toilet tissue, and Kleenex, Bobbie Pins, and nylon hose. They were tired of losing sons, fathers, husbands, and boyfriends. They were tired of driving long distances in old cars to jobs in far-away war plants. But the end was not in sight.

Mama said, "The war will be over eventually and we can have more of the things we want. I pray every day that it will end soon so Alex won't have to go, but that is out of our hands."

"I would like for this to be a good year for all of us," said Alex. "Every family in the world is faced with the same thing, whether they are rich or poor, black or white or yellow. We have to find happiness in our own families and our friends. I want us to find time to enjoy each other. I will do all I can to make my last year at home as pleasant as I possibly can."

"Alex, you deserve to have some fun," said Mama. "You've had to pitch in and do the work of the head of the household. I don't know how we could have survived without you. We have to make plans to carry on. We'll try not to make it the subject of every conversation, but it's something we're facing." Mama was looking at the fork that she turned over and over with her fingers on the table as she spoke. At last she raised her head and looked him in the eye. Alex saw a tear slip down her cheek and he quickly changed the subject.

"Is Daddy coming home tonight?"

"Yes, he should be here soon." He had been renting a room in Mobile to be closer to his job.

When they heard the bus stop, they all went to greet their father. He walked slowly up the path. They followed him into the house. He set his suitcase inside the front door and hugged each of them, asking about what was going on and commenting about their responses. It was a warm homecoming. Mama served his dinner in the kitchen and they sat around talking.

Alex told him about Willie. He offered condolences. He said he'd go over there as soon as possible.

Dad asked about Liz, who had moved away six months ago to find work in Pensacola. Mama said they had received a letter from her today. "She said she is doing fine and has met another young man she would like us to meet."

"Where is this one from?"

"New York, I think."

"Tell her to forget about him. I don't know why so many silly girls go for New Yorkers. Tell her she'll have to come home and find a nice young man right here in Atmore. Tell her in your next letter."

"Daddy, Liz is nineteen," Alex said. "She has a good job and is making her own way. I really think she is happy down there."

Dad looked at Alex. His children did not usually disagree with him. They listened and did what he said. He didn't make an issue of it. "She'll probably drop him in a week or two. Go ahead and tell her to bring him home. We'll feed him for a week-end." He went on to another subject.

"I don't want to get your hopes up, but I think I've found us a decent car. A 1938 Buick. It's clean and runs well. I gave the lady who owns it a $50 deposit. She wants $325 for it." Everybody held their breath. They wanted to hear all about it.

"That sounds like an awful lot of money for a six-year-old car," Alex said. "A brand new Buick only costs between six and seven hundred dollars. How many miles does it have?"

"Twenty-one thousand on the odometer. I think it's right. It hasn't been run much since the war started and it was kept in a garage. The interior is just like new, and the paint is perfect. No dents or scratches."

"Did you hear it run? Did you drive it?"

"Of course I drove it. It sounded good and it handled nicely."

"What about the tires?" Alex knew all of the things to ask.

"The tires are old, but they have pretty good rubber." A 1938 Buick was a huge step up from the rebuilt 1931 Chevrolet that the family owned. They were all excited.

Friday night Daddy drove a car home. It wasn't the 1938 Buick. It was a 1939 Chevrolet. He explained that someone had offered the woman $400 for the Buick and she took it. He searched all week for the Chevrolet.

Alex and Jed looked under the hood, and found a few problems. "We've worked on a Chevy before," Jed said. "I'm sure we'll be able to keep this one going."

Alex looked at the odometer and whistled. "It has 54,000 miles. That might not be all if they've tampered with it. At least Dad got it home without any trouble. We'll just have to work on it when things begin to break. Hopefully we'll be able to get the parts."

Bill Simmons rode up on his bicycle.

"Hi."

"Hey, yourself."

"Nice car."

"We like it."

"Guess what? My dad just got a 1938 Buick. He drove it home tonight. Only 21,000 miles. Beautiful paint job! Perfect interior. Runs like a top."

"1938? That's a year older than this one." Alex didn't want to let Bill know he was angry. *Why did it have to be Bill?*

"My dad got a great buy," Bill said.

"Drive it over and let's have a look."

"My dad drove it into the garage and locked the door. The keys are in his pocket. He knows how to 'baby' a car."

Alex smiled. His dad had parked his new car in the driveway and handed Alex the keys. It was great to be treated like a man.

Liz came home that weekend with her new boyfriend, Peter

Sanders. He was nice enough for a New Yorker, but Alex secretly hoped that Liz would break up with him. He didn't want her to move to New York. The family had always been close. He didn't like the idea of her being serious with someone who might take her so far away.

"Don't you think there's someone around here for you?" asked Alex. "You don't know anything about his family. What do you really know about him?"

"I know he is really great to me. He's been to college for two years, studying for the ministry. He told me about his family. He has two sisters in high school. His father is a postman. And I do care for him," she said.

"I wouldn't want to marry someone from another part of the country," said Alex. "People up North and out West are different from us. I'm glad I have a girlfriend right here in Atmore. I expect to get married and live here when I finish college."

Liz smiled. She had met some very nice people in Pensacola who were just like the people she had grown up with. She knew that Alex would feel differently, too, when he was forced to meet and mingle with people from other parts of the country.

There was always something happening on the farm to draw Alex's attention from his studies. Weather had been perfect for crops that summer. Just enough rain, just enough sunshine for corn and cotton and especially for peanuts.

When Dad came home the first week in September, he was pleased that the cotton had been picked and the corn was almost ready to be harvested. He walked through the peanut field and pulled up a few bunches of peanuts. The vines were full, but he noticed there were a few immature peanuts on each vine. He decided to wait one more week to begin plowing them up. Alex questioned his decision, pointing out that the vines were loaded with mature peanuts and only a few had not filled out. But Daddy said to wait.

The weather that week was hot and dry. The soil surrounding the peanuts hardened faster that Dad realized it would. When they started plowing, many of the peanuts broke off the vines and stayed in the ground. There were only half as many peanuts as they had anticipated. The whole family set to work pulling them from the vines, washing them, and getting them ready to boil.

Daddy dug around in the field to see how many peanuts were still left. Finding a large number, he thought of a way to recover some of his loss.

On Wednesday morning three weeks later, Alex stood in Mr. Hodnette's office asking to be excused for his absences on Friday, Monday, and Tuesday.

"Were you sick?"

"No, Sir."

"Did a close relative die?"

"No, Sir."

"Then you may not have an excuse."

"Then I guess I'll have to go home. I wasn't sick and nobody died." He was angry. He walked out of the office and headed toward the front door.

"Come back, Presswood."

Alex hesitated. He would quit school, finish up the crops, and then join the Army or Navy. Going to school and running the farm was almost impossible. And to have Mr. Hodnette refuse to give him an excuse without even hearing what had happened was the last straw. For a fleeting moment, Alex felt relief. How easy it would be. He put his hand on the doorknob and started to turn it when he felt a hand on his shoulder.

"I said, 'come back,' Presswood."

Alex walked back into Mr. Hodnette's office and waited for him to speak. "Just what is your excuse?"

Alex collected himself and let his anger subside. He chose his words carefully. "All of our hogs died and I had to dispose of the bodies."

"How many hogs died? How long does it take to bury a hog?"

"My dad bought 14 young shoats to eat the peanuts that were left in the ground after we plowed them up."

"Why did you leave peanuts in the ground?"

"We waited a week too long to plow them. One of the best crops we ever had. The ground was too dry so the peanuts were jerked off the vines and stayed in the ground. Daddy bought the hogs to fatten them on the peanuts."

"What happened? Did they eat themselves to death?" Mr. Hodnette chuckled. Obviously he didn't believe Alex's story.

Alex flushed. "No, Sir. They died of cholera."

"Cholera?"

"Yes, Sir."

"They weren't vaccinated?"

"Yes, Sir. Daddy had them vaccinated, but the dose must not have been strong enough. They got sick Wednesday night, but I came to school Thursday. By Thursday night two of them had died and most of the others were sick. I called the veterinarian, but he couldn't help. I spent all day Friday bathing them and trying to keep them cool. By the time Daddy got home Friday night, twelve more had died. We dug a huge pit to put them in. Mama and all of us helped. We poured kerosene on them and started a fire."

"Why didn't you just bury them?"

"Burning is better to keep cholera from spreading."

"How many did you lose?" a little compassion was beginning to show in the way he spoke.

"Every single one of those beautiful shoats died. I had to stay there and keep the fire burning."

"Who was the vet?"

"Dr. Shannon."

"I'll check your story. Meantime, I'll give you an excuse for a family emergency."

Alex was enraged. "I certainly did not make it up."

"I'll check."

"Alex, what's wrong?" Jeannie asked when she met him in the hall. "Where have you been? I've missed you."

Alex couldn't understand why Mr. Hodnette refused to believe what he had told him. He was insulted. He didn't even look at Jeannie.

"Alex, what have I done? What is the matter?" Tears were in her eyes.

Alex felt like screaming. He walked on, wearing an angry expression on his face.

Jeannie turned and walked away.

"It's not you, Jeannie. Come back." He was after her in a flash, but she darted into the bathroom.

At that moment Mr. Hodnette stepped into the hall. He looked at Alex sternly and motioned with his head for him to move along.

Alex gave him an angry glance and started toward class. He knew it was his fault, but he didn't expect Jeannie to react in that way. Alex didn't see her come to first period class. Her seat remained empty. Alex couldn't keep his mind on his work. He kept looking over to see if she had come in. When the bell rang, Alex glanced toward the back of the room. He caught a glimpse of her leaving. She must have come in late and taken a seat in the back of the room.

"Wait a minute, Jeannie." He ran to catch up with her. "Please let me explain." He could tell she had been crying, but she walked on down the hall, completely ignoring him.

"I can explain, Jeannie. I love you." She walked on.

Alex explained his absence to the next teacher. Jeannie's friend, Evelyn, heard him. She wrote a note and slipped it to Jeannie after class. "Talk to Alex," the note said. "He has an explanation."

Jeannie went into the bathroom. She stood in a corner, leaning against the wall with her arms folded across her stomach. She turned her eyes away when anyone tried to approach her. When the bell rang, she walked to her next class.

Jeannie still had no clue as to what had happened, but she began to feel remorse for being so cold. She wrote a note and passed it to Alex. The note simply said, "Can we talk?" He nodded briefly, but his expression was grim.

When class was over, Jeannie waited for Alex just outside the door. "I'm sorry," both of them said.

"A lot has happened," Alex said. Alex told her everything.

"I'm so sorry," she said. "I couldn't understand your walking away from me. I should have known that something serious had happened."

"Mr. Hodnette didn't want to give me an excuse. I felt like just walking away and never coming back."

"I'll help you get caught up if you want me to."

"Thanks. I don't know what I would do without you."

Toward the end of the day, Mr. Hodnette sent for Alex. "I checked with Dr. Shannon about your hogs. The doctor is concerned about an outbreak of cholera in the community. He said that you did the right thing burning them. He also said that the hogs were probably infected with the disease when your father bought them. You might be able to get restitution from the man who sold them to you. You should look into it."

"Thank you, Sir."

Alex appreciated the principal's concern, but he had not gotten over the fact that Mr. Hodnette doubted his explanation. "Mr. Hodnette, I wouldn't miss a day of school without a real reason."

"I guess you wouldn't, Presswood, but come over here." He showed Alex a stack of absentee slips that had come in during the month. "Every absentee costs us money. The state pays us for students who come to school, but not for the ones who are absent. I would have a lot more of these if I didn't keep a close check. Luckily, you were able to prove yours or you would have answered for three unexcused absences. And by the way, Alex, let us know if you have this kind of trouble again. We might be able to help." Alex was surprised. He just nodded his head and walked out of the office.

One Sunday, Alex was invited to Jeannie's house for dinner. He enjoyed the food and the company and said so. He was invited to come over the next week and pretty soon, he had a standing invitation for Sunday dinner.

After dinner, they played card games with Jeannie's parents. They taught Alex how to play bridge, a game that he would enjoy for the rest of his life. After bridge and dessert, Alex and Jeannie were able to spend time together. If they didn't have to study, they went for long walks or to a movie, or just sat in the swing and talked. On these Sunday afternoons, the war seemed far away and they were happy with the world.

The senior class felt they were missing many things they had looked forward to. They had enjoyed senior plays given by other senior classes. They petitioned for a play, but it was denied because the teachers were too busy rolling bandages, or filling in for jobs vacated by men who were drafted, or were helping out on farms. No one felt like taking on the jobs of casting, practicing, costumes, and scenery.

A group of parents was successful, however, in persuading Mr. Hodnette to let them give an after-game party for seniors and football players. "Our children have not had a single school party since they've been in high school. We can't deny them everything just because of the war. They will be expected to sacrifice their time and maybe their very lives in a few short months. We would like them to have some fun before they are hurled into such an uncertain future."

Bill Simmon's father was the one who spoke for the group. Bill became the hero for the moment and he gloated over the attention.

On the night of the party, Alex started dancing most numbers with Jeannie, but someone cut in every time. Bill wouldn't dance with anyone else but her. Jeannie knew that Alex was getting angry and she pleaded with Bill to stop cutting in. He only laughed. Finally Alex said, "Bill why don't you find your own girl? Jeannie is my date and I haven't finished a dance with her yet."

"Jeannie is the best dancer here. I'm sorry to spoil your fun, Old Buddy, but I like to dance too." Alex bit his lip. He wanted to knock Bill down, but he didn't want to be the one to ruin the party.

Alex thought about it as he walked over to the jukebox. He chose a song that he knew Bill liked and could sing fairly well. Alex announced he had a surprise. He said that Bill Simmons would sing the next song, "To Each His Own," and he added that Bill would sing requests after that. Bill was pleased. Bill smiled and bowed and moved close to the jukebox. Alex danced the whole number with Jeannie and clapped when it was over. Next he sang "Moon River" and then "Dark Town Stutter's Ball." Bill had fun. Alex and Jeannie had fun, too.

"That was the smartest thing you've ever done," Jeannie said. As soon as Bill finished one song, someone requested another. Evelyn sang with him and others joined in. The crowd had a wonderful time. Some danced, some sang, and some stood or sat just watching and listening.

On the way home, Alex stopped the car. "Jeannie," he said, "There's something I've always wanted to do. Something I haven't tried since the seventh grade." Jeannie waited. Alex reached into his pocket and pulled out an unopened pack of Camel cigarettes. "I want to smoke. I've watched my dad and other people smoke and they seem to enjoy it so much. I want to try it. I've always respected my parents' wishes and refrained from doing it, but I think I'm old enough now to make my own decision about smoking. Would you like to try?"

"I've thought about it, but I know my parents wouldn't like it. I'm curious about it. I know some of the girls in our class smoke."

"I didn't know anyone smoked."

"Some do."

Alex opened the pack. He took out a cigarette and placed it between his lips. He clumsily struck a match and touched the flame to the cigarette. He sucked in at the right time and managed to get it lit. He remembered well the last time he had done this and how sick he was, so he was careful not to let smoke go down his throat. He blew it out quickly. "Want to try?"

Jeannie giggled. She took his cigarette and held it between her index and middle fingers as she had seen others, mostly men, hold their cigarettes. She took a short puff and handed it back to Alex. He tried again, this time letting a small amount of smoke go down his throat. He coughed. Jeannie took another puff and she coughed. "We'll get the hang of it in a minute," Jeannie said.

"Let's go slowly. I don't want our parents to catch us before we even learn how to do it." Alex put the pack back into his pocket. "Maybe we can try again tomorrow." He told Jeannie about the time long ago when he was caught smoking by Bill Simmons.

"You told me you had lost $5 and Bill found it," she laughed. "And you never told me the truth in all these years."

"I tried to forget about it." They laughed.

Alex offered Jeannie a piece of gum before they went home. "I don't want anyone to smell smoke on us."

"We can always say that someone else was in the car."

"Who?" He wondered who among their friends was smoking.

"You can always say Bill Simmons," she laughed.

During the next few weeks, Jeannie and Alex learned to smoke. He rode the bus to her house and they went for walks to find a secluded spot to smoke. At first they felt guilty; smoking was one thing Alex's dad asked him not to do. However, Alex liked it. He wanted to smoke.

On Sunday afternoons when they played cards, Jeannie's father smoked a cigar while they played. After an hour or two, the young people found themselves almost screaming for a cigarette. When they went for a walk or a ride after the bridge game, they reached for a cigarette as soon as they were out of sight.

When spring came, Alex and Jed did the plowing and planting as they had done for many years. Now that Liz was gone, Marge had to assume many of the household chores. Mama had been asked to do some substitute teaching in schools nearby, which made more work for everyone.

Alex was concerned that most of the work would fall on Jed's shoulders after he was gone. This would be his last planting. He would not be around for the plowing and weeding in the summer or the harvesting in the fall. He encouraged his dad to cut down on the acreage, but Dad had plans to buy more cows and would not consider cutting down on any of his crops. Alex said that it would put a great burden on Jed, but he could not reason with his father. Dad had his own plans and his own goals.

Dave Presswood could not accept that his eldest son would be drafted. As the time for Alex's departure drew nearer, Dave became unreasonable. He believed that if he had more livestock, more land under cultivation, and more demands upon his son, he could plead before the draft board to have his son deferred until the growing season was over and the cows and hogs were fat and ready for market. His frustration increased when he went to the sale pen to buy more livestock and found that the prices for even the scrawniest animals had escalated beyond his ability to pay. He found fault with everything his family did and he argued with them about the slightest inconvenience. He argued with neighbors. He argued with drivers on the road. He made the boys redo jobs that they had done precisely to his instructions.

"What are we going to do, Mama? Daddy is acting like a mad man!" Alex exclaimed. "I don't want to have to worry after I'm gone that he will do any of you bodily harm. I am afraid for you."

On the way to the barn one morning, Alex dropped his cigarettes. He and Jed fed the cows, horses, hogs, and chickens. Alex had finished feeding and milking his cow, and was letting her calf suck before separating them for the day. Dad, who had the week off from work, woke up early and decided to walk out to the barn to see if he could assist the boys. He went into a rage when he saw a pack of Camels lying on the ground. He picked up a broom handle that was leaning against the wall and began swinging it in the air, shouting and going for Jed, who was milking a young cow. The cow was startled when she saw the raised stick and bolted out of the stall, knocking Dad backward into a gatepost. Dad's head hit the post and an old plow that had been left on the post fell down and cut his head. Blood gushed out over his face and head.Alex chased the runaway cow. Jed screamed when he saw his father and ran to the house for help. Mama came running to the barn, followed by a half-dressed Marge. Dad was unconscious, and had to be carried to the house. They took him up the steps, and into his bedroom. Mama grabbed a towel, dipped it into warm water and washed his face and hair. Dave made a groaning sound and slowly opened one eye. He tried to sit up, but fell back on the pillow when he saw the blood. Mama slapped his cheeks to try to rouse him. He opened his eyes again and spoke one word, "Stop!"

Alex rushed in. "What happened? Is Dad O.K.?" Alex had chased the cow down the road for a quarter of a mile before he was able to overtake her and get her turned around. He locked the cow and calf safely in the pen.

Dad motioned to Mama that he wanted to sit up. She propped him up in bed. The flow of blood from his head wound had stopped, but his shirt was streaked with blood.

"The cow I was milking bolted and knocked Daddy into a post," Jed said. "I was knocked over against the wall and the milk went everywhere."

"What made her bolt?" Alex asked.

"Daddy was swinging a stick."

Alex turned to Dad. "Swinging a stick? You have always told us not to swing sticks in front of a cow, especially a young one."

Everyone stood there in astonishment. Where did Alex get the nerve to talk to him like that?

"I intended to hit Jed with that stick. I found these." He held up the pack of Camels that he still clutched in his hand.

"Those aren't mine," Jed said.

"They're mine," Alex said. Everyone gasped. "It's my choice to smoke. In less than a month, I'll be joining the Navy. I'll have to make many decisions. I've chosen not to drink alcohol. But I do want to smoke.

"They're mine," Alex said. Everyone gasped. "It's my choice to smoke. In less than a month, I'll be joining the Navy. I'll have to make many decisions. I've chosen not to drink alcohol. But I do want to smoke.

"Daddy, you must accept the fact that there's nothing you can do to keep me from being drafted. I'm sorry. I would much prefer to go away to college next year. I still want to be a doctor, but that will just have to wait. I'm not afraid to go and I don't want you to be afraid either. What I am afraid of is that you won't be able to cope with the work that has to be done here. You can't expect Jed to do alone what we have done together the last few years."

Dave hung his head and said, "Jed, I'm sorry. I never thought Alex would do it."

Jed shook his head. "I didn't either."

Then Dave turned to Alex. "You're right," he said. "We'll have to cut back. I've been on edge for a long time. I promise to calm down. The war has changed so much. The hardest thing for me to bear is your going away. I wanted you to be a doctor. But this goes to show you just how little control you have over things that you believe to be your own. A person truly does not own anything."

Dad handed Alex his cigarettes. "These are yours."

"Thanks." Alex put them into his pocket. The idea of lighting up in front of his father flickered through his mind, but out of respect for him, he did not.

"You may take the car today. You can all go to school together. If you hurry, you won't be late."

The next few days whizzed by as they took their final exams and attended graduation. Alex's orders came a few days before school was out. He was ordered to go on the train to Birmingham. He would receive instructions there.

Many other boys who had graduated that week were at the railroad station. A crowd had gathered: fathers, mothers, brothers, sisters, sweethearts, friends and relatives came to say goodbye to their loved ones. Tears flooded everyone's eyes as the train pulled away with anxious young boys who were about to become men, and upon whose shoulders rested the destiny of the nation.

Jeannie stood on the platform and waved. The train slowly chugged out of view. She touched her cheeks with her handkerchief and brushed away the tears.

Bill Simmons stepped up to her. “Don’t worry. He’ll be back,” he said in a sarcastic voice.

“Why aren’t you on that train?”

“My birthday isn’t until next month,” Bill grinned. “How about us hanging out until I have to go?”

“I’ll be much too busy to ‘hang out’. I wouldn’t hang out with you anyway.” She turned and walked away. She didn’t see Bill again for a long time.

## *ALEX AND JEANNIE*
## ALEX JOINS THE NAVY

At the Birmingham railroad station, Alex and the others being inducted were met by personnel officers from all of the different branches of the military. Naval recruiting officers led the young men to the waiting buses. Over seventy young men destined to become sailors were driven to an induction center. They entered a gymnasium where hundreds of cots were set up. They were led to a row and instructed to place their suitcases on one of the cots. Alex stood by his cot nervously anticipating what would happen next. The inductees remained in the gym waiting further instruction.

Alex noticed that there were sailors wearing SP armbands stationed in various areas of the large room. The big, burley men whose size alone commanded respect carried Billy clubs on their hips. Alex had heard that thievery was rampant among sailors and was relieved to see SPs in the room.

Soon the induction process began. The young men were instructed to remove their clothing, line up and march down the hall to the examination area. Each man was examined from head to toe, had his head shaved, and ordered to hit the showers. Uniforms were issued and they returned to the gym.

Alex quickly dressed in his new white uniform. He and some of the others discussed how to roll and tie their ties properly. Alex had trouble with his webbed belt and brass buckle. His pants were a little bit too long and so were his shirtsleeves, but he felt like a real sailor. Alex was ready for anything his future held.

An officer swore in the new recruits. He announced that although the freshly dressed sailor boys looked great in their new white uniforms, they were unsuitable for the long train ride ahead of them. They were to change into their dungarees and to put their white uniform and the rest of the gear they had collected into their duffel bags.

The new sailors were issued bags in which to put all of their civilian clothing. "You won't have any need for civi's where you are going." they were told.

"We'll return these to your parents. Write their names and addresses legibly on the bags."

The inductees were marched into the mess hall for chow. They had just enough time to eat before boarding the bus and returning to the train station.

Darkness had fallen by the time the trip to California had begun. Alex was lucky to get a window seat. As soon as they were out of the city and away from all of the lights there was nothing to see except the occasional light in a farmhouse, or a small town here and there. Alex soon fell asleep, leaning on a small, thin pillow that was given to him. It had been a long and tiring day. He was not happy about leaving his family and friends behind, but he was excited about his first journey away from home, and the opportunity for travel. He knew he would be home in twelve weeks, so he felt good as the trip began.

Alex knew that where he was headed was a long way from home. He could not have anticipated how tiring the trip would be. The train rattled, shook and groaned. The bumping and banging woke him and made it difficult to get back to sleep. The seat was hard, the pillow thin, and he was not used to sleeping sitting up.

When daylight came, he felt better since he could look out the window and watch the scenery. But after looking at mile after mile of trees, fields, and pastures whizzing by, misery and boredom set in.

At various cities along the way other frightened eighteen-year-olds, answering their country's call, joined Alex on the train.

Alex took advantage of each stop, and left the car. He wanted to stretch his legs, breathe a little fresh air, go to the bathroom, and perhaps get a candy bar and a coke. Most of the young men were strangers to each other but they conversed as they mingled on the train and on the station platforms. Alex overcame his reservations about speaking with strangers, and began talking to his traveling companions. No one was willing to admit that they were on the greatest adventure of their lives. Nor would they admit that they wished their families and friends, and especially their sweethearts, were sharing this experience with them. Many of the young men had never traveled further than a few miles from where they were born.

At last they reached San Diego. Alex grabbed his duffle bag, climbed down from the train and looked around. He listened carefully to instructions being barked over loud speakers. He followed the instructions and walked to a waiting bus, boarded, and sat down. The bus delivered the tired young men to their barracks. He stood in line and waited to be assigned a place to sleep and to store his gear. He found out very quickly that good listening habits, which he had acquired in high school, were essential to his survival. He also learned quickly that written instructions were to be read at once, memorized, and followed to a tee if he was to avoid being dressed down by his superiors. Being on the bottom of the pile, so to speak, made almost everyone his superior.

Alex easily adjusted to basic training and the many restrictions involved. He had always gotten up early on the farm, worked from daylight to dusk, and was disciplined to accept responsibility. He was in good physical shape. He learned quickly to use and care for his weapons, and he learned what was required of him as a member of the United States Navy. He took his classes seriously. He studied the manuals and was determined to be the best sailor that he could possibly be. As in high school, Alex endeavored to excel in every phase of his training. He found it difficult, however, to keep his personal belongings spotless, his shoes mirror clean, his bed flawlessly made, his blanket folded perfectly. Every time he thought his bed was perfect enough to pass inspection, he found the sheet hanging lower on one side or the other or his pillow placed slightly off center, or his blanket slightly wrinkled. His squad leader called these things to his attention before inspection each day and Alex quickly corrected them. When his twelve weeks of basic training were over, Alex had mastered these skills. He had learned to eat the poorly prepared food without complaining, to take his turn cooking, peeling potatoes, and cleaning the latrine.

Alex had time at night to write letters to his family and to Jeannie. With each letter he wrote to Jeannie, he realized how much he loved her and how much he missed her. He daydreamed about his upcoming leave, and about being able to see her again. He began counting the weeks, the days, and the hours until he could journey back to his little town in southern Alabama.

Alex discussed with his friends the different modes of transportation available. They argued about the fastest, most reliable, and most comfortable carriers. Each method had its drawbacks, but each man seemed to have fixed in his mind just how he would travel. Many of them thought that hitchhiking was the fastest and cheapest, though servicemen in uniform traveled at a reduced rate on public transportation. Others preferred to 'hit the rails' and take their chances on the bone-crushing, rickety, jerky, shaky railroad cars. Air travel was out of the question; as the cost was too great, most airports were small, and were only in larger cities.

Alex decided to try the bus. When he saw his ticket, he began to wonder if he had made a wise decision. It was as long as his arm. He would have to change buses seven or eight times and lay over at bus stations at almost every change. Alex was told that he might make up time by hitchhiking from some of the towns or cities to the next. He decided to leave as much of his gear as he could in his locker. He would travel with as small a bag as he could get by with in case he found it expedient to try to hitch a ride along the way.

When the great day finally came, Alex was ready to go just as soon as his leave papers were issued. He took a shuttle to the bus station and arrived there only moments before his bus began loading. He was lucky to get a seat. Before he had settled in, a young woman with a baby and a small child climbed up the steps. Looking around, Alex saw that all seats were taken. He relinquished his seat to the very appreciative young woman. She sat down with her two children on her lap.

She explained that she had been visiting her husband, who had never seen the baby. Her husband had lost a leg several months before while fighting the Japanese in the Philippines. She was so glad to have him back from the war zone, alive, that she accepted his loss of a limb as a blessing.

Later, when a seat became available, Alex sat down and closed his eyes. The humming of the wheels soon put him to sleep and he slept for over an hour as the bus moved steadily along. Alex got off in Blythe, California. He walked into the station and inquired about the departure time of his next bus.

"Five hours," said the desk clerk.

Alex didn't want to sit in the bus station for that long, so he asked directions to the highway where he could, hopefully, catch a ride. He was directed to a spot near the edge of town where servicemen, seeking rides, often stood.

It was late afternoon when he approached the four sailors and a soldier who stood at the spot, each one hoping to save time by being picked up. Alex greeted them. The soldier, Joseph Burns, was headed for South Carolina, the same direction Alex was going. They decided to walk a little farther down the road together, separating themselves from the others. They had walked about a quarter of a mile when an oil truck stopped and offered them a ride. The driver said he was going fifty miles and would be happy to give them a ride. Alex and Joseph introduced themselves as they climbed into the seat next to the driver. Conversation flowed smoothly and in a little more than an hour, the driver slowed down.

"I'm sorry to put you out in the dark, but I'm turning off right up here," He brought the truck to a stop. Alex and Joseph thanked the driver and got out. They began walking. Two minutes later a car stopped.

"I am going to Phoenix," the driver of the old Ford car shouted. "You are welcome to ride with me."

Alex and Joseph looked at the car and at each other. They said at once, "Thank you. We'd appreciate it." They hurried to get into the car.

"I saw the truck let you out." The older man, who introduced himself as William Davis, apologized for his old car, and remarked that it was impossible to get a better one.

The boys expressed their gratitude for the ride and assured him that they were thankful for it. They explained that the five-hour lay over motivated them to try to hitch a ride instead of sitting in the station killing time.

"Can either of you boys drive?" William Davis asked.

"Yes," Alex said. "I would be glad to help with the driving."

When he slowed down and stopped, Alex slid behind the wheel. William pointed out the switches, the brakes, and the clutch, and then sat back to enjoy the ride. Alex started off with a jerk, but soon had the car running smoothly. He enjoyed driving. The Ford reminded him of the car he and Jed had restored.

There was little traffic on the narrow road, which while not paved, was hard and smooth. "We'll be going through some mountains between here and Phoenix," William said. "Have you driven across mountains before?"

"No, Sir, I haven't," Alex said.

"You just have to drive a little slower and keep your eyes on the road. Also, if it begins to choke, put it into second gear until you reach the top of the mountain, and then put it back into 3rd."

"How will I know when I have reached the top of the mountain?" Alex asked, looking out of the window.

"You can tell by the way the motor sounds and the car handles. If you have any trouble or don't feel confident, just wake me up and I'll take over. I have been driving for eight hours and I need a little rest."

"O. K." Alex slowed down a bit and kept his eyes peeled. "I'm surprised that this road isn't paved. Most of the main roads back home are paved now."

"They are working on a more direct route between Blythe and Phoenix, which will be wider and paved, of course. The war has slowed down construction so we'll just have to put up with this until we can put more time and money into it," William said. "Now, I'll try to get a little sleep. Be sure to wake me up if you need anything. By the way, I bought gasoline a few miles back, so you should be all right on that score."

William leaned his head back on the seat and was soon asleep. Alex noticed that Joseph, sitting in the back seat, was sleeping too. It gave him an eerie feeling to be virtually alone, driving a strange car on a strange road and knowing that mountains were looming up ahead. He hoped that he could stay awake for an hour or two anyway.

When Alex first realized that he was starting across a mountain, he began to panic. His hands got sweaty and his neck felt prickly. When the car began to cough and choke, he put it into second gear and reduced his speed. He kept his eyes glued to the road, afraid to look toward either side. He prayed that he would not meet another car until he got to the other side of the mountain.

When the car reached the peak, the sound of the motor changed. It no longer made a grinding sound, but sounded steady and quiet. Alex shifted back to third gear and began to relax. *That wasn't so bad,* he thought. Suddenly the car began to move faster. When Alex realized that they were speeding down the other side, he began to apply the brakes.

"Go easy on the brakes, son," Even in his sleep, William knew what was happening. He knew that it would burn the brakes out if they were used too much on the descent down the mountain.

Alex tried to take his foot off the brakes, but the car was going too fast. He kept putting on brakes and taking them off, putting them on, taking them off, as the car whizzed down the mountain road. His hair was standing on end as he realized that he wasn't able to slow the car as it rolled faster and faster around curve after curve until finally they reached the foot of the mountain and the car slowed its self.

*That was the scariest thing that has ever happened to me!* Alex thought. *But I made it! I hope there won't be another one for a while.* He began to enjoy the ride again.

Soon Alex realized that they were beginning to climb. He was not happy about the prospects of another hair-raising experience, but he felt he could do it again. He changed gears and chugged, chugged, chugged to the top of the mountain, then braced himself for the ride down the other side. He tried to apply the brakes sparingly, but they were going so fast that he couldn't take his foot off them. When they finally reached the foot of the mountain, Alex smelled something burning. He applied the brakes again and his foot went to the floor. He pumped them once, twice, but his foot again hit the floor.

Since Alex was giving the car no gas, it finally rolled to a stop on its own. That was when Alex saw what was burning. "The car is on fire!" He screamed and jumped out. William and Joseph fell out behind him.

"What can we do?" Alex cried excitedly as he darted here and there trying to think of something to do.

"Pee on it!" William, who had already started wetting the brakes, ordered.

It took Alex some time to unbutton the 13 buttons of his sailor pants, but he made a steady stream for nearly a minute. He had been wishing for a rest stop for the last hour. William and Joseph, who had also helped to quench to fire, stood back and examined the damage.

The fire was out—now what? Alex was petrified. Would William be angry enough to leave him and Joseph on the mountain road alone? He had not seen another car since they had hit the mountains. He just stood there, waiting to see what William would do.

William walked around the car, looking it over as he went. Then he spoke, "You are lucky, Boy," he said. "You managed to get us over the mountain before this happened. I think I will be able to drive it now. I believe there is a gas station up ahead. We'll let a mechanic look at the brakes before we start over the next mountain. We'll be traveling between mountains for the next twenty or thirty miles so I can get along without brakes until we get to the station."

"Will he be open this late?" Alex asked.

"If he isn't, we'll wake him up."

Joseph had little to say about the fire, but he seemed very nervous about riding in a car that had no brakes. "I don't think I want to ride thirty miles in a car that doesn't have brakes, especially at night," he said. "You can go on with this fellow if you want to, but I think I'll take a chance on getting another ride." He had been watching a set of headlights that appeared and disappeared on the winding road behind them. Joseph grabbed his bag out of the car and continued up the road. "You coming?" he yelled to Alex.

"I'll stay," Alex answered.

In a few minutes the car reached them. It slowed down and the driver asked if he could help.

"Let me see if I can crank it," William said.

When the car started, William stepped over to the other vehicle. "Thank you," he said to the driver. "I think we can make it to the station. There is a soldier walking up the way. He didn't want to continue with me because my brakes are bad, but I am sure he would appreciate a ride."

"I'll watch for him," the driver said. He started down the road.

"Why didn't you go with him?" William asked Alex.

"Well, I feel like I am responsible for your trouble and I don't want to leave you alone out here."

"I appreciate that," William said. "I'll do my best to get you to Phoenix by midnight so you can get another ride, either on the bus or hitch-hiking." They began to move slowly toward Phoenix.

The mechanic was just closing his shop when they reached the station. He went right to work on the brake job. Another car pulled up and the driver asked if he could buy some gas. When he saw Alex standing there in his uniform, he offered him a ride.

"I am going to Phoenix," the driver said.

Alex looked at William who said, "Take the ride, Son. You have a long way to go. I'll be all right now."

Alex thanked William, shook his hand, grabbed his bag, and climbed into the waiting auto. The new driver introduced himself as Herman Alvord and said that he was anxious to reach Phoenix before midnight. He had an appointment early the next day with a group of cattle growers who supplied beef for his meatpacking company. Since his company provided meat products for the government, he was allotted gasoline and tires so he could use his car to travel from place to place, procuring beef, pork, lamb, and even buffalo for his business. He had a reservation in a Phoenix hotel. He asked Alex if he would like to spend the night with him, to keep him company.

"Oh, no, Sir," Alex said. "I am anxious to get to Phoenix and catch my next bus." Alex explained that he had decided to hitchhike, rather than wait at the bus station for his next bus.

"Then you won't mind sitting in the back seat where you will have more room, will you? I might find another young man who would enjoy having a nice room to sleep in tonight."

Alex felt uncomfortable. He was, far from home, in the car of a complete stranger who was looking for male companionship for the night. Had it been daylight, he would have asked the man to let him out, but to be alone in the dark on an unfamiliar roadway was more frightening than being in the car with this strange person. Herman stopped the car and Alex quickly got into the back seat. "You don't have to be afraid," Herman said. "I often pick up servicemen on my trips. I invite them to share my hotel room because I realize they are having a rough time, being away from their family and friends. I feel that a night in a clean, respectable room would be a treat. I am a married man. Having a woman share my room would not be acceptable at all."

Alex found his tongue. "Thank you, Sir," he said. "I am really pushed for time. I have only a three week leave and over a week of that will be spent traveling. If I can get to the bus station on time, I can be on my way tonight." He still felt uneasy, but he accepted Herman's explanation and hoped it was the truth.

"Where is your final destination?" Herman asked.

Alex hesitated. He didn't know if he should reveal to this man just how far he was from friends and family, but he decided to play it straight. He answered that he was going to Alabama.

"I have never been to Alabama. I suppose it isn't too different from Arizona, is it?"

"I think it is quite different," Alex said. "We get much more rainfall than you do here and there is much more vegetation. Why, you can ride for miles without seeing a tree out here, but in Alabama there are trees everywhere. There is a great difference, Sir."

"Perhaps after the war, I can take a trip to Alabama," Herman said. "Sounds like that is something I would like to see."

"It is a very beautiful state," Alex said. "I am very excited about going home. I only wish I could stay."

"The war won't last forever; you'll be going home to stay before you know it."

"I certainly hope so."

Their conversation ended for a while. Herman seemed to be looking for something.

"There is a major crossroad up ahead and servicemen are often waiting there for rides." He slowed the car down. Sure enough, there were two soldiers waiting.

"I am going as far as Phoenix," Herman called to them. They hurried to the car and got in, one in the front and one in the back with Alex.

"How long have you been waiting?" Herman asked.

"We have been here for almost an hour," one of the soldiers said. "We certainly do appreciate your stopping."

"You are welcome," Herman said. The young man in the front seat was a talker and he kept a lively conversation going.

Alex thought about the events of the day: hitching a ride on an oil truck, then another one across the mountains, driving over two mountains, brakes on fire, putting the fire out with pee, and being picked up by this unusual person. Well, at least he wasn't alone now. He drifted off to sleep and didn't wake up until he felt someone shaking him and saying that they were at the bus station in Phoenix.

Alex got out, stretched his legs and arms and yawned. He picked up his bag and walked around the car to shake Herman's hand and thank him for the ride. Herman thanked him for the sacrifice he was making for his country. He wished Alex good luck and drove away. Alex saw that one of the soldiers was still in the car. He walked into the station, thankful to have arrived safe and sound. He knew he would not be likely to take another chance at hitching a ride on this trip.

"Your bus will be here in twenty minutes," the station agent told Alex. Then he took a closer look at Alex's ticket. "You were scheduled to make connections with a bus that does not arrive for four and a half hours. How did you get here ahead of schedule?"

When Alex explained that he had hitched rides, the agent was concerned. "You did save a little time, but you took a great chance. You really never know what might happen out there. You had already paid for the bus ride, so you didn't save any money. My advice is to get a book or magazine and pass the time reading. It's much safer."

"I will take that advice." Alex hurried over to the lunch counter and ordered a hamburger and a cup of coffee, remembering that he had not eaten since lunch.

Alex was standing outside when the Greyhound bus pulled in. He found a seat, adjusted it, and was sound asleep before the bus left the station. He did not wake up until the bus pulled into Tucson, three hours later. He followed the crowd into the station for the twenty-minute rest stop. He went to the rest room then went outside to wait.

"You'll change at Las Cruces," the driver informed Alex as he boarded the bus. "We'll get there about noon."

Alex was glad to be moving again. He curled up on the seat and was soon asleep again and didn't wake up until daylight. He was pleased that a pretty young woman had taken the seat beside him while he slept. They talked amicably. She was returning to college for her senior year and was looking forward to seeing her friends on campus. She pointed out interesting landmarks as they zoomed through the countryside. The time passed quickly.

Alex's connection at Las Cruces was at the station when his bus arrived there. "You'll change again in El Paso," the driver told Alex. No wonder his ticket was as long as his arm.

Alex stayed on the next bus all of the way across Texas. There were stops along the way at San Antonio, Houston, and other Texas cities, and at Lake Charles and Baton Rouge in Louisiana. It took a day and a night to reach New Orleans. Alex was tired. He knew his journey was almost over.

After waiting only forty minutes, Alex was on his way to Mobile. The bus followed the coastal route, past beautiful beaches and lovely old pre-Civil War mansions. Alex enjoyed the scenery. In Mobile, he began to get nervous. In about an hour, he would be home.

Alex's whole family was at the station to greet him. He was excited to see his parents and Jed, Liz, and Marge, but he was disappointed that Jeanne wasn't there. He hoped to see her soon.

The few days at home went very quickly. Alex spent time with Jed on the farm, enjoyed home-cooked meals, and hurried to Jeannie's house whenever he could. The last night of his leave came too soon.

### *JEANNIE AND ALEX GET ENGAGED*

Alex held Jeannie in his arms, stroking her bare shoulders and back. He moved his hands slowly across her breasts and heard her gasp. He felt her snuggle closer to him as he kissed her cheeks, her eyelids, and her forehead. Her slender body trembled next to his. Alex knew that Jeannie shared the ecstasy that he felt. She had clung to him, kissing him with passion as he felt her body melt into his, her arms and legs holding him and her whole body moving with his; every cell crying out to be to touched and soothed. And then the almost inaudible sound of climatic response followed by deep relaxation filled him with the greatest happiness he had ever known. He had loved her before, but this was more wonderful than he had ever dreamed. He wanted this moment to last forever.

Alex felt Jeannie gently push him away as she reached for her clothing scattered about in the car. She dressed silently, brushed her long brown hair, and fell back into his arms, clinging to him again, kissing him with warmth and tenderness.

How long Alex had waited for this moment! They had been sweethearts, pals, buddies, and now they were lovers. They had spoken of their love. But they had never made love before.

And now they must part for the duration of the war, and that seemed like a lifetime. Alex was leaving tomorrow. He needed to tell Jeannie that this was forever, but words would not come. At last his lips started to obey his heart. He promised that he would return. This was the beginning of a wonderful life together, and their love was complete. The war would not last forever. He would be back to her.

Alex felt tears on his neck, hot and wet. Through her tears, Jeannie whispered, "I love you." She kissed him on the neck, on the cheek, and on the lips, sweet tender kisses that he would remember forever. Jeannie had stopped trembling now and he knew that she was ready to face the inevitable. They must say good-night and good-bye."

In the darkness Alex slipped into his pants, and pushed his arms into the sleeves of his shirt. Jeannie helped. She buttoned the cuffs and handed him his tie. Alex opened the door. They slid out of the back seat and stood there for a while, locked in another loving embrace, clinging to each other, feeling their bodies pressed together, knowing it would be their last night until he returned from the war. Slowly they walked around to the front of the car. Alex opened the door and helped Jeannie in. She reached in her bag for her lipstick.

Alex lit a cigarette as he walked around the car. He must regain his confidence to walk her to the door and face her father. *Well, she isn't his little girl any more,* Alex thought. *She now belongs to me.*

Alex and Jeannie talked all the way home. They had so little time to plan. Jeannie would go on to college as she had planned. Studying would help to pass the time. If Jeannie earned her degree while Alex was in the service, she would be able to work while he caught up with his education. Jeannie promised to write every day and Alex promised to write as often as he could.

As Alex pulled up in front of Jeannie's house and turned off the car, he finally managed to say the words every girl wants to hear. "Jeannie, will you marry me? Will you wait for me?"

"Oh yes, Alex, I will wait for you forever. I will marry you. I love you."

Inside the house, Alex asked Jeannie's dad for her hand. Her mom woke up, and the exciting news quickly spread to the whole family. It was true. It was official. They would be married when Alex returned home.

Jeannie walked with Alex to the door and out on the porch. They had a long, last kiss. She cried. They parted. She would not go to the railroad station tomorrow. His final parting belonged to his family. She would not be there. She could not share the parting with anyone.

Jeannie stood on the porch and watched and waved until Alex was out of sight. "Damn the war!" She sobbed. "Damn the war!"

Alex drove home slowly. He decided to wake his parents and tell them the great news. He knew they would be happy that Jeannie had promised to marry him. His emotions ranged from ecstasy to depression, a combination that was difficult to handle. He did not want to return to San Diego. He dreaded the trip. He hated having to leave his family and Jeannie, yet he felt the greatest elation because of his commitment with Jeannie.

A light had been left on for Alex in the kitchen. He poured a glass of milk and sat down at the table. Love made him tingle from his head down to his toes. The memory of their love was overwhelming. At least he had that much. In his mind, he could still feel her warm body pressed against his. He remembered every curve. The feeling would last forever. Alex finished his milk, rinsed the glass, and left it to drain on the counter.

Alex climbed the creaky stairs and knocked on the door of his parent's room. He felt a flush of panic as he realized what he was about to tell them. What would they say to their eighteen year old son who had just become engaged? He hoped they would share his joy. The door was opened quickly and he walked in. His mom slipped back under the covers as he sat down on the edge of the bed. They waited for him to speak.

"Mom, Dad," he said. "I asked Jeannie to marry me and she said yes. She's going to wait for me until I come home."

He watched his mother's face flush red as a wide toothy smile appeared. His father beamed.

"I am so glad," they both shouted. His mother hugged him and his dad did too. A hometown girl would bring their son back after the war. Many young men were marrying girls from other states, even other countries and would not return home to raise their children near their grandparents. It was a relief for Alex's parents to know that Alex had definite plans to come back home.

"I think you have chosen wisely, son," Alex's father said. "I think Jeannie is a wonderful girl and I know she will be the perfect wife for you." His mother echoed his approval.

After chatting for a few moments and making a few last-minute plans about breakfast and the trip to the railroad station, Alex went to his room.

Alex decided not to wake Jed and Marge; he'd tell them about his engagement first thing in the morning. He looked around at the familiar surroundings, taking in each and every detail of the room that had been his for eighteen years.

Sitting on the bed, Alex focused his attention on his poster collection. "Pinups" the guys called them: Veronica Lake, Betty Grable, Susan Hayworth, June Allison, and photos he had collected from notebook binders at school, and a few from magazines. He also had war pictures: tanks, guns, B-29's and other planes, tankers, and cutters. Alex recalled where he had gotten every picture; many of them were from Jeannie.

Alex got up and stood in front of the dresser. He reached out and began gathering the movie ticket stubs and snapshots of friends from school that had been tucked behind the mirror. He wrote names and dates on the backs of the photos. He put everything in a pile on his table. Then he began taking his pinups down. He found a box in his closet and laid his mementos carefully in it. He would ask his mom to put them in the attic until he came back. It would be better to have everything put away in case he didn't come back. It would be easier on his folks if he packed up his belongings himself. They might even want to rent his room out now that he would be gone for good. Many people were having great difficulty finding living space. He'd speak to Mama about that before he left. Packing his treasures took longer than Alex expected. Each item had memories: memories of high school and especially memories of Jeannie.

Jeannie, Jeannie! How he missed her already. If only they could have spent this last night together. He picked up the yearbook and slowly turned the pages. There was Jeannie, smiling her broad, friendly smile. She was a beauty! She was also caring and thoughtful and understanding. And she was fun. Jeannie had written beside his picture "To my best friend since fifth grade." He smiled, "Friend, lover, and now she is going to be my wife."

Alex understood why Jeannie didn't want to go to the railroad station to see him off, but he longed to see her again. He longed for one more kiss, one more hug, one more caress. He wondered how long it would be before they could love again?

Alex heard the clock in the living room strike one. He knew he had to get some rest. Going to bed was hard. Going to sleep was harder.

Alex did not know where he would be sent. Plans for his squad had not been disclosed after basic training. He only knew that he would return to San Diego and he guessed that he would serve on a ship in the Pacific, though he knew anything was possible. Alex felt disappointed that he would not be going to Europe. Friends who had served in Europe told about visiting London, but he knew it would be hell no matter where he had to go. Hell because of the danger. Hell to be away from home, and hell because he couldn't be with Jeannie. Thinking about what was in store for him kept him awake for a long time.

Alex's thoughts drifted to his brother and how much more work he would have to do. Alex knew that Jed would have to shoulder a larger load. James Edward, Jed for short, had been Alex's shadow for many years. Jed had started out holding the plow lines while Alex ploughed the field and he brought water and snacks. They had been pals as well as brothers. Alex knew that Jed would take up where he left off and help their father plant, cultivate, and harvest the crops as well as the dozens of other chores that must be done. Since their father was still committed to his defense plant job, Jed had the management of the farm almost to himself, quite an accomplishment for a fifteen-year-old ninth grade student. Their father had seen to it that Alex and Jed learned how to manage a farm. It was a major part of their education. He also instilled in them a desire to have a career other than farming, hoping that they would have the knowledge they needed to lead successful lives. Alex knew he would be missed, but he also knew that life would go on without him. At last he fell asleep.

Alex heard the alarm go off in his parents' room. He knew they wouldn't mind if he stayed in bed until time to get ready to go to the train station, but he wanted to get up. He dressed in work clothes and went out to help with the milking and chores. Alex did the milking while Jed fed the pigs and chickens. Jed was pleased about his engagement to Jeannie.

"I guess you can't count on me after the war, Jed. I will have to get a job as soon as I finish college, so I won't come back to the farm. Jeannie and I didn't have time to make any definite plans, but she'll go on to college while I am away."

After congratulating his brother, Jed said, "I like farming. I suppose I will stay with Daddy as long as he wants me to. I may decide to make my living farming. I haven't decided if I want to go to college or not."

"I know it will be hard on you, going to school and doing so much of the work here, but you should at least finish high school. If things don't work out on the farm, you will need a good education to see you through. You may even want to go to Auburn and learn how to be a prosperous farmer," Alex grinned. "Just promise me you will not drop out of high school."

"I plan to finish school," Jed said resolutely. "I know my grades aren't the best, but I usually manage to pass. I don't think Mother and Daddy would allow me to quit school anyway."

"Marge is the scholar in our family anyway," Jed said. "She may go on to college. I'll help send her if she wants to go."

"You have a lot of responsibility for a boy your age, Jed. You mustn't tie yourself down though. You need to have some fun, too."

"I do, football games, a little hunting, baseball now and then. But I enjoy the work here on the farm. I like the smell of the dirt when I am plowing and I like being outdoors all day."

"Well, just try to make the best of all of this. I love you and Mother and Daddy and Liz and Marge. I wish I didn't have to go."

"We'll miss you. Since Liz has gone to work at the Naval Air Station in Pensacola, there are only four of us. But don't worry, we'll make out all right."

"Mama will have breakfast ready. We'd better go on to the house," Alex said, picking up the milk bucket.

Alex hesitated a moment, looking across the fields. He knew that he would never return as a working member of the family. It made him feel sad. Except for the sadness in his heart for his loved ones, however, he was excited about the future. Alex had worked hard on the farm for a long time, for as long as he could remember. But he did not have the love for farming that his brother had. He wanted to see what lay beyond the horizon, and being in boot camp had given him a glimpse of the outside world. He liked it.

Marge was setting the table when her brothers returned from the barn. The expression on her face showed how she felt about Alex's leaving. Alex walked over to her, put his arm around her shoulder and guided her silently into the living room. Alex wanted a few minutes to say good-bye to his favorite sister who would not celebrate her seventeenth birthday until next year. Marge and Alex had always been close and he would miss her. Marge was pleased about his engagement to Jeannie and said so as she hugged him.

"Marge, you have always been special to me. I will miss you. I want you to continue to work hard at school. You'll graduate in a few months and will probably be halfway through college before I return. Do your best, and be careful about boys. There are so few boys left in high school, but you'll meet some in college as soon as the war is over. Anyway, be careful."

Marge felt embarrassed. She just nodded. "You be careful, Alex. I'll miss you." They hugged again and then joined the family for the very special breakfast Mama had prepared.

Their breakfast together was enjoyable. There were huge servings of eggs, bacon, grits, biscuits, butter, Mama's own fig preserves, coffee, and milk. Every one was very congenial and pleasant and no one mentioned Alex's leaving.

### *ALEX RETURNS TO SAN DIEGO*

After breakfast everybody rushed around, clearing the table, straightening the house, making the beds, and getting dressed. Then they piled into the car for the ride to the train station. Alex and his father had discussed travel arrangements, and they had decided he should make the trip by rail. The train took a little longer and was a little more expensive, but it seemed better than the way he got home. "I hope you will never try hitch-hiking again. You might save a few hours' time, but you could get into serious trouble."

"I am afraid I agree with you."

They stood on the station platform waiting for the train. They said little. Each one was thinking of how he would fill the void Alex's leaving would produce.

When the train arrived, Alex hugged everyone and quietly walked up the steps. He turned around and waved. Marge was crying. Mama's eyes were dry, thank goodness. She had hugged him and kissed him, and patted his back, but no tears had appeared in her soft gray eyes. Daddy had hugged him too, and had wished him good luck. Jed started to shake his hand, then grabbed him and hugged him as he held back the tears. Liz was not there to see him off because she had to return to her job the day before. They all stood there and watched and waved until the train began to roll away. Alex saw Daddy put his arm over Mama's shoulder as they walked toward the car.

Two blocks from the station, Alex spotted Jeannie's car. She was standing beside it, hoping for a last glimpse of him. He didn't know if she had seen him or not, but he waved until she was out of sight.

Alex closed his eyes and leaned back in his seat. A feeling of helpless despair engulfed him. Where was he going? What would he be doing? How could he stand to be away from his home, his loved ones, especially his Jeannie? He didn't want to be on this train. He didn't want to leave his home, his town, his friends, or his loved ones. He dropped his head into his hands. He hadn't cried in a long time, but he had to fight to hold back the tears.

A hand touched his shoulder. "Cigarette?" asked the sailor sitting beside him, offering Alex a Lucky Strike. "Thanks," Alex said. "I smoke Camels." He dug in his pocket for his own cigarette, but he accepted a light.

"What is the name of the town?" The sailor asked.

"Atmore, Alabama. I have lived here all of my life."

"I'm Bud Henson," the sailor said. "I am from Buford, Georgia. I am on my way to New Orleans. My ship tied up there last month and I was lucky enough to get a seven-day pass. I had five days with my family."

"Alex Presswood. I'm headed for San Diego."

"How long will it take to get there?"

"Four days and nights."

"You'll have a sore butt," Bud said, shaking his head.

"You're right about that. I just hope I can make my connections. I have to change in New Orleans, Houston, and El Paso"

"How long do you lay over in New Orleans?"

"Four hours."

"Would you like for me to show you around the French Quarter? That's what everybody wants to see."

"Sure," Alex said. "There wasn't time to see anything when I came through on my way home."

"We'll be in New Orleans about fifteen hundred this afternoon. I don't have to be back to my ship until nineteen hundred, so we can look around for a couple of hours."

"As long as I am back in time to catch my train," Alex said, checking his ticket.

"How long have you been in the Navy?" Bud asked.

"I just finished boot camp. I graduated from high school on May fifteenth and was on my way May seventeenth.

"I've been in for three years," Bud offered. "I'm thinking about staying in the service after the war is over and making a career of it. I can retire at thirty-seven."

"That would be nice, retiring at thirty seven, but I am in only for the duration. I am already thinking about getting out and getting on with my life."

"I suppose staying in is the easy way out, but I haven't decided what I want to do."

"I know what I want to do. I have always wanted to be a doctor and I am anxious to get to college and begin studying."

"I've had enough studying," Bud said. "At least I thought I had. I am afraid I didn't take school very seriously. I did a lot of goofing off. I am really sorry for that now. Opportunity only knocks once, my dad always said."

"It probably isn't too late. Some people seem to be taking advantage of the new GI Bill of Rights. You can finish high school and then go on to college if you want to."

"Nah, I've had enough. Besides, I am so far behind, I'd never catch up."

Alex started to ask Bud about some of his experiences as a navy man when he heard a commotion at the other end of the train. Alex looked around in time to see a soldier hit the floor and an angry marine punch him when he tried to get up. Another marine held the first one back while the soldier got to his feet. The soldier then lunged toward the marine who moved aside and let the soldier take another tumble, this time falling across a seat occupied by a large, redheaded soldier. The redhead jumped up and the first soldier hit the floor again. Then a very lovely young woman appeared, returning from the restroom. Alex smiled, realizing that the two had been fighting over the girl. Then came the shrill whistle of the ever-present M.P. who marched the soldier and marine to the next car, telling them to leave the young lady alone.

"Watch what happens next," Bud whispered.

In a couple of minutes, the M.P. returned and sat down beside the girl. He asked her for her name and address, which he wrote down, then sat talking with her for half an hour.

"Looks like the M.P. won this one," Bud laughed. "I think I'll be an M.P. myself."

Then Bud began to talk about himself.

"I've been on the Ranger for two years. We're in New Orleans waiting for some engine parts to arrive. We didn't expect to be there more than a few days, but it's taking a lot longer than we thought. It seems that airplane, jeep, and tank parts have priority over parts for a ship. It's hard to understand. Of course, I'm grateful for a few days with my folks. But leaving again was hard."

"Hardest thing I've ever had to do," Alex agreed. "I got engaged, last night, and it's killing me to have to leave her."

"Congratulations. Hope it works out for you."

"I know it will. We have known each other since the fifth grade. We've been good friends for years. And now we're planning to spend the rest of our lives together, if this lousy war ever ends." Alex was surprised that he was talking so freely about his personal life to a perfect stranger. He wanted to talk about it. It just came naturally.

"Did you give her a ring?"

Alex sat up straight. He hadn't even thought of a ring, with so many other things to think about. "No, I will have to send it to her."

"I happen to have a ring I need to get rid of," Bud said. "I felt pretty confident about my girl, too. I bought a ring for her. But she wasn't ready to accept it. I thought you might want to buy it." He put his hand into his pocket and pulled out a tiny box. He opened it and showed Alex. An attractive gold mounting surrounded the small diamond.

Alex admired the ring. "It is very pretty, but I don't have the money right now. Thanks anyway." Then he added. "You should keep it. She might decide that she wants it later on."

"I doubt it. You see, she knows that I want to stay in (the Navy) and she doesn't want the life. You're sure you don't want the ring?"

"I'll have to pass on it. I'd like for us to pick one out together."

"O.K.", but don't forget that a ring on her finger sends a message to the other guys." Bud put the ring back in his pocket.

"That's true. Maybe I can send her one for Christmas."

Silence fell between the two sailors as the train rumbled on. Alex closed his eyes, and was soon asleep. Bud decided to circulate through the crowded car to try and find someone he knew.

When the train began to cross Lake Poncetrain, Bud returned and woke Alex. "You don't want to miss this. Crossing the lake on the train is like being out on the ocean on a ship, there's water as far as the eye can see, on both sides of the train."

Alex yawned and stretched. “Thanks,” he said as he looked around. “What a sight. This gives me an eerie feeling. It is just like being out on a huge lake in a boat. I am glad you woke me up.” He stood up and looked out the windows on both sides. “This is great!”

Then they passed through a swampland. Tall green grass grew in the wet low land, covering the ground for miles. Long legged water birds stood in the shallow water, waiting for frogs or crayfish to appear. If lucky, they ended up with a tasty morsel in their beak. Large blackbirds sat on bushes, watching for bugs or flies. Alex got a kick out of watching them. It reminded him of the creek near his family farm.

Then Alex was aware that the train was slowing down. He could see the outline of tall buildings in the distance as the skyline of New Orleans came into view. Alex was impressed by the height of some of the buildings. He was glad they had reached New Orleans in the daylight so he would be able to see some of the sights.

When the engine pulled into the station, the train came alive. Soldiers, sailors, marines, and a few civilians lined up in the aisles ready to hop off the train. Alex held on to his bag as he joined the group of anxious young men in the depot. He found a locker, deposited his bag, and followed Bud out the door. He was excited about having someone show him around the city. “We’ll walk down to the French Quarter,” Bud said. “There will be enough time for a stroll down Bourbon Street. I’ll take you to Jackson Square to see the statue of Stonewall Jackson and the St. Louis Cathedral. Then we’ll go to the French Market for a cup of coffee. Even at this time of day, their coffee is special. There is so much to see in New Orleans.”

Alex and Bud pushed their way through the crowded streets. Alex took in the quaint shops, the second story porches with their ornate iron grillwork, the beautiful flowers growing in pots on every doorway, and the people walking up and down the streets. He was surprised to see horse-drawn carriages giving rides to curious passengers on sightseeing tours of the city. They stopped in front of a bar and watched a beautiful girl with long black hair dancing on a tabletop. Sailors and soldiers clapped and cheered as she twirled around in her lovely red skirt, revealing beautiful, long legs and scanty red tights. Alex gasped. Bud looked for a table, but he couldn’t find a vacant one, so they walked on.

"You'll see worse than that if you hang around this town," Bud said when he noticed Alex's astonishment. "Maybe you can stop on your way back home."

"I think I would enjoy seeing it with Jeannie," Alex said. "We might even come here on our honeymoon."

When they reached Jackson Square, they heard a band playing "Alexander's Rag Time Band." As the small band approached, Alex and Bud saw only tired-looking old men and a few women. Absent were fresh young faces that one would expect to see in such a band. They stood for a few minutes and listened. Bud put a dime into a hat held out by an old woman, and they walked on. An artist painting street scenes attracted Alex's attention. The artist flipped carefully through his collection, trying to interest the boys in purchasing a painting, but they declined. Even though they couldn't spend the few dollars they had in their pockets, they admired several paintings. The boys walked past vendors of various items: food, flowers, umbrellas, raincoats, and trinkets for souvenirs. Bud pointed out the beautiful St. Louis Cathedral and the statue of Stonewall Jackson on horseback in the middle of the square. They walked on to the French Market.

Alex looked around the small café and wondered why it was so famous. There were many items for sale; woven baskets, hand-made toys, clay objects, pets, potted plants, rugs, but he wasn't impressed. Bud explained that it was very old and had been a slave market in pre-Civil War days. Alex nodded. "I suppose it looks different when there is no war."

Then they sat at one of the little tables and ordered coffee. Bud insisted that Alex try the coffee and doughnuts. "I've never tasted coffee like this before," Alex said as he sipped the strong, black chicory coffee with thick cream floating on top. "Not bad, though." He enjoyed the doughnut and ordered another one.

"I think I had better head for the railroad station," Alex said when they had finished eating. "I'm glad I got to see all of this. Thanks for letting me tag along with you."

"My pleasure," Bud said. He gave Alex directions to the depot, shook hands with him, and wished him luck. Alex walked toward the station looking in shop windows. He had enjoyed the time with Bud, but he was concerned about missing the train that would carry him back to San Diego. The punishment for being absent without official leave, AWOL, even just a few hours, had been discussed many times during basic training. He knew he didn't want an AWOL charge on his record. If he missed his train, he would really be in trouble.

Alex looked at his watch. It was only six-thirty. His train was not scheduled to depart from New Orleans for nearly two hours. He felt confident about getting to the station on time and walked leisurely. Then he entered a drug store and casually surveyed the array of books and magazines for sale. He picked out a Reader's Digest and a Look magazine. He also selected a number of picture post cards, reading them and laughing at the amusing ones. While at the cash register, Alex glanced at the clock. The long hand was on the ten and the short hand was on eight. He looked at his watch. It said six-thirty. He shook his watch and put it up to his ear. It wasn't ticking. Sweat broke out on his brow. He threw down the items he was about to purchase and dashed out to the street. A clock on the corner verified that it was ten minutes to eight.

Alex began running down the street as fast as he could. He wasn't sure how far it was to the station, but he knew he just couldn't miss that train. He had planned to get to the station in time to go to the head and freshen up before boarding, but not now. As he ran along, he tried to remember where he had left his bag, and where the door to the tracks was located. His mind raced ahead, planning every move he must make when he reached the depot.

A policeman on the corner blew his whistle and called out to him to stop. Alex was terrified. Was it against the law to run down the street?

The policeman ran his hands up and down Alex's clothing, checking for weapons or evidence of stolen objects, before he began questioning him. "Where are you going? What is your big hurry?"

"Train," Alex managed to say through great gulps of air. "Watch stopped," he sputtered breathlessly. "I can't miss my train."

"When does your train leave?"

"Eighty-thirty."

The policeman looked at his watch and shook his head.

Just then a taxi drew up to the corner. The policeman blew his whistle and motioned for the driver to pull over. "Take this young man to the train station and forget about the fare."

"Be glad to," the driver said. "Right on my way. Hop in, young man. You'll be at the station in no time."

"Thank you." Alex sank into the seat. He had hardly caught his breath when the driver said, "That's the station just ahead. You were only a couple of blocks away."

"You saved my life," Alex said. "I thought I had plenty of time until I found that my watch had stopped. I was scared to death that I would miss my train and be AWOL."

"We couldn't let that happen." The drive pulled up to the curb, hopped out, and held the door for Alex. "Run on in there and collect your stuff. Have a good trip."

"Thank you!" Alex said.

"Good luck and keep safe," the driver shouted as he rolled away.

Alex rushed into the station. He had just enough time to go to the restroom, collect his bag, and locate his loading zone before the train arrived.

On the train Alex sat down. He remembered the food his mother had packed into his bag. He ate a sandwich and settled back in his seat. The train dashed across the mighty Mississippi following the fleeting glow of the setting sun, carrying him to an unknown future. A feeling of depression crept over Alex. His eyes began to water and his skin felt cold and clammy. The realization of his desperate situation struck him. He did not want to leave the ones he loved. He wanted to go back to the safety of the little town that he knew so well.

Alex realized he was crying. He jumped up and raced to the bathroom. He tried to regain his composure as he stood swaying in a corner. The train rattled, clanked, and jarred him back and forth. He told himself that he had no choice. His life was in someone else's hands. He had to go on; he had to follow orders. There was no escape, and no going back.

Alex felt a hand on his shoulder. He turned around and faced a soldier who was a few years older than he was. Tears were in his eyes too. "You are not alone. We will all have to make the best of this situation. I had to leave my beautiful wife and two wonderful children, a son and a daughter. But we have a job to do sailor, and it will take all of us, everything we have to offer: our energy, our devotion, and even our lives to protect the ones we leave behind. You can do it. You have to do it." And he left.

Alex washed his face and went back to his seat. On the way, he looked at the faces of his fellow travelers. He realized that everyone was suffering and yet they were laughing and talking and showing each other pictures of the ones they were leaving behind. He still felt sad, but he knew he had to come to grips with his feelings. He knew he had to devote everything he had to the job he had been trained to do.

Alex turned to his seatmate and asked for a light. With shaking hands, he lit his cigarette and offered one to the sailor beside him. They fell into conversation as the rickety train carried them ever westward.

They pulled into Houston at five in the morning. His next train wouldn't leave until eleven o'clock. Alex followed the crowd to a restaurant at one end of the terminal. It was a long wait, but finally he took a seat at the counter.

"We're out of eggs," the waitress said before he could ask, "but I can fix you a hamburger."

Alex ordered two hamburgers and coffee.

"We're out of cream and sugar. Can you drink black coffee?"

Alex said, "Yes" and she poured him a steaming cup of the blackest coffee he had ever seen. She tipped the cup over and spilled coffee on the counter.

"I'm sorry," she said as she grabbed a rag and wiped the coffee up. "I'm getting a little shaky. I have been working since three o'clock yesterday afternoon."

"Why so long?"

"My replacement didn't come in; I don't blame her. Her husband is leaving today. She just had to spend their last night with him."

"I don't blame her," Alex said.

The wait for the hamburgers was as long as the wait in line. Finally they arrived. Alex ate them and drank his coffee. He paid a dime for the coffee and fifteen cents each for the hamburgers, and then wandered out into the waiting room. He looked at the signs hanging on the walls. He spotted the ones directing him to the restrooms on the second floor. He wearily climbed the stairs, used the toilet, and washed his face. Then he went back down to the waiting room and looked for a place to sit.

Alex bought some picture post cards and began writing to his folks and to Jeannie. He decided to number the cards and letters he wrote to Jeannie so she would know if she was receiving all of them. He wrote number one in Houston. Then he numbered six other cards that he would write as he went along.

Long before the eleven o'clock, scheduled time for his train, Alex was waiting on the platform. At first there were only a few people milling about, but the platform became crowded as time for the arrival of the train approached. Alex recognized some of the faces he had seen on the last train, but no one spoke. Everyone was anticipating getting aboard and finding a seat. After a long time, Alex looked at his watch. It was eleven thirty. The crowd became restless and noisy. They pushed against each other as tired legs began to hurt and buckle. The anxious travelers moaned and groaned when the stationmaster wrote on the blackboard that the train was delayed and was not expected until twelve-thirty. A few of the more restless in the crowd wandered back into the station, hoping to get some rest or a bite to eat. Alex didn't budge. He wasn't going to give up his chance to get a seat on the train. He shifted his weight from one foot to the other. At twelve-fifty the engine finally came into view.

Relieved at the sight of the train, Alex's spirits picked up. He had shaved in the washroom in the depot and had washed his face and combed his hair, but he felt sweaty and dirty after standing in the hot sun for over two hours. He was tired, he was uncomfortable, and he wanted to sit down. The engine went by, the baggage car and five coaches rolled past the station. At last the train stopped and the door opened. Alex felt a surge of bodies pushing against his, forcing him up the steps and through the narrow doorway. He stumbled toward the first empty seat and wearily sat down. *It was worth the wait*, he thought. His body became adjusted to the seat and his muscles relaxed. He realized that he was hungry and thirsty. His mother's preparations came to the rescue again. An orange, a peanut butter sandwich, and a few sips of water from the thermos hit the spot.

Alex leaned back in his seat and went to sleep. He slept soundly for an hour and a half, restlessly aware of people talking and laughing and making noise around him. When he opened his eyes, he was surprised to see that they were still at the Houston station. "What happened?" he asked of no one in particular.

"We are on a sidetrack," his seatmate answered. "I think they are adding more cars to the train. You have to expect these delays."

"I know. There's a war on," Alex said. "That's everybody's excuse."

It was three o'clock in the afternoon when the train finally began to move. Alex calculated the hours before he was due to arrive in San Diego. He could only hope that he would make it by twenty hundred Friday evening. "It's Wednesday now. I won't worry about being late, not now anyway," he said to himself.

The trip across Texas seemed endless as they went through farmland and past huge cotton fields. Crowds of cotton-pickers were pulling their heavy sacks up and down the rows gathering the fluffy white bolls and putting them in their sacks. Alex knew the feeling. They were hot and sweaty and tired, but hopeful that at the end of the day they would have a little change to jingle in their pockets. They passed through pasture, where huge herds of cattle were grazing. He saw an occasional cowboy riding on a horse, checking fences or checking on water holes for the cattle. He saw oil wells and mesquite trees and dry desert land with tumbleweed blowing about. They passed mile after mile of boring, uninteresting countryside. The beautiful blue sky seemed endless, and the land looked hot and dry. Alex slept. He read. He talked with the people near him. He slept some more. He tried to convince himself that this was better than what lay ahead, though that thought gave him little comfort. He closed his eyes and thought about Jeannie. He talked with her in his mind, telling her that he loved her and missed her and about the plans he had for their future. He thought about his family, especially about Jed. Jed was a very special brother, a rock. He knew that Jed would step into his shoes and carry on just as he had always done.

At ten o'clock the next day the train pulled into the El Paso station. At last they would be leaving Texas. Alex was so stiff, he could hardly move. He had left his seat only when it was absolutely necessary because he was afraid someone would take it. Now he stretched his arms and legs to try to get his muscles to relax and the blood to circulate through his body. He stumbled out of the train, took great gulps of fresh air and stamped his feet. He tried to orient himself.

Alex looked up and down the platform, reading signs. He found the bulletin board and checked his schedule. The train for San Diego would arrive in two hours. He found the restaurant and made his way to the counter. He decided to try a barbecue beef sandwich and coffee.

"Make that two sandwiches," he said as he realized how hungry he was. His mother's provisions had been consumed on the long trip across Texas and food on the train was expensive. He hadn't eaten for several hours.

Alex looked for the men's room, hoping there would be a shower he could use. After a shower and a shave, he felt better. He returned to the loading zone and waited for the train to arrive. He felt a little anxious about getting another seat as the waiting area began to fill up, so he stayed put and hoped he had chosen the right spot.

This train proved to be a little less crowded than the one across Texas. Alex found a window seat. He was relieved that they were at last out of the state of Texas and began to think that the trip would soon be over. He didn't know that a third of the trip was yet to come and some of the most boring stretches of land lay in New Mexico and Arizona. Texas had fields, ranches, cow country and a city or two along the way. Now, however, they were traveling through desert. There was nothing to see but dry sand, dry grass, an occasional cactus or mesquite bush, and a few tumbleweeds. Alex tried to sleep, but he wasn't tired. He tried to read, but that made his head ache. He looked around to see what the other travelers were doing. He saw a bunch of guys huddled together. He left his seat and drifted over. They were playing craps. Alex watched for a long time before he was invited to join in.

Alex had never played before. He decided to try his hand. He admitted that he didn't know how to play, but was told to try anyway.

"You'll learn as you go," they said and handed the dice to Alex.

"Just throw them," one boy said, "See what comes up."

Alex threw the dice and got a two and a six.

"You lose!" they shouted. "Pay up!"

Alex looked surprised. "I really don't know how to play. I don't know what I am trying to do." Then he asked, "How much do I have to pay?"

"We're playing penny ante," somebody said. "Throw in a penny."

Alex found a penny in his pocket and threw it on the pile. He stayed in the game until it was his turn again. He threw a seven the next time and was told that he had won so he didn't have to put a penny in.

The game continued for an hour, until there was quite a large pile of pennies in the pot. Then someone shouted "MP's!" Immediately the group dispersed and somebody threw a sweater on the pile of pennies.

"What's going on here?" The M.P. asked.

"Do you see anything going on?" a sailor asked.

"It wouldn't be hard to guess what is going on, but I don't see any evidence," he said. "You boys know gambling isn't allowed on the train."

"Oh, we weren't gambling," the same sailor said. "No, we weren't gambling."

"O.K., see that you don't."

Alex went back to his seat. Another sailor sat beside him. "Canasta isn't forbidden," he said. "Let's get up a game of Canasta."

It didn't take long for two more players to be found. Someone pulled down a suitcase from the luggage rack and began dealing the cards. Alex was fond of card games and grateful for a break from the monotony of the trip. The boys played until darkness and finally decided to call it quits.

"Let's go to the dining car," Alex's seatmate, Jackie James said. "I have enough left to have one good meal before we get to San Diego. Do you?"

Alex looked in his billfold. "I guess I can afford one meal."

Alex looked at the menu. "Buffalo steaks! I've never had buffalo steaks, have you?"

"Sure, I've had them before," Jackie said. "I'm from Oklahoma and we find them on the menu often. Go ahead and try them. They are a lot like beef. I'll have one, too."

"Well, what do you think?" Jackie asked when Alex tasted the steak.

"Not bad, but I prefer beef steak."

"I guess I do too, but I don't mind them for a change." The boys finished eating and went back to their seats.

"Have you ever heard of television?" Jackie asked.

"What is that?" Alex asked.

"Well, it is hard to explain. I'd say it is something between a radio and the movies."

"What do you mean?"

"I saw one at a science show. It is a box something like a radio, but it has pictures like you see in the movies. The pictures are smaller, of course."

"What do you do? Just sit around and look at little pictures like in the movies?"

"Something like that. You buy the set like you buy a radio and set it up in your living room. You can watch pictures right in your home."

"Do they cost much money?"

"I believe you could get one for four or five hundred dollars. The guy at the show said it wouldn't be long before everyone would have one in their home."

"Four or five hundred dollars?" Alex exclaimed. "I doubt that they will catch on. That's too much money."

"I think it is a wonderful idea. Look how much money you'd save, not having to go to the movies."

"It would take a lot of movies to add up to five hundred dollars," Alex said. "No, I don't think it will ever catch on."

"Time will tell. They're coming out with something new every day, just simple things that will make life easier. Take steel wool, for instance. My mom was delighted to find out about that."

"And ball point pens, simple things."

The boys chatted for a while longer and then Jackie began to yawn. "I think I'll take that empty seat and stretch out.

It wasn't much later when the train pulled in to Phoenix. A

huge crowd of people was waiting on the platform. As they began to board, all of the vacant seats were filled and some of the passengers were left standing in the aisles.

The rest of the trip was unpleasant and uncomfortable. Alex felt guilty that he had a seat when he saw other people obviously suffering because they had been standing so long. He moved over closer to his seatmate and let a sailor share the seat. Others were doing the same thing and finally everyone had a place to sit. Sleep was impossible now as the train jerked and jostled the passengers as it moved down the tracks. He leaned his head back and closed his eyes, but there was too much noise for him to fall asleep. He was miserable. *I'd take hitch-hiking over this,* he thought, but it was too late for second thoughts now. He had to pee, but he was squeezed in too tight to get up and he was afraid he wouldn't get his seat back. Finally, he just had to go. He made his way to the restroom. When he got back to his seat, he found the sailor who was sharing it was sound asleep, taking up all of the room on the seat. He took his bag down from the luggage rack and walked to the end of the car. He stood for a while swaying back and forth with the rhythm of the train, holding onto a pole near the door. When he got too tired to stand, he sat down on the floor and leaned against his bag. Would this ride ever be over?

At last Alex fell asleep. He slept a long time and woke up to find that he was stretched out in the aisle and people were stepping over him as they went back and forth to the restroom. The sun was coming up and it was getting lighter outside. Alex decided to see if he could get his seat back, but he found it occupied by two other sailors.

When they reached Riverside, the train stopped. Alex was surprised that even more people boarded. Now there were people standing in the aisles, some balancing themselves on the arms of seats already occupied by three people. *It can't be much farther*, Alex told himself.

At last word began to circulate that San Diego was only a few miles away. Alex felt the train slowing down. The cars swayed less, the noise decreased, and the train finally rolled to a stop. The jolt of the final braking sent people flying into each other, but there was not enough space for anyone to fall down. At last, the ride was over.

Several buses were at the depot to pick up the sailors and take them to the Naval Station. Alex picked up his bag and made his way to a bus. He found it hard to walk. He had been on the train for so long. His ears hurt, his legs hurt, and he was hungry, thirsty, and tired. *I never intend to make this trip again,* he thought. *If I ever get home, I will stay there, no matter what.* Alex couldn't decide which he wanted more, a hot shower, a decent meal, or to be able to lie down on a bed. As usual, the decision was made for him. "You have one hour to shower, dress, and get to the mess hall. After dinner, you will be given further instructions. Alex followed orders and was ready to march to the mess hall on time. Hot food, even hot Navy food was delightful. Before he left the mess hall, he listened to instructions from the C.O. "The following units will report immediately to the Missouri which is waiting at the dock: Units #176, #138, #109, #127. Other units will wait in their quarters until further notice."

Alex was in Unit #108. He was both relieved and disappointed. He would have time to write to Jeannie, but he knew that waiting around would be boring.

"At least, I'll have one more night to sleep in a bed. I'm ready for sleep," he thought as he fell in with his squad to march back to his quarters. Before the unit dispersed, the C.O. announced that there was a memo to be read and digested by each member of the group before he hit the sack. The memo was an explanation of their orders. Unit 108 would be assigned to a ship that had not arrived yet. Each member must be thoroughly familiar with his responsibility. The exact date for the arrival of the ship had not been disclosed and members of #108 would be able to get passes to leave the base until specific orders were received, which could be from one to fifteen days. Men were ordered to read the bulletin boards twice a day for further orders. Also, pay envelopes would be available the next day and the pay line would form at 0900 in the mess hall.

## *SHOPPING FOR A RING*

Alex felt a slight relief. Pay day! Passes! And hopefully a few days before leaving. He would have time to shop for a ring. He remembered what Bud Henson had said about the message a ring sends and decided to use his pay to purchase a diamond ring for Jeannie.

At 0900 the next morning, Alex stood in line, waiting for his pay envelope. Men in his squad, dressed in white uniforms, were lined up alphabetically. Alex was near the middle of the line. Since this was the base where he had his basic training, Alex was familiar with the procedure. After receiving his pay envelope, he picked up a pass and continued to the bus stop. He had been waiting only two or three minutes when the bus arrived. Half a dozen other sailors, whom he had seen, but did not know, joined him.

Alex's buddy, Clarence Garfield, usually went into town with him, but Clarence had returned late last night and he wanted to rest and write letters home. Alex felt comfortable being alone this time. He was going to a jewelry store to look at engagement rings and he preferred to do this alone. He had never shopped in a jewelry store before, had no idea what a ring would cost, and he didn't want anyone looking over his shoulder. Alex stepped off the bus when it drew up to the curb in the center of town. He glanced at his watch, noting that it was ten-thirty. He decided to look in the show windows of all of the jewelry stores along the street before going inside. Several stones caught his eye, but most cost more than he could afford. A sailor about to be shipped out on a mission didn't have much credit along the streets of San Diego. Most stores were reluctant to show their wares to young Navy men who wore no stripes or bars. Alex calculated the money in his envelope and the few dollars that he had been able to save. The diamonds that he could afford were very small indeed, though they were enhanced by attractive mountings.

Unable to find anything that he would feel proud to present to Jeannie, Alex stepped into a soda shop and slipped into a booth. He ordered a BLT and a coke. He began to weigh his options. Alex wanted a beautiful ring for Jeannie, but he was aware that beautiful rings were beyond his reach at the moment. However, he wanted to give Jeannie a symbol of his love that would please her and would send out a signal that she had accepted his proposal.

When Alex finished his lunch, he walked out on the street and began once again to gaze into jewelry store windows. At last he decided to enter a small shop where an elderly woman stood guard over the merchandise. She was wearing beautiful rings, bracelets, a lovely broach, and diamond earrings. Alex was intimidated by her appearance, but was encouraged by her warm smile. He began to explain his mission. She understood his predicament. She stood thinking for a moment, and then she carefully pulled out a tray of rings for Alex to examine.

The saleslady knew that the young sailor standing before her would be unable to purchase the precious stones that she had to offer, but she saw no harm in letting him examine them and have the experience of touching them and wishing. He picked up one ring after the other, admired it and asked the price.

A large one-carat solitary was his favorite. How it sparkled in the brilliant light in the showroom. He knew this was the ring he wanted for Jeannie. He turned it over and over examining each facet of light before he looked at the patient saleslady. She patted his hand gently as she said, "That ring costs $750."

"It is the one I want," Alex sighed, "but I would never be able to buy such a beautiful one as that."

"You will some day," the lady said. "You are young now, but someday, you will come back and ask for it. It is beautiful, and worthy of your bride-to-be, I am sure."

Bride-to-be. Yes, Jeannie was his bride-to-be. He had never thought of her in just those words.

Each ring that Alex examined was carefully replaced in the tray. There were rings with tiny diamonds that he could have afforded, but Alex wanted to give Jeannie a ring that she would be proud of; a ring that would reflect his love and admiration and that would be a symbol of the life he hoped he could provide for her. He would just have to delay purchasing the ring until he could save more money.

"May I suggest a more modest gift for you?" the gray-headed lady said. "A locket is a gift that most girls cherish and they are less expensive. I'll be glad to show you some." She reached for a box on a shelf and brought out a collection of lockets, inviting Alex to examine them. Alex hesitated, at first, but then he decided that a locket would be a more appropriate gift. He chose a small gold, heart-shaped locket with delicate hinges and a tiny spring opener. The lady wrapped it in white paper with tiny pink roses and handed it to Alex. Feeling satisfied with the gift, but disappointed that it wasn't a ring, Alex again stepped on to the sidewalk. He would mail the gift tomorrow. At the bus stop, Alex bought a newspaper and sat reading it while he waited for the bus. When he glanced up from his paper, he almost fainted. Coming toward him was a beautiful girl. She had long brown hair, brown eyes, a tall lovely figure, and a beautiful face. It was Jeannie. But it couldn't be Jeannie. He blinked and started to call her name, but he was too astonished to speak. She walked right up to the bench where Alex was sitting and took a seat beside him. She didn't even glance at him, but took a book from her coat pocket and began reading.

Alex couldn't take his eyes off her. His hands began to shake. Looking carefully at her face, he discovered that she had freckles on her nose. Jeannie had no freckles. Alex looked at her feet. She had the smallest feet he had ever seen. Jeannie's feet were larger. But she did look like Jeannie. He noticed that she looked up each time a bus came to the stop. She watched until all passengers for the stop had stepped off and the bus began to move.

After the fourth bus pulled up and stopped, Alex saw a look of panic cross her face. Tears welled up in her eyes and in a moment he heard muted sobs. He had to speak to her. "Miss, is there anything I can do to help you?"

The Jeannie look-alike shook her head and continued crying. Then suddenly she turned to Alex and asked, "Are you from the main base?"

"Yes," Alex answered, and again asked if he could help her.

"You may be able to help me," she whispered. "I was supposed to meet my boyfriend here at one o'clock, that's thirteen hundred for you, but he hasn't shown up. I must give him my new address and phone number so he can call or come over. It is nearly two o'clock and I have to go back to work. I can't wait any longer."

"Can't you mail it to him?" Alex suggested.

I don't know his address and he expects to ship out tomorrow or the next day. I won't be able to get in touch with him." She was crying again. "His name is Donald Ray Atkinson. Do you happen to know him?"

Alex thought, *There must be 15,000 men at that base; how could I possibly know him?*

"I am afraid not."

Then the girl began writing something on a small slip of paper, her name, address, and phone number and the name of her friend. "You are my only hope." She looked so heart-broken and pleaded so earnestly that Alex took the paper and promised to try to find Donald Ray Atkinson and give him the message.

"My name is Mary Driscoll." She stood up. "Please do this for me. And by the way, what is your name?"

"My name is Alex Presswood, Mary. I don't know what my chances of finding your friend are, but I will try."

"Oh, thank you." She kissed him on the cheek and walked away.

Alex felt as if he had seen a ghost. He had seen a beautiful girl who looked so much like Jeannie that he almost cried out to her. He had sat beside her and heard her speak. It was like a dream, but here he sat with a small piece of paper on which was written the name, address, and phone number of the girl and the name of the person who should receive the information. Alex had taken the paper and had watched her walk away. He folded the note and slipped it into his billfold.

Alex held the package with the beautiful gold necklace in his hand. He felt good about his purchase. "I should have enough to buy Jeannie a pretty ring later. If I go aboard a ship, I won't have to spend my money for anything. I can save it all and I'll get her a ring when I get back." Alex was satisfied with his decision.

Just then Alex's bus arrived. As he boarded the bus he caught sight of Jeannie's look-alike hurrying down the street.

Alex reached his barracks; he went directly to the bulletin board as he had been instructed to do. The daily bulletin contained 18 items and he began reading from the top. (1) Fire drill at 1530, everyone must participate. (2)Sickbay closed from 1600 until 1700 except for emergencies. (3)Parade on Thursday. Reading down the list, number fourteen, Squad #108 be prepared to ship out by 2300 this day. Alex had to force himself to read the last four items, then he found himself running at break-neck speed to his bunk.

Most of the members of Squad 108 were already cramming their possessions into duffel bags. It took Alex less than thirty minutes to do the job. Getting packed for immediate departure was practiced over and over during basic training, so now it was automatic.

Alex sat down on his bunk and took out a cigarette. Clarence sat beside him, looking pale and anxious. Both boys smoked. "No phone calls," Clarence broke the silence. "All missions are so secret we can't even tell our parents we are shipping out."

"That makes it very hard on our folks. Of course, they always think the worst is happening."

"I would like to know just what is happening to us. All we know is that we are going aboard a ship. We don't even know the name of the ship."

"We have time to write a letter or two," Alex said as he searched through his bag for paper and a pen. "I suppose we can let our folks know by mail that we are shipping out and that we are well at this point."

"That's a good idea, except that I wrote to everybody this morning."

Alex wrote to his parents and to Jeannie. Hopefully they would get his letters and would know that his address would be different. They had been instructed to use the Fleet Post Office as their return address.

Alex finished his brief letters and mailed them just before going to the mess hall. A little later, they were lined up and marched down to the dock to board their ship. Now they were truly going to war.

## *JEANNIE GOES TO COLLEGE*

Jeannie sat quietly looking out of the window, listening to the hum of the engine. She decided to sit in the empty seat just behind the driver. This was her first long ride on a bus and being alone, she felt secure and protected near the operator. Her father wanted to take her in the car, but was unable to get the extra gasoline for the trip. A middle-age woman sat beside her, but she slept most of the time and had little to say when she was awake.

Jeannie reflected on the events of the last few days. She could not believe all that had happened. She had made a list every day of the things that she should accomplish, but there was always something left at the end of the day. Buying clothes was an impossible job. She had to find someone to make her skirts and dresses from material that was almost as scarce as the few ready-made garments she found. She had several sweaters and blouses that she had worn in high school. She also found a few new ones.

She and her mother had walked all over town looking for sheets and towels. There were none in the stores. Her mother finally bought some unbleached domestic material and made sheets for her, but they were rough and had an unpleasant odor. Towels were simply not to be found. Her aunt Betsy gave her three.

The war had been going on for three long years. Jeanne had a summer job working in a store and had listened to complaints of customers who could not find things they wanted. They complained about the stamps they needed to purchase shoes, gasoline, and sugar. Panties with elastic waistbands were no longer made, and they had to resort to wearing ones with buttons or drawstrings. Silk stockings were no longer available and neither were silk slips and fancy bras.

Jeannie was glad that she had been able to finish most of her shopping before Alex came home on leave. She only had to be concerned about packing her trunk and suitcases as the time for departure came near.

Jeannie's mind wandered back to the night before Alex's leave was over. It seemed like a long time, but it had been only two weeks. She had received a card and a letter from Alex. He told about his slow, uncomfortable trip across the country; about his visit to the French Quarter in New Orleans, about the layovers and sidetracks, and crowded trains. He told her how much he loved her and missed her. She felt warm and exciting when she thought of their lovemaking. She could still feel the strength of his arms holding her tight and his tender kisses that sent chill bumps up her spine. She loved him. She wanted to marry him. The thought of not being able to see him for a long time brought tears to her eyes. How would she ever get over her longing to be with him?

Alex had been her idol since fifth grade. All of the girls liked him, but Jeannie captured his attention. One day she whispered the answer to a question he didn't know and saved him from being embarrassed. He had written "Thanks" on a note and had flipped it to her. When Miss Baxter, their teacher, eager to relieve the monotony of the lesson, caught sight of the note, and rushed down the aisle to retrieve it, Jeannie casually put her hand over her mouth, coughed, and pushed the note through her lips and under her tongue. When Miss Baxter asked Jeannie to give her the note, Jeannie opened her hand revealing nothing and denying any knowledge of a note. Miss Baxter returned to her desk. She had been outwitted. Alex and Jeannie laughed about the incident many times, and both acknowledged that this was the beginning of their friendship.

As Jeannie sat watching the countryside slip by, she thought about Alex and remembered how close they had been over the years. She had never dated another boy, never paid attention to anyone but Alex. They had had fun on the bus, in school, and after school. He didn't have a lot of money, but his wonderful personality made up for that. Jeannie was so proud to be seen with Alex. He was handsome, smart, and he made her and everyone in his presence comfortable. When his sister sprained her ankle in physical education class one day, he helped her up the stairs. He always checked to be sure his brother and sisters were on the bus. He carried her books and helped her with her coat. Everything about Alex was honorable. Jeannie knew she could trust him with her life. She loved him so much.

Jeannie thought about how anxiously she had awaited his letters when he was in basic training. She had read each one over and over and had poured out her heart to him in her letters. Their love had grown during the summer and when he came home on leave, they could not resist the temptation to go all the way. Thinking about it made her feel warm and happy. How long would she have to wait for him to come back? She could not even imagine, but she was sure that the wonderful memory of making love and his precious letters would keep her love alive until he did return.

Jeannie was disappointed that Alex didn't have a ring for her, but he had mentioned in his letter that he wanted to find the perfect one and hoped that she wouldn't mind waiting until he found it.

Jeannie accepted these conditions but she desperately wanted a symbol, even a small one that would give assurance that his promise was real and would be evidence that she had made a promise also.

At last Jeannie dozed off. The bus stopped to pick up passengers who waited beside the road and it pulled in to stations at every town and village. The 165-mile trip to Montgomery was scheduled to take nearly seven hours. In Montgomery, she would change coaches for the remainder of the trip to Tuscaloosa. Jeannie had left Atmore at 5:13 A.M. and didn't expect to reach Tuscaloosa until 5:00 P.M. She had been told exactly how to make the change in buses, but she felt uncomfortable about finding her way around a large bus station. It wasn't easy traveling alone for the first time.

Suddenly the heavy motor ground to a halt. "Everybody out!" the driver said. "We're in Montgomery."

All around, people were waking up, stretching, and reaching for baggage on the shelf above the seats. Jeannie stood up and reached for the suitcase that she had placed overhead. A friendly soldier said he would get it for her and she smiled and thanked him.

Stepping down from the bus, Jeannie blinked in the sunlight. She followed the other passengers into the station and looked around. A timetable posted on the wall just inside the door gave the time of departure of the bus to Tuscaloosa.

The bus station was a long room. At the end, nearest the door and ticket window, were rows of seats, most of them taken by men in uniform. At the other end of the room Jeannie saw a lunch counter and several tables and chairs. To her left were the restrooms. Straight ahead was a door to the street. Along one wall were rows of lockers where suitcases and packages could be deposited and locked up safely.

Jeannie got in the line for the restroom. Mothers with little children, a few older women, and several girls who looked like they might be students were ahead of her in line. No one spoke to her; everybody was preoccupied. She hoped there would be enough time to get a sandwich before she had to board the next bus.

Jeannie had combed her hair, washed her face, put on fresh make-up, and tucked in her blouse. She felt fresh and alert as she walked out of the restroom. She crossed the room to the lunch counter and took her place on the line that was waiting to be served. On the wall over the counter was a huge display of available items. She decided to have a hot dog and a Coca Cola.

Jeannie looked around the crowded room. For the first time in her life, she was alone in a crowded room. So many people were moving about, carrying their possessions in bags, bundles and worn suitcases. Service men were everywhere and young mothers with babies, some sleeping, some crying, following their husbands from one end of the country to the other, desperately trying to keep their families together until the inevitable move to the war zone would separate them for months, for years, or forever. Everyone was trying to grasp a fleeting moment of happiness in the little time that was left.

Jeannie walked around balancing her food and her suitcase, looking for a seat or at least a corner where she could eat in peace. A sailor offered her his seat, but she declined. She had been told to stay away from strangers, especially servicemen. She found an empty space on a wall and took possession of it. She put her suitcase down, leaned against the wall, and began to eat.

Jeannie had taken only one bite of her hot dog when she felt a tap on her shoulder. She glanced around and found that she was standing face to face with none other than Bill Simmons. "What are you doing here?" She almost shouted.

"I'm following you," Bill said.

"Bill Simmons, you are not!" She wouldn't put anything past Bill Simmons.

He laughed. "I'm on my way to Birmingham. My call came last week. I'm going to be in the Army."

"Congratulations! I thought you'd be a 4-F, Bill. I'm surprised they'd let you in the Army."

"Low blow. Actually I won't know if I will pass my physical or not. I do wear glasses, you know."

Jeannie remembered the "glasses incident" in high school and smiled. "That probably won't make any difference. Why are you traveling on the bus? I thought everybody went to Birmingham on the train."

"Not everybody. I missed the train. Our car wouldn't start when my dad was getting ready to take me to the station. I had to call a taxi, but before it got there, the train pulled out. I was lucky to catch a bus. Now I am waiting for my connection on to Birmingham."

Jeannie smiled. "Some people have the rottenest luck."

"What do you hear from your boyfriend?" Bill asked.

"He is fine. He was home on leave and left again two weeks ago. He got back to California okay. He said that the trip was tiresome and he was glad when it was over."

"I saw him. He had on a white uniform. I'm surprised that you two didn't get married when he was at home."

Jeannie blushed. "Well, we didn't." By then Jeannie had finished eating her hot dog and looked around for a trash can. "I have to go out back now," she said. "Good luck—and keep safe."

"Wait, don't go so fast. I want to tell you something. You know I am I crazy about you, Jeannie. If you ever decide to drop your boyfriend, I surely would like to take you out."

"Not a chance," Jeannie hurried out to wait for her bus. *The nerve of him,* she thought. *I would have to be desperate to go out with the likes of Bill Simmons. Not only desperate, but also crazy.*

Jeannie was shaking when she walked out the door. She glanced at the clock. She opened her purse and looked to see if her ticket was still there. It was. She found the loading zone for the Tuscaloosa bus and got in line. There were thirty or forty girls in line waiting for the bus: only girls. They all were dressed in pretty summer dresses and wore high-heeled shoes. Jeannie was glad that she had worn her high heels. She glanced around to see if Bill had followed her outside. She didn't see him, but she didn't stop shaking until she was seated on the bus and it was getting ready to pull out.

At last they were moving. How she wished that Alex could have been on this bus with her. For years, she had dreamed of going off to college with Alex. He had always wanted to be a doctor and she wanted to be a teacher. Alex would have to wait until the end of this dreadful war to begin studying. When she got her degree, she could get a job and work until he finished college, then they could start the family that she wanted so much.

On the bus, Jeannie sat beside a girl who introduced herself as Lee Ann Jones. They talked about life at the University of Alabama.

Lee Ann was a junior, majoring in education. She described the program and told Jeannie about some of her classes and her teachers. "Of course, most freshmen have to take the basic curriculum, no matter what their major is. They may take an elective or two their freshman year, but everybody takes English 101, 102, and 103 and basic science, math, history, physical education, music, art, and social studies."

"All of those subjects every day? How can you do it?" Jeannie asked in surprise.

"You don't meet all of your classes every day; you alternate. Some classes meet Monday, Wednesday, and Friday, others meet Tuesday and Thursday. And when you aren't in class, you are free to go to your room, the canteen, walk around the campus or visit the library, whatever you want to do."

"I don't believe it, not having someone standing over you, telling you what to do all of the time!"

"Actually, many students can't handle the freedom. They spend their time socializing and having fun and neglect their studies. Then, when exam time rolls around they aren't ready. Be sure you don't let that happen to you."

"This is certainly going to be different from high school," Jeannie said.

"Yes, like night and day. But it doesn't take long to get into the swing of it. Just be sure to keep up with your daily assignments and study for tests. You'll be all right."

The girls talked about their friends and families, their boyfriends, and their hometowns. Time went quickly. As they approached Tuscaloosa, Lee Ann began to point out places of interest. Few students on campus had cars, so they walked everywhere they wanted to go—to church, to the movies, or to restaurants. She pointed these out to Jeannie.

A large group of girls was at the station, waiting for the bus that would take them to their dormitories. Lee Ann met some of her friends and introduced them to Jeannie. They chatted while they waited for the bus. "The bus will take us to our dormitories, then it will return for our luggage," Lee Ann explained. "You will get your room assignment at the office, if you don't already have one."

"I have my room number. I'm in Tutwiler Hall," Jeannie said.

"Then we'll be in the same building. I'll help you find your way around."

Soon everybody was getting out of the bus and scrambling to find their rooms and their friends. Lee Ann directed Jeannie to her room and disappeared down the hall.

It was all so easy. Jeannie's feelings of apprehension subsided and she began to relax. Her roommate was already in the room getting settled, and she greeted Jeannie warmly. Her name was Mary Ann Braxton. The girls spent the rest of the day getting acquainted, putting their things away, and getting used to the idea that they were, indeed, college students at last.

There was a knock on the door. The two girls from across the hall introduced themselves as Patty Phillips and Susan Grace. They talked about their majors and about how excited they were. They had left their door open, and were soon joined by other neighbors, Frances Beck and Jimmie Sue Carpenter. During the next half hour they exchanged pictures, hometowns, and people they happened to know in common, laughing gleefully when they discovered that they had mutual friends. All of the girls on the second floor were freshmen and everybody was anxious to become acquainted. Lee Ann and her roommate dropped by. After quick introductions, Lee Ann offered assistance in registering the next day.

"Registering for the first time is a dreadful experience. It is very different from high school. You should get to the administration building early. People start getting in line by six-thirty."

"What are the lines for?" Jeannie asked.

"You said you are going to be an education major. Well, you have to find the line for the education department. You will be assigned to a counselor, who has to approve your courses. She will give you cards to fill out for each of the subjects you will be taking. Then you have to go to the gymnasium where all of the instructors will be sitting at tables around the room. You find the instructors who are teaching the classes you want. They will check your card and sign it. If the class happens to be filled, you will need to find a different instructor."

"How will we know who to go to?" Patty asked.

"Don't worry. You will be given instructions all of the way. Just pay close attention. When all of your cards are signed and your schedule arranged, you go to the registrar's office and pay your bill. You pay for your room and board at the same time."

Two other girls had drifted in and they, too, were listening intently to every word.

"Lee Ann, thank you so much for explaining it." All of the girls echoed Jeannie's thanks.

"I remember how difficult it was for me that first time. I'm glad to help you. Now let's all get a bite to eat before we go to bed. It is just nine o'clock and the dorms aren't locked until eleven on Sunday nights. We have time to go to the canteen."

The girls grabbed their billfolds and followed Lee Ann to the canteen, located in the basement of the recreation building. It had a long counter with stools, all of which were occupied at the moment. Behind the counter several young black men were making hamburgers and hot dogs. There were about sixteen tables, arranged in the large room. Many were occupied, but the girls found a couple of empty ones and pushed them together to accommodate their group of ten. The noisy hum of voices was occasionally interrupted by sudden outburst when old friends greeted each other for the first time since the end of the spring quarter. Most of the occupants were girls. Jeannie noticed a table where two boys were sitting with five girls who were desperately vying for their attention. A young man on crutches came in; one leg was missing. Jeannie flinched, realizing that Alex could return in the same condition.

Their hamburgers were ready. Jeannie had forgotten how hungry she was. She was thrilled to be on campus at last and knew that she would make some really good friends. Already the girls were laughing and giggling as if they had known each other all of their lives.

Lee Ann looked at her watch and announced that they had just enough time to get back to the dorm before the doors were locked.

Lee Ann said goodnight on the second floor and went to her room on third floor. "Be sure to get up early and be ready to get started," she reminded the freshmen as she began climbing the stairs.

Mary Ann and Jeannie got ready for bed. Jeannie wrote to Alex. She had much to tell him.

Thanks to Lee Ann's instructions, registration went very smoothly. Jeannie completed seven cards and stood in the long, winding line that led to the registrar's office. Behind Jeannie was a veteran, back in civilian life because of an injury. His name was Walter Anderson. He was from Bay Minnette in Baldwin County, about twenty-five miles southwest of Atmore. They talked about football teams and swimming holes and how hard it was to find shoes, cigarettes, candy, and coffee. Walter had graduated from high school in 1938 and took a job with the CCC for several years, where he had planted acres of pine trees throughout southeast Alabama and built parks and roads around lakes. He had gone into service in 1941, just before the war broke out, hoping to serve only one year. He ended up spending three years, getting wounded, and finally getting discharged that spring. He decided to take advantage of the GI Bill and return to college to maybe become a lawyer.

"I'll give it a try, anyway," Walter said. "It has been quite a while since I have been in school, but I think I can handle it."

The line moved along. Walter talked with the girl behind him and Jeannie talked with the girl ahead of her. All four chatted about the illustrious Governor of Alabama, Big Jim Folsom, and the war. When they reached the payment window Jeannie filled out the check her father had given her. It was for $184; her first quarter's expenses. Then she started back to the dormitory.

Mary Ann was already in the room. She was lying on the bed with a hot water bottle on her stomach. "Cramps," she said. "I always get them the first day."

Jeannie caught her breath, but said nothing. She quietly checked her calendar. Today was September 9. She was supposed to start her period on the eleventh. She hated having a period, everybody did, but that was life. *Well, OK,* she thought. *I had almost forgotten.* She'd keep it in mind now.

"Did you take an aspirin?"

"I took Stanback. I should be all right in a few minutes."

"Have you had lunch?"

"I don't feel like eating. You go ahead."

A lump came up in Jeannie's throat. She was hungry, but she didn't want to go to the dining room alone. She didn't know whom she'd sit with.

Mary Ann saw the look of horror on Jeannie's face. "I don't

blame you. I wouldn't want to go alone either. Why don't you see if Patty and Susan have gone?"

Jeannie knocked on her neighbor's door. Nobody answered. Then Mary Ann said, "I feel better now. I'll get up and go to the cafeteria with you. I am getting hungry myself."

Relieved, Jeannie sat down and waited for Mary Ann to get dressed.

"Don't forget your meal ticket and your key," Mary Ann said when they were ready to go. There was much to remember.

Food was served cafeteria style. They picked up their trays, silver, and glasses and selected items that they wished. They could choose between french-fries or mashed potatoes and peas or beans and cornbread or rolls. Only one meat dish was offered at each meal. They found a table with two available seats and sat down, introducing themselves to the girls already seated.

It seemed to be an unwritten law that everyone complained about the food. Jeannie's mother had warned her about this and had told her to refrain from criticizing it. "Either eat it or leave it," she had said, "but don't waste your mealtime complaining."

Back in her room, Jeannie wrote to Alex again. She wanted to share everything with him. She missed him. She wrote to her parents, her sister, and friends. She didn't know when there would be time to write to family and friends after classes began. She knew she would write to Alex every day, no matter how much studying she had to do.

The next morning when Jeannie got up, she felt strange. Her stomach was upset and she threw up after breakfast. "I guess I'm not used to the food," she explained. "I've never had this problem at home." She went to her first class, but had to dash to the restroom again before it was over. After upchucking again, she felt better.

By second period, Jeannie felt fine. She found her classroom for English 101. As she glanced about, she was surprised to see Walter Anderson. She took a seat next to him and smiled. He said, "Hi!"

"Oh, hi, I didn't know we'd be having classes together."

"Everybody has to take 101. This class fits my schedule."

"Your major is law?"

"I haven't decided, for sure, at this point. I'm also interested in business. I just signed up for general studies for now. I don't have to commit to a major until later."

Professor Raintree entered the room and everyone's attention focused on him. Jeannie glanced at Walter. He was handsome. He reminded her of Alex. Maybe they could be friends.

Professor Raintree was giving a brief outline of the course. "English 101, 102, and 103 are required for graduation from the University of Alabama. English 101 deals with grammar, 102 with literature, and 103 with composition. This first quarter, we will learn all there is to know about grammar. You may believe that you learned all there is to know about the English language in high school, but I believe there are a few points you might have missed. You will have homework assignments daily, quizzes weekly, and a final test. He wrote the name of the text on the blackboard and advised everyone to make every effort to acquire the text as soon as possible. He gave an assignment, passed out an outline of the course, and dismissed the class.

"We'd better get over to the bookstore and get our books before they are sold out," Walter suggested.

"Where is the bookstore?" Jeannie asked.

"I'll show you." They walked down the hall together.

They purchased their books and discovered that the Post Office in an adjacent room. Jeannie rented a box. It still wasn't time for the next class.

"Let's get a drink," Walter suggested. They entered the canteen.

"I'll pay for mine." Jeannie looked in her purse for a nickel. "I'd like a Coca Cola."

"I have it." Walter stepped up to the counter.

"Thanks, but I'd rather pay," She didn't want a stranger to buy her drink. He might get the wrong idea.

"OK," He took her nickel. "Will you sit with me anyway?"

"Sure." She sat down and waited for Walter. She noticed that he limped a bit as he walked toward the table.

"What do you think of the professor?" Walter asked.

"I couldn't tell in the short time we were in class. I hope he is as good as my high school English teacher, Miss Hodnett."

She asked Walter what he thought of the professor.

"I have an idea he will be a tough one. I will really have to study for this class." Walter looked over the outline Professor Raintree had handed out. "English has always been hard for me. How about you?"

"I have always liked it. I made out all right in high school."

"Girls do seem to have a knack for the subject, but boys do better in math—at least that is what I have been told." She knew he was just making conversation, but she listened and responded with a nod.

"It really is strange, going back to school again. I thought about it for a long time before I decided to do it. I really think it is the best thing for me to do, considering my leg. I have to do something that I can handle as a cripple."

"What do you mean a cripple? You seem to walk just fine."

"I took a bullet in my left leg and it had to be amputated. I have an artificial leg."

Jeannie was surprised. "I am sorry. I wouldn't have guessed. You walk so well."

"I was in the hospital for three months. They taught me to walk on it. I was lucky. Some guys lost both of their legs or arms. Some had their faces blown off. Yes, I was lucky. I won't talk about it anymore, but I can't get it off my mind."

"Maybe being in college will help. You will be so busy studying that you won't have time to think about the war. There will be things to do on campus."

"I hope so."

Jeannie glanced at the clock at the end of the room. She fished her schedule out of her purse. "My next class is at ten o'clock. I have history in room 207."

"I have science in 112," he said. "We'd better go."

They said good-bye and hurried off in different directions.

The rest of the day went smoothly, but Jeannie was very tired. When she finished her classes, she took a nap: something she never did at home. She slept for three hours, waking up just in time for dinner. All through the meal, she yawned. "I can't seem to wake up," she said as she excused herself, emptied her tray, and made her way back to her room. She lay down again and was fast asleep when Mary Ann returned.

"I don't know when I have ever been so exhausted," Jeannie said when she finally woke up.

"Do you mind if I play some records?" Mary Ann asked.

"Maybe some music will help me to wake up. Please, go ahead. I like to listen while I study."

The music did seem to help. She sang along quietly with Lanny Ross and Vaughan Monroe while she did her math assignment. But she had difficulty keeping her eyes open to read all of her assignments. Jeannie was perplexed. She blamed it on the long bus trip, the frustrations of registration day, getting used to her classes. She remembered that her period was supposed to start tomorrow. That was it, she was sure.

The next morning, Jeannie upchucked her breakfast, felt drowsy in her classes, and went to sleep the minute she came in from class. And her period didn't start. "All of the excitement of the last week or two is making me late," she told herself. She tried to shrug it off.

When her period hadn't started the next day, Jeannie thought she would mention it to Mary Ann, but she decided to wait a little longer.

That night Lee Ann came down to visit. The girls sat talking about the events of the last few days. Patty and Susan came in too. Patty had a letter from her boyfriend and wanted to share it with everyone. They were having a great time when there was a knock on the door.

"Is Lee Ann here?" a quiet voice asked.

"Sure, come in," Lee Ann said, before Jeannie had time to answer. The new girl introduced herself as Betty Lou Mimms. Now there were six girls sitting on the beds, talking.

Betty Lou couldn't wait to tell her news. She turned to Lee Ann. "I have terrible news, Lee Ann. Terrible. Madge isn't coming back."

Lee Ann looked shocked. "Madge has only two quarters to go. Why isn't she coming back?"

Betty Lou whispered in Lee Ann's ear. Lee Ann caught her breath. "Oh, no!" She cried.

"What is it" the other girls all said together.

"I may as well tell you. It'll get out anyway. Madge is pregnant."

"Oh God!" Everyone gasped.

"What happened?" Lee Ann asked in a loud whisper.

"She got pregnant when her boyfriend was home on leave. Now he is overseas. They can't get married.

"What is she going to do?" asked Lee Ann.

"What can she do?" Betty Lou answered with a question. "They won't let her come back to school and she is too scared to tell her parents."

"Where is she?" Lee Ann asked.

"She is with her sister in Jacksonville, Florida. She called me from there."

"My God! How could she let that happen?"

"Her boyfriend was at home on leave. He knew he was going overseas. And they just went all the way. She loved him so much," Betty Lou said in a whisper.

"It could happen to anyone," Lee Ann said quietly.

"It couldn't happen to me," Mary Ann said. "I have better sense than to do that. Besides, it takes more than one time."

"Maybe not," said Susan.

"I am sure it does," Mary Ann said convincingly. "I think it is a sin to do it before you are married and anyone who does it is trash."

"That's what I have always been taught," said Betty Lou, "but times are different now. If your boyfriend is going away and won't be back for months, maybe years, some people just can't help it."

"Well, I certainly can," Mary Ann said. "I'll never give in until I have that ring on my finger." She held up her hand and pointed to her ring finger.

"Her life is just ruined." Betty Lou said.

"She must have loved him an awful lot," Patty said quietly. "I feel sorry for her and I don't even know her."

"She's a very nice girl and a good student," Lee Ann said.

"How can you say she is nice?" Mary Ann asked sarcastically.

"Can't you hear what we're saying?" Betty Lou said. "She loved him. And they were planning to be married when he got back."

"That's no excuse." Mary Ann just wouldn't let up.

"What would you do if it happened to you?" Susan asked. "I think I would just die."

"It isn't that easy," Patty said. "I think death would be the easy way out, but then you would have another sin to answer for."

"What would you do?" Jeannie asked. She had been quiet, just listening to what the others had to say.

"What would I do?" Betty Lou asked. "I guess I would go to my aunt in Memphis. I am sure she would help me out, if it happened to me."

"It happened to a girl in my neighborhood," Susan said. "She told her parents and they hired a guy to marry her. Then when the baby was born, they got a divorce."

"I guess that would be the easiest thing to do," Betty Lou said, "but I wouldn't be able to tell my parents. I couldn't hurt them that much."

"I think I would just get rid of it," Lee Ann said.

"You mean, have an abortion?" Susan asked in surprise. "I could never do that. That's murder."

"I think my way is best," Mary Ann said stubbornly. "Save yourself until you are married. And besides, a man loses respect for you if you go all the way."

"I admit, that is the safest way to handle it, but when you love somebody so much, so very much, you just want to give him your whole self as a pledge to show him how much you love him," Patty said.

"Nobody but a slut would do that," Mary Ann said.

"Have you ever been in love?" Lee Ann asked Mary Ann.

"I've had my share of dates," Mary Ann said "But I never let anyone touch me."

"Mary Ann, when you are truly in love with a man, you will be willing to lay down your life for him."

"But, if he loves you, he won't expect you to go that far. He wouldn't ask you to make the sacrifice."

"I think this discussion could go on all night but none of it would make a difference. I do feel for Madge. Maybe her boyfriend will come back and marry her," Susan said.

"Fat chance," Mary Ann just had to say.

"I have some more studying to do," Betty Lou said. "Good-night, All." And she was gone.

One by one the other girls got up and left the room. Jeannie fell into bed and was asleep immediately.

Jeannie was sick to her stomach the next morning after breakfast. She quietly went to the bathroom and threw up. After that she felt better. Today was the thirteenth of September. "I know my period will start today," she tried to convince herself, but she was beginning to worry.

## *JEANIE MARRIES WALTER*

On Friday afternoon, Walter called and asked Jeannie to go to a movie with him. Her first impulse was to say No, because she hadn't intended to date anyone. But she needed to go out and have some fun. She would explain to Walter that she was engaged to Alex. She needed Walter as a friend. So she said yes and went to the lobby where Walter was waiting.

"I've called a taxi already," Walter said.

"May we share your cab?" a stranger asked. "We're going to the movie and it would save us some time if we could ride with you. We'll share the cost."

"Sure," Walter said and introduced Jeannie and himself. The stranger introduced himself and his friend. Sharing a taxi was a common practice for students. They chatted about the weather, the campus, and the war. The other young man was classified 4-F and it was evident by his thick glasses that he suffered from poor eyesight.

The movie was Thirty Seconds Over Tokyo with Van Johnson. Jeannie cried through the last half of it. It was too real, too close to home. Walter held her hand and tried to comfort her, but he was suffering also. His war experiences flashed through his mind.

"I am sorry, I don't feel like talking," Walter said after the movie. They returned to campus via taxi and Walter took her straight to her dorm.

"I understand," Jeannie assured him. "Thank you, anyway."

"I'll try to pick a different movie next time," Walter said. "Cowboys and Indians would have been better for me." He kissed her on the cheek, and said, "I'll see you soon."

By Saturday, September 14, Jeannie knew she was in trouble. She slept late. When she woke up, Mary Ann had already gone out. She wrote to Alex and went to the Post Office. Her spirits lifted when she saw several letters in her box. One was from Alex. This was the first letter she had received at school from him. She held it to her heart and tears clouded her eyes. She waited until she was in her room to read it.

Her hands trembling, she tore the envelope open and began to read. It was a short letter, hastily written.

"Jeannie, my love," he began. "I have received four of your wonderful letters. Thank you for all of them. How I miss you. How I wish I could be starting college with you. I have news, I am being ship-CENSORED. I will be on board the CENSORED. I don't know where we will be going or how long we will be gone. Jeannie, if you have a problem, or need to talk to someone, go to my mother. She is a great lady. She will want to see you. My family will treat you like one of the family. I only wish I could be with all of you. I love you with all of my heart, and I will count the days until I get back home to you. I will write as often as I can. Address my mail c\o Fleet Post Office, San Francisco. Just be sure to write my numbers correctly so I will get your letters. I can't live without them." He signed it, "All my love, Alex"

Jeannie felt numb. Alex was gone. What could she do? She was too frightened to cry. What could she do? What must she do? She put the letter into a book and began to straighten up the room. She piled her clothes up and took them to the laundry room. Thank goodness, no one else was there. She had to think. She knew she was pregnant. She thought about the way her body felt. Her breasts were slightly swollen and they were tender. She had been having morning sickness. She was sleepy most of the time. She had been such a fool. Mary Ann was right. Nobody but a fool would make love before they were married. Who could she turn to? Who would help her? She had no one. She could never tell the girls. She wouldn't tell her parents. She had to find help somewhere.

Jeannie finished washing her clothes and hung them out to dry. She went back to her room. Mary Ann was there studying. Jeannie opened her history book and tried to read. She couldn't keep her mind on the ancient Greeks. She read every paragraph over three times before she could comprehend its meaning.

At last Mary Ann said, "It's time for lunch. Would you like to go to the dining room?"

Mary Ann wanted to talk. She missed her family. Jeannie listened politely, but said little. Mary Ann was so concerned with her own homesickness that she didn't notice that Jeannie was quiet. She didn't notice the worried look on her face. Lee Ann came over to their table and sat down.

Betty Lou had a call from Madge. "Madge had an abortion. Her sister took her to a woman who does that," Lee Ann talked quietly.

"Will Madge come back to school now?" Mary Ann asked.

"No, she is going to transfer to the University of Florida in Tallahassee. She couldn't come back here."

Jeannie turned pale. "What an awful thing to happen," she said.

"I am sorry," Mary Ann said. "Although . . . . ."

Lee Ann got up and left the table. She didn't want to hear what Mary Ann had to say. She had noticed Jeannie's expression.

After lunch, Mary Ann announced that she was going downtown. She wanted to do some shopping. She asked Jeannie to go, but Jeannie declined.

Jeannie had to think. She sat on the bed, just looking into space. She thought of her options. She couldn't disgrace her family. They must never know. She couldn't tell her older sister. She wouldn't understand. Maybe she could find someone to do an abortion. Or hire someone to marry her. She had heard of homes for unwed mothers where she could live until the baby was born, then put it up for adoption. How would she feel about giving her baby away? Her and Alex's baby. She thought about Alex's mother. Calling her was a possibility, but people would find out. Her parents would find out and the whole family would be disgraced.

There was a knock on the door. "There is a telephone call for you," a stranger said.

"Thank you," Jeannie said and hurried down the hall to the phone. How she wished it were Alex, though she knew that a call from him would not come for a very long time.

It was Walter. He apologized for last night. Would she like to go for a walk?

She'd love it. Could she tell Walter that she was pregnant or that she was afraid she was? Would he help her?

They walked across the campus. She let him hold her hand. He talked about the time he had lost overseas. He talked about being lonely, and about how glad he was to meet her. They sat down on the grass and he put his arm over her shoulder. He told her about his family how they had grown apart since high school. He had lost both of his parents. His father died of flu and his mother had cancer. His older sister had married and moved out west. Jeannie told Walter about her family. They talked about religion and about their hopes and dreams for the future. And then he kissed her.

Jeannie kissed Walter back. Maybe Walter would fall in love with her. Maybe he already had. Maybe he would want to marry her.

"Oh, Jeannie," he whispered. "Oh, Jeannie."

*Not too fast now,* she told herself. She moved away gently.

He talked of love. "I have never had a real girl," he said. "I didn't think I could fall in love so fast. But, I think I love you, Jeannie. You are beautiful. I feel wonderful when I am with you. Oh God, Jeannie, I do love you. I have waited so long for a girl like you. Could you love me too?"

She did have feelings for him. His kisses made her feel warm. She wanted to melt into his arms. "Oh, Walter, I can't believe this is happening." They kissed again, a long, passionate kiss. Then she gently pulled away, kissed his cheek, and looked straight into his eyes. "I can love you," she whispered. "I think I do love you."

Walter could not let the spell slip away.

"Jeannie, I know it is awfully soon to ask, but things happen fast during wartime. Jeannie, will you marry me?"

Jeannie caught her breath. She looked at Walter. What choice did she have? A door had opened. Could she really learn to love this man as she loved Alex? Did she dare tell him what had happened to her? Should she tell him? Could she get away with not telling him?

He waited for her reply, watching her face, her eyes for clues.

At last she whispered, "Yes, Walter, I will marry you."

They kissed again.

"When?" She asked.

"Tonight. I want to marry you tonight. Let's go ahead and do it. We'll go to Mississippi."

"Tonight?" she gasped.

"I'm serious. Yes tonight."

"I know we have some things to work out. Where we'll live. What we'll do, stay in school or drop out. I can find a job and go to work. I promise, I will work it all out. Trust me. The GI Bill makes a lot of provisions for servicemen, especially those who have a serious injury. It will be all right. Do you need to go back to your room for anything?"

"I need to change clothes and get a few things."

"OK," Walter said. "But don't change your mind." He walked her back to the dorm and kissed her cheek. "I love you," he said.

Mary Ann had returned from town and her purchases lay on her bed. Jeannie glanced at the packages and saw that Mary Ann had bought a lovely white, rayon blouse that would look pretty with her blue suit. Jeannie picked it up and held it up to her. She wanted to wear it. She really wanted something new, and something borrowed, but did she dare take it?

Mary Ann popped in. "Where have you been, Jeannie? I've been looking for you. I'm going to the football game with a guy in my French class. He has a friend. Would you like to go?"

"Oh, no thank you," Jeannie said. She didn't offer an excuse. "But I'm sure you will have no trouble finding someone else to go."

"I really don't have time. They are waiting in the lobby. I guess I'll just have to go with both of them." And she was gone.

Jeannie looked at herself in the mirror. "I don't believe I am doing this," she said to herself. "But I have to. I have no choice. And I do like Walter a lot. He reminds me of Alex. He is tall and handsome."

Jeannie left the room wearing her blue suit and Mary Ann's new blouse. Mary Ann was a little like a sister, and sisters borrow each other's clothes. She just had to borrow that blouse. She'd return it later.

Walter had borrowed a car. They drove to Lucedale, Mississippi and were married that night. Jeannie could have her baby. She knew she could really love Walter, and she would be forever grateful. She was saved. She had done what she had to do and no one would ever know.

It had happened so fast. Reality began to seep in. Jeannie's parents. Her family. Alex. Alex's family. How would she tell them? She lay in Walter's arms shivering. She could not share her secret with anyone, not her parents, not Walter, not even Alex.

Walter was gentle. He knew it would take time for them to build a real marriage. He was surprised that Jeannie had agreed to marry him so soon, but he was thrilled that she did. He was fond of her. He loved her, he knew he did. They had similar goals in life. He was dedicated to a one-woman-for-life philosophy and he would make it work. Jeannie was beautiful. She listened to him. She spoke highly of her family. He liked everything that he had seen about her. He felt good. No regrets.

Jeannie was grateful. This man had saved her. He would be the father of her child. No one would know any different. She made love with Walter whenever he wished and he wished often. And when she was ready to reveal that she was pregnant, he would have no doubt that he was the father.

Jeannie moved out of her room in the dormitory. Her roommate gave her a shower. The few friends she had made gathered around and wished her well, perplexed as they were about her sudden marriage to a man she hardly knew. They remembered her declarations of love for Alex.

Lee Ann followed Jeannie to the borrowed car she was using to transport her things to the one-room apartment she and Walter had found. "I know something is wrong," Lee Ann said. "I won't pursue it. But if you ever need a friend, you can call on me. Strange things happen in wartime and we have to do what we think is best." She held Jeannie's hand in both of hers, and squeezed it. Jeannie drove away, saying that she would keep in touch and that they'd see each other around campus.

Walter helped Jeannie hang her clothes in the small closet they would share. They had a small kitchenette, a table and two chairs, a bed and an old-fashioned rocking chair. The bathroom that they shared with another couple was down the hall. "We'll have to have a bookcase," Walter said. "I'll try to find one tomorrow."

Jeannie wondered how they would survive in such a small area. Of course, they had the whole campus. They could study in the library, eat in the dining room, and visit with friends in the canteen. Jeannie bought and served breakfast every day. The meal tickets took care of lunch and dinner. Walter helped with the chores. He took out the trash, helped make the bed, and dried the dishes. They went to their various classes during the day, meeting in the canteen occasionally for a Coke. They talked a lot.

Jeannie was beginning to develop a great affection for this kind, gentle man. She gave him no reason to doubt her devotion. She went to the bathroom when she felt sick in the morning, but this was happening less often now. Her anxiety had quieted, and her body was becoming adjusted to her condition.

One morning, five weeks after their marriage, Jeannie announced that her period was late. Walter tried to convince himself and her that this was only because of the excitement of the previous weeks. She made an appointment with the doctor, who confirmed her suspicion. They decided that it wouldn't change their plans.

Jeannie still had not told her parents about her marriage. She began to mention Walter in her letters to introduce him over a period of time. She would take Walter home for Thanksgiving. She would tell them about the marriage at that time. At Christmas, she would tell them about the baby. It wouldn't be easy, but with a baby coming in May, she had to let her parents know.

"Walter," Jeannie whispered one evening just before Thanksgiving, "I must write a 'Dear John'. I have put it off as long as I can. I must do it now. We've been so busy. And now that we are having a baby, I can't put it off any longer.

"I wondered when you would tell me," Walter said. "You are too beautiful not to have had someone in your life before. I love you for telling me, but spare me the details. I'll go out."

Walter got his sweater and walked out. Jeannie began to write.

"Dear Alex," she wrote. "This is the hardest thing I have ever had to do. I met a wonderful man. We fell in love and we got married.

His name is Walter Anderson from Bay Minnette. He is a student at the University. I am so sorry our relationship had to end this way. All my best wishes go with you for a safe return. Love, Jeannie."

Jeannie left the letter on the table for Walter to read, and got into bed. She did not expect to sleep, but she was weary. Later, she felt Walter shaking her and she opened her eyes. It was after midnight.

"Jeannie, Honey, I read your letter. Sweetheart, it is too harsh. I have seen men go berserk when they received a 'Dear John.' There really is no way to make him understand, but you must be more compassionate. You haven't told me much about your relationship, but I know you are a wonderful person. You are kind and sincere. I have wondered how you could accept my proposal of marriage so soon. But I didn't care then, and I don't care now. Only, we must be honest with each other.

"Jeannie, I went to see the doctor tonight. He told me the baby is due in May, not the last of June. He also confirmed that I could never have a child. I had mumps as a teenager, which rendered me incapable of fathering a child. I had hoped the doctors had been wrong, that I could father a child, but that isn't the case."

Jeannie's body stiffened. She started to speak. She had to defend herself, somehow.

"Don't say anything yet, Jeannie. Your letter to Alex proves that you are willing to give him up. I understand that you were in a desperate situation, not knowing where Alex was; where he was going-the FPO address gave that away-or when he would return. I gather that he doesn't know about the baby. I know you could have had an abortion. Many girls have taken that route. But you were willing to risk marrying a stranger to save the baby, to save your reputation, and to save your family the embarrassment of an illegitimate child. I have no doubt that Alex would have married you, if and when he returned.

"Jeannie, I love you. I want you to be my wife. I want to be the father of your child. Your secret will be a sacred trust between us. Jeannie, will you stay with me? Will you remain my wife?"

All of this time, Walter had been talking to Jeannie's back. She slowly turned around and sat up. He sat beside her. Her arms went around him and she nestled her head against his chest. "I couldn't tell you. I couldn't tell anyone. I thought I could keep it a secret. I didn't mean to deceive you. I meant to do everything I could to be a good wife, and I hoped you would never know. I can't believe anyone could forgive such deception. I am relieved that you know.

"Walter, Alex and I had been friends since we were both in the fifth grade. We made love the last day of his leave, the only time. And he will never know that I became pregnant."

"Don't tell me any more, Jeannie. Just answer my question. Will you stay with me? I promise to be a good husband and a good father to the only child I will ever have. And I promise that I will never mention it again."

"Thank you for understanding. Walter, I was in deep trouble and marrying you was my only hope. But I did not make my decision lightly. I made a promise to you, and I do plan to keep that promise, as long as I live. I love you now, but I am sure our love will grow as it has grown every day since we were married. Not only do I love you, but I owe you a great debt. You saved my life.

"I will do everything I can to make it up to you. But if you change your mind, please stay with me until after the baby comes."

"Jeannie did you hear what I said, Darling? I want you for my wife forever. Will you be my wife?"

"Yes, Walter, I will be your wife."

"Now let's rewrite that letter to Alex."

## *ALEX GOES TO WAR*

Alex stood on the dark deck of the USS YORKTOWN. The night was quiet and peaceful. At last he enjoyed a few moments of solitude, something unknown since he had come aboard two weeks ago. Anchored in the harbor were destroyers, aircraft carriers, and other battleships. At dawn they would be on their way to search out and destroy the enemy. Tonight reminded Alex of home when the farm animals lay in the pasture, resting and slowly chewing their cuds. He shivered as he thought about where he was. Just four months ago he graduated from high school and left the next day for boot camp. The few short weeks in boot camp, taught him about being a sailor, mostly how to take orders.

He had learned to shoot an antiaircraft gun and how to peel potatoes. And he had learned to march. Now, here he was, on a ship far out in the Pacific Ocean, so far from home; so far from Jeannie.

Alex thought of the seven-day trip from San Diego to Hawaii. His first day aboard a sea going vessel was the most memorable experience of his life. The moment the ship slipped out of the San Diego docks Alex felt exuberant. Standing at the rail watching the waves break against the bow of the ship, feeling the soft spray in his face, tasting the salty mist, Alex could think of nothing in his life to compare. It was Alex's first ride on the open water and he was caught up in the experience.

Clarence, who was standing beside Alex, was enjoying himself too, but he reminded Alex that they must go below and find their quarters. He caught Alex's arm and gave a little tug.

"Come on, let's get squared away. We have to get our gear stored and find a place to sleep."

Clarence took the lead as the two novices made their way below deck. A master-at-arms led the boys to a dark, damp compartment, lighted only by naked light bulbs, hanging loosely every ten or so feet apart. Most of the top bunks had been taken but they found two lower ones and tossed their duffle bags on them. It was smoky and their eyes burned. Alex coughed.

"You'll get used to it," the master-at-arms said. "You won't be with us but a few days anyway."

After locating the head and washroom, the boys looked for the mess hall. They arrived just in time for the evening meal. They fell in line and had their bowls filled from a huge pot of vegetable soup. Then they took sandwiches and coffee from trays on a stainless steel counter, found seats, and began to eat.

"I guess we are settled in," Alex said casually after they had finished eating. "Let's go up on the deck again. I could use some fresh air."

Up on the main deck, as Alex breathed deeply the cool, clean, fresh air, he felt himself getting sick. Over to the rail he dashed. After throwing up, he was so weak he could not stand up. His legs let him down to the deck. He collapsed to the deck, leaned against the rail, and groaned in agony.

"I'll help you to your bunk." Clarence helped Alex to his feet.

Feebly, Alex made his way to his bunk, leaning heavily on Clarence, and lay down. He pulled his knees up and closed his eyes. His head was swimming. His bunk was rolling over and over and round and round. He had difficulty breathing. He hurt so bad, he wanted to die. He lay still with his eyes closed. At last he fell asleep.

Clarence did not get seasick. He wandered back out on the deck and watched the waves. There was nothing to see but water, sky, and a few soft clouds in the distance.

Alex felt fine when he woke up an hour and a half later. He thought he'd try to write to Jeannie. As he pulled some paper and a pencil out of his bag he came across the necklace that he had bought for her. He wondered when he would be able to send it; he'd inquire about the procedure for mailing packages. After writing a quick letter to Jeannie, Alex got ready for bed.

The next morning, Alex skipped breakfast, wanting to be sure that his stomach had settled. He thought he would never eat again if it meant another bout with seasickness.

"Our unit has to assemble on the fore deck," Clarence said when he returned from breakfast. "It was announced in the mess hall. We have to be there at 0615, that's in ten minutes."

"OK," Alex said, "I'm ready."

"We have a job for you," a seaman started. "You didn't think we would give you a free ride, a holiday, did you? We keep our men busy. That way they stay out of trouble." He was holding a tool in his hand, one that Alex was not familiar with. "This is a paint scraper. We have some boats that must be scraped and repainted. Your job is to scrape. I want every speck of white paint removed from every boat. Two of you will work on each boat, except you, Presswood. Since we have an uneven number of men, you will work alone. When the others are finished, you will be given some help."

The sailors were told where to pick up the scrapers and other materials they would need. Alex was shown his boat. It was a lifeboat, about fourteen feet long. He set to work right away, glad to have something to do. Alex had never scraped paint before, so he did not know how long it would take him. He decided that he would complete his task, alone, in the same time as the others. He tried to anticipate the length of time it would take him and figured he could complete the job in one week. The sun beat down, but there was a cool breeze blowing. Sweat collected on his eyelids and forehead and he brushed it away with his arm, occasionally using his handkerchief. Since he had no one to talk to, he could concentrate wholly on the scraping. When half of the first board was scraped, Alex stopped and reached for a cigarette. He enjoyed his smoke, and returned to work. He did not stop again until he noticed that it was time for lunch. He joined the others and headed for the mess hall.

"This isn't what I expected to be doing on this ship," one boy said. Several echoed his complaint. Alex ate quietly and paid attention to how his stomach was reacting to food. He never, ever wanted to go through what he had yesterday. After eating, he went to the head then back out on deck. He stood by the rail and had a cigarette before returning to his task. Alex's competitive nature demanded that he do an expert job of removing the paint, in record time. He paused. He was surprised to see an officer standing nearby, watching him. Nervously, Alex went back to scraping. "I guess I am doing all right," Alex thought. "At least he didn't say anything." When the officer walked on down the deck and out of sight, Alex stopped for a cigarette.

One more board and I will be on schedule, Alex thought. He continued to scrape, sand, chip, scrape, sand, and chip.

"Hot damn, Presswood, you are going after it, ain't you?" He heard someone say. "You think you're gonna be paid for this crap?"

There stood Jake Newman, a buddy he had met in Boot camp. He walked over and shook hands with his friend. "I like to see a job through," Alex said. "If I get this finished, it can be painted again before we leave the ship. Anyway, it helps to pass the time."

The officer whom Alex had seen earlier appeared. "Presswood, report to my office at 0800 tomorrow morning." He said and walked away with no explanation except to hand Alex a card. He was Lt. Brower, legal officer.

Alex panicked. What had he done? He thought about everything he had done and said since he had come aboard ship. He could think of nothing that he had done wrong. Perhaps he had not saluted an officer. Had he taken too many breaks from his scraping job?

Alex showed the card to Jake with a questioning look on his

face. "Don't understand it." All Jake could offer was "You'll find out tomorrow."

Alex and Jake noticed that everyone else had cleared out of the work area. Alex looked at his watch. "It's time for dinner." The boys made their way to the mess hall. Jake and Alex caught up on what they'd each been doing since boot camp. Clarence sat with them and heard about Alex's orders for the next day. Clarence was as puzzled as the other two boys.

"I think I will write a couple of letters," Alex excused himself. He wrote to Jeannie and to his parents. He told them about his ship, about becoming seasick, and the job he had been doing. He didn't mention his orders to report to Lt. Brower. He'd wait until he found out what that was all about.

Then he tried to find the Post Office. He saw no one he could ask, so he walked around, trying to locate it on his own. He followed another sailor with letters in his hand. The post office turned out to be a chute with a slot in the crew's reception room. On his way back to his bunk, Alex noticed several mail chutes where he could have mailed his letter.

"A movie is being shown on the fantail," Clarence said when he returned. "Do you want to see it?"

"Sure." They walked together to the far end of the ship. There were seats for the officers and staff. The enlisted men sat on the deck, some on up-side down buckets, but most sat Indian style on the hard, steel deck. The movie was an old Three Stooges film. Alex laughed at their antics and was glad he had come. After the movie, he surveyed the star-studded sky. Alex liked being out on the top deck where he could enjoy the fresh salt air. He was getting used to the ship's constant motion. Alex and Clarence headed back to their bunks where Alex produced a few candy bars he had tucked away. Alex ate his bar slowly. He did not want a repeat performance of last night's meal. "I guess I'm O.K. now."

When Alex appeared in Lt. Brower's office the next morning, he was dressed in his white uniform, shaved, showered, and shoes polished. Alex was waiting beside the lieutenant's desk when Lt. Brower entered. Lt. Brower noticed Alex's appearance and his promptness. Alex saluted. Lt. Brower saluted and barked, "At ease!"

before he began explaining why he wanted to see Alex. He did not tell Alex that he had been impressed by the work he had seen him do the day before.

"Presswood, did you finish high school?"

Alex answered in the affirmative and added that he had graduated in May.

"I offer my congratulations. A high school diploma is quite an asset." I need someone to do a job for me and I think you may be able to handle it." Pointing to a large desk stacked with folders, he explained that these were records of the men on board the ship. They had been sent to him randomly and needed to be in alphabetical order. "They must be put into boxes because we don't have enough file cabinets to accommodate all of them and I need my desk for a conference tomorrow. Do you think you can do it?"

"Yes Sir."

Alex walked over to the desk and began sorting through them. The lieutenant left the room.

Alex spent a couple of hours placing the stacks of folders on the floor in alphabetical order. He then started alphabetizing each stack. He worked another hour.

"I think I'd better have a break," Alex said. He went to the head, got a drink of water, smoked a cigarette, and then went back to work.

Alex surveyed the job he had been doing. Suddenly, he thought, "This is the first time since I've been in the Navy that I have been treated like a responsible person. I had to think! I had to figure out how to do this job. Man! This is progress."

Alex had finished alphabetizing the folders, placed them in boxes, and labeled the boxes before Lt. Brower returned. He had also dusted the table and arranged chairs around it.

"What is your rating?" Lt. Brower asked Alex.

"I am a gunner's mate, Sir," Alex answered, wondering why the officer had not noticed his chevron.

"Were you drafted or did you enlist?" was his next question.

"I was drafted," Alex answered.

"I was wondering if you would be interested in switching over to regular. You'd have a good chance of getting into Officers Training and begin climbing in the Navy."

"I intend to stay in the Navy for the duration only. I am anxious to get out and go to college as soon as the war is over."

"I see," Lt. Brower said. Then Alex noticed that his folder was on the lieutenant's desk. "A career in the Navy isn't half bad," he said. "I have been in since 1938. I'll be able to retire in 1958 and I'll still be a young man."

"I have always wanted to be a doctor," Alex said. "I am willing to do my share in the war effort, but I want to go home after the war is over. I want to go to school and become a doctor, get married and have a family."

"Good luck with your plans," Lt. Brower said. "Thank you for helping me today."

"Will that be all, Sir?" Alex asked.

"Yes. You are dismissed."

"Thank you," Alex said and saluted. Things were looking up. The lieutenant had actually thanked him.

Before putting Alex's folder back into its box, Lt. Brower opened it and wrote. "Gunner's Mate Presswood is prompt, capable, conscientious, and dependable. Recommended for OCS."

The next day, Alex returned to his lifeboat. Nobody had bothered it.

By nightfall, Alex had completed the first half of the boat. The job was perfect. He had scraped off all of the white paint and had gone over it with sandpaper. It was totally ready for a new paint job. Tomorrow he'd start on the other side.

It took Alex two more days to remove all of the paint from the other side of the lifeboat. He was glad they had another day before reaching Hawaii. *Now I can get a little rest,* he told himself.

"You have done a good job here," Alex was told. "Now you can help the other teams finish their boats. We want all paint removed so these boats can be painted."

Alex couldn't believe his ears. *I've worked my butt off so I could get finished and have a little rest and now I have to help the others.* He was fuming. *I have learned a lesson today I won't soon forget. I'll never be an eager beaver again. I'll work, but I won't try so hard. This isn't high school.*

# Reunion

The USS YORKTOWN was ready to leave when Alex's ship sailed into the harbor in Honolulu. Alex and the other sailors from Squadron 108 were rushed aboard and directed to their quarters. They set to work immediately doing the jobs that they had been trained for, relieving sailors who had been in the battle zone for as long as two years and those being returned to the States for long overdue leaves and reassignments.

As Alex stood enjoying the solitude of the evening, he became aware of three men approaching. He recognized Clarence at once, but he did not know the other two. Clarence said, "We've been looking for you." He introduced William Jenkins and Ray Adkinson. "Would you like to play Bridge with us? We haven't had a chance to play in days."

"I am afraid I'm a little rusty," Alex began. "I haven't played Bridge since that one night in Boot Camp when we had a couple of hours to kill."

"We're amateurs," Ray said, hoping to persuade Alex to join them, "but we love the game. We need a fourth."

"Ok," Alex said. "Where are we playing?"

Few sailors were interested in the game. Canasta was the game that was "in" at the moment. Alex enjoyed Canasta, but liked Bridge much more.

The four men found an empty table in the crowded recreation room and sat down. Ray produced a deck of worn cards and spread them in a fan for determining partners and first dealer. William and Alex played against Clarence and Ray. Conversation was limited to bids and comments about the game at first because each one was concentrating on rules and strategies. After a few hands they began to relax. Alex was impressed with his partner's knowledge of the game and his ability to remember the cards that had been played. William modestly admitted that he had been playing since he was ten and that he had been the champion at Old Dominion University in Virginia where he had attended before the draft caught up with him.

"You can teach me a lot," Alex admitted. "Playing with a champion is bound to improve my game."

"I have been playing only a few months," Ray said. "I met this girl, Mary, at the U.S.O. in San Diego who had the patience to teach me. I could have gone for her, but I have a girl at home. I had to break it off. The last date we had, I just didn't show up."

They enjoyed several hands, but didn't bother adding up the score. It seemed obvious that William had won.

"We'd better break this up and hit the sack," Clarence said. "I hope we can play again soon."

"Five o'clock tomorrow, my place," Ray said. They all laughed. Ray's "place" was just like theirs, a bunk in a 5 x 8 compartment with three other guys.

They didn't get together for several days. One day Ray came by Alex's bunk and sat on the edge. Alex could tell he had something he wanted to share. "What's up?" He asked.

"I got a letter from my girlfriend. She said she'd marry me when I get home. God! I can't wait."

"I know the feeling," Alex said. "My girl is waiting for me, too."

"A girl I met in San Diego took my mind off Sara for a few weeks. She was nice. But I know Sara is for me. She is so beautiful and so smart and so everything. I'll show you her picture."

Ray took out his wallet. He removed Sara's picture. "Here is Sara."

Sara was beautiful. She was blond with a beautiful smile and laughing eyes. "That's the girl for me," Ray beamed.

Suddenly a whistle sounded, and the loudspeaker blasted the order "BATTLE STATIONS EVERYONE, BATTLE STATIONS! BATTLE STATIONS!"

Alex reached the top deck and began passing huge shells to his gunner, Martin Scholtz. Out of nowhere appeared three Japanese planes, one of them headed straight for the YORKTOWN. The blasts from the anti-aircraft guns were deafening. The plane was hit. It exploded, sending red-hot shrapnel raining across the deck. Alex fell back. His head hit the deck, and for a moment he was too stunned to move. Flames engulfed the whole deck and were moving toward an unconscious Martin Scholtz. Alex sprang up, grabbed Martin around the waist, and dragged the 160-pound man away from the flames. He pulled him 20 feet across the deck and through an open hatch, leaving a trail of blood from Martin's bleeding arm. The metal hatch closed just as flames reached the opening. Two corpsmen came running up with a stretcher and relieved Alex of his burden. Down to the sick bay they rushed the wounded gunner.

Alex returned to the deck to resume firing the gun. A crew of fire fighters had already extinguished the flames on the deck and was standing by to make sure it didn't re-ignite. It was surprisingly calm. The planes were gone. The guns were quiet. Across the water, Alex saw another ship burning; thick, dark smoke was pouring from it. It was only then that Alex thought of himself. He ran his hand through his hair and realized that it felt different. His hair had been singed and the back of his hand had been burned. *Nothing to worry about,* he thought.

Alex stood beside his gun, watching and waiting to see what would happen next. At last the message came over the loudspeaker. "We were attacked by three Japanese fighters. There were no direct hits. All planes were downed. We will cruise toward the burning ship to search for survivors." Then, "Return to your quarters."

Alex went to sickbay to check on his gunner. He could not see him, but was told that he was seriously injured. Martin would remain in sickbay until he was better. Alex was assured that Martin would recover, thanks to his effort in getting him to safety.

The doctor noticed that Alex's hair had been singed and his hand was burned. "I'd better check you out," he said. "Your hands need bandages and ointment. I can't do much about your hair, but it will grow back. I don't think you need to stay in sickbay.

"By the way, you may have earned yourself a Purple Heart for saving a life," the doctor said.

"I didn't do anything heroic. Anybody would have done what I did."

"I am sure you will get some kind of citation," the doctor said. Alex returned to his quarters. He was exhausted and fell right into bed.

The next attack came three days later. The YORKTOWN usually cruised the waters along with at least one or two other battleships and destroyers. Their orders were to protect the battleship and aircraft carriers. Planes took off from the flat tops headed for Japanese strongholds in the Philippines, the Coral Sea, and even Japan itself.

In a heavy fog their ship had drifted out of range of their companion vessels. Radio communications had been discontinued because of suspected enemy subs in the vicinity. When the fog finally lifted, the YORKTOWN was totally alone. Everything was quiet; no sounds were heard but the slopping of waves against the side of the ship. In the bridge, the ship's navigator diligently plotted their position, but the radio communicator received no messages from the fleet and sent none. The radio receiver picked up signals that indicated that they were not alone, but they had no way of telling if they were being approached by friend or foe.

The captain came to the bridge. "We'll sit tight for the present. Wait until they make a move." For four days the men waited in silence, not knowing where the rest of the fleet was. "I know they are out there," the captain said, "and so is the enemy, so we will wait."

Then the call came. AIRCRAFT SPOTTED. MAN YOUR BATTLE STATIONS. MAN YOUR BATTLE STATIONS! WE ARE ALL ALONE THIS TIME, MEN. DO YOUR BEST!

Every man moved. In seconds every man on board was in position to fight for his life. Six Japanese planes were headed in their direction. As each plane came into view, huge anti-aircraft guns went into action. Every plane was hit before it was able to attack the ship. Four of them hit the water. Two left the area.

"OK. Now, try to locate the fleet," the captain's ordered.

Radio communicators began at once to send messages to the other ships in the fleet. The YORKTOWN had drifted ninety miles from the nearest ship.

"Waste no time catching up with them," the captain ordered. "Being alone out here with those planes is not my idea of a responsible mission. Every man's life on this ship is at stake. We are in a vulnerable position and I do not like that at all."

Alex made his way to the upper deck. He met Steve, one of his classmates from San Diego. They spoke of the battle the day before and the speed at which they were traveling.

"I heard that the skipper is upset about our being so far from the others. He is afraid we'll run into something we can't handle,"

Steve said.

"I'll feel a lot better when we are closer to the others. We aren't helping them out here and they aren't helping us," Alex said.

"I am getting anxious about getting mail from home," Steve said. "My mother had to have an operation and I don't know how she is."

"That has to be tough on you," Alex said. "I'm waiting to hear from my girl. It's been over 3 weeks. I've read the last one fifty times. I read every letter until I have it memorized. I still get a thrill from reading them over and over."

"I guess we all do if we are lucky enough to have a girl." Steve agreed.

"I'd better go below. I want to check on my gunner."

"He had a close call," Steve said. "Are you the one who pulled him to safety?"

Alex just said, "Yeah," and walked away.

Alex was on the deck enjoying the fresh air when he spotted another ship. Not knowing if it was one of their fleet or an enemy vessel, he became anxious, but remained calm and watched and waited. Since no alarm was sounded, he knew that it had to be friendly. Others stood with him and watched as the YORKTOWN continued toward the ship. Other vessels came into view, assuring Alex and the others that they were rejoining the fleet. A huge sense of relief flushed over him. All around him men were crossing themselves and uttering quiet prayers of thanks for their return to the safety of the fleet.

### *DEAR JOHN*

Two days later there was mail. Each man clutched the letters he received with shaking hands, and moved away to a quiet spot to read undisturbed. Alex had several letters, one from his mother, one from his brother, three from Marge, one from Liz, and two from Jeannie. He quickly read the letters from his family. His mother wrote about the farm. She included a message from his dad who left the writing to her. Jed wrote about school and football games and the war bond drives that students were encouraged to participate in. He said he had begun buying stamps and hoped to fill a book before Christmas, maybe two. Liz told about her life in Pensacola. Marge talked about her classes.

Alex waited until he was in his bunk to read Jeannie's letters. He noticed that the post dates were several weeks apart, but assumed that other letters just hadn't reached him. He read the older letter first. Jeannie wrote about her classes, her roommate and her new friends. She mentioned that she had not been feeling well in the mornings. She assured Alex that she was adjusting to her new life, but that she missed him desperately. She promised to write as often as she could and hoped that her mail would reach him to reassure him of her love and commitment. Alex felt happy as he finished the first letter.

Then Alex opened the second letter, expecting it to be newsy and chatty and as warm as all of her letters had been. Every letter from Jeannie had made him long to be with her, and had given a surge of love and happiness that made him tingle with excitement. He loved her so much.

Alex opened the second letter and read it. He could not believe his eyes as he read the words she had written.

*Dear Alex,*

*I hope this letter finds you well. I am fine, but am very busy. The subjects that I am taking aren't really hard, but the assignments are quite long. We have to read fifteen or twenty pages in each subject. In ways, college is easier than high school because you don't have to meet every class every day. There is variety in the schedule that makes it more interesting and gives more time to do homework assignments. We have a lot of reading and papers to write. I am enjoying the work.*

*Alex, I have to tell you about something that has happened. I know that it will hurt you. I am sorry, but things have changed. I met a man who had returned from service. He looks so much like you and reminds me of you in every way. We met the first day I arrived at the University. We talked a lot. I don't know how it happened, but I fell in love with him. When he asked me to marry him, I said "Yes." I wish I didn't have to tell you this and hurt you, but you have to know. Walter Anderson is his name. He is from Bay Minnette. He played football for Bay Minnette High. Walter is going to be a lawyer, so he'll be in school a long time. He is going to college on the G.I. Bill, which pays all of his expenses. I don't know where we'll live. Alex, please forgive me. I didn't mean for it to happen this way, it just did. God Bless You.*

*I will always love you, Jeannie*

Alex felt like a railroad engine had hit him. He was numb. He felt tears gushing down his face and he heard himself sobbing. Never had anything shocked him like this. Jeannie, his Jeannie, was married to someone else. Someone she had just met. He had only been gone for six weeks! How could this happen? How could he bear the pain of losing her? Could this be some kind of joke? No! Jeannie would not joke about something like this. He put his head under his pillow and sobbed.

Alex had to find someone to talk to. He couldn't bear this news alone. He dashed up to the main deck, looking for someone he knew. No one he knew was on the deck. He returned to his quarters to look for Clarence and found him in the head, shaving.

Clarence looked at a shaken Alex. "What is the matter?"

"Oh God! Jeannie is married. She married another guy she just met. I can't believe it. We were engaged. How could she do this?" Alex fell to his knees and cried like a baby.

"I am so sorry, Alex. It's the worst pain imaginable. I remember feeling like my insides had been sucked out when my girlfriend dumped me. Go ahead and cry, it will make you feel better."

"How could she do it? It doesn't make sense. She has been my girl for eight years, going on nine. I have never looked at another girl. I haven't thought of anything but getting back to Jeannie ever since I left home."

"Come on, Alex," Clarence said. He tugged on Alex's arm and helped him up. "Wash your face. It'll make you feel better. I have been through this and I know how awful it is; I promise you, you will survive. It will take time, but the pain will get better as the days pass. Right now you will just have to live with the fact that you can't count on Jeannie any more."

"I can't do that. I can't live without her."

"Yes, you can. You will survive," Clarence consoled him.

Alex washed his face. "I have to lie down." He fell into his bunk and into a fetal position. Clarence threw a blanket over him. He cried himself to sleep. Two hours later, Clarence woke him up. "Alex, you have to go on duty. Wake up." Alex remembered the letter immediately. "Oh God! How can I go on? I lived for Jeannie." He fell back on his bunk, closed his eyes, and felt tears filling them.

"You have to go," Clarence said again, shaking his shoulder. "You'll be in trouble if you are late."

Alex stood on shaky legs. He went to the head and washed his face. He dressed, picked up his hat and made his way to his station. He stopped in the galley for a cup of coffee. His hands were shaking so hard he couldn't hold his cup. He spilled coffee with every step.

"Hey! Look what you're doing!" he heard someone shout. "You're spilling coffee all over the floor."

Alex set his coffee down and grabbed a mop. He wiped up the spills and started toward the upper deck.

"You forgot your coffee, Bud," the sailor called. "What's the matter with you?"

Alex didn't answer. He went up to the top deck and began cleaning the gun that had been fired in the last battle. Every gun had to be torn down, one at a time, cleaned, and reassembled. It took a long time to clean them. Alex kept his mind on the job, concentrating on each piece of metal that he cleaned, oiled, wiped dry, and replaced. He was alone at the moment. At least he didn't have to try to make conversation.

After four hours, another sailor relieved Alex. He headed toward the galley. He picked up a tray and selected food, and sat down. He ate a few bites, but after a couple of minutes, he dumped his tray and went back to his quarters. He wanted to read Jeannie's letter again; maybe he had missed something.

Alex picked up the letter. At once, he was sobbing. He folded it and put it under the mattress. "I can't believe it. I can't believe it. I can't believe it."

Steve walked by. "What is the matter, man?"

"I can't talk about it." Alex rushed out the door. He went to the head and washed his face. He smoked a cigarette. "I may as well go back to work," Alex said to himself.

Days and nights ran together. Alex worked and slept and worked and slept. He smoked one cigarette after the other. He avoided his friends. He read Jeannie's letter over and over, trying to find a clue as to why she did what she did. He could not believe that her love could have ended so abruptly, so totally, so finally, and he never even had a hint that this might happen.

"Care for a hand of bridge?" Clarence asked about a week later.

"Not yet," Alex answered. "I'm not up to bridge yet."

A few days later, Alex forced himself to go to a movie. He enjoyed it. Later, he joined a couple of his buddies for a cup of coffee and he began to talk about the letter. The boys listened. They told of similar experiences. They tried to help Alex find the answer to the mystery. They concluded that girls were fickle and couldn't be trusted.

That night Alex wrote to his parents. He had not felt like writing to anyone since he had received Jeannie's final letter, but he thought that his parents would be worried. He told them about Jeannie's marriage. He told them that he had been shocked and that he had grieved, but that he was accepting the fact that Jeannie was no longer a part of his life. He'd concentrate on his work and forget about the future for now. When he finished it, Alex felt better. He would never forget Jeannie. He would learn to live without her.

A few days later, as Alex searched for his extra pair of socks in his duffle bag, he ran across his wallet. He picked it up and looked through it. His eyes fell on a torn piece of paper on which was written the name Ray Adkinson. He thought about the name for a moment. He turned the paper over and found another name and an address. Mary Driscoll, 1672 Los Anvers Place, San Diego 24, California.

"Mary Driscoll. Mary Driscoll," Alex repeated. And he read "Ray Adkinson" again. "Those names sound familiar, but I can't place them," he thought. He put the paper back into his wallet and went on looking for a pair of socks. "Maybe I will remember who they are later."

Clarence popped his head in. "Feel like bridge today?"

"Sure," Alex said, pulling on his socks. He picked up his wallet and followed Clarence to Ray's bunk. They sat cross-legged on the floor and used the floor for a table.

"Sorry about the accommodations," Ray said. "The rec room was full."

"Don't worry about it," Alex said. "We'll be OK."

"Ready for a few hands?" Ray fanned the cards out so each player could choose one. Alex and William were partners again and Clarence and Ray were partners. Ray won the deal.

Alex watched as Ray dealt the cards. He made four neat stacks, then pushed a stack toward each player. "Mary showed me how to do that," Ray said casually. "It keeps the cards from scattering in case the table is bumped."

Alex drew in his breath. "Ray, I think I have a message for you."

"Message for me? What do you mean?"

Alex told about meeting a girl in San Diego at a bus stop. "She said she was waiting for someone who didn't show up. She asked me if I thought I might be able to get a message to a sailor who was due to ship out. She wrote down her name and address. Her name was Mary Driscoll and the guy was Ray Adkinson." Alex took the note from his wallet.

"What?" Ray looked surprised. "You ran into Mary that day? I couldn't face her. She was a nice girl, but I had decided that I wanted to marry my girl from home."

## *WAR ENDS IN EUROPE*

Alex replaced the torn paper in his wallet without a word. Ray had mentioned in an earlier conversation that he had become engaged to a hometown girl. What a strange coincidence.

Alex remembered that Mary Driscoll was a Jeannie look-alike and he wanted to see her again. He would write to Mary. Alex began to plan what he would say. Thinking about Mary got his mind off Jeannie and he began to feel better. He fell asleep quickly and slept the whole night through; something he had not done for weeks.

Just before dawn the next morning, Alex was awakened by a loud horn blast signaling an emergency. He hit the floor one second and threw his clothes on the next. His feet were in his shoes and he was on his way to his battle station within two minutes, falling in line behind a sailor who had been on watch. The sound of running feet resounded through the vessel as every man on board rushed to his assigned area. Alex reached his station and stood at attention, waiting for instructions. All was quiet now as every man stood motionless, waiting, watching, and wondering.

No guns sounded. No planes appeared on the horizon. Anxious sailors relaxed as the minutes ticked by. At last there came an announcement.

GENTLEMEN: I HAVE A TELEGRAM TO READ TO YOU. PRESIDENT ROOSEVELT DIED YESTERDAY AND HARRY S. TRUMAN, THE VICE-PRESIDENT, HAS BEEN SWORN IN AS PRESIDENT. ALSO, WE HAVE WORD THAT THE WAR IN EUROPE IS RAPIDLY COMING TO A CLOSE.

A recording of the "Star Spangled Banner" was played while every man stood at attention, most with tears in their eyes. President Roosevelt was the only President they remembered. His death was a shock. Tears were also tears of joy. No news could be more welcome than the news that the European theatre was coming to an end.

When the ALL CLEAR sounded sailors up and down the deck looked at each other, not knowing what to say. They reached for their cigarettes and lit up. The men who were not on duty made their way to the mess hall or the head. "I could have used just a few more minutes of rest," Alex said to Clarence. "But, now that I am awake, I may as well stay up. I thought it was an emergency drill. I certainly did not expect this news. Wonder what happened."

"I suppose they will let us know as soon as they find out themselves," Clarence said. "I have some good friends over in Europe. They'll be headed home soon, I hope. I wish it was us."

"It couldn't come too soon to suit me," Alex said. "This damn war has really messed up my life."

After washing his face and hands and combing his hair, Alex went to the galley for breakfast. A steaming cup of coffee helped to clear his head. He walked through the breakfast line and enjoyed the smell of the food. He was hungry. Other mornings, he had gone through the motions of eating and emptied half of his food into the garbage can. But today, he ate heartily and enjoyed the conversation with the guys at his table who were talking excitedly about the prospects of war in the Pacific theater coming to a close also. Everybody wanted to go home.

"MAIL CALL ON MAIN DECK" a voice screeched over a loud speaker. Again the sound of rushing feet was heard as sailors, anxious for word from loved ones, made their way to the main deck.

Alex followed the crowd. He hoped to get a letter from Jed, Marge, Liz, or his parents. He could not help but hope for some word from Jeannie, but he was trying hard to push her out of his conscious thoughts.

Alex listened for his name to be called. He did get some mail: a letter from his mother, one from Jed and two letters from Marge. He stepped over to the rail to begin reading. He read his mother's letter first. She had news about the farm. They had found a young boy to help Jed. She told about seeing Jeannie's parents at church, but didn't say that she had talked with them. Daddy had resigned himself to the reality of Alex's being away, but he was quieter than usual. She said, as she did in all of her letters, that she missed him and prayed for him every night.

Next Alex read Jed's and Marge's letters. Marge wrote about school, homework, friends, and some thoughts about her future.

Alex felt better after reading his mail. He glanced at his watch and realized that it was time for him to go on duty. He was surprised to see his gunner, Martin Scholtz, waiting for him. Martin had been in sickbay ever since he was hit five weeks ago. Alex had visited him there several times, but had not seen him in over a week. Alex was shocked by Martin's appearance. His head and arm were still covered with bandages. He had lost a lot of weight and looked gaunt.

"I came by to thank you for saving my life and to say good-bye. I'm leaving for the States this afternoon."

Alex extended his right hand, but Martin wanted to hug him. He pulled Alex toward him with his good arm and embraced him, patting his shoulder and back.

"I am so sorry man," Alex said. "But I am glad you are going home."

"Me, too," Martin said.

Alex took out a cigarette and offered one to Martin. He lighted Martin's first and they stood for a few minutes enjoying a smoke together.

Martin left and Alex set to work cleaning and lubricating his gun. "War is Hell," he said under his breath. Later he heard a helicopter approach and watched it land on the forward deck. Martin boarded the craft. Martin waved and Alex saluted. *The war is over for him,* Alex thought. He continued cleaning his gun.

*JEANNIE'S BABY IS BORN*

Jeannie watched Walter walk up the path to the door. She detected a slight limp that indicated a tiring day for the handsome man whom she admired, appreciated, and loved dearly. He was generous, witty, good natured, and concerned for her feelings and her condition.

He worked for high marks in all of his subjects. He had taken a job as a dispatcher at a local taxi company and worked four hours a day to supplement their income. The income from his job meant they could afford a night out every now and then.

Jeannie's family had agreed to continue paying her tuition, meal ticket, books and some clothes to the extent they had expected to if she had remained single through her college years. Walter received benefits from the G. I. Bill plus benefits as a disabled veteran. They were able to buy the things they needed for themselves and to prepare for the baby. They even managed to put a few dollars away for a rainy day.

Jeannie felt the baby move inside her. She had mixed emotions about the baby she was carrying and about the changes it had forced her to make. It was hard for her to remember the love for Alex that had brought her to the point of uncontrolled passion that was resulted in the life that was pulsating inside her. Reflecting on the events leading up to their lovemaking, she knew that she had wanted it to happen. She had loved Alex for a long time. If only they had taken precautions, life would have been so different.

And now another man had taken Alex's place. Never in her wildest dreams had Jeannie thought that she could love another person as completely as she loved Walter. Their few months together had been happy. In the early weeks of their marriage, Jeannie had felt such overwhelming relief that the life inside her would not cause shame for herself and for the family she loved so much. Walter had saved her from the grief that would have destroyed her, her child, and her family. In the weeks that followed, Walter's tenderness and love had led her to love him as deeply as she had loved Alex. The memory of her love for Alex began to fade until he was no longer a focal point in her thinking. Yet, the knowledge that the squirming, kicking little organism inside her was a product of her love for Alex haunted her every hour of the day. The knowledge of the pain and grief she had caused Alex never left her and she knew that it never would.

Walter saw Jeannie waiting for him on the screened-in porch. He tapped on the door playfully before he entered. The look of tedium disappeared from his face and was replaced by a bright smile when his eyes fell on the face of his beautiful bride. She rushed to hug and kiss him and welcome him home. It was eleven- thirty P.M. He was glad to be home.

"Thanks for waiting. I expected you to be fast asleep."

"I finished my term paper and was resting a bit," she said. "I made some cookies this afternoon and some lemonade. Would you care for some?"

"Sure, your cookies are always good, but I would prefer a glass of milk, if we have some."

Jeannie poured a glass of milk and presented a plateful of cookies. Walter took several.

"Hard day?" she asked.

"Not hard, just long. So you finished your term paper. Can I read it tomorrow?"

"I'd like that. I don't have to turn it in until Monday. I am trying to finish as much of my work as I can before the baby comes. I'll have to miss at least a week, maybe more if there are complications. I just hope it comes on Friday so I will have two weekends to recover. I talked to the Dean and he said that students could be excused a week to have a baby, especially since you are a vet."

"Well, today is Friday. How do you feel?" Walter asked.

"I don't think this is the day. I think I would have some warning."

"You should be able to count the time to the day maybe, even hour, if you had relations with Alex just one time," he said.

Jeannie had never been angry with Walter before, but his remark caused a surge of fury inside her. Walter had never even hinted that he didn't believe her when she told him that she and Alex had made love only once—on his last day at home. A look of anger and disbelief froze on her face and she began to cry.

Jeannie ran down the hall to the bathroom, closed the door, and locked herself in. She sat on the toilet seat and sobbed. When she stopped crying, she just sat and thought. What if Walter didn't really believe her?

Walter tapped on the door. He had been outside waiting for her to stop crying. After a second tap, she opened the door, but she couldn't look him in the eye.

"What did I say to upset you? I didn't mean to hurt your feelings."

"Walter, you have never questioned the fact that Alex and I made love only once. I told you the truth. And I have figured out the exact day the baby should come, if it comes on time. Next Wednesday is the due date, but it could be a day or two earlier, or later."

"I didn't mean to indicate that I didn't believe you, Honey," Walter said. "It was a poor choice of words. Please believe me. I am a little tired."

"I overreacted. You are right; I should know the exact date."

Walter held her close. "I love you. Let's go to bed. I have some good news."

"OK." When they were in bed, she said, "I do need some good news."

"I found a bigger apartment for us today," he said. "It has two bedrooms and a bathroom. We'll have a room for the baby and we'll have the privacy of our own bathroom."

Jeannie sat up. "Where is it? What does it cost?"

"Honey, I'll worry about the cost. You'll see it tomorrow. It won't be vacant until the end of the semester, but that's only two weeks away. I made a deposit tonight."

"Before I even saw it?"

"Honey, it's nice. I heard about it this afternoon and went right over, looked at it, and put down the deposit. Apartments are hard to find. I have been looking for a larger one ever since we got married. Neither of us likes sharing a bathroom and I know you will like it."

"I didn't mean to question your judgment. I know I'll like it. Can I see it tomorrow?" Jeannie snuggled back under the cover.

"Yes, I asked the present tenants if I could bring you over tomorrow at 10:00 o'clock. Can you be ready by ten?"

"Sure." Jeannie yawned and rolled over to go to sleep.

At one A.M., Jeannie felt a surge of pain similar to cramps. The pain lasted only a few seconds, so she went back to sleep. An hour later, she felt another pain. It hurt more and lasted longer. She caught her breath and sat up in bed. A slight "Oh" escaped from her lips waking Walter.

"What is it?" He cried. He sat up and nervously pulled the string to turn on the overhead light. He saw a look of panic on Jeannie's face.

"I think I've started labor," she whispered.

"How do you know?" Walter did not know whether to touch her or not. He wanted to hold her in his arms, but was afraid it would cause her pain. "Do you think I should get you to the hospital?"

"I'm not sure. I felt a pain about an hour ago and just now I felt another one. Let's just wait and see if another one comes."

Walter watched her for a few moments. "What do you want me to do? Shall I pack your bag?"

"I've been packed for over a week. Anyway, this may be a false alarm."

Walter reached for the cigarettes that lay on the bed table. He lit one for himself and one for Jeannie. They smoked quietly, waiting for another signal from the baby. Fifteen minutes later, Jeannie cried out when a sharp pain hit her and lingered for several seconds.

"Jeannie, I'm going to call the doctor," Walter grabbed his pants and thrust his legs into them. "Where is the number?" He asked.

"It's on the mantle, on the left side."

Walter grabbed the index card with the number of Dr. James Craig neatly written on it and dashed out the door and down the hall to the telephone. Dr. Craig answered on the first ring and spoke calmly to Walter. "I was half expecting you to call tonight." He listened carefully as Walter related the events of the past few minutes.

"Bring Jeannie to the hospital," Dr. Craig said. "It probably will be several hours before the baby actually comes, but I think it is on its way. Drive slowly and carefully. I will meet you there."

Walter was reassured. Dr. Craig had delivered many babies in his nearly thirty-year practice. He was one of the few doctors left in Tuscaloosa because all of the younger ones were serving in various branches of service. He was reliable and respected. Jeannie and Walter felt confident with his care.

Walter tiptoed into the room and asked Jeannie how she felt. She smiled. "Maybe it's a false alarm."

"Dr. Craig seems to think that this is the real thing. He wants us to meet him at the hospital. He thinks we should go right away."

"I have to go to the bathroom," Jeannie slowly got to her feet. She carried a flashlight to light her way in the dark hall. As she sat on the toilet, she felt a huge gush of water flow from her. "Walter!" Walter ran to her.

"What is happening?" She wailed, pointing to the wet floor.

"Your water must have broken," Walter said. "Did you have another pain?"

"No, not yet."

"I'll carry you back to the room," Walter said.

"I think I can walk," she said and slowly began to shuffle her feet along toward the room, Walter supporting her with his arm around her waist.

She stopped suddenly, grabbed her stomach, and bent double in pain. She stood trembling in her tracks until the pain subsided. She heaved a sigh of relief and moved on to the room.

"My suitcase is in the corner beside the chest. Please get it for me. I'll wear my maternity dress in the closet," Jeannie said. "I feel OK enough to walk to the car, I think, but would you help me with my shoes?"

Walter put Jeannie's shoes on her feet carefully and gently. He held her arm tightly as they made their way to the car Walter had managed to buy, opened the door, and helped Jeannie in. When he reached the driver's side, he heard Jeannie scream.

"We'll hurry," Walter said, "but these rough streets will slow us down."

Jeannie felt every bump in the street as Walter drove toward the hospital. "You can slow down," Jeannie said, then screamed when another pain hit.

"Just a little farther," Walter said. "I can see the hospital lights now."

A nurse stood near the door with a wheelchair ready to help. Walter and the nurse lifted Jeannie into the chair. "I'll take her to the maternity ward," the nurse said. "You stop by the office and sign her in."

The registrar handed Walter papers to fill out. "Your wife will be well taken care of here. Have a seat in the waiting room and we'll let you know how Mrs. Anderson is doing. Don't be nervous. Dr. Craig is with her."

Walter sat alone in the quiet waiting room. Stacks of magazines lay on tables beside rows of chairs. He didn't feel like reading; he just sat there and thought.

Walter wasn't really worried about Jeannie. She was a strong girl, young, and healthy. He knew that she would experience unbelievable pain and wished that he could do something to help relieve it, but all he could do but sit and wait. He began to think of the circumstances that had brought them to this point, her giving birth to another man's child, a man who knew nothing about the baby, and never would. Jeannie had promised to stay with him, but what if the baby looked just like his father, would she be reminded of him every time she looked at the child? Would she be able to keep her promise? Was he asking too much? Beads of sweat popped out on his forehead. What a chance he had taken falling in love so quickly. He did love Jeannie. He wanted to go to her, to reassure her, to comfort her.

Finally the doctor came into the waiting room. "Mr. Anderson, your wife just had a fine little boy with a great set of lungs. Both are doing nicely. You can see the baby as soon as he is cleaned up and you may go in and see your wife when she is in the ward. No need to stay after that. She needs rest." Then the doctor added, "You'd better get some sleep, too. Sleep tends to be an elusive commodity when there is a new baby in the house. I know. I have had six."

Walter approached Jeannie's bed, leaned over, kissed her, and whispered that he loved her. "How do you feel?" he asked. *Dumb question*, he said to himself and felt foolish for asking it. "We have a boy," he said before she answered his question.

"A boy. Have you seen him?"

"No, but Dr. Craig said he was fine. I'll see him when I leave. The doctor said I should go home so we both can rest." Jeannie had already closed her eyes so Walter slipped out of the room and walked down the hall to the nursery. In a basket near the window was a small bundle with a tiny head showing. ANDERSON BABY was written on a piece of cardboard, attached to the basket. Walter looked at him for a few moments, and then walked on down the hall. He was tired and sleepy, and so relieved that the baby had finally been born. Now Jeannie could be his and his alone. It would probably take some time for him to "connect" with the baby. He would do his best to be a good father. He called Jeannie's parents, saying that the baby had come early and that mother and son were fine.

When Walter visited Jeannie that evening, they discussed what name they would give the baby. "Can we name him Walter?" She asked. "I like Walter Daniel Anderson."

"I would be honored, is Daniel a family name?"

"No, I just like it. We could call him Danny."

"It isn't his father's name is it?" Walter asked.

Jeannie understood. "Walter, I honestly don't know Alex's middle name."

"OK. Walter Daniel Anderson."

Walter was surprised at how quickly he was able to assume the role of father. He passed out cigars and received congratulations from his friends and classmates. He helped with the chores and cooked meals while Jeannie was convalescing. He changed the baby's diapers and watched for any signs of illness.

Jeannie had difficulty facing the fact that she was a mother. She felt that a load had been lifted from her shoulders when the baby was born, but being a mother at nineteen was a blow. This wasn't what she had planned. She regarded this little person as an intrusion into her life. She became moody and withdrawn. She did not want to nurse the baby, but put him on a formula as soon as he was born. She also resented having to wash the baby's clothes and his diapers. The baby was always there, needing to be fed or cuddled or changed.

Jeannie was tired. The doctor had let her go home when the baby was five days old, instructing her to stay in bed for at least two more days. But she had so much to do that she ignored the doctor's instructions and resumed her regular schedule the day after she came home from the hospital.

Walter helped all he could, but he was carrying a full load at school as well as working at night. Final exams were coming. Knowing that the semester would end in just a week gave them both heart. They pushed themselves a little harder, slept a little less, and somehow found the strength to do all that had to be done.

One night, Jeannie put her work aside and sat down to write a letter to her mother. She told her that the baby's coming earlier than expected had thrust a greater burden upon Walter and herself. Sharing this with her mother made her feel better. She said that premature babies often slept most of the time. It was important to convince her mother and family that Danny was Walter's baby. She never wanted them to know what had happened.

That same day a package arrived from her mother. It contained three little outfits, two-dozen diapers, baby powder, a rattle, a bottle and a nipple. Jeannie carefully examined each item in the package.

Jeannie's mother invited her, Walter, and the baby to come home for summer vacation. Jeannie felt good about the invitation, but a visit would be impossible at this time.

With exams finally over, Walter and Jeannie breathed a sigh of relief. They packed their things and moved to their new furnished apartment. They were excited. They were amazed at what they had accumulated in the past eight months. They placed the baby's bed in the second bedroom and set up a used changing table that had a storage place for his diapers, oils, and creams.

Walter tirelessly waited on both Jeannie and the baby. He knew the advantage of having a place for everything and keeping everything in its place and he found places for everything.

Walter often hopped out of bed when he heard the baby cry at night. He held Danny tenderly as he gave him his two A.M. bottle and patiently patted his back until the expected burp finally came, then laid him down carefully on his soft bed.

Jeannie was grateful for his unsolicited support. Her love for her husband grew every day.

### *JEANNIE AND WALTER TAKE BABY DANIEL TO ATMORE*

She left Daniel lying on a blanket on the floor near the door. It was the coolest spot in the apartment and Jeannie left him there to play with his hands and feet. He was growing so fast. He couldn't hold his rattle yet, but he hit it every now and then as he stretched and kicked his little legs. Jeannie glanced at him every few minutes as she went about her work. As soon as she finished, Jeannie fell to her hands and knees, and played with the baby. She loved him and loved taking care of him. Any feelings of resentment subsided and she found herself becoming irrevocably attached to Daniel.

Jeannie decided not to go to school in the summer. She stayed at home and enjoyed being a wife, mother, and housekeeper. She had learned to cook and took pride in preparing meals for her husband who was taking courses during the summer.

Walter accelerated his education taking summer classes and extra hours during the fall and winter semesters. He planned to graduate after the following fall semester. He would stay in school for two more years to get his law degree.

Jeannie would be a sophomore in the fall. She should have her B.S. Degree in Education at the same time Walter finished Law School.

"Honey," Walter said when he came home from work. "I don't have to go to classes for the next four days. Let's go to visit your family for Independence Day."

"You don't have to work?"

"No, I arranged to take off from work, too."

"Do we have the money?"

"We can manage."

Jeannie was delighted. She was anxious for her family to see the baby. She had written about his weight and color of eyes and hair, and the shape of his chin and nose. She was quick to point out that Daniel had some of Walter's features, but he favored her more. He was a beautiful baby and she would be pleased to show him off.

"When can we leave?" Jeannie thought of all of the preparations she would have to make.

"As soon as you are ready," Walter replied, already searching in the storage area for the suitcases.

"I'll pack tonight and we can leave tomorrow morning. Could you make a formula for the baby while I get things together?"

"I can do that," Walter often made the baby's formula and knew exactly what to do.

"Do we need to call your mom?" Walter asked.

"It is so hard to get through. Mom asked us to come and spend the summer. I am sure we'll be welcome."

"OK. We'll leave as soon as we can in the morning. Some of the roads are so bad; it will take nearly all day to get there."

Jeannie packed her and Walter's things into one large suitcase and the baby's into a smaller one. It didn't take long for her to have everything ready and set beside the front door.

Jeannie had not seen her family since Christmas. The Christmas visit had been difficult. That's when Jeannie quietly broke the news that a baby was expected in June. It was awkward for her family to turn their affection from Alex whom they had known for many years, to a total stranger who was now Jeannie's husband.

But Walter was easy to like. His manners, his attention to Jeannie, his wit and charm soon won them over. Walter became a family member as the shock wore off. They assured Walter that he was welcome and that they looked forward to spending more time with him. The baby was not discussed but it was mentioned in letters exchanged in the following months.

Jeannie and Walter were now taking their infant son to meet his grandparents. He would be admired, scrutinized, and loved. Jeannie felt confident that her and Walter's secret would never need to be revealed.

The trip from Tuscaloosa to Atmore was long and hot and tiring. Starting out on a 180 mile trip with a tiny baby was a bit scary, but they both felt the need for a vacation and Jeannie, especially wanted her family to see her baby.

Walter had carefully planned their route the night before they left, considering several possibilities. They could go northeast to Birmingham, and then turn south on highway 31 that was paved most of the way to Atmore. The distance was greater than the southeast route to Montgomery. The roads on the Montgomery route were not as good, some portions of which had not been paved. The other choice was to head directly south on Route 43, which was mostly unpaved, but was considerably shorter.

Walter decided to take the shorter, more direct route, though he knew driving would be more difficult. Actually, the hard, red clay surfaces were adequate in dry weather and it had been dry for at least a week and a half. Also, there usually was less traffic to contend with on the unpaved roads. He thought that the trip would take most of the day and planned for an early departure.

Jeanie picked up a couple of cardboard fansjust as she walked out the door, knowing that they would need them when they stopped to eat. Eat! She had forgotten to make sandwiches and pack fruit for the trip. She quickly put together peanut butter and jelly, bologna, pimento-cheese sandwiches and three apples and an orange. They could stop for drinks on the way. Then she dashed out to the car where Walter was waiting.

"Are you ready?" Walter put the lunch basket in the car.

"I think so," Jeannie started to get into the car.

"Where is the baby?" Walter asked.

"The Baby!" Jeannie screamed.

They both laughed as they re-entered the apartment. Walter picked the sleeping Danny up and carried him to the car. He put him into Jeannie's arms and walked around to the driver's side.

They were off. The sun rose behind them as they traveled out of town on the clear July morning. Outside of town, they increased their speed. Jeannie looked at her watch. Six fifteen. She couldn't even guess how long it would take to reach the checkpoints Walter had marked on the map. They reached Eutaw within the hour and were soon headed toward Demopolis when Jeannie motioned Walter to stop. She held her nose and pointed to the baby. While Jeannie changed the baby's diaper, Walter took a little hike into the woods.

"We'll stop at a gas station for you," he said when they were ready to go again.

They stopped at Demopolis for drinks and bathroom. Walter filled the gas tank, not knowing when they would find another station. He carefully counted out the gas stamps and money. He had saved several stamps during the previous weeks and had been able to buy a few from people who had extras.

Soon after they started again, they caught up with a Model T Ford that was chugging along at a snail's pace. The narrow, curvy road meant they could not easily pass. Every time Walter tried to get around the Ford, a car, truck, or a wagon came into view. Small particles of red dust rose from the car ahead of them. It was impossible to see well enough to pass the other car. Walter slowed down, putting more distance between the two cars. They rolled the windows up, but the bright sun made it hot inside the car.

Jeannie remembered the fans and began to fan Walter and the baby, until her arm finally got so tired she had to quit. Walter smiled. "That felt good."

"Let's just stop and let that car get ahead of us," Walter said at last. "At least we can open the windows and let some cool air in."

They stopped beside a creek and walked down to the water. "It looks clear but I don't think I'd drink it. A wet handkerchief sure would feel good on my face." Jeannie took a few minutes to wash out the dirty diaper in the stream.

"I guess we can go again." Walter said after a short rest. Two more cars went by. "They seem to be traveling fast enough. I feel better after a little break."

Walter munched on an apple as he drove along.

With less dust in the air they could travel with the windows open.

They stopped at a store in Linder for drinks. Jeannie fished a dime out of her purse for the two Cokes she found in the cold drink box, and handed it to the gray-haired man behind the counter. Her hands were freezing when she lifted them out of the icy water where the drinks were kept cool.

"Last two Coca Colas I have," the man said. "They get picked out nearly as fast as I put them in the box. It is hard to get them nowadays."

"We're glad you had them," Jeannie said. They drove away taking the bottles with them.

"We'll stop for a sandwich after a while." Walter realized that it had been quite a while since breakfast. "Let's put the baby on the back seat, then you can take a little nap. I may need help with driving later on."

"I'll just hold him," Jeannie said. "I'm afraid he'll fall off the seat."

"Not if you put the blankets under him and sort of chock him. He should be all right and you can get some rest."

They stopped at Dixon's Mills to check the tires and the oil. They bought two orange drinks for lunch and drove on to a shady spot outside of town.

"We're just about halfway to Atmore," Walter said, folding up the map. "We should be there by four o'clock."

After lunch Jeannie said, "I'll drive for a while."

"OK," Walter said.

Jeannie pulled back into the road. She was soon driving along at a pretty good pace.

Jeannie gained speed as she went along. She didn't notice the dog that had wandered into her path until it was too late. She swerved to miss it and ran off the side of the road into a sand bed. The car stopped with a jerk.

Walter woke up with a start. "What happened?" The baby began to scream. He had bounced on to the floor, landing face down on the pillow. Jeannie grabbed him up and hugged him. He wasn't hurt.

"What happened?" Walter asked quietly this time.

"A dog jumped in front of me."

Walter saw the dog trotting off toward a house in a field. "I'll see if I can get us back on the road."

An old farmer approached with a team of mules. "I seen what

happened. Glad you didn't hit my dog. I'll help you get out of the sand." He hitched the traces to the bumper and led the mules forward. Jeannie and Walter pushed while the mules pulled. In a few minutes the wheels were out of the sand and back on the road.

"Where you going?" the old man asked.

"We're going to Atmore," Walter said.

"On leave from the Army?" he asked next.

"No, Sir, I've been discharged. Lost a leg. My wife and I are students at the University of Alabama."

"Well, I'm glad you're back. My boy ain't coming back. That's why I'm so particular about that dog. It was his."

"I am so sorry," Jeannie said. "I certainly hope your dog wasn't hurt."

"He don't seem to be hurt, Ma'am," he said. "You just be careful. All sorts of animals roam these parts."

"Thank you for your help," Walter said, offering the man a dollar.

"You're welcome, and no charge." The old farmer led his mules across the field toward his house.

Walter was behind the wheel when they started again. Danny stayed in Jeannie's lap. "I hope that was our last hold-up," he said.

They reached Grove Hill and turned east toward Frisco City. Jeannie started to get excited when she saw road markers pointing familiar towns. They came to a detour sign and men working on a bridge over a small creek. Walter turned the car onto the narrow road indicated by a large black arrow. It was little more than a trail through the woods, full of ruts, holes, and bumps. Their car jostled slowly over the rough road. At the crossing Walter drove the car through the shallow water and heaved a sigh of relief when they were safely on the other side.

Soon they were crossing the Alabama River. Jeannie looked down from the high bridge to the river below. She squeezed Danny, who was sleeping in her arms.

As they got closer and closer to Atmore, Jeannie told Walter about the friends and relatives that they were likely to see.

They finally pulled up in front of Jeannie's parent's house. No one was home. The family car was not in the garage. She told Walter to put their things in her old room and she went to the kitchen. Had dinner been started? Had they already eaten?

Everything was in its proper place. The back porch revealed a few magazines and newspapers scattered on the floor. They must have hurried out of the house for some reason.

Jeannie went next door. The maid, Millie, was in the kitchen. She came to the door, saw Jeannie, and invited her in, hugging her and admiring her beautiful baby.

Mr. Presswood was killed this morning in a wreck, right downtown. I expect your folks have gone out there or to the funeral home."

"Killed!" Jeannie exclaimed. "Alex's father! Oh no! What happened?"

"They said Mr. Presswood didn't hear the train whistle. The train was late, and I guess he just thought it had already gone past. Anyway, he drove right in front of it. His car was knocked forty feet down the track."

Jeannie rushed out of the house without saying Good-bye. She held Danny close, tears streaming down her face. Walter held her and let her cry. "A close family friend was killed in an accident this morning," she sobbed.

"Do you want to go and look for them?" Walter asked.

"I can't go. I can't go," she cried. Walter didn't understand, but he did not question her.

"Let's sit on the back porch."

Walter tried to comfort her. She sat quietly in the rocking chair, gently rocking the baby back and forth. She had loved Mr. Presswood. He had been her friend. And she loved Mrs. Presswood. Now she couldn't go to them—to try to give comfort, even to express sympathy. She wiped her tears. "I am sorry, Walter. They were friends of the family. I have known them a long time."

"I understand, Sweetheart. I really do. So much in life is out of our control. Nobody wants bad things to happen, they just do."

"Walter, this is my fault. I made a terrible mistake that has ruined all of our lives. I am so sorry." She looked at him through puffy red eyes. "How can I ever make it up to people I love?"

It had been less than a year since Jeannie had gone away to college, leaving friends who were happy that she and Alex would be married. They would not yet have forgiven her for abandoning her childhood sweetheart.

"Jeannie, sometimes we just have to walk away. Nothing you can do or say can change what has happened. I love you. I know you love me. We will put the past behind us and move on. It will do no good to tell anyone what happened. Nobody else needs to know. We will do our best to make a wonderful life together. Don't spoil what we have by telling anyone the truth. I will stand by you."

They heard the front door slam. The teary family exchanged hugs and kisses, happy and excited to see each other. Grandparents, aunt, and uncle each took a turn holding and cuddling the tiny new family addition.

"Did you hear what happened?" Jeannie's mother quietly asked her when they went to the kitchen to start dinner.

"Yes, Millie told me."

During dinner no one mentioned the tragedy. Instead, they asked about the trip, the roads, the apartment, the classes Walter was taking, and the car. Jeannie asked about the things that were happening in Atmore. Mr.Carlson mentioned the possibility of a new telephone company. A young man, Bill Corman, was talking about buying the company and expanding the service in Atmore.

Walter thought it was strange that they chose to avoid the subject of the accident. Jeannie did not explain. She did not want Walter to know the connection with the family.

Danny had slept while they were eating, but afterward, he cried. He needed a bath and bottle before bed. Jeannie and her sister, Beth, went up the stairs to get him ready.

Walter helped clear the table and offered to wash the dishes. Mrs. Carlson wouldn't hear of it. He sat down and talked while she washed them. Mr. Carlson and Jimmy took the trash out, and then fed the dog and rabbits. They talked about what had happened to Mr. Presswood and if Alex might be coming home for the funeral.

Danny was bathed and changed. Everyone wanted to hold him. Jeannie was delighted to have so many anxious arms to hold Danny; it gave her a break. After being passed around from one loving relative to another, fed, burped and changed, Jeannie thought it was time for bed. He slept soundly in the bed they made for him in the bottom dresser drawer.

Jeannie and her mother sat on the back porch discussing the accident, funeral and the possibility of Alex's coming home when the phone rang. Alex's sister, Marge, called to tell them that Alex would not be able to come. The Red Cross had not been able to locate his ship, which probably was in the war zone.

"When will the funeral be, Mother?"

"Tomorrow. Alex can't come so there is no reason to delay.

"Alex's family must hate me."

"They were heartbroken. They had looked forward to having you as a member of their family. They were dumbfounded when you married someone else."

"I didn't mean to hurt them. I would like to go to the funeral. I liked Mr. Presswood."

"I don't think that would be a good idea. I don't think they would appreciate it."

"I feel sorry for Mrs. Presswood. She is so kind and good to everyone. That family has had its problems."

"More than you know. She won't have anyone left at home but Jed when Marge goes to college."

"Is Liz coming to the funeral?"

"I don't think so. She lives in Pennsylvania now and is expecting her first child."

Jeannie leaned back in her chair and closed her eyes. She cared deeply for the Presswoods and wanted to be with them. However, she knew that any expression of sympathy from her would be rejected.

Walter joined Jeannie and her mother on the porch. He had had a shower and was dressed in pajamas and robe. The conversation changed to the weather, the mosquitoes and the Fourth of July celebration. The merchants had decided to keep stores open since the Fourth fell on Saturday, their big day every week. There would be no fireworks.

Mr. Carlson, Jimmy, and Beth came out and sat on the steps. A gentle breeze provided a little relief from the hot July evening. Fireflies flashed their tiny beacons as they flitted about over the lawn delighting them and lifting their spirits. They talked about the baby. Everyone agreed that he had Jeannie's features, but his hair favored Walter's.

The baby cried. Jeannie rushed to check on him, Beth at her heels. Jeannie's mother followed and the three women rocked and cuddled Daniel until he went back to sleep. Then they all decided to go to bed.

Jeannie, Walter, and the baby stayed at home while Jeannie's family went to the funeral. She would keep her presence in the town as low key as possible. She realized that her whole family was under pressure because of her marriage. If they only knew what Walter had done for them when he agreed to accept her child as his own!

Jeannie had dinner ready when the family returned. They had gone to the church service, the cemetery, and to the Presswood home to extend condolence. They returned at 5:30 and were pleased to find that dinner was ready. They rushed upstairs to change into cooler, more comfortable clothing while Jeannie and her mother set the table and fixed drinks for everyone.

Little was said about the funeral. Jeannie was dying to know who was there and how they looked, but dared not ask. Mrs. Carlson did mention that Thelma Presswood held up well during the funeral, but broke down at the cemetery and had to be helped to the car. Jeannie hoped that her mother would talk with her about it later.

Early the next morning Jeannie took the baby for a stroll in a carriage the family had borrowed. It was old and rickety, but Jeannie managed just fine. She headed for the drug store. She was hoping to do her shopping and get back home while it was cool and before the stores got crowded. She had just finished paying for her items when she turned around and came eye to eye with Alex's mother. "Mrs. Presswood," she gasped.

"Hello, Jeannie. How are you?"

Jeannie burst into tears. "I'm so sorry, Mrs. Presswood. Could we sit down and talk for a minute?"

Mrs. Presswood hesitated, but she followed Jeannie. They sat in the secluded corner booth so they could have a private conversation.

Jeannie did not know what to expect from Mrs. Presswood. A dressing down was possible. Perhaps she would get it. At least Mrs. Presswood did speak to her.

"How have you been?" She asked.

"I have been well. I finished my first year at the University. And as you can see, I have a baby boy. We named him Walter Daniel. We call him Danny."

Mrs. Presswood looked at the baby for a long time, and then looked questioningly at Jeannie. "He is beautiful. He looks like you, I think."

"Mrs. Presswood, I have not told anyone the truth about my baby. I need to tell you, but I must have your assurance that no one else will ever know."

"I think I know, Jeannie. He is Alex's son, isn't he?"

Jeannie took a deep breath.

"Please keep my secret, Mrs. Presswood."

"I promise, I will never tell anyone. Tell me about your husband. Will he be a good father to this precious child?"

"His name is Walter Anderson. He is a wonderful man and a wonderful father. Walter cannot have children of his own, so he has accepted this child as a gift from God. I don't think Danny will want for anything, especially love and attention. Walter wants to be a lawyer. I am going to be a teacher. Danny will have the best of everything.

"Mrs. Presswood, I did not plan for this to happen. I loved Alex. He doesn't know that the baby is his and I don't want him to find out. I was lucky enough to find a man who would accept the responsibility of my child and I intend to keep my commitment to him. Can you understand? Can you forgive me?"

Mrs. Presswood did not answer for a long time. "Jeannie, you did the right thing. The war has caused all of us to make changes and accept things that we could not accept before the war. In a way, I am glad you told me this; in a way I am sorry. I don't think Alex should be told about this child. Yes, Jeannie, I can forgive you and I realize that it took a lot of courage for you to tell me about this. Alex will never hear of it from me."

"Alex told me that if I needed anything I should ask you for advice. I could not bring myself to tell anyone I was pregnant. Marrying Walter seemed to be the right decision. I am so glad to tell someone whom I could trust."

"Take care of my grandchild, Jeannie. If Alex doesn't come back, at least I will know that his son will carry the bloodline, even if it is under a different name. Perhaps I will see the boy from time to time. I will be looking for him."

Jeannie put her hand on the older woman's arm. "I promise to let you know every time we come to town. I will arrange for you to see Daniel when we are here. I am so sorry about Mr. Presswood. I didn't think it would be proper for me to go to the funeral, but I am sorry."

"I understand." She kissed Jeannie on the cheek and stood up. "The best of luck to you."

Jeannie now had a secret she would have to keep from Walter. It bothered her, but she felt good about telling Alex's mother why she had married so suddenly.

Jeannie and Walter joined her family at the town's Fourth of July picnic in the large vacant area behind City Hall. Tents had been set up for food and drinks. Some families had brought their own picnic lunches and sat on blankets. Jeannie's family spread their blanket under one of the few trees in the area.

Most of the participants in the celebration were white, but a few blacks congregated at the far end of the open field and were laughing and talking among themselves.

"I wonder who invited them," Walter heard a woman say. "Why can't they have their own celebration somewhere else?"

Walter walked over to her and said, "Excuse me Madam, but I overheard your remark. They have as much right to be here as anyone else. The Negro population has lost thousands of their young men in this war. If it hadn't been for a black man, I would not be here today. A black man saved my life. He found me on a battlefield, bleeding, unconscious, and carried me to safety. As far as I am concerned, everyone is welcome."

"I just never did like to mix with them," she cast a scornful glance in the direction of the group of blacks. "They just shouldn't be here with us."

Walter bit his tongue, sat down beside Jeannie and remained quiet for a while. "People just don't appreciate what others do for them," he said.

"What are you talking about?" Jeanie asked.

"Nothing, I guess." He was afraid he would cause a commotion if he said any more, and he didn't want to embarrass his wife and her family.

At noon, the mayor stepped up on an improvised stage and spoke about the war's effect upon the country and about the sacrifices that the young men of the city had made. He read off a list of names of men from the community who had been reported killed or missing in action and those who had been seriously injured. He praised them for supporting their country and for laying down their lives to defend it. The sober crowd sat quietly, feeling the impact of the message delivered by one who had served as mayor for as long as they could remember. “These are sad times,” he said, “trying times. But we can look forward to the day when this war will be over and our town and our country can live in peace and prosperity.”

After the speech, the high school chorus sang the Star Spangled Banner and other patriotic songs. Then there were speakers from the VFW, the American Legion, and the Red Cross. Later, in the absence of a band, records were played, beginning with patriotic songs and then changing the pace to lively, happy tunes that helped to put the crowd into a more relaxed mood. Everyone began to mill round, greeting friends and neighbors and enjoying the activities. Many of them wandered back to the stores and did their shopping or went to the theater to watch a movie.

Jeanie’s mother suggested that they walk back to their car and rest. The hot sun was beating down and she was afraid the baby would be too hot. Everyone agreed except Beth and Jimmy who asked to be allowed to stay and watch the games and races that would be held during the afternoon. Mrs. Carlson gave them permission to stay, but Jeannie was glad enough to be going to a cooler spot.

“Would you like for me to take you home? I can come back later for the children.” Mr. Carlson offered.

“That sounds great to me,” Jeannie said.

Later, Jeannie’s mother asked if the two young parents would like to go out and leave the baby with her. They accepted without hesitation and began to plan what they would do on their first night out. “I would like to rest awhile before going out again,” Jeannie said.

Jeannie and Walter had a very happy afternoon together. They went first to the field where the games were being played and watched the games and races. Then they went to a movie, staying for the double feature. Then they went to the drug store for a dish of ice cream.

Jeannie and Walter were sitting at a table in the drug store, having a banana split, when a group of young people came in. Marge was in the group. Marge saw Jeannie. She waved slightly and said an unemotional, “Hi”, and turned away. Jeannie returned the greeting, and then lowered her eyes. She wanted to embrace Marge and express her sympathy, but she was afraid to. She didn't know what Marge's reaction would be. One tear rolled down her cheek. Walter saw it, said nothing. He put his hand over hers for a moment.

The next morning, Walter packed the luggage in the car and made a little bed for Danny on the back seat. They planned to start back to Tuscaloosa right after breakfast. Jeannie had gotten up early, packed the suitcases, given Danny a bath, and dressed for the trip. She helped her mother with breakfast while the car was being loaded.

"Jeannie, I'll say that marriage is good for you," her mother said. "You certainly have taken control of your life and have learned to do things around the house."

"I guess I really wasn't much help when I lived at home, was I?" she said. "I have learned a lot. Walter has been very patient and helped me along. I don't know what I would have done without him." Jeannie was setting the table and checking on beverages for everyone,

"Are you two really happy?" Jeannie's mother asked. "Your marriage was such a surprise, shock really, to everyone, and your father and I, in particular, are concerned about your happiness."

Jeannie looked at her mother. "We couldn't be happier, Mother. Walter is good at everything he does. He is a good student, he helps me with the housework and with the baby. He works hard at his part-time job. And we are in love. I can't believe it, because I thought Alex was the only one for me, but I love Walter with all my heart."

Mother hugged Jeannie. "I just wanted to be sure you are happy and that he is good to you."

"The best, Mother. You have nothing to worry about. We are happy."

On the way home, Walter asked Jeannie the same question. He wanted to know if Jeannie felt remorse for having to break away from her family and friends and return with him to the life they were sharing at the University of Alabama. He asked if she was really happy, or did she find she was grieving for her lost love. Walter needed to be reassured that Jeannie would keep her promise now that the baby had been born and the legitimacy of her child was accepted in her hometown.

"I am a different person from the one I was a year ago," Jeannie said. "That person was in deep, deep trouble and was rescued by a wonderful, understanding, unbelievable man who has made my life happy original goal was a desperate attempt to hide the truth about my pregnancy from the world. You have done this for me, and so much more. There is no doubt in my mind that you love me and I am happy about that. I hope that we can continue our educations as we have planned and find jobs and enjoy life together until 'death do us part' as we promised on our wedding day."

"I am glad to hear you say that, Jeannie. You are truly a jewel. I know that your family and friends care for you and miss you. I hope we can visit them often. When we finish college, hopefully, we can get jobs near enough to Atmore that you can visit whenever you wish."

## *ALEX AND MARY*
## ALEX SIGNS UP FOR OCS

That night Alex took Mary's address out of his wallet. He wrote a brief letter, explaining who he was and a little about and his background. He mentioned that he was lonely and would like to hear from her. He headed for the mail chute. He lit a cigarette and started through the door.

"Douse that cigarette!"

A startled Alex thought, *Man, that was close*. Smoking was not allowed outside at night. Even a tiny light might attract the attention of an enemy vessel.

"Mail it tomorrow. Mail isn't picked up until afternoon anyway."

"You were watching me?"

"I just noticed that you were writing for a change."

"I haven't felt like writing lately. I got a "Dear John" a few days ago."

"More like a few weeks. Time just stands still when you go through something like that. I'm glad you're over it."

"I don't think I will ever get over Jeannie, but I have to pull myself together and start living again."

"You'll get over it, believe me. It just takes time."

A couple of weeks later, Alex received a letter from Mary. She wrote about herself, her job, and a little about her family. She was working at her uncle's dental office and going to Del Mar College at night. She rented a room from her uncle across the street from the college. She had yet to decide on a career. She sent a picture of herself and asked for one of Alex.

Alex answered her letter immediately. He hoped to hear from her again soon.

Alex played Bridge with Clarence, Ray, and William every few days. He didn't mention to Ray that he was writing to Mary even though Ray had assured Alex that he had broken off completely with her. The company of the players, the games, and Mary's letters helped to lift Alex's spirits. Day by day he began to pull himself out of the depression that had consumed him. Enemy planes were spotted and shot down from time to time, often enough for the men to be well aware of their mission in the Pacific. The ship they were protecting was carrying troops and supplies from Hawaii to Luzon. Also in the fleet were aircraft carriers that launched planes that were loaded with bombs and headed for Japanese strong holds in the Philippines. They were totally alert to the danger they were in, but tried to focus their attention on enjoying the card games and each other's company, except when a battle was actually raging.

Soon Alex began writing to Mary every day, telling her what he was doing and what he was thinking. He told her about the farm in Alabama and how the whole family had to work together to make ends meet during the depression and how the war years had divided the family as they tried to cope with changes and limitations imposed on them. His father's job had taken him away from home, his sister moved away, and greater demands were made of the ones who remained at home. He told her that his ambition had always been to be a doctor and he hoped that some day he would pursue this course. When the mail arrived, there were letters from Mary. She wrote to him every day also. Since she was working and going to college, her letters were usually hastily written, but Alex got the idea that they had much in common and he knew he wanted to spend time with her.

On the first day of July 1945, Alex was summoned to the Captain's quarters. He dressed in his best uniform and sat twisting his hat in his hands as he waited for the captain to begin. The captain had ordered him to sit down while he attended to a more pressing matter.

At last the Captain tuned to Alex. "There is a vacancy in OCS starting August 20 in San Diego. You have been submitted as a candidate. Would you like to go?"

Alex was astonished. The idea of spending a few months on dry land was appealing. "Yes, of course, Sir."

"Lt. Brower highly recommended you. You will leave by helicopter next month. Check with me Saturday morning by 0800 for your orders."

"Thank you, Sir." Alex stood and saluted his Captain. He went directly to his post and began working on his gun.

"Presswood, why are you dressed up?" asked Able Saxton, his new gunner.

"I had to see the Captain."

"I heard. Congratulations. You are going, aren't you?"

"Yes, I will have to stay in the Navy a little longer than I had planned, but I'm in no great hurry to get back home now. My girl married someone else and I'm not ready to deal with that yet."

"At least you will get out of this "Hell Hole." When you come back, if you have to come back, you'll be an officer."

"Won't that be something?"

"Yes, it will. I'm glad you have the opportunity. Now, go and change your clothes before you get that uniform all grimy. You've got fifteen minutes. Alex hurried away to change. He could hardly believe his good luck. Now he'd have something to write home about!

*WORLD WAR II ENDS*

By summer 1945, the war had escalated in the Pacific. There were daily attacks from enemy planes. Every man had to be prepared to fight both day and night. As soon as the "ALL CLEAR" sounded, the men had to clean the guns, then they fell on their bunks to rest. Everybody was edgy. Able and Alex started sleeping on deck beside their antiaircraft guns.

Harvey Johnson, a communications officer found Alex there. He asked Alex to follow him to the communications center where Alex was surprised to see the chaplain.

Harvey closed the door and told Alex to sit down.

"I am so sorry to have to tell you this news. We received a wire from the Red Cross. Your father was killed in an automobile accident on July second."

"Today is July the eighth. The Red Cross has been trying to reach you but I'm sure you know why they could not get through."

Alex was motionless. He was shocked. He finally asked, "H-H-How?"

I'm sorry, we don't know. As soon as we get in touch with the Red Cross we'll ask for details, but right now we have to maintain radio silence."

Alex extended his hand. "Thank you, Sir, I understand." Harvey offered Alex a cigarette.

"I loved my father. We all did. He worked very hard especially since the war started. I don't know how my family will survive. It's going to be hard on them."

"Do you have family, any uncles, aunts, or cousins, who can help?" the Chaplain asked. "Usually at a time like this friends and relatives come to the rescue, and we find solace in our God. Have faith that He will see them through. They'll manage. They'll have to."

"I guess so. My uncles, aunts and cousins will be there for them. I have two sisters and a brother and close friends and neighbors who will help."

As the news sank in, Alex sobbed. Harvey and the chaplain sat quietly and let him express his grief. Alex stood up and made his way to the door.

"Thank you, Sirs," Alex wiped the tears from his eyes. He somehow made his way to his bunk where he cried himself to sleep.

Mail finally reached the Yorktown. Alex had letters from his family. Each member told him in his own way about the accident and how he or she was dealing with the loss. They reassured Alex that everything was under control. They told about the funeral and about how everybody had been there for them. The preacher was a great source of strength for all of them. He visited often and was available when they wanted to talk.

Alex also received three letters from Mary. Her letters were newsy. She told about her relief that the spring semester was over, but she had decided to attend the summer session with only a one-week recess. Alex checked the calendar and smiled. The summer session was half over. Attending classes and working kept her busy during the day and studying kept her busy at night. She expressed concern for Alex's safety and hoped he would be out of the war zone soon.

With the war in Europe over, more planes, ships, munitions,

and men headed for the Pacific. That the Japanese would eventually surrender was a given. Only when was the unknown. Japanese planes continued to attack ships in the area trying to keep reinforcements from reaching the Marines.

Alex realized that had he not agreed to go to OCS, he would most likely be able to go home in a month or two. But since his "Dear John" letter he was not ready to go home.

Just before Alex was scheduled to leave the ship, news of the dropping of the Atomic bomb and the Japanese surrender reached the YORKTOWN. Everyone heard the news over the intercom. They all dropped what they were doing and jumped up and down and shouted. Many men dropped to their knees and thanked God. The captain allowed the jubilation to continue for about fifteen minutes, and then he called for order over the loud speaker. He asked for silence while the chaplain offered a prayer of Thanksgiving. Then the merriment began all over again.

Life was about to change for every man on the ship. Alex would be one of the first to leave. Others would return to their homes and families. A great sense of accomplishment filled the crew. They had put their lives in danger and had faced their country's enemies. The dismay over being drafted and separated from family and loved ones gave way to a sense of pride. They would go home, hold their heads high, praise each other, and face a new and different world.

On August 19, Alex was summoned to the Captain's quarters. The captain handed Alex's orders to him, shook his hand and wished him well.

"Good luck. You will be leaving at thirteen hundred hours."

"Thank you, Sir." Alex saluted his captain then hurried to get his things packed. *Everything I own is in this duffel bag*, Alex thought as he got ready to leave.

Alex said good-bye to his bridge partners before going to the forward deck to wait for the helicopter. Things were happening too fast.

Upon arrival in San Diego, Alex received orders with specific instructions. He was assigned a room on the base that would be shared with five other sailors. It was a stark room with single bunks, a table and chairs. There were racks where they could hang their coats. There were windows, but no curtains, just drab, mustard colored adjustable shades.

Alex surveyed his space and laid claim to a bunk by throwing his hat on it. He placed his duffel bag beneath the rack nearest his bed.

*I guess I'm settled in*. He lay down on his bunk for a nap while he waited for his roommates.

In less than two hours all of the sailors had arrived and claimed their spaces. A sailor called for attention.

"I'm Wayne Purvis and I have been designated captain of this room. I will receive instructions and notices, and will pass them on to you. Classes begin tomorrow morning at 0600, so we will have to get up and be ready for breakfast by 0500. The head is downstairs and mess hall is at the north end of this building. We will dress in clean, white uniforms for class. We will march in formation wherever we go. We can receive a one-day pass in three weeks if we complete our courses. In three months we must know everything about being an officer in the United States Navy. It is now time for mess. Fall in!"

The six men lined up and Wayne opened the door. Lines of men were filing down the hall. Wayne instructed his group to proceed down the corridor.

After mess the squadron marched back to their room. They were given permission to use their time to read or write letters since they had yet to receive their assignments.

Alex wrote to Mary, explaining that he was back in San Diego for training. He said he hoped to see her, but that the first chance for a pass would not be for three weeks. He asked for instructions to her home and for her phone number. He was disappointed that he would not have more free time. Alex really wanted to see Mary again.

Mary sent instructions and invited Alex to call as soon as it was possible.

The three-weeks passed quickly. Days were filled with instruction and the evenings with reading, studying, and written assignments. Physical conditioning was not neglected. They marched to the parade grounds for calisthenics and laps around the field. Each evening before dinner they played soccer or softball. At the end of the third week, Alex received a twenty-four hour pass.

*ALEX MEETS MARY*

Alex picked up his pass at four o'clock Saturday afternoon. Mary met him at the main gate with a beautiful happy smile. She kissed him and led him to the car she had borrowed from her dad.

"Since your time is limited my parents have invited you to spend the night at our house. My brother is in the Army, so you may use his room. Would you like to come?"

"I would like that very much. That is very kind of your parents."

"They are the greatest. They miss my brother and they will enjoy having you visit."

"I hope that goes for you, too," Alex said.

Mary's smile grew wider. "It does, of course. I am so glad to meet you at last. I feel that I already know you. We have been writing for over four months."

"Your letters have been a life saver for me, Mary. I looked forward to every mail call, hoping there would be a letter from you. And you didn't let me down. Thank you."

"Writing was a pleasure. Every night when I finished my homework, I just wanted to tell you what I was doing. I'm afraid my letters were boring; I didn't do much except work and go to school."

"I am sorry I couldn't tell you about what we were doing. I can tell you now. We were shooting at Japanese planes that were trying to blow us out of the water. We were one happy bunch of sailors when they finally announced that the war was over."

"We all sat with our ears glued to the radio for days, waiting for the final blow. The Atomic Bomb was such a surprise to us, and certainly to the Japanese. Everybody was running around kissing everybody when they announced the surrender. What a happy day that was!"

"That certainly was happy for me, just as this day is. I finally get to spend time with the girl whom I have thought about every day for the last four months. By the way, your pictures do not do you justice."

Mary laughed. "Neither does yours."

They had been driving for half an hour when Alex said, "Are you sure you know where you are going?"

"Yes, we live in a small town called Santee. My great-grandparents were some of the original settlers of Santee. My parents were born there and lived there before they were married. My grandfather was the mayor for a long time and now, my father is. My father has a ranch outside the town."

Mary's parents greeted Alex warmly. "We are so glad to finally meet Mary's new friend," Mrs. Driscoll said. Alex and Mr. Driscoll sat on the porch and chatted while Mary and her mother got dinner on the table.

"We would like for you to join us at the square dance tonight," Mrs. Driscoll said.

"I'm afraid I don't know how to square dance," Alex said.

"We'll teach you," they all said together.

"It's easy. Every Saturday night, dances are held in the school gymnasium," Mrs. Driscoll said. "Everyone is invited and nearly everyone in the community comes. It has been a life-saver for families who have lost sons, fathers and sweethearts in the war. The love and concern for each other has made it a little easier for those who are grieving. And we also share in their happiness."

Alex was a little nervous about his inability to square dance.

"Don't worry, Alex, it is easy to learn square dancing. Listen to the calls and do what everybody else does. Just follow us."

"Mary, tell him what he needs to know to get him started," Mrs. Driscoll said.

"Sure," Mary said.

She explained *Honor your Partner, Honor your Corner, Do-See-Do*, and *Promenade*. "You just have to listen to the caller and do what he says. They take a few minutes to show what to do when there are new dancers. We need to find a place near the caller."

"I am afraid it sounds complicated to me," Alex said.

"You'll catch on."

When the fiddlers arrived and began playing and the caller began the calls, Alex did catch on. Soon he felt like a pro.

"See, I told you it was easy," Mary said. "Everybody has so

much fun at the dances. I know you will love it."

"It is fun, but it is exhausting," Alex said after the third dance.

"OK, Alex, let's sit the next one out."

A middle-aged woman approached Mary and put her arm around her waist. They talked in a quiet voice for a moment before Mary introduced Alex to Mrs. Griffin.

Mrs. Griffin squeezed Mary's hand. She looked at Alex. "Mary had promised to marry our youngest son who was killed during training last year." Tears filled her eyes.

"I am sorry." Alex put his arm around her shoulder and hugged her. He was reminded of Willie Ray Coons' mother and the sorrow she had borne the year before.

Mary showed Alex around the school. She introduced him to family after family and now understood the special looks they gave her and the sincerity of their expressions of pleasure in meeting him. They knew that Mary had grieved along with the Griffin family and were glad to see that she was now ready to move ahead with her life.

At ten-thirty, the lights blinked three times, signaling that the dance was almost over. The band, made up of local fiddle players, harmonica players, and a bass fiddler, would play two more dances. The caller invited everyone to join in. Young mothers gathered up their children to get ready to leave, while the older men and women squared off for the *Texas Star*, then the *Virginia Reel*. Everyone laughed and hugged each other when the dances were over.

On the way home, Alex remarked that he had had a wonderful time. As soon as he had learned to Do-See-Do, Honor his partner, and Promenade, he had no trouble doing the dances.

"We hope you will go with us again," Mr. Driscoll said.

Mary's parents retired to their room, leaving the young couple alone for the first time. They sat on the porch and enjoyed the cool, fresh air. They had much to talk about.

Alex told Mary about Jeannie. "Finding your address in my wallet helped me come to grips with my feelings. Jeannie's last letter was a shock. But now, being here with you, Mary, I can put the past behind me. I can have joy and hope again."

Mary said that her life was over when she heard of the Robin

Griffin's death. After a couple of months, her girlfriend had persuaded her to go the USO in San Diego, and try to find solace in helping young men who were far from home. She had danced with them, played games with them, and just talked and listened to them. She had met Ray Atkinson at the USO. They had played cards a few times and had had several dates. She had moved to her room near Delmar College the day before she met Alex at the bus stop. She had promised to meet Ray there to give him her new address. That is when she gave the note to Alex. She laughed. "How naive of me to think that you might happen to know Ray."

"I actually did meet Ray. We were assigned to the same ship. I saw your picture fall out of his billfold, but didn't put two and two together until I came across your note in my wallet. We played bridge. He told me that you had taught him to play. He also told me that he had become engaged to a girl back home. That's why he didn't meet you that day."

"Why didn't you tell me?" Mary asked.

"I thought it was better not to mention to you or to Ray about what happened. And I must say that I am glad that it did."

"I lost Jeannie because I waited too long. Now I have put all of that behind me. I am falling love with someone else. I am not going to wait this time. Mary, I want to ask you to marry me. I know the time has been short, but I know I love you. Will you marry me?"

Mary had developed a great affection for this handsome young man. Writing to him every day and looking forward to his letters had brought joy back into her life. But could she honestly say at this moment that she loved him, and was it enough to marry him? She hesitated.

Before she could answer, Alex went on. "I'll understand if you don't want to give me an answer tonight. Just, please, don't say 'No' until you have had time to think about it."

"There are a couple of problems that we would have to work out. One, Atmore is all of the way across the country. Two, I am not yet sure that I really love you. Time has been so short. I do feel wonderful when we are together. I am comfortable being with you. I have read your letters over and over and I think we have a lot in common: goals, hopes, and dreams. My parents have read your letters, too, and they like you."

"We can work our problems out. I love you enough to do whatever is necessary to be with you."

"At least, we go to the same church," Mary said. "Religious differences are one of the hardest obstacles to overcome in a relationship, but we have that one licked.

"Speaking of religion, my parents will expect us to go to church with them tomorrow. We'd better go to bed so we can get up in time. Breakfast is served at nine o'clock on Sunday mornings."

Alex pulled Mary to him and gave her the kiss he had been dying to give ever since they met at the Naval Base.

"Oh, Mary, please say "yes," I love you so much."

"I will answer you tomorrow."

After Alex had gone to his room, Mary slipped into her parent's room. She sat on the edge of the bed and told them of Alex's proposal.

"I know I haven't known him very long, but I think I love him. He is really good-looking. He is smart enough to have been picked for OCS. His letters have been wonderful. He doesn't have a lot of money, but I think he has potential. He had planned to be a doctor since he was very young, but isn't sure he'll go through with that now. The war sort of messed up his life and his father won't be there to help him through school. Well, what do you think?"

"Mary, Dear, you have known Alex such a short time. You are just getting over Robin's death. I know you have been corresponding for several months, but that isn't the same as dating." Mary's mother didn't want her only daughter to make a mistake. "Also, he lives so far away. Alabama, didn't you say?"

"Yes, but Alex said we could work that out."

Mary's daddy said, "I don't have to tell you what an important decision this is for you." Remembering that he had fallen in love with his wife the first time he saw her, he added, "but I don't think it has to take forever to tell if you care for someone. Alex has written about the things he likes and dislikes and he seems to be a well-brought-up young man. You need to give yourself time to evaluate him and to be sure he is the man you think he is."

"Time is so short. He will be in San Diego only nine more weeks, and he may get only one or two leaves during that time. I like him a lot. I really think I love him. But this is a hard decision to make."

"You will have to let your heart be your guide. You need to consider your plans and how you would have to change them," her daddy said. "I really like him, what I have seen of him, but you are the one who must be convinced."

Mary's mother had gotten up and was looking in the mirror. "My hair is a mess." She started to brush it. "Yes, he is a handsome young man, and he seems to be a nice person, but I am afraid he will take you away from us. I want you to live here, in southern California, so we can see you often."

"Is that your only objection?" Mary asked.

"That is the most important one."

"I told Alex I would think about it. Thank you for not being mad."

"We are happy for you, Honey. We are only concerned about your happiness and welfare. Now, go to bed and get some rest. We'll go to church together in the morning," her mother said.

Mary took all of Alex's letters out of the box she was saving them in. She read all of them again and looked at the pictures he had sent. She thought about what a wonderful person he was and how lucky she was to have met him.

The next morning before anyone else woke up, Mary tiptoed into the room where Alex lay sleeping, leaned over and kissed his forehead.

"Oh, J-?" He started to say Jeannie.

"Mary! You woke me up!"

"Do you mind?"

"Oh, no, no," he said, pulling her down to him and kissing her. "You just surprised me." Then he moved over and she slipped into bed beside him.

"Oh my, this is so wonderfully cozy and warm, but I just want to talk," she said. "We have had so little time to be together."

"Do you have an answer to my question?"

Mary started to say, "What question?" But she decided to be serious. "I think I do, but we must clear something up. Would you be willing to live in California? I mean, make your home here?"

"I must say that thought never entered my mind. I have always planned to live in Alabama. I thought that when I get out of the Navy we'd make our home there."

"It would be very hard for me to leave California. This is my home. My parents expect me to live here, to raise my family here."

"And you wouldn't consider going to Alabama?"

"For a visit, maybe, but I don't think I would want to live there."

"Oh, Mary, I don't want to give you up, but I am not sure I could make such a drastic change. There's no chance you would change your mind?"

"I have to know that you would live here," she said. "I can't give you an answer until I know."

"Are you saying that you would marry me if I promised to live in California?" Alex said.

"Yes, that is what I am saying."

Alex sat up and felt around for his cigarettes. Mary rested her head on his shoulder.

"Mary, I am not ready to make that decision yet. I love my family very much and I am not sure if I can make such a drastic change."

Mary blinked back tears and started to go.

"Don't leave me," he said.

"I have to go back to my room. My parents will be getting up soon." She tiptoed across the room and out the door, leaving Alex alone to think.

Alex lay back. This was a decision he didn't think he would have to make. He fell asleep and dreamed of Jeannie. They walked hand in hand across an unplowed field. She looked so beautiful with the wind blowing her long hair across her face. Suddenly she dropped his hand and looked at him for a long time. Then she began to run. Faster and faster she ran across the field. She ran deep into the woods and disappeared into the trees. He ran after her, calling her name, but she was gone.

Alex woke up and realized that he had called her name aloud. His own voice woke him. He had to face the truth. Jeannie was gone. She was really gone. The real Jeannie was gone. He had lost her forever.

Alex smoked another cigarette. His life had changed. His love had changed. If he did not promise to live in California, he would lose Mary. He couldn't bear the thought of losing Mary.

At nine o'clock, Mary knocked on his door. "Breakfast is ready."

Alex joined everyone in the large kitchen. They chatted about the weather and the few clouds drifting across the sky that were likely to bring rain. Alex admitted that he loved to square dance and hoped he could do it again. Everyone seemed a little nervous.

Alex cleared his throat. "Mr. and Mrs. Driscoll, I have fallen in love with your daughter. I asked her to marry me and she said she would if I would agree to make California my home." As he turned to look into Mary's eyes, he said, "I have decided that I will live here when I get out of the Navy if it means that I won't have to give Mary up."

Mary jumped up and ran around the table to hug Alex and to kiss him. "My answer is yes!" she said.

"I would like to get married as soon as I get my commission, in nine weeks," Alex said.

"Only nine weeks to plan a wedding," Mary's mother said.

"I would prefer a small wedding," Alex said.

Mary agreed. "We don't have time to plan a big wedding. My friends are scattered all across the country anyway."

"We'll see," Mrs. Driscoll said resolutely. "Now it's time to go to church. And by the way, let's keep this in the family for a few days, at least. I have to get used to the idea."

The next nine weeks passed quickly. Alex graduated and received his commission as a Warrant Officer and was immediately assigned to a ship. Mary spent the time going to school and helping her mother plan the wedding. They had decided on a small wedding in the Driscoll home. Even so, everybody had to have new outfits, the bridal gown had to be selected and altered, flowers had to be ordered, announcements printed, and a pianist invited to play. Mary's mother insisted on new drapes and fresh paint for the living room. Food and drinks had to be ordered. Licenses had to be purchased and the minister contacted. There was something to be done every day. Mary's mother finally announced the day before the wedding that everything was ready.

Alex and Mary's one-night Honeymoon was spent in a hotel

near the base. One night of loving and making love filled both of them with the greatest happiness they could ever imagine. They were in love. They belonged to each other. They were beginning a life filled with joy and hope. During the consummation of the marriage, Mary became pregnant.

*WARRANT OFFICER PRESSWOOD*

Alex's ship was ready to sail when he arrived and requested permission to board. Wearing his Warrant Officer's uniform--white pants, white shoes, white hat and stiffly starched white jacket gave Alex's ego a boost and filled him with confidence.

Mary had lain in bed feeling giddy as Alex donned his spotless new outfit. She was sad to see Alex go, but at least the war was over and he wouldn't be in danger.

Alex had spent most of his time in San Diego at the base and their courtship had been limited to telephone calls, letters, and occasional twenty-four hour passes. Their hasty decision to be married caused both of them to have doubts but these disappeared as they saw the joy in each other's faces. They both knew that this was right.

Alex and Mary said, "I do" before a beautifully decorated fireplace in the Driscoll living room. A few close friends and relatives gathered to witness the event and to wish them well. Mary's best friend came from Texas, and was her bridesmaid. Mary's father stood beside Alex.

None of Alex's family attended the wedding. Alex had not been able to break the news to his family that he was getting married and had promised to live in California. He could not bring himself to tell his family that he would not be returning to Alabama. He knew it would break their hearts. He had not been able to find the right words to explain his grief after his break-up with Jeannie, and his ecstasy over finding Mary. Mary was so much like Jeannie, yet was herself a warm, loving person. How could he make them understand?

Mary had driven her father's car to the base and was given permission to walk with Alex to his ship. After a lingering good-bye kiss, Alex hurried aboard. A sad, but smiling Mary, waved until he disappeared from sight. Mary walked slowly back to the car; tears filled her eyes. She didn't know where Alex was going or when he would be back, but she knew that he would be back.

Alex found that his cabin had a small closet in which to store his uniforms and shoes, and a small vanity with drawers for his shaving gear, and other personal belongings. He placed a picture of Mary on the vanity and lay down to read the bulletin that he found under his door. It contained a diagram of the vessel, schedules for watches, duty and meals, when hot water would be available and when lights could be turned on. He was told to memorize the entire bulletin, as it would acquaint him with the vessel.

Alex read the bulletin and laid it aside. He was anxious to learn their destination and his responsibilities. He stood up, stretched, and looked at his watch. It was almost noon. He decided to begin memorizing his material so he would be familiar with the ship and would be able to find his way around. *How different could ships be*? He thought. Picking up the bulletin, he started up to the deck to continue studying. He opened the door and stepped over the threshold. He bumped his head on the doorframe, fell back, and the paper flew out of his hand. A gust of wind carried the bulletin into a passageway and dropped it down a shaft to the deck below. Alex realized that his knowledge of the ship was not complete when he could not find a way to reach the lower deck. Panic hit him. He tried to locate the stairs. Then a door opened beside him and a sailor appeared holding his paper.

"I dropped that," Alex shouted excitedly. Then gaining his composure, he said calmly, "May I have that bulletin, please?"

"Of course, Sir," the sailor said.

Alex was startled. The voice was familiar. He looked quickly at the man holding the paper. "Earl Maddox!" he shouted.

"Presswood, is that you?" Earl said excitedly. "When did you come aboard?"

"Just this morning," Alex and Earl shook hands. Earl was from Atmore and had attended the same high school as Alex.

"So you are a Warrant Officer?"

"Yes, I just got commissioned last Saturday," Alex said.

"And you ended up on this tub."

"Yep, my first assignment."

"I've been on this ship for two years. I am on the last leg of my duty. I get out at the end of the month."

"Lucky you! I've signed up for two more years."

"That's all right for you young guys," Earl said. "But I'm getting old. I want some of that Alabama soil under my feet."

Earl was just two years older than Alex and he called himself an old man! He smiled. "That sounds great to me. There's nothing like Alabama soil. But I'm not going back to Atmore to live."

"What do you mean?" Earl asked.

"I promised my wife I would live in California after the war. So I'll only be going back home to visit."

Earl was flabbergasted. "You're married? Jeannie wants to live in California?"

"No. Jeannie wrote me a 'Dear John'. I married a girl from San Diego and promised her that we would live in California."

"Well, that is a surprise. I thought you'd be plowing that Alabama farm land for the rest of your life. I can't believe it." Earl shook his head.

"I am sure I would have been going back if Jeannie hadn't dropped me, but now I am happily married and looking forward to settling down in Southern California."

"Well, good luck and congratulations on your marriage and your commission. I have to get back to the mess hall and start serving dinner." Earl walked away. "See you around."

Alex took the bulletin, folded it, and put it into his pocket. He headed for the upper deck to have a look around and was surprised to see that they were already out of sight of land. He had no idea where they were going or what this mission would be. Sooner or later it would be revealed. In the meantime, he'd keep his eyes and ears open and try to figure it out. Alex unfolded his bulletin and again began to memorize its contents. Maybe next time he'd be able to find the stairway to the galley.

After studying for a few minutes, Alex folded the paper and returned it to his pocket. He would wait until he was familiar with the ship to follow the instructions to destroy the notice.

Alex went to the mess hall. He loaded his tray and began eating. He hadn't finished his meal before he knew he was going to be sick. He was glad he now knew where the head was and he made a beeline for it, doubled over with pain.

The next two hours were spent in his bed with his head spinning round and round until he finally fell asleep. He was awakened by someone knocking on his door. He jumped up. His sickness had dissipated.

A sailor handed Alex a note from the captain. He was expected to report to the captain at fifteen hundred hours.

Alex looked at his watch. He had ten minutes. He rushed to the head to wash his face and comb his hair. He knocked on the captain's door at exactly 1500 hours.

The captain introduced himself and welcomed Alex aboard. "I am Captain Penn Moore. Welcome aboard. We do not yet know what our mission is, but I do know it is confidential. I do not know where we will end up. My orders are sealed. I cannot open them until certain things have been accomplished." He didn't elaborate on the 'things' and Alex didn't dare ask. "Your assignment is simple. You are in charge of all of the guns on this ship. You will make sure that they are ready at all times. Of course, you will have a crew, but you are responsible for keeping them in ship-shape. We hope that we will have no need for guns, but they must be maintained at all times.

"We will become better acquainted as time goes along. I like to maintain a friendly atmosphere on my ship. All I ask is respect and fulfillment of your duties."

"Thank you, Sir," Alex said.

Captain Moore handed Alex a book. "This explains your duties. Read it at once and become familiar with its contents."

"Yes, Sir."

"You are dismissed."

Alex saluted and turned to leave. He wanted to begin reading at once, but instead he decided to go aft, meet his crew, and have a look at the guns. He was pleased to find that the guns were the same as on the Yorktown. He would have no trouble maintaining them, but he would have more guns to inspect. He introduced himself and met his crewmen. There were four gunners and four mates on both the forward and aft decks. He questioned the sailors about their experience and knowledge of the guns and was satisfied they were capable of operating and maintaining them. Alex spoke to each of the men individually and was surprised when every one informed him that they would be leaving the ship soon. They all were being discharged. *I suppose I will have a whole new crew when these men go. I hope they don't all leave at the same time.*

"When do you expect to leave?" Alex asked each crewmember. He was told that they would leave at different times. He would have experienced people aboard long enough to break in the new crew as they went along.

Alex decided to begin reading the manual the captain had given him at once to become better acquainted with his duties.

That night Alex wrote to his family. He had to tell them about Mary and his decision to live in California. It was imperative now because he had met someone from home and had told him that he was married and planned to make his home in California. How could he do it without breaking their hearts? It would be hard to tell his mother.

He questioned his decision. He really was being selfish when he asked Mary to marry him without consulting his family, but it was too late for second thoughts. *What a fool I have been, a perfect fool. How am I going to handle this situation?*

Alex wondered about his love for Mary. He had known her for such a short time. But he was married and had promised to stay married until death parted them. Mary depended on him. He had given her his word. He could tell them that. He could tell them that he really loved Mary. "I must never doubt that I love Mary," he said to himself. "I love her. She loves me."

It was a long letter. Alex wrote about what he had been doing and how proud he was to be a warrant officer. He told them about meeting Earl Maddox. Finally he got around to tell them about Mary. He told them how badly he was hurt when Jeannie married someone else and how miserable he had been. He detailed how he had met Mary and how much she had meant to him. He decided to wait until his next letter, or the next to tell them that he would make his home in California, but he would have to tell them before Earl did.

The next morning Alex mailed the letter on his way to the aft deck. The ship was moving steadily south, toward the Panama Canal. The sailors began to speculate where they were going and why.

*We could be headed to New Orleans*, Alex thought.

He wondered if it would be possible to get a pass to go home from New Orleans, so he could tell his family about his decision to live in California. Telling them in a letter would be difficult. He began composing a letter in his head. He would write it all down tonight.

Late the next afternoon the ship steamed into the Gulf of Panama. Alex was excited about having the opportunity to sail through the Panama Canal. He had studied about the canal in school, but never expected to go through it. He got goose bumps when he realized he was about to see it.

As the ship crossed the Gulf of Panama and entered the canal from the Bay of Panama, the deck became alive with sailors. Every off-duty sailor and officer came on deck to observe the passing.

Alex found himself standing beside Earl Maddox. Earl had made several trips through the canal already and knew what to expect. He explained the operation to Alex.

"It takes about eight hours for the ship to travel the fifty miles from the Pacific to the Atlantic Ocean," Earl said. "It's better to make this trip in the daylight so you can see the country side. Too bad we have to go through at night." In a few minutes Earl said, "I think I will hit the sack now. I have to roll out early in the morning."

"I don't want to miss any of this," Alex said. "I'm going to stay up here until we reach the other end of the canal."

"I'd do the same thing if it were my first time." Earl walked away.

Alex sat down on the damp steel deck. Other men were sitting down enjoying the fresh air, not wanting to miss a moment of this experience.

At daybreak the ship steamed out into the Caribbean Sea and started toward the Gulf of Mexico. Following its course on his compass, Alex realized that they were sailing toward Texas. In Corpus Christi the men were given 24 hour-passes while the ship took on supplies. Alex went ashore for a few hours.

Alex wandered through the city. He gazed out at the beautiful blue water of Corpus Christi Bay. Palm trees and flowering hibiscus reminded Alex of California and made him miss his wife. He bought picture post cards and wrote quick messages to Mary and to his family before returning to his ship.

The ship sailed past Galveston and on to New Orleans. Alex asked for and received permission to go ashore long enough to call his family. They would not be in port long enough to receive a pass.

Alex dreaded the call. He felt sure that his letter announcing his marriage had reached his family, but he had not heard back from them. He could imagine how deeply they were hurt. His need to talk to them was greater than his fear of reprimand.

Alex met Earl on the upper deck. Earl turned to him and offered him his hand. "This is the end of the War for me, Presswood."

"Congratulations," Alex said and asked Earl to visit his mother and tell her that he was fine. He would try to reach her by telephone while they were in New Orleans.

"I'll visit your family," Earl promised. "And I'll tell them that you are trying to reach them."

"Man, I wish I were going with you. I wrote to my family about my marriage, but I really wanted to talk to them face-to-face and make them understand."

Earl shook his head. "It was a shock to me. But I am sure they will accept it. You couldn't help what happened. So long, Buddy" He patted Alex's back--and was gone.

In New Orleans Alex found a telephone and dialed the operator. He waited for her to make the connection. It took seven minutes for the Atmore operator to respond and several minutes longer for the connection to be made. At last the operator signaled that his party was on the line.

"Hello, Mama," Alex cried. "Did you get my letter?"

"Yes, Alex, we got it. Is it really true? Are you married? We just couldn't believe it."

"It is true, Mama. Everything happened so quickly. Mary is wonderful. I am anxious for you to meet her. We will come for a visit as soon as we can."

"A visit, Alex? A visit? We want you to come home to stay with Mary, of course."

"I had to promise Mary that we would live in California. I had to or she wouldn't have married me."

Alex could tell that his mother was crying.

"I love you, Mama. Don't cry."

The phone went dead.

"I'll write," Alex said, but he knew she couldn't hear him.

Alex felt the blood drain from his face. He walked slowly back to his ship. He went straight to his cabin to write his mother.

Their lives would never be the same. Alex was on his own now. He had a wife. And he would live happily, he hoped, with his wife over two thousand miles from his family. Alex was still having trouble dealing with that idea. How could he expect his family to give their approval and blessing? He knew he couldn't. Yet, there would be no going back.

Alex wrote to Mary, declaring his love for her and telling her how much he missed her. He still did not know where the ship was headed. If the captain knew, he had not shared the information. He only said that they were on an important mission.

The ship sailed out of the Gulf of Mexico, around the tip of Florida, and up the east coast of Florida. They steamed into Jacksonville four days later. At mail call, Alex received several letters from Mary, one from Marge, and one from his mother. He opened his mother's letter first.

Tears came to his eyes as he read: tears of sorrow, tears of relief. He knew that his mother and siblings had composed the letter together, but Mama had written it.

*"Your decision to live in California gives us great pain and sadness, but we will try to understand. It is hard for us to accept the fact that you will always be so far away. We had looked forward to seeing you settle down in Atmore and raise your family here, but that isn't to be. We are happy to know that you have found a girl whom you love and who loves you. We will always love you, miss you, and look forward to your visits. If you change your mind and decide to move back to God's Country, we would be very happy. Please write to us often and let us know how you are getting along. We would like to see pictures of Mary. Ask her to write to us.*

Next Alex read Marge's letter. She was furious. Marge said

that Jed was upset too. Alex hoped that time would eventually bridge the chasm that his marriage caused. He would have to write often.

Alex lay down on his bunk to read his wife's letters. She told him what she was doing and how her studies were going. She mentioned that she felt exhausted much of the time. Mary's next letter mentioned that she had had a fainting spell on campus after skipping breakfast that morning.

In her third letter, Mary said that her period was late, but she thought that was only because she had been under so much stress for the past few weeks. She went on to tell Alex that her brother was expected home soon. She declared her love for him and said how much she missed him.

Alex's ship made stops in Savannah, Charleston, Norfolk, New York, and Boston. Never having been on the east coast, Alex was excited about having the opportunity to spend a few hours in each port-of-call. As long as the men did not get into trouble, they received passes when not on duty. They could see the sights, walk through the parks, and see a movie or a play. In Boston, Alex saw the Old North Church and the statue of Paul Revere and other American Patriots.

Alex wrote to Mary.

*I'm thrilled to see the places that we learned about in school. I don't know what this trip is all about, but I'm very glad we are making it. I only wish that you were with me and we could share the experience.*

Alex received news that Mary was pregnant. Mary was excited. Disturbing was the word that crossed his mind. He hadn't expected to start a family so soon.

Mary's doctor told her that she would have the baby in early August. She would finish the semester at Del Mar College and then move back in with her parents until Alex returned.

"A baby!" Alex said aloud to himself. "How can I go to college and become a doctor if I have a baby to support?"

Alex's life changed once again. His plans to continue his education--eight years or more of college--would have to be reconsidered. He would have to make other plans for a career. He sat looking at the wall, thinking.

Alex went ashore and placed a call to Mary. They talked about how she felt physically and mentally. He reassured her that he loved her and was happy about her news.

His love for her was as strong as ever. Hearing her voice thrilled him. Jeannie seldom entered his consciousness now that he had Mary, but in his dreams he still had difficulty separating them.

After Boston, they sailed to England. That he had been ordered to go to London excited Alex. He and Lt. Marshall Johnson were ordered to deliver a message from the captain to The Deputy Minister of Defense. Alex and Lt. Johnson delivered their captain's message to a courier and waited ten minutes in an outer office. The courier returned and told them that it would be several hours before a response to the message could be prepared. They could leave the building but were to return in six hours to pick up the papers for their captain. They were given identification badges granting them the privilege of visiting London for the day.

Alex and Lt. Johnson hoped to take a guided tour of the city, but were informed that tours were not available because of labor shortages and post war rebuilding, remodeling, and reconstruction of devastated buildings. Wherever they walked there were barricades across streets and sidewalks where carpenters were hard at work repairing holes in walls, broken windows, broken down doors, and roofs and walls. It had been over a year since the last bombing, but much work still had to be done.

"I would at least like to have a look at Buckingham Palace," Alex said. "I would like to tell the folks at home that I've seen it."

"Let's try to get a taxi to drive us past," suggested Marshall. They hailed a cab.

A taxi stopped and they got in. "We would like to see the Palace," Alex said.

"You are Americans?" The driver asked.

"Yes, Sir," they said together.

"Welcome to London. I'm sorry, but I cannot take you there. No one is allowed to go within a mile of the Palace. The streets are all blocked off."

"The war has been over nearly a year," Lt. Johnson said, "Why is it still restricted?"

"We still have to be careful."

"Well, thank you anyway." Alex and Marshall started to get out.

"Come on, I'll give you a ride. How much can you spare?"

Alex and Marshall discussed it and decided they could spend five dollars each.

"I'll bring you back to this spot in an hour. You will have a grand tour of old London town, and a story or two to boot. We owe a lot to our American friends and I will show you a good time for an hour." He clicked off his meter and put the car into gear.

In the hour that followed, Alex and Marshall had the most memorable trip of their entire lives. The driver drew their attention to points of interest and told stories of how the brave men and women had endured the nightly raids from German aircraft. More than 30,000 people had been killed and immeasurable damage had been done to buildings. The driver showed them the London Bridge, the British Museum, which opened in 1759, the crumbling remains of the old Roman Wall built nearly two thousand years ago, Old Bailey, the Central Criminal Court, the site of the House of Commons which had been destroyed by bombs, St Paul's Cathedral, and building after building that showed evidence of the relentless bombings that London had endured. As he drove along, the driver talked about catastrophes the city had endured from the time of its founding by first century Romans, followed by the determination and fortitude of the stalwart London citizens who rebuilt their city.

As the hour's tour came to an end, Alex and Marshall felt overwhelmed. They had seen so much that they knew they would keep in their memory forever. "I know one thing," Lt. Johnson said, "Someday I would like to come here on my own when I have more time to visit."

"Let's shop for souvenirs for our wives before we have to go," Alex said. Each bought a present for his wife before returning to collect the reply for their captain.

"Where do you suppose we will go next?" Alex asked as they headed back to their ship.

"My guess is that we will head back to the States for a while," Lt. Johnson replied. "I think we will have to go into dry dock and have our engines overhauled before we begin the secret mission the captain mentioned. I bet that what we just did--delivering that message and waiting for a response--is part of our mission. And have you noticed, we have a whole new crew."

"In other words," Alex said, "all of the men who served aboard this ship in the war zones have been replaced with fresh new personnel. Even Captain Moore. And you. How long have you been on board?"

"I have been on board since last September," Marshall said thoughtfully. "But actually, the change of personnel isn't really strange, considering that most of the men were drafted for the duration."

Mid-April found the ship in Seattle, Washington where major components were replaced. The crew remained aboard.

It had been five long months since Alex had seen Mary. The letters he received told him about everything that was happening in her life. She sent pictures of herself every week. She was wearing pretty maternity clothes that she and her mother made.

Mary was lonely and begged Alex to try to find a way to come home even for a few days or hours." Alex looked at the map and pondered over the possibility of going from Seattle to San Diego. No one from the ship had received more than a three- day pass and Alex was afraid he could not make the trip in seventy-two hours.

*I'm afraid to risk it,* Alex wrote to Mary. *It's just too far to go on a three-day pass.* Alex thought of having Mary meet him in San Francisco, but was worried that would be risky, too. Passes were not issued until Friday afternoons and could not be reserved ahead of time. But after talking with Mary on the phone, they decided to take the chance.

Alex checked on hotels in San Francisco and chose one that was just across the street from the Greyhound Bus terminal. He reserved a room and told Mary where to meet him. They agreed that if Alex didn't arrive by noon Saturday and Mary could not reach him by phone, she would catch the next bus back home Saturday evening.

Mary arrived first. She had boarded the bus in San Diego at seven o'clock Friday morning and arrived in San Francisco at six-thirty Friday evening. She found the hotel and checked in.

# Reunion

It was still light outside, so Mary decided to take a walk and look for a restaurant. She went to the coffee shop in the bus station, which was near her hotel. She had a sandwich and coffee and bought snacks for later. She bought a couple of magazines to read while she waited for Alex to arrive.

Before crawling into bed, Mary showered and dressed in a lovely nightgown she had bought for the occasion. She checked the locks on the door and windows. Looking out of the window, she could see people moving on the streets below. She was glad her room was on the fourth floor, but she felt lonely in this huge city.

Mary was awakened by city noises. Several times during the night when she heard fire truck and police sirens, she sat straight up. She decided to leave a light on so she wouldn't be frightened if she woke up again. She picked up a Reader's Digest and began reading. Eventually, she fell asleep and did not wake up until she heard a knock on the door.

"Alex, is that you?"

"Open up, it's me!" Alex reached down to pick up his bag.

Before he knew what had happened, the door opened and he was knocked to the floor. Mary had intended to jump into his arms, but she jumped just as he had bent over. They found themselves on the hallway floor hugging and kissing, and trying to tell each other how happy they were to be together again. At last Alex was able to get to his feet, pick up Mary, and carry her into the room.

"It took me fourteen hours to get here. We'll have approximately forty hours together. Forty wonderful hours to be with my beautiful wife. Thank you for coming."

"Thank you for arranging it," Mary said, pulling him down beside her on the bed. Lovemaking was awkward at first. Alex was afraid he would hurt Mary or the baby, but she assured him that she and the baby were OK.

They talked about everything: her studies at college, her feelings about becoming a mother, and what they both had been doing since he left. They dressed up and went out for dinner and to a movie Saturday evening. They enjoyed the sights on Sunday.

Sunday evening arrived before they knew it. They had not talked enough, laughed enough, or made love enough, but their love for each other had been renewed and strengthened.

By the middle of June, the work on the ship was complete. Captain Moore announced that they were headed for Hawaii. In Hawaii, they joined a fleet and set sail toward Japan.

When the captain was ready, he called all of his officers together. "What I am going to tell you is a secret. You will not reveal our assignment until it has been accomplished. Then the whole world will know."

"There is a small island in the Marshall group called Bikini. The United States will drop an atomic bomb on that island to study the effects of an atomic blast on the island. The dangers could be considerable, but we must know the effects of our powerful new weapon. We need to know how much harm will be done and how long the land will be affected. We are doing this test in cooperation with our allies. Every living thing has been moved from the island and relocated on other islands in the area. Local fishing vessels have been employed to move every man, woman, child and animal from the island. We are here to help protect the fleet in case of retaliation by our enemies. We will be anchored twenty-five miles from the island, and we will be able to observe the detonation. The entire crew will receive protective gear and are hereby ordered to wear it as long as we are in any danger of fallout from the bomb. The test will take place tomorrow. We do not know for sure what the range of the blast will be, so we must take every precaution."

The next day, Alex stood on deck, wearing his protective gear, and watched the mushroom-shaped cloud rise in the distance. Fearing that the wind would blow radioactive material toward his ship, Captain Moore ordered every man to his cabin for the next twelve hours.

Word got around that the mission had been a success and that they would be heading back to the States. Before he arrived in San Diego, Alex learned that the government was releasing men who had served two years if they were willing to give up their commissions. It took very little thought for Alex to elect to become a civilian. He would have less time on the G.I. Bill for his education, but he would work that out later. He knew he would find a way to go to college somehow. Getting back to his family was of utmost importance at this time.

Alex's son had been born while Alex was at sea and he was anxious to get home to see him. Mary named him Jules, a name they had agreed upon when they were in San Francisco.

Alex had signed the necessary papers for his release from the Navy before the ship sailed into port. With all of his earthly possessions again packed into his duffel bag, Alex stepped ashore, a free man, a civilian. Mary and the baby were waiting at the dock while her mother and father and brother stayed in the car. Alex couldn't keep his eyes off his beautiful son. He held him and kissed him and cuddled him in his arms. He finally placed the baby into the arms of his mother-in-law and slipped away for a few quiet moments with his beaming wife.

After spending the first month at Mary's parent's home, they moved into a small apartment of their own. Alex could go to college for two years on the G.I. Bill. After that, they would both get part-time jobs and continue their education.

### *ALEX AND MARY GO TO COLLEGE*

Mary had been able to complete one year of college before Jules was born. She was excited about going back to school and had decided that she wanted to be a librarian. She enjoyed studying and liked to work with books and research materials. She and Alex had decided that they would both go to college for the next year and see how it worked out. If they were able to find part-time jobs and could juggle everything, they would be prepared for good jobs in three or four years.

Alex had given up his desire to be a doctor, he had to consider another career. He wanted to be a good father and husband and spend time with his wife and son, so he looked for a course that would require less college preparation and, hopefully, be less demanding on his time.

Alex decided to study business administration because his counselor said it offered many employment opportunities and was general enough that he could branch off into different fields.

Mary's mother had become totally involved with the baby from the minute he was born. The baby filled the void left when there was no further need for rolling bandages and knitting sweaters for the Red Cross. She became a surrogate mother enabling Mary to pursue her studies and work part-time waiting tables in town. Mary sometimes cried because she had so little time to spend with her baby and her husband. She also shed tears when her homework assignments piled up and seemed impossible, but she reminded herself that studying would be over in a few years.

Alex was aware of Mary's frustrations. Mary expected to make top grades in all of her subjects. Alex, who was working part-time as a mechanic, was also carrying a full load of college courses and he also expected to excel in his classes. He found himself wondering if the goals they had set for themselves were realistic. But they persevered.

Since Mary was a year ahead of Alex, they had no classes together. They met in the library during free periods where they did most of their studying and enjoyed each other's company. They arranged their schedules so they could have lunch together every day and sometimes sit under their favorite tree to chat.

Alex knew that the wonderful spark of love that had brought them together had to be kept alive if theirs was to be a successful marriage. Too many of the hasty wartime marriages were ending in divorce because the adjustments were too great. Alex had felt that he had to fill the void that was left by Jeannie and had decided to marry Mary before he really comprehended the position he would be in. It was a spur of the moment decision to marry her and to promise to live in California.

Neither Alex nor Mary had any idea of the difficulties they would have in trying to build a strong, lasting relationship. They were young. They felt love for each other but they wanted reassurance. They had gone into their marriage with unanswered questions. It was their strong commitment to themselves and their desire to build on that commitment that made it possible for them to survive the years of hardships that they had to endure. Mary and Alex talked about the possible failure of their marriage. They both were determined to make it last, not only for themselves, but also for the precious little boy who was so dear to them both.

The time they spent in college was a period of growth. Support of each other was an essential part in the success of their life together. The reality that they were still together at the end of their college years attested to the fact that they both had determination and character. By the time they graduated the love that had been the basis for their commitment to each other had flourished and grown into deep affection and trust. They were totally devoted to each other.

Mary had chosen their first apartment soon after Alex separated from the Navy. She wanted to begin making a home for her husband and son. She chose a place near her parents; who were like a rock. They were always available to care for Jules when they were needed.

It was hard to make ends meet. Their furniture had come from attics and storage rooms of friends and relatives. They depended on public transportation until Mary's uncle gave them his old car. Alex had to buy all new clothes when he gave up his uniform. Life was difficult, but they were happy.

Mary graduated a year before Alex and quickly found employment in the high school from which she had graduated. Though her job was demanding during her working hours, she was free of homework and study. She had more time for her husband and son, and the money she made was a welcome relief. She insisted that Alex give up his part-time job and limit his mechanical activities to keeping their old car on the road. Even though they both wanted a better car, they decided to wait until after Alex graduated and began working full-time.

The year went fast. Jules was an active little boy. Alex and Mary enjoyed watching him grow. Loving grandparents, his uncle Bill, and his parents surrounded him. Jules was almost four years old when Alex received his baccalaureate degree, sixteenth in a class of 240. "Not bad for a peanut farmer from Atmore, Alabama," Alex chuckled.

Alex was offered a position in the Metropolitan Life Insurance Company's Los Angeles office. Accepting the position would mean a move. It would be a dramatic change for Jules. Alex had other offers, but he felt a kinship with insurance because it had been his father's business. He qualified for several positions in the company and the salary possibilities were beyond his expectations.

## *JOBS IN LOS ANGELES*

After much soul-searching, Alex accepted the job with Metropolitan. Although Los Angeles was less than a hundred and fifty miles away, a comfortable distance for frequent visits, they were reluctant to break away. They had been happy living near Mary's family. They wanted their son to be surrounded by friends and relatives who offered love, companionship, and guidance.

Mary supported Alex in his decision. Alex had worked hard to earn the degree, which had helped to land him the job. He had kept his promise to live in California; breaking ties with his family and friends whom he loved. The offer from Metropolitan was by far the best one he had received and there were opportunities for advancement. Though it broke her heart to move away from her parents, Mary accepted it.

Soon after Alex graduated, Mary said good-bye to her old life and hello to a strange new world. They loaded their possessions into a U-Haul trailer and hitched it to the back of their car. They bade Mary's family good-bye and drove to their new home in Los Angeles.

Mary and Alex had located an apartment on a previous trip. Their landlady met them at the door to give them instructions: where to park the car, where to put the garbage, where their small storage area was, when to water the grass and when to mow it. She told them to keep the radio turned down so their neighbors would not be disturbed. She took a long look at Jules and sighed. "You will have to keep the boy quiet also. The older people don't want to be bothered by children." She showed them a small area where Jules would be expected to play. She finally left them.

"This isn't going to be like Santee. We should have taken more time selecting a place to live."

Mary tried to be optimistic. "Let's try it for a month or two. If we don't like it, we'll just move."

"I was not impressed with her rules and her insinuations about our inconsiderateness for others," Alex said.

"Perhaps the people who moved out gave her cause to be disagreeable."

"All we can do is give it a chance. We paid a deposit and the rent for a month. We'll have to stay a couple of months anyway."

Mary unloaded the boxes and set them on the back porch while Alex unloaded the furniture. They walked into the apartment together and discussed where to place everything.

There was a knock on the door. On the front stoop stood a young couple holding a picnic basket filled with food. They introduced themselves and presented the basket.

"I'm Julie Walker, and this is my husband, Bill. Welcome to Los Angeles."

"What a beautiful gesture," Mary exclaimed. "Thank you. And do come in."

"We left our son sleeping upstairs," Julie said. "We can't come in now. We have been watching for you all morning. Mrs. Dawson said we'd have new neighbors today. We are so happy to see that you are young, like us, and you have a little boy for our Steven to play with."

Jules appeared and was introduced. Julie bent down, shook his hand, and spoke to him, "Our little boy, Steven, will want to play with you," she smiled. "When he wakes up, you may come out and play with him while your mom and dad work. Would you like that?"

"Sure," Jules said. "We can play trucks."

"I'll come and get you when Steven wakes up from his nap," Julie said.

"I'll give you a hand unloading the trailer," Bill said. "I'm a bit of an expert. At least I've had lots of experience at it."

"How's that?" Alex asked.

"I'm with Western Electric. We get moved around quite a bit. Four times in the past three years," Bill said.

"What do you do?" Alex asked as they started toward the U-Haul.

"Train new recruits. I was in electronics in the Army and got hired a few days after I got out. I didn't have to go to school. Uncle Sam taught me what I needed to know."

"Lucky. I maintained and shot guns in the Navy. It didn't prepare me for anything in the real world."

"What line are you in?" Bill asked.

"Insurance. I just got my degree in business last week and landed this job right away."

"Your first job?" Bill asked.

"I'm afraid so."

Alex and Bill lifted the dresser and carried it into the house. Then came the bed, the sofa, the kitchen table and chairs. "This old stuff could use a new coat of paint," Alex said. "Maybe we can get it done on weekends."

"You'll be buying new now that you have a job. That's the way it works. Soon you will be hanging out at the furniture store looking for new stuff."

"Sounds like the voice of experience."

"It started on my first pay day."

"It could happen with us too, but Mary is pretty attached to this old furniture. Her friends and family gave it to us. There's a lot of sentiment attached."

"Mark my words," Bill grinned. "There's some mighty pretty furniture out now. Women have a hard time resisting it."

"We'll see." They finished unloading the trailer and stopped for a Coke. "Thanks for your help," Alex said.

"Glad to. Now I have to go to the garage and get a part for my car. I broke a tail pipe last week."

"I can help with that. I worked as a mechanic part-time while I was in college."

"I may need your help. Want to go with me to the garage?"

"I'd better stay here and help Mary get squared away," Alex said.

Mary finished putting the pots and pans away and was unpacking dishes and glasses when Julie appeared again with a wide awake Steven, ready to play with his new friend. He carried several toys, including a truck, in a cardboard box.

"I'll watch Jules in the back yard while you get your kitchen set up," Julie said. "Steven will be happy to have someone to play with."

"This will go much faster if Jules is out playing. Thank you so much," Mary said. She kissed Jules on the cheek and he rushed out to join Julie and Steve in the back yard.

"Beds are ready," Alex said. "Do you know where the linen is?" Mary showed Alex the box that held the sheets and blankets.

The apartment was small. Many homes had been altered to make apartments for GIs and their families and many of them were still available though the war had been over for six years. This apartment was in a big old home that had been remodeled during the war.

"It will do for now." Alex said, putting his arm across Mary's shoulder as he surveyed what they had done.

"Let's go out and see what Jules is doing." Jules and Steven were playing in the sand box. Julie sat at a picnic table, reading.

"It's quiet." Alex said as they approached the play area. Mary and Julie fell into conversation while Alex dropped down beside Jules and began scooping up sand with him. Steven was building a roadway and Jules was trying to make a tunnel through the sand castle he had made. An old cast iron truck stood on the side of the sandbox.

"I'm going to take a load of logs to the building site," Jules pointed to a pile of sticks they had stacked up. "We are making a bridge to go across the river."

"This is very good," Alex said.

"Help us make the tunnel," Steven said. "Then we will be finished." Alex helped with the tunnel while Mary and Julie talked.

"I am hoping to find a job as a librarian in a school nearby," Mary said. "I dread having interviews in a strange place, but I want to work."

"I stay at home and keep house." Julie said. "We are expecting another baby in five months, so I'll have my hands full."

"Oh how exciting, do you want a girl or another boy?"

"It doesn't actually matter so long as it's healthy. I will be back to washing diapers and making formula. I love taking care of a baby."

"I love it, too," Mary said, "but I want to work. I have always wanted to have my own identity and my own money, but I want a family too. It is hard doing both, but I feel good about it."

"To each his own. I think it is good that we can do what we want. Bill and I decided before we got married that he would earn the living and I would run the home, and it has worked out just fine, so far. I like being available for Stevie."

"My mother has always helped us with Jules. When we were in college, she cared for him almost as much as I did. I'll be looking for a nursery nearby for now, and after next year, he will be in school. I feel a little guilty about not being with him all of the time, but he is cared for."

"There are several nurseries in this area and a high school four blocks over. Maybe there is an opening in the library there."

"I submitted an application when we came here for Alex's interview, but I haven't heard back. I'll have to call Monday and check on it."

"I'll be glad to watch Jules for you when you go on interviews," Julie offered. Mary hesitated. She was delighted to have the offer, but she wasn't sure just how to accept it. After all, she had only met Julie this morning.

"I'll pay you to watch him," Mary said.

"Nonsense." Julie said. "Jules and Steven will have fun together. I couldn't charge you for doing a favor."

"I really appreciate your offer; I will let you know when I need to go. If you ever need a sitter, I will be happy to watch Stevie as long as I am not working."

"Thanks, I may need help when I go to the doctor for my appointments. I have to go only once a month now."

"We can help each other then," Mary said.

When Bill returned from shopping, Alex asked, "Did you find a new tail pipe?"

"No, I found a used one though." Bill stepped over to Julie and gave her a hello peck on the forehead.

"Everything OK?" He asked.

"Sure." she said. "And the boys have played together very nicely."

"Let me see the pipe," Alex said. After examining it he said, "It's for a 1939 Buick?"

"Right. You know your cars."

"I have worked on a lot of cars." Alex said. Let's see if this thing fits."

When they left, Julie said, "We're grilling out tonight. Why don't you join us? You can start cooking in your new kitchen tomorrow."

"OK, if you let me help. You have done so much for us already."

"Let's see what we can get together."

"I have a couple of cans of baked beans and some potatoes. I'll make salad and tea," Mary offered.

"I have hamburgers and buns and some ice cream," Julie said. "We are in fine shape." She called the boys. "Steve and Jules, you'll have to come in now. We are going inside."

They looked at each other and started crying. "We don't want to go," they said.

"Julie's Rules," Julie said. "No boys in the play yard without a mommy or daddy."

"Mary's rule, too," Mary said. "We can't watch you when we are inside. Come along."

Julie patted her foot. She didn't have to say another word. Steven, then Jules stood up and walked toward their mothers. Mary noticed that Jules was several inches taller than Steve.

"How old is Steve?" Mary asked.

Three and a half," Julie said. "How old is Jules?"

"Four in August," Mary said. "He has always been large for his age."

The boys scrambled into the house ahead of their mothers. "We can be ready to eat in a couple of hours. Come on over when you are ready."

Mary knew it would take a little longer than usual to get going in her kitchen, since she had to remember where she had put everything. She found the potatoes and put them on to boil. She dumped the beans into a pan, added onions, brown sugar, and a couple of strips of bacon, and slid them into the oven. She was glad her mother insisted that she shop for groceries before they left Santee. She had everything she needed for potato salad.

"I think I am ready to try out the shower." she said to Jules. "Would you like to go first?"

Being the first to use the shower appealed to Jules. He said, "Sure," and began removing his clothes. Mary laid out clean clothes for him.

Alex came in shaking his head. "Tail pipe's all fixed," he said. "I don't know how Bill keeps that old Buick on the road. It is held together with seaweed and bailing wire."

"Maybe you can help fix it up," Mary said.

"If I have time. But I really think he wants a new one."

"I'm going to need a car to get to and from work, if I get a job."

"We could start looking around for something used."

"I thought we were getting a new one when you started to work," Mary pouted. She really thought they deserved a better car, but she was afraid to push Alex too far.

"I know, Mary, but let's wait a few more months. We both feel sure that you will find a job, but I want to know for certain. And there are lots of things we need." He was thinking about Bill's comment about their furniture.

"I am sure we can find many things to spend our money on. Let's just be careful and not get bogged down in debt like so many other people do."

"We'll be careful, but that seems to be the way people get the things they want. A dollar down and a dollar a week." They both laughed, but they knew it was the truth.

Jules dressed himself while his mother had her shower. She chose a sleeveless dress and slipped it on. Then she finished the salad while Alex got dressed.

"Do I need to wear a tie?"

"I don't think so." Mary looked in the closet and pulled out a sport shirt. "Here. Wear this."

Alex helped Mary carry the food. He took the hot pan of baked beans and Mary carried the salad.

"I'm glad we don't have to go far with this hot pan," Alex said. Jules carried tea in a pitcher that had a screw-on top.

There was a scream of delight when Steve opened the door. Both boys were shocked to see that they were dressed in identical outfits, little Navy blue pants and white shirts. Their shoes were even the same, Navy blue tennis shoes.

Julie had set the table on their back porch. They sat down and started passing hamburgers, salad, and beans. Julie served the drinks. For dessert, Julie had made a devils food cake, coffee for adults and milk for the boys.

After dinner, Bill asked, "Would you like to play Canasta?"

"I like to play Canasta," Alex said. "But I am really tired. Could we take a rain check?"

"I can understand that. Sure we'll play another day."

"We are going to the beach tomorrow," Julie said. "My cousin invited us to join them. They are picking us up at 7:30 in the morning, so we can have a long day there."

"Then you want to go to bed early, too," Mary said.

"Well, yes. Fairly early."

"You have been very helpful today," Mary said. "You have made a hard job easier. Thank you very much."

At the door, Bill said, "We'll look forward to seeing you often. Call on us if you need help." He shook Alex's hand.

"Nice folks." Alex said when they were inside their own apartment. "I think we will enjoy having them as neighbors."

"I'm glad they have a little boy for Jules to play with." Mary went to the kitchen to straighten up.

"Come along, Tiger," Alex said to Jules. "Time to hit the hay."

While Jules slept, Alex and Mary both wrote letters to their parents. Alex's family had reconciled themselves to the fact that Alex was established in California and would come home only for visits. They constantly asked that he bring his family for a visit. Going to Atmore was always in the back of Alex's mind.

"I wish we had a telephone," Alex said, "The phone company said that a phone would not be available for at least four months. I got us placed on the waiting list."

"Mrs. Dawson said we could use hers in an emergency," Mary said. "And I saw a pay phone outside a service station on the main street near that little shopping center. We can use that one if we need to make a call."

"I got used to having our own phone in Santee. Of course, we wouldn't have had one there if your father hadn't been the mayor.

"I think I like being on our own here, but I know it will be hard for your mother to adjust to our being away and for you to get used to being away from your family."

"Mom's a real trooper. Dad is too. But I'll miss them."

"We'll see them at Thanksgiving and Christmas," Alex said. "I'd sure like to see my folks at Christmas, but we'll have to wait."

"Maybe by next summer we will be able to visit them." She made a mental note to check on the cost of airplane tickets. She would need to know how much she would have to save for a trip.

The following week, Mary received a letter from the office of the Board of Education. She was advised that there were positions available for librarians in several high schools and in three elementary schools. Included in the letter were names and addresses of three schools in her area. She was advised to visit the schools, talk with the principals, and decide if she could accept a position in one of them. Then she was asked to notify the Board of her decision. If none of these schools suited her, other possibilities would be presented. Salary for all school librarians, based on education and experience, was the same. Base salary was $5,000 per year with an 8% increase for each year's experience. After three years of successful service, and appointment for a fourth year, she would be eligible for tenure.

Tenured teachers and librarians would be able to keep their jobs as long as they wanted them and could only be denied a position via a court order proving incompetence or a major infraction of published rules.

What an offer! More money than she had expected. A choice of schools, and a guaranteed position after three years of satisfactory work! Mary was elated. She could hardly wait for Alex to come home to tell him the news.

When Alex drove up, she dashed out to the car. She jumped up and down and laughed as she told him about the job offer. He kissed her and jumped with her. They continued laughing as they walked into the house.

Jules, who was in the play yard with Stevie, heard the laughter and came running. Alex picked him up and swung him in the air. Jules didn't know what was going on, but he knew that his parents were happy about something.

Alex looked at the letter from the Board of Education. He read the offer and noted the names of the schools. He went to the car and got out his map of the city.

"Let's drive by the schools to see what they look like"

He circled each of the schools on the map. They hurried to the car and started out to locate them. The school on Avalon Blvd. was on Alex's route to his office in Downtown Los Angeles and was near the Florence Avenue School where Jules would go to school later. Alex advised Mary to look at the Avalon School last so she would have some basis for comparison.

"Good advice," Mary said. "You think of everything."

"Right now I am thinking of dinner. How would you like to celebrate by having dinner out?"

"That's a wonderful idea if we can afford it."

"I think we can manage," Alex said. Alex still had to watch his pennies closely, but he knew things would be better as soon as school started.

Mary dropped Alex off at his office the next day so she could have the car to drive to the schools. Julie readily agreed to watch Jules.

To her delight, Mary found the Avalon School was cheery. She met the principal, the school secretary, and a few teachers who had stopped by.

Mary visited the library and was given an outline of her duties. She accepted the position.

"You will have to go to the Board of Education to sign a contract for the year," her principal told her. He called and made an appointment for her. "They will be expecting you in an hour," he said.

Mary found the building and was greeted by a secretary who had the papers ready. The whole procedure was completed in half an hour.

"You won't be able to meet the Superintendent today because he is in a meeting," the secretary told her, "but he likes to meet every one who comes in. You will have an opportunity to meet him later." Mary was elated. She had a job!

It was almost time for Alex to go home, so Mary stopped at his building. She went up in an elevator and knocked on his door. A stranger appeared.

"Excuse me. Am I in the wrong place?"

"This is number 406," the stranger said.

"I am sorry. I am on the wrong floor," Mary blushed. "I need number 506."

"One floor up. It is easy to get mixed up in this building," he said trying to put her at ease.

"Thank you." She hurried back to the elevator.

A few seconds later Mary knocked on Alex's door. He saw the apprehensive look on her face and guessed that she had had trouble with her job search. When she saw Alex, however, her face burst into an ear-to-ear grin.

"I will be with you in twenty minutes," Alex smiled. "Sit down and wait for me. I just have a few things to finish up."

On the way home, they passed by the Avalon School. Alex slowed down and Mary pointed out the windows of the library. They smiled. This was a great day. They both had good jobs. They could now begin building their lives together.

When Mary told Julie her news, she was delighted.

"Jules and Steve get along well together," Julie said. "Bill and I talked about it last night. I could keep Jules while you are at work. What do you think?"

Mary didn't have a ready answer. She thought for a moment before she said, "Have you ever kept children before, other people's children, I mean?"

"No, only my own."

"It sounds like a good idea, but I can't give you an answer right now. I will have to talk it over with Alex."

"I won't charge as much as a nursery school," Julie said. "In fact, I won't charge anything. I just want Stevie to have someone to play with."

"You are wonderful! Of course, I will pay you. It will be so much easier for me, not having to take him and pick him up. But I want you to be sure you can handle it now and when the new baby comes."

"If today was an example, it will be a lot easier for me to have a companion for Steve than to play games with him all day. Those boys get along like brothers."

"I really don't know what Alex will say. We had agreed to put him in a nursery school. We'll let you know."

"Good enough."

Later, Alex said. "Let's be careful about rushing into it. Maybe wait a week or two to be sure that they continue to enjoy playing together."

"You are so smart, Alex, I just didn't know what to say. We don't have to decide for sure right now."

Mary spent time the next few days looking at nursery schools. Many women, like Mary, had decided to have a career and a family too, so there were several nurseries to choose from, ranging from small ones with two or three workers to large ones with a larger staff. Also there were differences in philosophy; some were strictly play schools, while others prepared the children for kindergarten.

One nursery that she visited had too many children in an old wooden building. Another one was understaffed and located in a church basement on a busy street. A third one had a long waiting list.

"I can't seem to find the perfect solution," Mary said one night. "I think we better review Julie's offer. She lives close, she wants to do it, and Jules and Steve are still good friends. She keeps the boys in the play yard and locks the gate whenever they are inside. She spends time playing with them. She answers their questions and she sometimes reads to them. There are lots of advantages to this arrangement."

"Tell her tomorrow," Alex said. "We will have to work out a payment plan. What will we do when Julie has her baby?"

"I figured that out," Mary said. "Mom can come and stay with us and look after both boys. She'd love it."

"And just where would she sleep?" Alex grinned.

"We could buy one of those sofas that open out into a bed. She can sleep there."

"You are something else. We will never have to worry about a thing."

Julie was pleased when Mary told her of their decision. Mary agreed to pay twenty-five dollars a week. Julie would give Jules lunch and would try to have him take a nap each day. Jules could run right over to Julie's apartment each morning, relieving Mary of the extra task of dropping him off.

When school opened in September, Mary began work as the head librarian at Avalon High School and Julie assumed the responsibility for Jules while she was working. Alex settled into his position with Metropolitan.

*JED IS DRAFTED*

The war in Korea had been raging for over two years when Jed received his invitation to join. Until now, he had been able to get deferments because he was engaged in farming, which was considered an essential occupation. At last, however, the draft board informed him that it had to meet its quota for the county and he was one of the eight men who had to report for active duty. Jed was the only one left on the farm with his mother. Liz had gotten married and moved up north. Marge had gone to college. Alex was in California. Jed was unhappy about being drafted, but he decided to make the best of it. He requested and was granted 30 extra days to make arrangements for his crops and livestock. A young veteran, Lee Mason, and his wife and two children agreed to take over for him. The Mason family moved into his mother's house and she moved into town. Jed hoped to be back home by the next spring, resume his work as a farmer, and move his mother back home.

The young veteran did not have as much experience on a farm as Jed. He took over just when crops were being laid-by. Instead of spending his time mending fences, checking on insect damage, and getting everything lined up for the harvesting, he went fishing, did some hunting, played with his children, and loafed around the house. His wife didn't save the abundant fruit and vegetable crops by canning and preserving them. It was obvious within three weeks of Jed's departure that the farm was being neglected. Then it began to rain, welcome at first, but continued rains made the grass grow high and prevented even plowing in the garden. Cotton that was open could not be picked when it was wet and much of it fell to the ground and became unusable.

Thelma was upset by what she saw happening on the farm and

did what she could to save as much of the crops as possible. She wrote to one of Dave's brothers who came with a crew to pick cotton as soon as it dried out.

Lee Mason welcomed the help gathering the crop, but was surprised that most of the profit was used to pay for labor. By the end of summer, he had become disgruntled. He packed up his family and moved away, leaving a dirty house and a dirtier yard. Thelma had to hire someone to clean up the place before she could move back home.

That fall, Marge could not return to college because there was not enough money to pay her tuition. She got a job working in a store and made enough to support herself and her mother. She lived at home and she used the family car. She hoped that she would be able to go back to college in the second semester.

Thelma looked for someone to keep the farm going until Jed returned from the service. A neighbor, George Willis, came to the rescue. He agreed to do the planting, cultivating, and harvesting if Thelma would buy the seed and fertilizer. He would use his own tractor and farm implements. In the fall, they would share whatever profit they made, fifty-fifty. This promised to be a good solution.

Jed made an allotment to his mother. Since he had been responsible for his mother and the major part of her support came from him, he was able to have half of his pay sent to her. She was also the sole beneficiary of his life insurance policy in case anything happened to him.

Jed spent basic training at Camp Gordon in southeast Georgia after which he had a seven-day pass before being assigned to active duty. He was satisfied with the arrangements that his mother had made for the farm and tried to assure her that he would be back soon. He was sorry that Marge had to drop out of college, but he was very glad that she would be at home with his mother.

"Things are different in war time," Jed said to Marge. "We cannot win without the sacrifices of people like you and me. As soon as I get back, you can continue your education. I promise. But for now, will you stay here with Mama until I return?"

Marge felt trapped. She loved her mother and was willing to live on the farm, but how long would Jed be gone? How long would the war last? She didn't feel that she could make such a promise.

At last she said, "Jed, I can't promise to stay here until you return, but I will promise to take care of Mama."

"I couldn't ask more," Jed said. He knew that he would be going to Ft. Lewis near Tacoma, Washington, before going overseas. He hoped to be able to see Alex when he was on the West Coast.

"Tacoma is a long way from Los Angeles." He told his mother, "but I will do my best to get down to see him."

Jed's squadron was one of thousands that were awaiting transportation to the war zone. The men spent their time cleaning already immaculate equipment, polishing their belt buckles, and playing Poker and Monopoly. Jed put in for a leave to visit his brother whom he had not seen in nearly six years. "It would take an Act of Congress to get you a leave at this time," he was told.

Lady Luck smiled on him just this once. He was granted leave. He didn't know until later that the base commander was from Opelika, Alabama and Jed's request had come to his attention. "Presswood from Atmore, Alabama is granted a ten day leave to go to Los Angeles to visit his brother," the commander said to Lt. Stamos, who presented the request. Also, arrange for Presswood to travel on a plane. It's about time one of the hometown boys got a break."

Jed packed his gear in his duffel bag and was ready to go in minutes, leaving his buddies exclaiming their disbelief and hitting themselves in the head because they hadn't requested a leave.

"Lucky stiff," resounded throughout the barracks when they saw him hop into a cab and roll away.

Alex was delighted that Jed had been so lucky. He and Mary planed things for him to do in L.A. Since they were both working, they were limited in the activities they could do with him. He arrived on Thursday and would leave the next Friday, with only one weekend when they were free. Julie, who had already had her baby, came to the rescue.

"I'll get my cousin to watch the baby and I'll take Jed and the boys to Hollywood and ride through Beverly Hills. We can get passes to some of the studios and maybe see an actor or two. You four can do what you want on the weekend and I can entertain him next week. Anyone headed for Korea deserves a vacation and some fun before he goes."

"What would we do without you, Julie?" Alex said.

"You are good friends," Julie said. "And besides, I'll have a ball. I need a little R and R myself."

Alex hardly recognized Jed at the airport. "You have grown into a giant of a man! Look at you. Six feet tall, broad shoulders, and Mother's green eyes! You look great." He hugged Jed a long time.

There were tears in Jed's eyes. "Man, it has been a long time. You are a grown-up businessman, married with a son. I can't believe it."

Alex introduced Mary. Jed hugged her. "I've waited a long time for this. You are as lovely as Alex said you were. I am so glad to meet you."

Mary smiled. She introduced Jules.

Jed and Jules became friends at once. Jules had heard much about his uncle Jed who was a soldier now. He asked him questions about the Army and his uniform and the plane he had flown in on. Jed looked forward to becoming acquainted with his sister-in-law and his nephew and becoming reacquainted with his only brother.

Alex and Jed stayed up nearly all night talking and drinking beer. Jed had so much to tell about: the farm and their friends and relations. They laughed about things they had done before Alex joined the Navy. Jed talked about their father's accident and the difficult adjustments the family made when he was gone. Jed told him that Jeannie was living in Monroeville and that she and her husband came to Atmore from time to time to visit Jeannie's family. He mentioned that Jeannie had a son, not much older than Jules. Alex talked about his experiences in the Navy and about how hard it had been for him and Mary to go to college when he got out. They had to force themselves to quit talking and go to bed. Friday was a workday for Alex and Mary, and a busy day had been planned for Jed, so they reluctantly broke up their conversation and went to bed.

When Jed's furlough was over, it seemed to everyone that it had just begun. Both Jed and Alex would remember this visit as one of the highlights of their lives. Julie, Bill, Steve, and the baby went with them to the airport to see Jed off. Everyone had enjoyed the visit. They were sad when he had to go.

Alex shed tears as he hugged his brother. After Jed boarded the plane, Alex turned and walked back toward the car. He loved his brother. He loved his family. He loved Atmore, Alabama. He missed the old life and grieved for the friends and family members he might never see again. He was quiet.

"Daddy, Daddy, can we watch the airplanes for a while?" Jules asked. "Mommy said we could."

Alex was jolted back into the here and now. He loved this family. He was happy in California and satisfied with his job. He had a good life with his wife and son. He was happy. His love for Mary was deep. He was glad to hear that Jeannie was OK, and that she had a son, but he no longer thought about her.

"Sure, we'll watch the planes," he said. "You and Steve stay close to us. There is a lot to see and hear, but you can't go running around all over the place. We can stand by the fence and watch them fly in and take off. You can see the passengers and the baggage being loaded and unloaded."

Watching the planes was a new experience. Jules and Steve exclaimed every time they spotted a plane coming in. They watched them land and taxi down the runway.

"Time to go home," Bill said after a half hour watching planes. They all piled into Bill's new station wagon. "We'll stop for ice cream on the way."

## *THE ACCIDENT*

"I have a doctor's appointment after school today," Mary announced. "Nothing special, just a routine check-up"

"Would you like me to go with you?" Alex asked.

"I'll be OK. It's just routine."

It wasn't really routine, but Mary wanted to be sure before she told Alex. She suspected that she was pregnant but needed the doctor's confirmation. She wanted a little girl so much and had high hopes that she was going to have a baby. She was enthralled with Baby Susan, Julie and Bill's baby. She could think of nothing but having a little girl of her own.

That evening she announced to Alex that they were going to have a baby. Alex shared her joy and they celebrated by having dinner out, followed by a movie.

When Mary told her friends at school the next day, they were thrilled for her. "But you know that women, have to quit work after their fourth month of pregnancy," one of the teachers told her.

"When you begin to show, you will have to go."

Having to quit her job in the middle of the school year was unexpected. There were so many things that she had planned to buy as soon as they had the money. They wanted to find a larger apartment as well as a better car. Mary sighed. They would manage. The apartment would be OK for a while and so would the car.

Mary felt bad that the trip to Atmore would have to be postponed. She knew how much Alex wanted to go to visit his family and friends, but now there would not be enough money for the trip. Maybe Alex could go alone.

"We'll have to save all we can now for the things we'll need for the baby since you have to quit work in just three and a half months. I really don't understand why you will have to quit."

"Well, actually, I just have to take a leave of absence for the remainder of the year. If all goes well, I can go back to work in the fall."

Alex was concerned. Having Mary's salary had made it easier for him.

"Don't worry," he said, trying to put Mary at ease. "We will be just fine. And if necessary, I can do a little moonlighting. I haven't forgotten how to work on cars."

"I hope it doesn't come to that, besides, maybe you'll get a raise."

"I will be up for one in June. Everyone gets a raise at the end of his or her first year. Plenty of people get along with just one salary and I am sure we can too."

"We will continue to live here, I suppose. I would not want to move away from the Walkers anyway. They have become such good friends, just like family."

"And their little girl is so precious. Our little girl will have someone to play with."

"Don't get your heart set on a girl. It may be a little Jules."

"Either way, I'll be happy. And I will love being at home with

Jules for a few months before he starts kindergarten."

That night Alex wrote his mother to tell her that they were expecting a baby. He explained that since Jeannie had to quit work so soon, they would not be able to come home the following summer as they had planned. He knew she would be disappointed, but he couldn't help it. There just wouldn't be enough money for a trip. Alex invited his mother to come for a visit when the baby was born.

Mary's last week of school was hectic. She had to break in a new librarian as well as take care of her regular duties. She asked for her job back in the fall and was assured that she could have it. She left feeling good about the situation, confident that everything would get back to normal as soon as the baby was born.

Mary was delighted to be able to spend time with Jules. They played catch in the play yard. They took walks around the neighborhood and went for rides on the city bus, sometimes meeting Alex for lunch. One afternoon they walked to a park two blocks from their home. Jules played on the slides, the jungle gym, and the swings. He was reluctant to leave when Mary wanted to go, but after promising him five more minutes and reminding him that Steven would want to play with him, Jules consented and ran to Mary. Hand in hand they strolled toward the house.

As they approached the corner near their house, they saw Julie and Stevie coming from the opposite direction. Julie had wheeled the baby in her carriage to the neighborhood store and Steve walked along, holding on to the carriage as he had been taught to do. When Steve saw Jules coming down the street, he began running to meet him. Julie called for him to come back, but he was excited to see his friend. He darted right into the street and was hit by a car. Mary fainted. Julie left the carriage and ran to pick Steven up. The car stopped and together the driver and Julie put him into the car. Mary, still holding Jules' hand, recovered and looked at Jules who was screaming for his mother and for his friend.

Julie called out the car window for Mary to take the baby. Mary yelled that she would take care of her as the man who had hit Steven sped to the hospital.

Mary, holding Jules in one arm, pushed the carriage up the walk and into the house. Still holding Jules she went to the phone and called Alex. She then called Bill, who was in a meeting, and left a message for him. Then she dashed over to Mrs. Dawson's door. Mrs. Dawson answered at once and they ran to her car. Mary held the baby in her lap and kept her arm around Jules as they drove to the emergency room.

Mary found Julie and handed her the baby. Julie hugged her so tight that she woke up and cried. "Mary, I'm so scared," she cried. "My little boy may not make it. It all happened so fast." Julie's whole body was trembling. Tears were streaming down her face. Mary held her in her arms, her eyes blinded with tears. Jules hung on to his mother's legs, not knowing what to do. Alex and Bill arrived at the same moment, each taking his wife in his arms, giving comfort and strength.

"Where is he?" Bill asked.

"He's in the operating room," Julie blubbered.

"Is there anything we can do?" Alex asked. Julie shook her head.

They all found seats together in the waiting room. Jules sat in his mother's lap, his little body still shaking from fright.

"Will Stevie be all right?" Jules asked.

"We hope so," Alex said.

The man whose car had hit Steve sat with his wife, holding hands. Not only did they feel sorrow for the young family, but they were afraid of what could happen to them. Witnesses were there, but did they see that it was an unavoidable accident? Did they see the little boy streak out in front of them before he had time to stop his car? Would he be arrested for speeding? He may have been going a little too fast but thought he was observing the 30 miles an hour speed limit. And was his mind completely on what he was doing? And should he have taken the boy in his car? How could he have left him lying there? His little legs could have been broken when the front wheel hit him. All of these questions kept running through his mind. He and his wife had been asked to stay when he brought little Steve to the hospital. Hospital authorities called the police.

When the police officer arrived, he collected information. A lady who had witnessed the accident had arrived and volunteered to tell what she had seen. The policeman talked to her first. Then he spoke to Julie and to Mary. Then he turned to the driver of the car.

Mr. D'Ambra removed his insurance card from his wallet and handed it to Bill, who wrote down the name of the company and the policy number.

"I wouldn't have done this for anything in the world, if I could have helped it. I am so sorry," he was wiping tears from his eyes.

Friends and neighbors began to arrive. Bill's boss and some co-workers came to see if they could be of any assistance and to lend support. Julie's cousin and her husband joined the group.

The doctor came out and spoke quietly to the Walkers. "Your boy is badly hurt. We cannot be sure of the extent of his injuries yet, but both legs were broken. They have been set. We can't tell about possible internal injuries at this time. He is under sedation and is sleeping quietly. There is nothing you can do but wait."

"May we see him, Doctor?" Bill asked.

"Yes, just parents," he said, glancing around at the others who were anxious for news. "There is nothing you can do, folks," he said sympathetically.

Bill and Julie stood up. Julie was still holding the baby. She walked over to Mary and handed little Susan to her. "Take care of her for me." she asked.

"Of course, I will." Mary hugged Julie. "As if she were my own."

Everybody went home except Bill, Julie, and Julie's cousin and her husband. Mary had to fix dinner for Alex and Jules and take care of the baby. She kept hugging Jules and holding him close to her. She knew that Jules would never forget what had happened that day, but she would do everything she could to comfort him. Alex hugged him and held him on his lap.

For many days, Julie stayed at the hospital, running home just long enough to take a shower, change clothes, and hold her baby a few minutes. Every day she seemed a little more hopeful that her son would recover. The doctor gave her a little encouragement, but warned her that it could be a long time before he was fully recovered or that he could even declare that he was out of danger. Steven had not spoken but he looked at Julie and blinked his eyes.

Bill had dinner with Alex and Mary every day. He took the baby home for a while and rocked her. Then he brought her back to

Mary and went to the hospital. Mary noticed that Bill asked more and more questions about the accident. "I can't understand how you all just let my boy run in front of that car. Why couldn't you have stopped him somehow?"

"Bill, it happened so quickly. We saw them walking and then suddenly Steve took his hand off the carriage and started running. Julie screamed and ran after him. Jules and I screamed for him to stop. And then it happened."

"I would have had more control over him than Julie did. She didn't teach him to mind. She let him get by with too much."

"Bill, Julie is a wonderful mother. She blames herself, but she wasn't to blame. Nobody was. It was an accident."

"And now, if he lives, my boy will be a cripple the rest of his life. I can't face it. I love him too much."

"Please, Bill, Julie needs you now, more than ever before. Try to understand."

"I can't. I can't." He sobbed. "I can't face her anymore."

"You stay here with Alex and the children and I will go to the hospital." Mary grabbed her purse and dashed out the door.

She drove around a few minutes looking for a parking place. When she found one, she hurried up to Steve's room. Julie was sitting beside him reading a story. She held his tiny hand as she read. She quietly closed the book and got up to greet Mary. "Where is Bill?" she asked.

"He was tired tonight. He asked me to come to see you."

Julie blinked back tears. "He blames me, doesn't he? He hardly spoke last night. He just looked at Steve and shook his head."

"Julie, Bill's world has suddenly been turned around. Not only is Steve here in the hospital, but you are too. You aren't at home taking care of everything. He is looking for someone to blame for the whole change in his life. And there is no one to blame but you."

"It wasn't my fault, Mary. Steven was so excited when he saw you and Jules that he forgot everything I had ever taught him about safety. It just happened."

"I know, Julie, but Bill needs some help getting through this. Talk to your doctor. Explain to him about Bill's feelings. There are people who can help."

That night when Dr. Carter came, he suggested that Bill talk with the chaplain. "I will make an appointment for him. He may need some psychiatric help before this is over. It is hard to get through these things alone, and he is virtually alone with you down here all of the time. I will talk with him myself the next time he is here."

It took only one visit with the doctor and one with the chaplain to help Bill through his feeling of resentment toward Julie. They had a good marriage, strong love, and the chaplain convinced him that it was important that he work to preserve what he had.

"Your wife is broken up over this. She needs you now more than ever. Don't turn your back on her. You have a right to feel helpless right now, but we must have faith that your son will recover. If you continue to feel bitter come and talk with me again," the chaplain said.

Steve began to recover. He began to talk and to listen when his mother spoke to him.

"I think Steven is going to be all right. I was concerned about his head injury, but he seems to be healing. There doesn't seem to be any permanent damage to his brain. Steve is a little fighter, and he will be as good as new in a few months," said Dr. Carter.

"What about his legs?" Bill asked.

"After physical therapy, his legs will straighten out. He'll have a few scars, but he will recover fully. You won't be able to tell that this ever happened. He'll be able to walk and run just like every other boy his age.

Bill squeezed his wife's hand. "I am sorry I tried to blame you for this. I was just so scared that he would be ruined for life."

*RETURN TO SANTEE*

There was a party for Steve when he came home from the hospital. Julie invited people who had shown concern for the family while Steve was in the hospital. Each family brought a gift for Steve who sat in his wheelchair. He could not walk yet, but the doctor had assured Julie and Bill that it was only a matter of time.

Mary made an appointment with her gynecologist. She had back pains and headaches. She had had some dizzy spells and she felt weak. She told the doctor about the accident and how she had picked Jules up and carried him to the house. She mentioned the stress she had been under.

The doctor's examination was thorough. He had a grave expression on his face. He questioned her extensively about how she felt. He asked about different symptoms.

The doctor stepped out of the examination room, telling Mary to dress and meet him in his office. He also asked that Alex come in.

"Usually these mishaps occur in early stages of pregnancy—"

"What do you mean, these mishaps?" Mary asked.

"Mary, I examined you carefully. I cannot hear a heartbeat for the fetus. I am afraid that your baby is no longer alive."

"What?" Mary exclaimed. "Oh no, doctor, that can't be. I want a little girl. I felt her moving. I know she is all right."

"This is hard. The movements that you felt were caused from gas. The fetus can be moving, but you should be feeling kicking and stretching. And there is no heartbeat."

"I don't believe it, I don't believe it. I want a little girl. I can't accept this. I must have a baby girl."

Alex tried to comfort his hysterical wife. "Mary, we can try again. You will have your little girl as soon as this is over."

"I want a little girl now," she wailed. "A little girl just like Susan."

"I know you do. I want a little girl too, but we can't have it now. We will have to wait for a little while."

The doctor took both of her hands in his. He looked into her eyes.

"Mary, I am so sorry, I didn't see this coming. Your last check-up was perfect. But this little baby just couldn't make it. Now we have to attend to your health."

"What do you mean, Doctor?" She asked.

"Removing the fetus is the inevitable next step. You will need to be hospitalized overnight, tonight. Usually one or two days of hospitalization are all that is required. The sooner we do it, the better, because we want as little infection as possible."

With teary eyes, Mary asked, "Doctor are you sure? Are you really sure?"

"Yes."

"Can we go to the hospital now?" Alex asked.

"I will make arrangements and meet you over there in three hours." The doctor looked at his watch. "Go ahead and check in. They will have her ready when I get there."

Alex called Julie and asked her to take care of Jules until he could get home.

Mary was back home in two days. She sat and cried. Jules let her hold him for short periods of time, but she squeezed him so tight that he wiggled out of her lap and went to play.

Alex's work was becoming more demanding and he spent longer hours at his office. He bought a television to help to entertain Jules and get Mary's mind off of the baby.

Mary showed little interest in the set at first. She watched as it was being installed, but still sat and flipped through the pages of a magazine that lay on the table. She complained that the apartment was too small for it and that she would have no time to watch. She didn't want to have to darken the windows in order to see the screen. And she knew it cost too much.

Alex was a little disappointed because of Mary's lack of enthusiasm, but was justly rewarded by Jules' excitement. Jules had seen television at the Sears Roebuck Store. He followed the installer around and asked questions as he patiently waited for images to appear on the screen.

Jules was transfixed as dim images materialized before his eyes: a movie right in their own living room. He sat cross-legged right in front of the set and had to be coaxed away from the screen. "This is great!" he exclaimed.

"I have to go get Steve," Jules cried, when the picture had been adjusted. "He will want to watch this."

In a few minutes, the whole Walker family had assembled in the tiny room to see the picture and to exclaim about the wonders of the great new invention. Julie placed Susan in Mary's outstretched arms as she joined Jules and Alex on the floor. Steve sat in his wheel chair and Bill stood beside him.

Mary hugged and patted the baby, but her eyes wandered toward the screen where OUR MISS BROOKS was explaining why she was late for work while the sides of her book bag moved strangely, revealing the presence of a kitten she had rescued on her way to school. Everyone laughed as she kept nudging the satchel out of the line of vision of the principal. As she walked down the hall to her classroom, the kitten escaped and dashed into the principal's office. By the end of the program, Mary was laughing along with the others. After a few commercials, Jack Webb announced that he was Joe Friday and that he was in hot pursuit of a dangerous criminal. He and his partner always caught their man on DRAGNET.

By this time, Mary was more relaxed and was enjoying the show as much as anyone else. She slipped out of her chair and gently carried the sleeping baby to her bed, laid her down, and tiptoed to the kitchen.

In a cabinet, Mary found a jar of popcorn. She poured oil into the pan, added a handful of popcorn, and shook the pan vigorously until the final pop. She served it to her guests, each one reaching for handfuls of the tasty morsels.

After that, Steve spent a lot of time watching TV with Jules, sitting in his wheelchair at first, but eventually slipping down to the floor beside Jules. Later, he got braces and began walking with crutches. Each day his mother rubbed and manipulated his legs, pulling them gently to stretch them and help them grow. Julie could do this while they watched television. Mary held and rocked little Susan. Mary and Alex felt comfortable with their friends who had become family to them.

"I know you are getting attached to little Susan," Alex said one evening. "She has helped you to get over our loss, but please do not transfer all of your love to her. I don't mean that I am jealous or that I think you are neglecting Jules in any way. I just want you to realize that we or they might decide to move away and it would be hard on you and the baby if that should happen. Do you understand what I mean?"

"Yes, I understand. I do love her like my own. When school starts, I will be so busy that I won't have time for her."

"I don't mean to tell you what to do, Sweetheart, but perhaps you could find something that interests you, like bowling or horseback riding, or something to help you break the tie."

"Maybe I will go to the library and find a couple of books to read. Jules and I could go to the park and hang out together if I can pull him away from the TV set."

"I guess I created a monster with that, didn't I?"

"Not exactly. I think it was a wonderful idea. We all enjoy watching it. I guess I am hooked on some programs myself. It's a great way to kill time. I find myself working extra hard in the mornings so I will have time to watch in the afternoon."

"I am glad you like it."

One day Bill came home with big news. When he had everybody's attention, he said, "I have gotten a promotion!" Before they could offer congratulations, he said, "Now for some bad news. I am going to be a branch manager for Western Electric, in Phoenix, Arizona."

Julie and Mary caught their breath and looked at each other. "Phoenix!" they said together. "Oh Bill!"

"I guess we always knew it would come," Bill said, "but we didn't know when. We were hoping it wouldn't be so soon."

"Couldn't they find a place for you here?" Julie said, "Phoenix is so far away."

"That is exactly what I said when my boss told me. He said I could take it or leave it. The company needs me in Phoenix."

"Well congratulations," Alex said at last, "that's great for you. Of course, it stinks for us."

"Stinks is right," Julie said. "When do we have to go?"

Everyone held their breath. "The first of July. Three weeks."

The three weeks flew by. At last the day of parting arrived. They hugged each other and cried and promised to keep in touch. Then they were gone.

That night Alex lay on the bed reading the newspaper. Mary stood at her dresser, removing her make-up. Jules slept in his bed.

"How would you like to move back to San Diego?" Alex asked.

Mary hesitated a moment, then leaned down to Alex and kissed him. "I would love to go back to San Diego. But why? Are you O.K. at work?"

"Oh, everything is fine at work. I have just been thinking about going into business for myself. Maybe open my own agency. And I thought you might like to move back closer to your family."

"Yes, I would love it."

"I didn't like moving, not even just a hundred miles away from all of your family and friends. I want Jules to grow up around his grandparents and his uncles and aunt."

"Do you suppose we could possibly to do it before school starts in September? Then you can start the new school year down there and Jules can too."

"That depends upon whether I can get a job or not."

"From what I read, teachers aren't having any trouble finding jobs, and that goes for librarians, too.

"We will have to wait a little longer to buy some of the things we want," Alex said. "But I should be going strong in a short time. The fellows at work said it isn't difficult to get started if you are willing to start small and work hard."

"Then you really think we'll do it?" She felt butterflies in her stomach.

"We'll start working on it tomorrow."

"I'll call my folks," Mary almost shouted as she ran to the phone in the kitchen.

Mary's mother answered the phone. When she heard Mary's news, she said, "This is perfect. Nothing could make me happier. Nothing. I didn't want to mention it before, but your father has not been well lately. He has to have an operation for gallstones. It will be good to have you near for moral support."

"Why don't we go down this weekend and see if we can find jobs?" Alex said.

"I'll pack tomorrow," Mary said. "This is exciting."

Mary had everything packed and was standing at the door when Alex got home. She had sandwiches made so they wouldn't have to take the time to stop for dinner. They could eat on the way. They locked the door and left. Jules sat between them in the front seat.

"I am so excited," Mary said. "I have such a good feeling about this."

It turned out to be a very profitable weekend. Mary was offered and accepted a job in the same school she had worked in before. Alex stumbled into an unbelievable employment situation. Following a lead given by a friend in Santee, he met an aging gentleman, Henry Yardley, who wanted to retire, but had no one to take over his faltering insurance agency in San Carlos, a few miles from Santee. Mr. Yardley had expected his son to take over the business he had worked years to build, but he had not returned from Germany after the war. After years of handling the business alone, Mr. Yardley had almost decided to give up his business. He was very happy when Alex approached him. They worked out a deal that was perfect for both of them. He offered Alex his entire business for no money down. Alex would pay Mr. Yardley ten percent of the net profit as long as he lived. They signed a contract and Alex agreed to begin work the first of the following month.

All Mary and Alex had to do now was to resign from their jobs in Los Angeles, pack up their belongings and move back to Santee. They would stay with Mary's mother again until they found a place of their own.

"I noticed several small houses for sale as I was driving around looking for Mr. Yardley," Alex said. "Wouldn't it be wonderful to have our own house and a yard with trees and flowers? Big enough for Jules to have his own room? We have lived in apartments so long."

"That would be wonderful."

The telephone was ringing when Mary and Alex reached their home in Los Angeles. Alex was carrying Jules, who had fallen asleep in the car. "You answer it," Alex said. "I'll put Jules to bed."

Alex's mother was on the phone. "I have been trying to reach you all day," she said. She broke down crying.

"Come quickly, Alex," Mary called in a loud whisper. "Something is wrong."

"Who is it?"

"Your mother." Mary handed him the phone.

"What is it, Mama?"

"Oh, Alex. It's Jed. He was killed in Korea."

"No! No!" Alex cried. "No!"

"What is it?" Mary said.

"It's Jed. He was killed."

"I can't tell you any more," Alex' mom sputtered. "I'll call later." She hung up.

Alex sat down. His sobs could be heard throughout the apartment. Mary cried too. "How awful," she said, "I can't believe it."

Time stood still. Alex tried to imagine what had happened. At last he began to think about what the next step should be. When he was able to speak again, he said, "I'll call Mama back and try to get some details. I really can't believe this has happened."

"The telegram was delivered this morning. It just said they were sorry to inform us that Jed had been killed in action and that more information would follow," his mother said.

"Are they returning his body?" Alex asked. "Are you going to have a funeral? Do you want me to come home now?"

"Yes, they will return his body and we will have a funeral when it arrives. Don't come home until we get more information. It could be weeks before his body gets here."

"Are you all right, Mama?"

"Well, yes I am O.K., everybody has come. The neighbors, friends, relatives, and Liz and Marge are here. We are all in a state of shock. Liz came last week for a visit. There really isn't anything we can do except be sad together."

"I'll come if you need me." Alex really wanted to be with his family.

"Come if you want to, but there is nothing you can to do, Alex. The preacher has been here and prayed with us. Jed's girlfriend is in hysterics and she has been in and out all day."

"I will talk it over with Mary," Alex said, "And we'll let you know. I can't believe that my only brother is gone."

"Alex, if there was anything you could do, I would insist on your coming right away. But you are so far away. And I do want you to come when we have the funeral. That is why I think you should wait. There are a lot of things you will need to help me with later on. I'll need help deciding what to do with the farm, but I don't want to deal with that now."

"I understand, Mama. I am glad that the others are with you. I am sorry I live so far away. I miss all of you so much."

Mary held him. Her mind went back to the time she had heard that her fiancé had been killed. She remembered the grief of everyone who had loved him. She couldn't imagine what her life would have been like if Robin had not been killed. She had loved Robin, but her love for Alex was so deep. Life must go on.

Alex did not go to work the next day. He wanted to be available for his mother in case there was word about his brother's body. He also wanted to be with his wife and son to comfort them and to be comforted by them.

The following day Alex went to work and talked with his supervisor, John Jacobson, about his plans to move to San Diego.

"Let us know if you change your mind," Mr. Jacobson said. "You can keep your job if you should want to." Alex thanked him, but said he was pretty sure he would not.

Mary went to the Superintendent's office to present her resignation. She was sent to the office of the director of personnel, Mrs. Watson. "This certainly comes as a surprise," Mrs. Watson said. "We have held your job for you while you were on maternity leave. How is the baby?"

"We lost the baby," Mary said.

"I didn't know that; I am sorry. We had expected you to return. We don't have to let you out of your contract since you did not notify us before May first that you wouldn't be back. That means we are not obligated to give you a recommendation."

"I didn't know until last weekend that I would not be coming back. My husband and I are returning to San Diego. We want to raise our son near his relatives to give him a little more stability."

"I can understand that, but I wish you had given us a little more time to find a replacement. Qualified librarians are not easy to find."

"I am so sorry to put you in a difficult position, but I think it will be best for my husband and me."

"Thank you for coming in," Mrs. Watson said. "And best of luck to you." Mary thought that she had been disrespectful, but it didn't really matter because she already had a job. She didn't say that. She didn't want to say anything else to the lady.

That night Mary told Alex about the experience. "You said all of the right things," he said. "Anything else might have sounded sarcastic."

"And now we have to get packed up to move again. I doubt if we can get all of our stuff in a U-Haul this time. We'll have to rent a truck or maybe get a moving van," Mary said.

"Since you are not working, maybe you can take care of making the moving arrangements."

"I will get things started, but I'll probably need your help. I haven't had any experience with this sort of thing."

"You handle everything like a pro, my dear. But, of course I'll help."

Alex called his mother that night to ask if she had heard anything more about Jed's body. She said that there had been no news. She said that she had called the Red Cross, but they had no information. They did promise to try to find out what happened.

Alex told her that he and Mary were moving closer to Mary's parents. She was pleased. "I wasn't happy about you being in such a big city all alone," she said.

When he hung up, Alex said, "I would like to be with my family at this time. I miss them so much."

"Alex, why don't you fly home for a few days? We will be all right here. You need to be with them."

"I might consider it if the Walkers were still here, but I wouldn't leave you alone. Maybe when we move back to Santee I can go. If I went now, I wouldn't be able to go back when his body arrives. I want to go to the funeral. Maybe you and Jules will be able to go too." Alex was quiet. Mary realized that he was grieving, not only for his brother, but for his whole family.

When Mary told Jules that they were moving back to Grandma and Grandpa's house, he was thrilled. "I love my grandma and grandpa so much," he said. "When?"

"Let's get the calendar," Mary said. "I will show you just how many more days it will be. I think you can be a lot of help getting everything packed into boxes, don't you?"

"Sure. Where are the boxes?"

"I don't have them yet. Maybe we can get some at the grocery store tomorrow."

Although there were two more weeks before they would move, Mary began to pack. She hated to have her house in disarray, but it would help to have as much as she could ready. She stacked the boxes neatly in corners.

The move went smoothly. They rented a truck and hired a man

to help pack it and to drive it back when they had unloaded.

"We'll just put your things in the garage," Mary's mother said, "until you find a place of your own."

"I hope that will be soon. I don't like being in limbo."

"You are welcome to stay as long as you wish."

"Thank you, Mother. We'll get things worked out as soon as possible. We will be very busy. I hope you will be able to help us with Jules when we get into a jam."

"Taking care of my grandson is a pleasure. Any time."

"Mary went with Alex to his office to look things over. Mr. Yardley promised to meet them there. I really don't know where to start with my work," Alex said. "This is a new experience."

Mr. Yardley arrived. He looked much younger than Alex had remembered him. "You lifted a load off my shoulders, young man," he said. "I will be glad to help you get started."

"Thank you. I will need all of the help I can get."

"My secretary is coming to help you, too. For years I have depended on Mrs. Junket to keep things in order. My advice would be for you to hire her for as many days as she will work. She knows how to handle the business."

"I'm not sure I can afford a secretary. I didn't even think about that. I thought I could to do it alone."

"You probably can. But having a secretary frees you up to do much more than send out notices and service policies. Of course, injured clients want to see you at the scene of whatever catastrophe occurs. That is where you pick up a lot of new business. And you want as much visibility as possible. I belonged to civic organizations and attended meetings when I was younger, but I dropped out of things like that when my wife was sick. I never felt like becoming active again when she passed away.

"Anyway," he went on, "there are opportunities in this area that just haven't been tapped. Take real estate, for example. I think that a young man like you could get something started here in real estate. Main roads are being built out of San Diego to outlying areas like San Carlos. It's only a short ride into the city and people today don't mind riding a few miles out to a quiet neighborhood. You could change some of these cow pastures and small farms around here into beautiful living areas and people would flock to them."

Alex listened, but did not quite grasp the whole concept. He had planned to take over a failing insurance agency, try to revitalize it, and make a living. He didn't think he was ready to get involved in a real estate venture. "You have a great idea," Alex said, "but I don't have the capital to begin such a venture."

"It would take capital, but if you could get the right people interested, you could make a lot of money. There's a lot of building going on all over the country. People need places to live and the government guarantees low interest rates and low down payments. You might even be interested in buying a home for your family."

Mrs. Junket drove up in her 1951 coupe. She jumped out of her car and hurried in. "Hope you haven't been waiting long," she said as she rushed into the room. Mr. Yardley made the introductions then he said he had to run down to the hardware store and pick up some gardening supplies. "I will be stopping in from time to time to help you get things organized. Call me if you need anything. Meanwhile, you can depend on Mrs. Junket to get you headed in the right direction."

"He looks good," Mrs. Junket said. "All he needed was a few days rest. He worked so hard building this business for his son."

"What happened to his son?" Mary asked.

"Nobody knows for sure. The story goes that he fell in love with a German girl and stayed over there after the war. He didn't even come home for his mother's funeral. Mr. Yardley just lost interest in the business after that. He hasn't tried to expand or anything. I think he was just depressed. Selling the business to you is the best thing that could have happened to him and the business."

"Mr. Yardley said you would stay on for a couple of weeks to help me get things rolling. I certainly appreciate that."

"No problem. I will stay as long as you need me."

Mrs. Junket stayed after the two-week adjustment period. She knew the business, the system, and the customers.

"I really don't understand why Mr. Yardley didn't just turn the business over to Mrs. Junket," Alex said to Mary later. "She really keeps it going."

"She probably didn't want the responsibility. And Mr. Yardley probably wanted a young man to take his son's place."

"I guess so. But the business is not that great. I am going to have to get out and hustle to make it a success."

"I know you can do it."

"I have been thinking about what Mr. Yardley said about real estate. Would you mind my taking a real estate course? It would take me away from home at night for a while."

"Go ahead. Good idea. Mrs. Junket can keep things going in your office. This seems to be a good time for you to do something for yourself."

"I knew you would say that." Alex smiled. "As a matter of fact, I have already enrolled at San Diego State University for a six-week course being offered this fall. I only have to go one night a week and take a test at the end to get my licenses. I think it will be good to combine insurance and real estate. Mrs. Junket can take care of the insurance and I can take care of the real estate. What to do you think?" "I think it sounds like a winner, but you will have to work very hard."

"The problem is that this is going to limit my time with you and Jules. I hoped to spend more time with you, but I'm getting more involved in my work."

"Oh, I forgot," Mary said, "a letter came today from your mother. "I'm sorry I didn't mention it earlier."

"That's OK. Where is it?"

Mary handed the letter to Alex and went to check on Jules. He was still playing even though it was getting dark outside. She called Jules in for dinner and told him to wash his hands and put on a clean shirt.

"Mama said she had received a check from the government for $10,000 for Jed's insurance. She said she didn't know what to do with it."

"Did she say when they'd send Jed's body?" Mary asked.

"Nothing about the body," Alex said. "I'll call Mama tomorrow. It's too late tonight."

When Alex called the next day, his mom was anxious to talk about her plans. It had been several days since she had written the letter, so she had made some decisions on her own, though she welcomed Alex's advice. Thelma had managed the farm with the help of George Wills. Together they had produced a good crop and had made some money for both families. Thelma put away enough to buy the supplies they would need to get started next spring and had a little to spend.

"I saved all of Jed's money that he sent home. I put it away for him. I wanted him to have money to get started again when he came home. Since he isn't coming back, Marge and I have decided to use it to go to school. I am going back to Montevalo and take enough courses to renew my teaching certificate. I'm going to teach again. And Marge is going to the University. She hasn't decided for sure what she wants to study, but she knows she doesn't want to be a teacher."

"You amaze me, Mama. You really amaze me. Are you sure you want to start teaching again? It has been a long time."

"Alex, I am only 46 years old. I can teach for nearly twenty years before I have to retire. I want to be sure I can take care of myself when I am old."

"You have insurance money."

"Yes, I do have that but I invested it in government bonds. And when I am old, I will be independent."

"I will take care of you when you are old. You don't have to worry about that. You can come and live with us."

"I will always have a place to live, Alex. In his Will, Daddy left the farm to me for as long as I live. Then it goes to you, now three children."

"Daddy had a Will? I didn't know that."

"You didn't get a copy?"

"No. Nobody sent me one. Remember, I was in the South Pacific when that happened."

"I will send it tomorrow."

Before hanging up Thelma mentioned that she had had no word from the Red Cross, but she would let him know as soon as she heard anything.

Mary had gone ahead and given Jules his dinner. She had put him in the bathtub and dressed him for bed.

"I'll read to you as soon as I have my dinner," Alex said when

Jules asked for a story. "Why don't you watch TV for a few minutes?"

Mary cleaned up the dishes while Alex read to Jules. They both put Jules to bed then sat down to read the paper and relax.

"Jules said he would soon be able to read his own stories," Alex said. "He is learning so fast."

"I guess he is beginning to learn a few words in school," Mary said.

Alex and Mary stayed with her parents for a year. There was plenty of room in the big house and they all supported each other. Alex fixed broken hinges, painted walls and fences, and did whatever had to be done. Mary's mother was always available to watch Jules when his parents were busy. The year went fast.

## *ALEX EXPANDS HIS BUSINESS*

Alex found a construction company that was anxious to begin a development in the San Carlos area. He negotiated with landowners to sell their land for development. When the company began building homes, he acted as the real estate agent and sold the homes. When one area was developed, he moved on to another location. His real estate business proved to be profitable and his insurance company was making money for him and for Mr. Yardley.

"I made a good deal when I sold you my business," Mr. Yardley laughed. "You are making a killing and I am making enough to live on. I knew a young man could make a go of this business, but you have exceeded my wildest dream." He hastened to say that he wasn't complaining, he was just dumbfounded.

"It just happened to be the right time for all of this to happen. The real estate business and the insurance just fell into place and began to support each other."

"I am glad it happened this way. I doubt that my son would ever have turned this business around the way you did."

Their conversation ended when the telephone rang. Alex had to leave the office to help a customer locate a lot he had bought the week before.

Mr. Yardley walked out with him. "Have you picked out a lot

for yourself?" He asked.

"We decided on a place a few blocks over. We bought a lot over near the reservoir."

"Sounds good," Mr. Yardley said. "How is the Allied Gardens project coming along?"

"Moving right along." Alex said as he climbed into his car. *I owe that man a lot. I needed his business and his advice to get started. I am happy to hand him a check every month for the 10% he asked for.*

Alex took care of his customer, and then rode over to his own building site. He or Mary drove by almost every day to see the amount of progress had been made on their house. They expected to move into their new home before school started again. Then he went home for the day.

Alex and Mary took a few days off for a camping trip in the mountains. They had a favorite spot halfway up Cowles Mountain near a stream. They had camped there several times and always came home relaxed and rejuvenated. Mary shopped for groceries while Jules helped his father collect the gear and pack.

It was a warm, cloudless day. Alex wore light clothing, but he picked up a sweater just in case it got cool. He told Jules to get a sweater too. Jules came out of the house wearing his raincoat.

"I don't think you will need that," Alex laughed.

"I'll bring it just in case," Jules said.

Alex shook his head. "We'll come home if it starts raining."

By the time Mary returned with food for the trip, the pile of gear was beside the driveway. She backed the station wagon in and they loaded everything into it. There was barely enough space left for Jules to sit in the back seat.

"Oh, I forgot my fishing pole." Jules ran to fetch it. Mary went in to say "goodbye" to her parents. "Better take a jacket," her mother said. "It can get real cold on the mountain at night. And take the radio, Honey. You don't want to be completely cut off from civilization."

"I think that is the point of camping," Mary said, but she took the radio her mother handed her.

At last they were off. "We'll be there in time to build a fire and roast wieners for supper," Mary said. "And I got something special for dessert."

"Marshmallows, I'll bet," Jules said. "Yum, yum, I love toasted marshmallows."

"I really needed this trip," Alex said as they drove along. "I am tired. I have had a dull headache for three days."

"I am sure a rest is just what the doctor ordered," Mary said. "We'll just sit and relax the whole weekend."

They arrived at the campsite, set up the tent, gathered firewood, and started the fire before the sun disappeared behind the mountain. It was quiet. Mary put a blanket down near the fire so they could sit and watch the flames. She took out frankfurters and buns, placed one on a straightened clothes hanger, and handed it to Jules. Next she fixed one for Alex and one for herself. They sat and turned their wieners around over the fire until they were a light brown. Then they put them into a bun and added sauerkraut and mustard.

"Hot dogs taste so good when they are cooked outside," Alex said. "I think I'll need three or four of these."

"Have as many as you like." Mary poured Kool-Aid into paper cups and handed them to Alex and Jules. "The best part to me is that there are no dishes to wash."

After eating, they stretched out on the blanket. Alex coughed now and then. "I must have something caught in my throat," he said. The three of them fell asleep on the blanket, outside the tent.

It must have been midnight when they were awakened by heavy raindrops. A strong wind was blowing and they could hear branches falling all around. The darkness was penetrating. The moon that had been shining brightly when they went to sleep had disappeared behind dark clouds. Flashes of lightening lit up the sky. The roar of thunder was deafening. They jumped up, grabbed the blanket, and ran to the tent. Alex fumbled around and found the lantern. Mary closed the flaps on the windows and door, but they could feel the tent being blown by the wind. Pelting rain sounded like buckshot as it hit the tent. Inside the tent was dry, but they were scared. Jules clung to his father.

"I'm wet." Alex took off his shirt and put on a dry one. He also put on his sweater.

"I'm wet, too," Mary changed her shirt. "Jules, you'd better change too.

"I certainly didn't expect rain tonight." Alex coughed a few times.

"Are your pants wet?" Mary asked Alex.

"Just a little."

"I think you should change them."

"I'll be alright," he said, but Mary insisted. She had noticed that Alex's cough was getting worse.

They stayed awake listening to the howling wind and rain until the storm subsided. Then they fell asleep again.

When they woke up the next morning, all was quiet. Alex said he had pain in his chest. He was coughing more and began spitting out yellow mucus. "I'm getting a bad cold," he said when Mary asked about his symptoms. "I'll be all right."

Alex didn't feel better after breakfast and coffee. "I don't feel like doing anything. I'll stay here and rest. You two go ahead and enjoy the woods. Let Jules go fishing."

The creek had risen several inches during the rainstorm and the water was flowing swiftly.

"I doubt if any fish will be biting this morning," Mary said. "Jules and I will take a walk along the stream. We will be back soon."

Alex lay inside the tent. His head hurt, his chest hurt, and he felt like he had a fever. He tried to go to sleep again, but his coughing kept him awake. He took some aspirin, but he felt too weak to get up and walk around.

When Mary and Jules returned, Alex asked if they could go home. "I need some medicine."

Mary and Jules packed up at once. Alex tried to help, but he was so weak he could hardly stand up.

Mary drove home. Alex sat with his eyes closed. When they reached home, Alex went directly to bed and Mary stuck a thermometer into his mouth.

"His temperature is 103 degrees," Mary said to her mother. "I'm going to call the doctor."

Mary described Alex's symptoms to the doctor. "Bring him to

the emergency room and I will meet you there," Dr. Kempton said.

Mary and her father helped Alex to the car.

"Do you want me to go with you?" her father asked.

"No, that won't be necessary," Mary said. "Would you and Mom look after Jules?"

"Of course," they both said.

They reached the hospital within thirty minutes and were met at the door by an orderly pushing a wheel chair. Alex managed to climb from the car to the chair on his own.

After an examination, Dr. Kempton told them that Alex had pneumonia. Alex was sent to a room to begin treatment. Mary followed and helped him undress and put on a hospital gown. She stayed by his side until a nurse told her she would have to leave. She kissed the sleeping Alex and went home.

"Mary, Thelma called," her mother said as soon as she walked in the door. "She asked that one of you return her call at once."

Mary picked up the phone and asked for long distance. When she was finally connected, she told Alex's mother that Alex was in the hospital with pneumonia.

"I called to tell you that Jed's body will arrive tomorrow. We will have the funeral on Monday."

"I can't believe it has taken fourteen months for the government to get his body home," Mary said.

"They had buried him over there along with hundreds of others. They have just now been able to return him. It has been hard on all of us."

"Mrs. Presswood, Alex will not be able to attend the funeral. He is very sick. He'll be heartbroken. He wanted so much to be with the family at this time."

"The officers who accompanied Jed's body are staying for the funeral. They have arranged everything, so we have to go ahead with it. Everybody has been called to come to the service on Monday. We won't be able to delay it."

"I understand," was all Mary could say.

"Please keep me posted on Alex's condition. Let me know how he is getting along."

Mary promised to call the next evening. She offered her

condolences.

"I met him only once, but I loved him. And Alex loved him." She said that she wanted to meet the rest of the family and re-extended invitations to Thelma to visit. Then she called the florist and ordered an expensive wreath for Jed.

Alex was in the hospital a week. The doctor said that he had a serious case of pneumonia, perhaps because he was tired and overworked. He advised Alex to stay at home, in bed, for at least a week and be sure he had completely recuperated before he returned to work. He said a relapse would be worse than his original siege.

Alex did not want to spend more time away from work. He asked Mrs. Junket to come by every day and keep him informed of the day's activities. Even though he now had four secretaries to help him in his office, Alex depended on Mrs. Junket to manage it all. She was the one who kept his books. She collected the money, deposited it, and paid the company bills.

Alex slept late in the mornings and sat quietly on the porch during the long days. He read the newspapers and caught up on magazine articles. Mary's father sat with him and they discussed the progress that was being made in the valley. They discussed the problems that farmers and cattle raisers were having. "It was no wonder that farmers are selling their land to developers. They get large sums of money for land that they inherited or had bought for practically nothing." Farmers got so little for beef and the cost of feed was high, many of them were willing to sell off large portions of their land and simply retire from farm work altogether.

"Prices are going up on everything," Mr. Driscoll said. "I was looking at cars the other day. Did you know that they are asking over ten thousand dollars for a car these days, and they are getting it? I have never paid over $5000 or $6000 for a new car, and now they are getting that for a used car."

"Times are changing," Alex said.

Mr. Driscoll went on, "And groceries. We've never spent more than $12 or $15 a week for groceries before. But now, a week's supply cost between $25 and $30."

"We'd better start giving you more for groceries," Alex said. "I didn't realize they were so high."

"Oh, I didn't mean that you weren't paying enough. Mary and her mother work that all out. I am just commenting about how expensive things are getting. I paid 49 cents for a loaf of bread yesterday."

"Actually, it is all pretty relative," Alex said. "Mary is making a lot more now than she did her first year as a librarian. We make more; we pay out more. That's the way it works."

"I guess you are right. I guess I am getting too old for all of these changes."

"You aren't even fifty yet. Don't talk about being old."

Mary's father mentioned that he had seen in the paper that a large tract of land was for sale. "It was over in the Murray Reservoir region. I expect it would be a good investment. It may be a few years before anything comes of it, but most investments take a little time to pay off."

"I don't know how much land I could buy right now," Alex said. "We have a little saved up, but we are building our house."

"Banks loan money for the purchase of land. You have to have good credit and some money to put down, but is seems to me you have both. And both of you have good jobs. You might be able to swing a deal."

"I don't know. I have never liked to go too far into debt."

"It certainly pays to be careful. You have to decide just how great a risk you are willing to take."

"I'll look into it when I am on my feet. Dr. Kempton told me not to go out for a couple more days. I am feeling pretty good though. I could probably go out tomorrow or the next day. Where is the paper?"

Mr. Driscoll went inside, got the paper, and handed it to Alex. "I'm going to ride out to the ranch and check on things," he said, leaving Alex to read the paper.

Alex found the advertisement and read it. Jules came by and asked him how he felt.

"I'm getting better, but I'm still upset because I couldn't go to Uncle Jed's funeral. I really wanted to go and be with your grandmother. I am the only son left now."

"Maybe we can go to see her when you are well again," Jules said.

"I certainly hope so," Alex said.

Alex forgot about the property until the next week when the same ad appeared in the paper again. *It can't hurt to look.*

It was a good buy. The owner, Mr. Sasser, wanted to get rid of it and move back east. He had inherited it from his grandfather and after spending a year trying to fence it and fix up the run-down house on the land, he was ready to almost give it away. There were 260 acres of undeveloped desert land. Alex offered him $30 an acre.

"I will take $50 an acre," Mr. Sasser said.

"Forty," Alex said.

"Forty-five, that's the least I can take," Mr. Sasser said.

"I will have to get back with you," Alex said. He knew he would pay $11,700 if he could borrow the money. But he wasn't sure he could. He agreed to meet Mr. Sasser in three days and let him know if he had a deal.

"Offer him $10,000 for the whole plot," Alex's father-in-law said.

"I don't have $10,000."

"Could you pay back a $100 a month?"

"I'll have to discuss it with Mary," Alex said.

Mr. Driscoll surprised Alex by saying, "I will let you have the money interest free if you can pay back $100 a month."

Alex talked with Mary. "Why doesn't he buy it himself if he thinks it is such a good deal?" Alex asked his wife.

"Well, my father isn't in the real estate business; he is a cattleman, but he knows a good deal when he sees it. You are in real estate and he thinks it would be a good venture for you. For us."

"So do you think we could repay $100 a month? That's a lot of money."

"Let's get him down to $80 a month," she said. "We can pay more if we have to, but I don't want to be obligated for more than we can afford."

"I don't know if that piece of desert property is worth $10,000," Alex said. "It's a lot of money."

"Yes, it is, but we can probably at least get our money back, and Dad isn't charging us any interest. How can we lose?"

"OK, I'll see if Mr. Sasser will take ten thousand for the property.

I don't want to pay any more than that, though."

Mr. Sasser hesitated. "That's not quite $40 an acre. I don't think I can sell for that price."

"I'm sorry, I can't pay any more," Alex said. They shook hands and Alex walked toward his car.

"Give me your phone number," Mr. Sasser said.

Alex handed him his card. "I will think about your offer," he shook Alex's hand.

It was three weeks before Mr. Sasser called. They made a deal and Alex became a landowner.

## *JULES IS A TEENAGER*

The next few years rushed by. Jules was a great son. He learned to skate and swim and ride his bicycle. He was a Boy Scout and he played Little League. Mary continued to work as a librarian, and Alex's business prospered.

Every time the family planned a trip to Atmore, something came up that prevented it; one of the family got sick or there was stormy weather, or floods made travel impossible. Alex called his mother and kept in touch by mail, but he had not seen her in years.

When Jules was ten years old, Thelma came to visit. She had gotten her Bachelor's degree from Montevalo and finally had a free summer. She flew out and visited for six weeks. She and Mary adored each other and became friends at once. Alex had little trouble becoming reacquainted with his mother even though they had both changed.

Jules reminded Thelma of Alex when he was growing up. He was polite and considerate, just as Alex always had been. He asked his grandmother to tell him about his father, grandfather and his uncle Jed. She showed him pictures. Grandmother went to all Jules' little league games. She helped him with his chores and made his bed. They went to the movies together.

Thelma could not believe how much Mary looked like Jeannie, and how much Jules reminded her of Jeannie's son, Daniel. Daniel was about a year older than Jules, but they had the same build, the same walk and many of the same mannerisms. Their hair and eyes were the same color, and their smiles were identical.

Thelma kept Jeannie's secret, but she did enjoy knowing that Daniel and Jules were half brothers. She didn't want anything to upset the marriage that Alex and Mary so obviously enjoyed. She said nothing. She didn't even mention that Jeannie had a son and that he always came for a visit when he was in town. That was her secret.

When the six weeks visit was over and Thelma had to return home, everybody cried. They had enjoyed picnics, outings in the park, square dancing and sight seeing. Alex stood and watched until the airplane disappeared from view.

Alex's mother came every summer after that. Marge was able to accompany her for many of the visits. They visited the Grand Canyon, Hopi Indian Reservation, Window Rock and other Arizona attractions. They visited the California beaches, the wine country, and San Francisco. Alex tried to make up for the many years when he had not seen her at all.

The years of tranquillity began to erode when Jules entered junior high school. Little by little, Jules' grades began to drop. Alex and Mary noticed a difference in his choice of clothes, shoes, and the way he wore his hair. He began spending more free time away from home and sometimes he left before his chores were done. Mary was upset when three older boys rode into the yard on motorcycles. Jules took them up stairs and a few minutes later loud music blasted from his room.

*This is my house*, Mary thought. *I will not allow such grown-looking boys to invade it with loud, raucous music.*

She knocked on the door. Jules opened it. The boys were sitting on the floor, engrossed in the music. They were smoking cigarettes, and she was sure she smelled alcohol.

"Jules, come out into the hall please," she said calmly. Jules gave her a surly look, but did not move until the boy who seemed to be the leader gave a slight movement of his hand indicating that Jules should do what his mother had asked.

Outside the door, Mary began, "Jules, who are those boys? I have never seen them before. Where did they come from?" She didn't give Jules a chance to answer. "And they came up on motorcycles! I can not believe. . . ."

"Mom, they are my friends. They haven't been here before. They are visiting their cousin who is in my class at school. They are really nice."

"What do you mean, nice?" Jules had to smile.

"Mom, they are my friends. They are nice boys."

"I am afraid I do not agree with you, Jules. I don't like the way they are dressed and I don't like the loud music. Those boys look like bad, punky, low life characters."

"Please don't insult my friends, they really are O.K. guys," Jules said calmly.

"They don't look O.K. to me," Mary said.

"Mom, you just don't know them."

"Jules, they are smoking, playing loud music, and I am certain I smelled alcohol. You will have to get them out of my house." Mary tried to keep her voice down, but she was angry and felt that her house had been invaded.

The door opened. "I am sorry we have upset you Mrs. Presswood," the leader said politely. "We will go now." The three boys walked out the door with Jules following.

"Hey, I'm sorry." Jules said.

"That's O.K.," said the leader. "We have to leave now." They got on their motorcycles and roared off.

Jules ran upstairs to his room and slammed the door without saying a word to his mother.

Mary was shaking. She couldn't believe this was happening, and she wasn't even sure what was happening. She sat down at the kitchen table. She remembered her beautiful, innocent boy of just a few months ago. What had happened to him? How could she get him back? She had made him angry, so angry that he had slammed the door in her face. Now he probably wouldn't ever talk to her.

Talk to her. It had been a long time since they had had a long talk. When she asked about his classes, he said she was intruding on his affairs. He clammed up about his grades. He was passing; he just wasn't making the honor roll. You can't expect every child to make the honor roll every month, but she had expected Jules to do much better.

What had happened to the nice boys who used to play with Jules? Had they changed too or was it just Jules? What about the sweet girls who had been in the group? Where were they?

One thing was on her mind when Mary tapped on the door of Jules' room. She wanted to talk. To try to find out what was bothering him. She wanted to bring him back into her life.

Jules did not open the door. She knocked again, a little louder. Then she tried the doorknob. It was unlocked. She opened the door and stepped in. Jules was not there. She looked in the bathroom and in the closet, but he was not there either.

She noticed that one of the windows was unlocked. She couldn't believe that Jules would run away. She looked into his closet again. A few clothes were on the floor. Missing was Jules' jacket that he wore to school nearly every day. Mary pushed up the window and looked out.

Jules had been taught how to climb out of his window in case of a fire when he was younger. Now, the fire escape route had become a means for getting out of the house without his parents knowing it. Mary felt faint. How long had this been going on?

Mary dashed downstairs to the ground under Jules' window. His tracks led to the garage. She panicked when she remembered her car was in the garage with the keys in the ignition. She ran to the garage. Mary's car was in its place and the keys were there, but Jules' bike was gone.

Mary had several thoughts at once. She could get in her car and ride around looking for Jules. She could call Alex and tell him what had happened, upsetting him, maybe for no good reason. She could call the police, but what would they do? Jules wasn't really missing yet. She could go into the kitchen and start making dinner. Or, she could drive to the grocery store for milk and eggs that she needed for breakfast the next day.

Mary decided to go to the grocery store. Her gut reaction was to take a chance on Jules coming to his senses and returning home in time for dinner. She reasoned that she had been rude to his friends and might even owe them an apology. They were older; older boys smoked. And she wasn't absolutely sure that the smell was alcohol after all. She would wait until Alex came home before doing anything.

When she got to the grocery store she looked across the street toward the gas station. Mary froze. The three motorcyclists were there and so was Jules on his bicycle. Jules had not seen her. He was sitting on his bike talking to the one that Mary thought was the leader. Mary saw Jules reach in his back pants pocket and pull out his billfold. He opened it and handed the boy some bills.

Mary was horrified. Why had Jules given the boy money? Had he paid for cigarettes, alcohol, or something else? She wanted to drive over and yank Jules into the car when she saw him ride away, in the direction of home.

Mary had dozens of unanswered questions. Dazed, she went into the store and picked up the items she had come for. She had shopped at this store for many years and knew everybody who worked there by name and they knew her.

"How are you today?" the manager, Jens Schroeder, greeted her. When she responded with a smile and a quick "Just fine," he went on. "How is Jules doing?"

Mary said, "He's fine," not really believing it herself, but she didn't want to share her concern with the manager at this time.

"I need a bag boy," Mr. Schroeder said. "I was thinking that Jules might be the right age to be interested in the job."

"Thank you, Mr. Schroeder. I will ask him about it."

"If he is interested, tell him to stop by as soon as he can. I need to replace a young man next week."

"Thank you." She hurried to the checkout line. *That request couldn't have come at a better time. I'll have a talk with Jules.*

Jules was in the kitchen when she got home. "What's for dinner?" he asked.

"We're having lamb tonight," she said.

"Great," Jules said.

Jules needed a haircut. He was wearing a brightly colored shirt and a long chain hung around his neck. He was beginning to grow a fuzzy mustache under his nose and a little facial hair was visible. Mary wasn't happy with what she saw, but she knew she had to back away from the way he was dressed. Mention of his attire would only bring forth angry words.

"How is school?" she asked, picking a less personal subject.

"OK. Why?"

"I just wondered."

"School is fine. My grades are fine. Everything is fine." He covered the whole gamut. They wouldn't talk about school.

"Tell me about your new friends," Mary tried to phrase her remarks in a non-threatening way.

"There is nothing to tell."

"Where did you meet them?"

"They showed up over at Dick Jones' house. Dick is in my typing class. I think one of them is Dick's cousin."

"They seem older than you. Do they go to school?"

"Sure. They are in high school. Jake is good in art. He makes designs on T-shirts and sells them. He is making me one. He came over to look at my room to try to get an idea of what to put on my design. I paid him three dollars to make me one."

That explained a lot. Mary was relieved. "Were they drinking?" she asked.

"I think the little guy, Rudy, drinks. I haven't seen the others drink."

That didn't convince Mary, but she'd let it go. At least she knew why Jules had given Jake money.

"I talked with Mr. Schroeder at the grocery store. He said he needed a bagboy and wondered if you'd like the job."

"Bag boy is as low as you can get," Jules said. "You have to do a lot of stuff besides bagging groceries and helping people take their groceries to their cars. You have to help clean the floor and stock the shelves. I don't know if I'd have time to do it."

"Well, think about it. Go down and see Mr. Schroeder if you think you would like the job."

A few days later, Jules came in after school and announced "I made 96 on my science quiz today. It was the highest grade in class."

"That's something to be proud of," Mary said. "I can't wait to tell your dad."

"Also, I have a job for after school and weekends."

"You do?" Mary said, "Doing what?"

"I am going to be a bag boy for Mr. Schroeder."

"Congratulations!"

"I'll make a little spending money. He said he would pay me 75 cents an hour. I can work three hours each evening and five hours on Saturday. That comes to fifteen dollars a week. My allowance is five dollars and I get five dollars for mowing the lawn. Man! I will be making twenty-five dollars a week. I can't believe it."

"That is wonderful, Jules." Mary said. "That's a lot of money for a fourteen-year-old to make." *We will have to keep a close eye on how he spends it.*

Alex was pleased that Jules had made an almost perfect grade on his science quiz. He said that he would like for all of Jules' grades to be ninety or above.

"It was important for me to make good grades," Alex said. "I always tried to make the highest average in the whole school."

"In the whole school?" Jules asked. "How many were in your school?"

"There were between two and three hundred I suppose. But I don't remember for sure."

"Did you really make the highest grades?"

"There was a girl in my class who tried to beat me. Sometimes she won, and sometimes I did. But it took hard work, very hard work."

"Why did you work so hard? Why was it so important?"

"Well, I wanted to be a doctor. I had to prove to myself that I was smart enough to be one."

"Why didn't you become one then?"

"After I went into the service, I guess it seemed like more than I could do. My father died, your mother and I got married, and you were born. By then I decided to go into business."

"I'd never want to be a doctor," Jules said. "I think it would be too hard. I think I would rather be a business man like you."

"You have plenty of time to decide what you want to be. But try to make better grades. You won't be able to go to the college of your choice if you don't have a good record. You start high school next year. That is when you really need to start buckling down."

"That is what our teachers are always saying. They say you can't get a job today if you don't go to college."

"They are right."

"Oh! Did you hear? I got a job today."

"Now that is good news. But how do you think you will handle a job, school, and mowing the lawn, not to mention homework?"

"Mr. Schroeder said he will pay me 75 cents an hour. It comes to fifteen dollars a week."

"That doesn't sound bad. Then I won't have to give you an allowance."

That surprised Jules. "I thought I would keep getting my allowance," he said.

"I think that if you are making your own money, I won't need to give you an allowance."

"O.K.," Jules said. "I can still mow the lawn, can't I?"

"When will you do that?"

"On Saturday mornings, before work."

"You aren't leaving yourself much free time, but you can give it a try."

Mary had been listening to their conversation. She almost fell off the chair when Jules said, "May I have some money to get my hair cut? Mr. Schroeder said it's too long."

Alex wanted to be nonchalant, "How much do you need?"

"A buck-fifty." Alex handed him the money.

"One thing. Mom, please don't shop when I'm working. Could you shop when I am at school?"

Mary was shocked; she had thought it would be so much fun to see Jules working and having him take her groceries to the car.

"Well, why not?"

Jules blushed. "It would be embarrassing."

"I usually shop in the morning anyway."

"Thanks, Mom. I'm off to get a hair cut."

Mary thought about how much Jules had changed. They had been close when he was younger. Now he was growing away from her.

Alex tried to explain, "It is a boy's thing, Sweetheart. In order to grow up to be a man in a man's world, he has to break ties with his mother. I am sure he feels the loss as much as you do, but you both have to let go. In a few years, a fine young man will come back into your life. Be patient. You still have to be there for him. You may have to do even more for him sometimes, like fix his meals at a different time to accommodate his activities.

"However, we must demand respect. We must never allow him to speak to us disrespectfully, and he must do what we ask of him. The trick of course is to be careful that our expectations are reasonable."

"I just love him so much," Mary said. "I am afraid he could get into trouble."

"We have brought him up the best we know how. We will now have to trust him to do what we have taught him. But we have to be there to pick up the pieces when he makes a mistake and falls apart."

"Maybe having a job will help. At least he is finally getting a haircut."

Jules came home about an hour later with his new haircut.

Mary was surprised, "You got a haircut?"

"Well yes, this is the new style," Jules replied.

Alex started to say, "It doesn't look any shorter," but refrained. He said "Nice haircut." Mary and Alex exchanged glances.

The roar of a motorcycle in the driveway ended the conversation. Jake was there with Jules' T-shirt.

"Thanks, this is really great. Come on in." Jules introduced Jake to his parents.

Alex bit his tongue and said, "Pleased to meet you. Have a seat."

Jules and Jake sat down. In an effort to make conversation with Jake, Alex asked him about his motorcycle. Jake asked Alex to come out and take a look at it.

It was a Harley Davidson, several years old, but a beautiful bike. It was obvious that it had received the best of care. It was clean and shiny, and had no dents or scratches. Alex was impressed.

Jake started it up, revved the engine for a minute and then shut it off. It's easy to ride."

Alex asked Jake how long he had owned the motorcycle. Jake explained that he had bought it used and had it only a few months. Alex began to tell Jules that he didn't want him riding a motorcycle because it was too dangerous.

"Oh not at all," Jake said. "A cycle is as safe as a car, and as easy to ride as a bicycle. Actually, it is easier to handle than a car or a bicycle. You can go places on this Harley that you could never reach in a car and you don't have to wait in long lines of traffic when there is a hold up. I would ride this baby anywhere. Try it," Jake offered.

Alex had always wanted to ride a motorcycle, but had never had the opportunity. He was reluctant, but when Jake insisted, he decided to try.

Jake showed him the starter and the gears. He showed him how to give it gas and how to stop. He assured Alex that it was simple to ride. "Just go easy to start with."

Alex rode slowly out of the driveway. He rode to the end of the block and turned the corner. The boys could hear him on the next street and they watched for him to round the corner on the opposite side of the house. He approached the driveway going a little too fast. When he put on the brakes, the motorcycle skidded. Alex could not keep it from falling over onto his left leg. Jake quickly grabbed the handlebars and pulled the machine up. Alex could not get up. He was experiencing the worst pain he had ever felt. Jules ran into the house, yelling for his mother. Mary could not pick Alex up; he just lay there on the ground in too much pain to move.

Mary dashed into the house and called the doctor, who was their neighbor. He came immediately.

"We'll have to get him to the hospital." He called for an ambulance.

Jake called a wrecker. He had failed to explain that the motorcycle really belonged to his Uncle, who didn't know that Jake had taken it out for a ride. Jake suddenly decided to leave the scene.

Alex's leg was broken in two places. He would have to stay in the hospital for at least two days and wear a cast for six weeks. He would need therapy for weeks after that.

"I can't believe I was so stupid. STUPID! STUPID! STUPID!"

"More stupid than you think," an officer who was standing at the door said. "I am Officer Rodriguez. The cycle you wrecked belonged to a man in Long Beach. It was reported missing over a month ago."

"WHAT?"

"Would you mind telling me what happened."

I only rode around the block and back. I guess I was just going too fast in the driveway. I put the brakes on too hard."

"I am puzzled, Mr. Presswood, about the circumstances surrounding this incident. Why were you riding a stolen motorcycle?"

"I didn't know it was stolen."

"The driver of the wrecker said that he was called to pick up a motorcycle at your address. When he got it back to the shop and ran the registration he found that it had been reported missing a month ago. I am afraid I will have to book you, Mr. Presswood."

"I can explain," Alex said, looking at Jules.

"I will explain," Jules said. He told about his friend delivering the T-shirt that he had ordered, and about their looking at the motorcycle together.

"Jake insisted that my father take a ride on it. He said that it was his. My father certainly did not steal that motorcycle."

"Where does Jake live?"

"I don't know." Jules looked scared.

"Officer, my husband would not steal a motorcycle," Mary said. "It happened just as they said. He had no idea that the motorcycle was stolen."

"Do you know this Jake? What is his last name? Where does he live?" the officer inquired.

"I only know that his cousin is in one of my classes. I met him at his cousin's house."

"What is the cousin's name? Where does he live?" the officer asked again.

"Dick Jones. On Lake Street, down near the warehouse."

"That isn't a very good neighborhood. I will check it out. Meantime, Mr. Presswood, don't leave the hospital until I get back with you."

Alex's face was white. He had never stolen anything in his life. He thought, J*ust wait until I get my hands on that punk Jake.*

"I think I better call my lawyer," Alex said.

Jules looked at his father, tears in his eyes.

"I didn't know," he said.

"We will just have to find out who this Jake person is. I will take Jules down to Dick Jones' house. Maybe he will know Jake's last name," Mary said.

"Don't you go down there!" Alex ordered. "Leave it to the police and to my lawyer. Maybe Jules can find something out about Jake at school tomorrow, but I don't want you going there. You might get into trouble."

Mary did not have to be told twice.

"You two go on home. I will be all right here."

"Will you have to go to jail?" Jules stood up.

"My lawyer will take care of that. He won't let them take me to jail." Alex tried to sound confident, although he knew there was the possibility he would be arrested.

The next morning, Mary found an article on the front page of the newspaper about the incident. Though the article presented the facts just as they had been stated to the police, the headline read "Missing Motorcycle Found in Local Businessman's Driveway." Mary shivered. *Alex and Jules must not see this paper*. She hid it.

Mary had made arrangements for a substitute in the library so she could spend the day doing what she could for Alex. She hurried to the hospital as soon as Jules left for school.

Alex's lawyer, Lester Van Camp, was sitting beside the bed talking to Alex.

"All we have to do is to locate this Jake kid and make him admit that the cycle was in his possession," he said. "We'll find witnesses who have seen Jake on it. We'll have it cleared up in no time."

Mary kissed her husband lightly and gave him a gentle hug.

"Thank you, Lester," she said.

"Don't worry, Mary. It is surprising how easily an innocent person can get into trouble. Tell that to your son," Lester said.

"I have a lot to say to that young man," Alex said.

"Sometimes situations like this turn a kid around. They realize how quickly they could get into trouble and how difficult it could be to get out of it," Lester said.

Later the officer came by.

"I have not been able to find a boy named Jake who rides a

Harley. I found a boy called Dick Jones on Lake Street, but he said he didn't know anyone named Jake. Is there anything else you can tell me that will help me that will locate this Jake?"

"I know something," Mary said.

Alex and Officer Rodriguez looked at her.

"I saw three boys on motorcycles at the gas station on Mission Pass and Francisco Streets. Jake was with them. I saw Jules hand Jake the money to pay for his T-shirt."

"When was this, Mrs. Presswood?" asked the officer.

"Two weeks ago yesterday."

"Have you seen any of those boys on their cycles anywhere else? Can you think of anyone who might know them?"

"I have not seen them before or since the day they came to our house."

"Oh, they came to your house?" the officer asked in surprise.

"Yes, they came that day - - two weeks ago when Jules ordered the T-shirt."

"Then you could identify them."

"Yes, I think so."

The telephone rang, and Mary answered it.

"Ms. Presswood, come to the emergency room at once," a female voice said.

"What is it? What has happened?"

"Your son is here. He was injured at school."

"Oh, my god," Mary said.

"What happened?" Alex asked.

"There was an accident at school. Jules is in the emergency room."

Officer Rodriguez dashed out of the room ahead of Mary.

"I will be back," Mary yelled to Alex, who could do nothing but watch her go.

Jules was lying on a gurney. He had been brought in by ambulance. The school principal, Mrs. Fletcher, stood nervously by.

"He was attacked this morning in the locker room. Two large boys jumped him. One of the boys had a baseball bat, but several other students disarmed him before he could hit Jules with it. They got in some pretty hard blows before they ran away. They jumped on motorcycles and disappeared. We called your home, and the maid told us you were here with your husband.

Mary looked at Jules. His face was covered with blood. His eyes were shut and his nose was bleeding. He had been kicked in the ribs and stomach. There were two large bumps on his head.

"They worked him over good. Do you have any idea what this was all about?" Mrs. Fletcher asked.

Officer Rodriguez stepped forward "We're pretty sure it has something to do with this motorcycle business. Did anyone know the assailants?"

"I didn't take time to question anyone. We concentrated on getting Jules to the hospital. Jules is the last person I would expect to have this kind of trouble," replied Mrs. Fletcher.

Jules needed stitches above his eye, on his chin and on his lip. He had lost one tooth, and had another broken. Mary cried.

"We will put him in your husband's room. It will be easier for you to help them that way," the nurse said.

Jules was all situated in Alex's room when Officer Rodriguez came in to talk with Jules. "Was anything said when they attacked you?"

"They said 'This will teach you to keep your mouth shut'."

"Can you describe who attacked you?"

Jules described the boys who had come to their home two weeks earlier. He only knew their first names, Rudy and Buzz, and where they went to high school.

"This should be an easy case to crack with the information you have been able to give us. We will get to work on it immediately. Mr. Presswood, you may go home when you are released from the hospital. You should call the precinct later today or tomorrow for an update. Also we'll cruise by your house to be sure everything is all right there." Turning to Mary he added, "I wouldn't go home alone, Mrs. Presswood. Wait until your husband and son are ready and keep your doors and windows locked. We'll try to get these goons in custody right away, but be careful."

When Officer Rodriguez left the room, Alex looked at his son. "I am sorry this happened. You and I both did something foolish. You forgot to check out your friends and I forgot to act my age."

Jules listened. "I'm sorry, too," he said. "I will be more careful. I will study more and maybe make the highest average in my high school at least once."

"You will have a lot of competition, Jules, but it is a worthy goal. We have always asked you to do your best. You are blessed with good looks, a great personality, and a brilliant, well, sometimes brilliant mind. A winning combination.

"Think about your future. You can enter a high-paying career with the same effort as entering a lesser paying one. Just make up your mind to work hard and believe in yourself."

Alex could see that Jules was paying less attention to him and more to the pattern on the window curtains. He apologized, "I am sorry son. I got carried away."

"I am listening, Dad. I want you and Mom to be proud of me. I got beat up today because I thought those guys were cool with their shiny motorcycles. Now I know how they got them, and I don't even want to think about motorcycles. I don't know exactly why they beat me up, though. I didn't do anything to them."

"The policeman must have gone to Dick Jones' house looking for Jake. Dick probably called Jake and told him you had squealed on them. You were getting mixed up with a pretty rough bunch."

"I am glad I found out about those guys."

"Just be careful picking your friends. I'd rather you stick with the kids around the neighborhood. Most of them are on the same wavelength as you."

The doctor came in and examined Alex's leg. "You can go home if you want to. You will have to stay off of that leg for three or four days. I will be by later to check on you."

Later, Officer Rodriguez called and said that they had found Jake and the other boys. Everybody heaved a sigh of relief. Jake's uncle was responsible for the thefts.

Jules was as good as his word. He began to turn his life around. He gave up his job as a bag boy when he decided to go out for football in high school. He spent time on the bench for the first two years, but had become a valuable player by his junior year. He was hoping for a football scholarship, so he put effort into the sport. He also made outstanding grades, but never was able to reach his goal of having the highest average in school, not even for one semester.

Every summer, Thelma came to visit. She taught during the school year in Atmore, but looked forward to her summer in California. Alex grew closer to his mother during these times. She always brought news of people he knew from his youth and she met his friends who shared his life in California. Mary's mother and father became good friends with her as well. They visited each other often and took short trips together. Jules brought the greatest joy to his grandmother. She was able to smooth off the rough edges when conflicts arose between parents and son, and she displayed a never-ending pleasure in hearing his dreams.

Jules told his grandmother about the lovely Mexican-American girl he had fallen in love with. She had long black hair, gleaming white teeth, dancing dark brown eyes, and rosy cheeks with deep dimples. She loved to dance and sing. She went to see Jules in every football game. She even watched him practice. When Thelma saw her picture, she was struck by her extraordinary beauty, but made no comment for a moment.

She was Mexican; probably Catholic. Finally she said, "She is very beautiful." But Thelma had difficulty identifying with this Mexican girl. She asked, "Have your parents met her yet?"

"Well, they haven't met her yet, but they have seen her. I know they will like her. Everybody does. She is smart; makes better grades than I do."

"Have you been out with her?"

"Oh yes. We have been dating off and on; dances, parties, movies, for a couple years now. But I would like to ask her to go steady with me."

"Maybe you should introduce her to your parents before you ask her to go steady. Going steady is a commitment."

"Yes, I know that. But I know what they would say."

"What?"

"That I am too young. To wait and think about it. And they might not like her being Mexican and Catholic."

"Those are serious considerations," Thelma said.

"I love her. I want to marry her someday." He was not embarrassed to share such serious thoughts with his grandmother.

"What do you think?"

"I think young love is so special. But you are very young. And the difference in religion is a concern. And you have another year of high school, your most critical year."

"Maybe if you and my parents met Juanita, you would understand why I love her," Jules said.

When Thelma met Juanita, she knew why Jules had deep feelings for her. She was radiant, bubbly, and simply charming. Mary had invited Juanita to a special dinner that she had arranged for a few of Jules' friends. She set the date for three days before Thelma was to return to Atmore. Thelma later told Jules that she thought his choice of a steady girlfriend was perfect, and gave her wholehearted approval. Mary and Alex invited her to visit often.

### *VIETNAM*

Jules' plans for college were overshadowed by the conflict in Vietnam. America had committed itself to fighting Communism there. Jules listened to the arguments against the war. He read about young men burning their draft cards and refusing to go into the armed services. Some of his teachers spoke against the war; even held demonstrations. Others were in favor of backing the government no matter how great the sacrifice. Many young men were slipping off to Canada to hide until the war was over. Some were bravely marching away, never to return.

Alex grieved that his only son was facing such a monumental decision. World War II had changed his life forever. He had hoped and prayed that his son would not have to go to war. Wasn't the United Nations supposed to ensure that fighting would not break out again? He loved his country, but it broke his heart to think that his son might have to give his life in a foreign country fighting for a cause that was not clear.

Jules had a choice. He could go to Canada. It would cost him his American citizenship, but going to Vietnam could cost him his life.

"For once in your life, I can not tell you what to do, even though I love you with all my heart. Your mother and I will be devastated no matter whether you choose Vietnam or Canada. We will help if you decide to leave the country. I will not consider you a coward if you choose that course," Alex said.

*I am beginning to sound like my father. I never realized how hard it was for him to let go of Jed and me. I still cannot think about Jed.*

The night before Jules' eighteenth birthday he announced that he had made a decision. Alex and Mary held their breath as they waited to hear what Jules had to say.

Jules began by saying that he had worked hard in school preparing for college and for life. He said he had enjoyed the conveniences and privileges of being a member of the greatest country in the world. "If I give up my American citizenship, all that I have worked for will be in vane. I have taken from my country all that it has to offer, and now I must give back. If I survive, I'll continue my education. I will go to the post office tomorrow and register for the draft."

Mary cried. She would have cried no matter what he had decided. His life was on the line either way. "I am proud of you, son. You are brave. I will miss you. I will write and send care packages. Most of all I will pray." The tears rolled down her face as she spoke.

Alex could not speak. He stood up, shook his son's hand and hugged him.

Thelma arrived for her annual visit a week before Jules was to leave for basic training. She was glad that her grandson had chosen to serve his country. Though she had lost Jed, she felt that a man should fulfill his obligation of citizenship and answer the call to defend his country. She would have supported Jules if he had made a different choice, but she was proud that he had the courage to face the dangers of the war.

Jeannie's son, Daniel, had also chosen to take up arms for his country the year before. He was currently in Vietnam and his anxious mother awaited word from him every day. Since Jeannie had moved back to Atmore, she had taught in the same school as Thelma. She and Thelma saw each other every day. The secret bond between them was shared with no one.

Alex and Mary grew even closer in the next two years. They read the newspapers, watched television, and went to the movies to see war pictures. They worried and they worked hard. Mary spent long hours in her flower garden. She planted watered, weeded and wept. Anxiety consumed her. She leaned heavily on Alex for support.

Alex planted vegetables, sharing them with friends and neighbors. He felt productive tilling the soil. He tried to remember the tricks of the trade that he had learned as a boy on his father's farm.

Mary and Alex resumed their participation in weekly square dances held at the schoolhouse in Santee to get their minds off their son being in the war. Alex began teaching a Sunday school class. They filled every minute of the day with activities. Mary understood why her mother had rolled bandages and crocheted Afghans during World War II; anything to keep your mind off your son's plight.

When Jules tour of duty was completed, Alex and Mary met him at the airport. Mary shed tears of joy and ran to greet him with hugs and kisses. They were both anxious to tell him how much they missed him, and how relieved they were that he was home again.

"Where is Juanita?" Jules asked as he looked around.

"She chose to wait for you at home. I don't think she wanted to share you," Mary replied. "We will drop you off at her house and you two can drive over for dinner later."

Jules' luggage appeared on the conveyor belt. He grabbed it and they headed for the car.

Thelma and Marge flew out for Jules and Juanita's wedding. The young couple was so much in love that they decided to marry despite the fact that they were both still in college. Alex and Mary agreed to support them until they both were graduated.

After graduation, Jules decided to work with his father. Alex now had one of the largest and most profitable insurance/real estate businesses in the area. Alex represented several different insurance companies. He sold auto, homeowners, and life insurance. He also bought and sold real estate. For starters, Alex turned over the auto insurance to Jules. Alex would eventually teach him how to handle other phases of the business. Jules and Alex were happy working together.

*THE REAL ESTATE INVESTMENT PAYS OFF*

A real estate investment firm contacted Alex about purchasing the land that Alex and Mary had bought 20 years before. Mary's father had helped them to make the deal when they had first moved back to Santee. Over the years they thought little about the land. Alex smiled. *Who could possibly be interested in that worthless tract?*

Alex investigated the investors. What he found made him reel. The New York firm was buying large tracts of land and improving them by building golf courses, artificial lakes, and swimming pools. They split up the tracts into quarter acre plots and sold them for five thousand dollars apiece. Alex's 260 sixty-acre plot was worth a great deal of money.

"This can't be happening to me."

The New York firm sent out a team. Alex asked Jules and his attorney, Lester Van Camp, to meet with them as well. Lester warned him to not set his hopes get high. After all he had paid only $10,000 for the entire tract of land. Under normal circumstances, $100,000 dollars would be considered a very handsome profit on his investment.

When the team arrived they first went to the site. Though it was located in the desert it still held promise. The proposed highway that would run nearby would make it more accessible to prospective buyers. There were Mesquite trees growing in the area, evidence of underground springs from which water could be pumped. Also, there was other undeveloped property in the area that would be available to them in the future.

Alex's brain was spinning. His lawyer thought he should ask $100,000, but Alex had a gut feeling that he could get much more. Losing the deal would be a disappointment, but not making as much as possible would be a shame. Alex could tell that they were interested. "What is your asking price for the whole 260 acres?"

Alex asked $7,000 an acre. They all knew Alex would come down. But how much?

"We are prepared to offer you $500,000 dollars for the whole tract," One man said.

Alex's lawyer, who was trained to show no emotion, sucked in his breath. He couldn't let the team know he was impressed with their offer.

"You can have the entire piece of property for $1,250,000- - a million and a quarter," Alex replied.

Jules squirmed.

"We will have to meet with our board," the man said. "We will let you know in about a week." The men shook hands and left.

"Are you crazy, Dad?" Jules said. "They offered you a half million dollars for that piece of wasteland. I can't believe you turned them down."

"We will see, Jules. I have a feeling they'll pay a lot more than they offered. After all, they are expecting to make millions on the project. What I asked is fair."

Lester was unconvinced, though they had offered five times what he had expected. Maybe Alex was right. If so, he would have the pleasure of working with a wealthy man.

Alex had not talked to Mary about the inquiry. She had stayed late one evening at work and had friends over another night. Though it was constantly on his mind, Alex could not seem to find the right time to tell her. He did not want to set her up for a fall if the deal failed. When he came home that night they talked.

At first Mary was indignant that Alex had not accepted their offer.

A profit of nearly $500,000 was inconceivable and Alex had turned it down. She sat there and stared at him. "I don't believe it!"

"Let me explain, Sweetheart," Alex began. "I have worked on enough of these projects to know that there are big bucks to be made. This company will make between five and ten million dollars on the lots alone. If they build on them and sell their houses at a profit, which they will, they stand to make even more. They will pay for the land."

"But what if they don't?"

"We own the land. What would keep us from developing it ourselves? We could end up with several million dollars."

"Why haven't you thought of that before?"

"I have been so busy with other things that it hadn't occurred to me. I have been giving it some thought now that someone has shown interest in it."

"Alex you are nearly sixty years old, do you think you should undertake something that big?"

"Maybe I won't have to. Maybe they will give me what I am asking."

Alex was right. Within a week he received a letter stating that they would give him $1.2 million for the property. Alex called Lester immediately and had him draw up the papers.

"I wish Daddy had lived to see this day," Mary said. "It was all his idea to buy the property. Mother would have been excited too."

"We owe it all to your father. Mary, I want to tear down your old home in Santee and build you the house of your dreams. Maybe one you haven't even dreamed of yet." They both laughed. "You will have everything you have ever wanted. It will be a shrine to your parents and a reflection of my love for you."

"That would be wonderful. You know how much I love it there. I will plant flowers all over the valley."

Jules and his father worked together as a team. Jules not only learned the insurance business and had taken over all the responsibility for it; he also learned the real estate business. But life with the beautiful Juanita was over.

Juanita had become a nurse. During their ten-year marriage she worked the various shifts at the Alvarado Hospital Medical Center, while helping to maintain the home she and Jules had built near Sunshine Park.

She had lost three babies that she and Jules had conceived. Her disappointment turned into blame and she decided to end the marriage.

Five years later, Jules met and married a lovely blonde girl named Agnes Kenwick. She was a buyer for a large San Diego department store. She was a successful career woman, two years younger than Jules. They were happy. A son, whom they named David after Jules grandfather was born after three years of marriage.

Agnes took a leave of absence from her job and became a full-time mother. Her pleasure in caring for her son was evident to everyone who knew her. When David was four years old, she took courses to hone her marketing skills and went back to work. She juggled work, day care, and parenting, as did most of the other women in her generation.

David became the focal point in Alex and Mary's lives. They showed him off to everyone they knew and loved spending time with him. His little feet were always running and his curiosity knew no limits.

*MARY*

Mary loved the home that her husband had built for her. She gave up her job as librarian and spent her time enjoying her grandson and working in her flower garden. Most of the landscaping on the seven-acre plot was done by professionals and maintained by a full time gardener. But Mary had her own garden that she planted and cared for. She enjoyed planting seeds and watching them grow into flowers, which she cut and brought into the house. Fragrance from the rose bushes that outlined her garden wafted through the window and into the house.

Mary's housekeeper, Maria, had worked for her for years. She and her husband lived in an apartment Alex had built for them. Maria attended to most of the household chores, including some cooking and laundry. Maria was dependable, and she was loved like a family member. Maria's help made it possible for Mary to have the time to take part in community activities and take leadership roles in civic organizations.

It was not surprising that Mary was asked to run for mayor of the city of Santee, a position that had been held by her father many years earlier. Mary considered running for the position, but there had never been a woman mayor and she didn't want to be the first. She declined, but asked the committee to consider Alex.

Alex accepted the nomination and ran for mayor. He campaigned hard with Mary at his side. He beat out the high school principal as well as a local pharmacist. Alex served two terms as mayor and then ended his political career.

Alex was aware that Mary's health was failing. She had lost weight, and felt weak. She tried to hide brief dizzy spells and momentary black outs. When she finally consented to seeing a doctor, he found that she had a serious deficiency of B-12. Her disease was identified as pernicious anemia and treatment began immediately. Mary experienced problems with walking and balance and had to limit her activities.

After many months, her condition improved, but she never regained her enthusiasm for life. She limited her activities to playing quiet games. Bridge, which she and Alex had enjoyed for years, became a chore so they changed to less stressful games like rummy and canasta.

Alex's concerns for Mary kept him close by. He knew that even the slightest cold was a threat to her condition.

When a cold turned out to be a virulent strain of the flu Mary became seriously ill. The virus caused pneumonia, which claimed her life within twenty-four hours.

Alex was dazed. Jules and Agnes led him through making the funeral arrangements. When it was over, he walked around the house like a zombie.

Jules made Alex come to work every day. He insisted that Alex attend to clients that he could have serviced himself. Jules and Agnes took him out to eat, and had him eat at their home. They took him to watch David's baseball games. Alex's friends dropped in to visit often.

"I don't think I will ever get past this grief," Alex said to Jules. "It will be hard to go on without her."

"I miss her too, Dad."

Alex shook his head. "Your mother and I worked hard at making our marriage work in the early years. But we were happy. We built our lives around each other and you."

Jules replied, "You were both wonderful parents. I am lucky to have had the two of you."

## *RETURN TO ATMORE*
## INVITATION TO A REUNION

Alex went to square dances and stood on the sidelines. He accepted friends' invitations to dinner and spent the evening talking about Mary. He went to work every day, but found it hard to concentrate. He often left the office in the afternoon and took David fishing.

One day in February, Alex received a letter inviting him to his fiftieth high school class reunion. It was hard to believe that fifty years had passed since high school. Life really is short. *How quickly the years slip by*, he thought. He laid the letter aside and went about answering other mail. It lay on his desk for several days before he picked it up and read it again.

The reunion would be held in his old high school auditorium. The old school building had been replaced by a larger, more modern one and was no longer used for classes. The letter explained that the building had been renovated and rooms were used for meetings by civic organizations, political meetings and church groups. Seats had been removed from the auditorium and it provided space for a gymnasium that was sometimes used as a banquet room for special events, like weddings and anniversaries. The old library and other rooms were also set up for smaller gatherings. Several years earlier Alex had been asked for a donation to help with the cost of the project.

Alex looked at the date of the reunion. It would be held in June, a week after school ended. Would he know anyone after all of these years? It had been a long time since he had even thought about his former classmates. He was sure they had not thought about him. What would they find to talk about? Would they remember how poor he had been, how he couldn't play football because he had to hurry home to the farm? How he had fixed up an old car and driven it to school sometimes.

Alex would like his classmates to know he wasn't poor now.

He wanted them to know he had become a millionaire. He wondered how they had turned out. Had they been able to reach their goals? He smiled when he thought about the prophecy. What had they said he would be? A doctor? What a switch he had made.

Alex told Jules about the invitation. "You have to go, Dad, you have to. You have planned to go back to Atmore for as long as I can remember, but never have. You deserve to go."

"I don't want to go alone," Alex said. "I had always planned to drive across the country with you and your mother. I wanted it to be a family trip."

"And I have always wanted to go. Every time we had to cancel I was disappointed."

"Would you go with me?"

"Let me look at my calendar. I'll see what appointments I have in, when did you say, June? What date?"

"June thirteenth."

"I will let you know tomorrow or the next day," Jules said. "I would really like to go."

"Call me as soon as you can. I'll have to let the reunion committee know if I can attend." Alex was anxious.

Jules set aside the month of June to accompany his father on the trip to Atmore. David's school would be out for summer vacation, so he would be able to go with them.

*THE TRIP TO ATMORE*

Alexander Presswood lowered the window of his brand new Lincoln Towncar and handed the teller a check. "I would like to have cash, please. I called this morning and was assured that there would be no problem getting cash."

"Of course Mr. Presswood," the teller replied. "Actually we have it counted out for you, in hundreds, twenties, tens and fives as you requested."

"Thank You," Alex said.

"Be careful with all of that money," she felt compelled to say. It wasn't unusual for customers to ask for large amounts of cash when they were on their way to Las Vegas, but Alex Presswood had never asked for a large amount of cash before. He had been banking there for nearly forty years and often chatted and passed the time of day as he made transactions from his car or from inside when it was convenient.

The teller leaned over and took a lingering look at the other man in the front seat and the young boy in the back. They were looking at a road map and speaking quietly.

"Yes, I'll be careful," Alex said. Noticing the questioning look on the teller's face, he said, "Meet my son, Jules, and grandson David. They are going on vacation with me."

"Nice to meet you," she smiled. "I am glad you introduced them. I was afraid for a moment that something may have been wrong."

"Thank you for your concern."

"Have a good trip." Alex pulled away as another car drove up behind him. He drove his car into a parking space in the bank parking lot to count the money.

"All here," he said as he smiled at his son. "Exactly $5,000."

"Why did you bring along so much cash, Dad? Wouldn't it be safer to use traveller's checks or credit cards?"

"It probably would," Alex said. "I have always dreamed of starting out on a trip with enough cash in my pocket. I do have a couple of credit cards if I need them. I will be careful, I assure you."

David leaned over the front seat to watch Alex. He said, "May I hold it for just a second? I have never seen so much money, Grandpa."

Alex hesitated.

"I'll give it right back. Let me hold it for just a second. Nobody will believe that I held $5,000 in my hand."

Alex could not see how it would hurt to humor his grandson. He let him have the thrill of actually fingering the bills. He handed David the large money envelope and watched as he flipped it open, put his hand inside and pull out a handful of bills. David examined them and put them back. Handing the envelope back to Alex, he said, "Thanks Grandpa. I will never wash my hands again." Both men laughed.

"When I was your age, I doubt if I had even touched a $10 bill."

"You must have been poor when you were my age," David said. "I have had lots of $10 bills."

"Yes, we were poor. Everybody was poor when I was growing up."

"Tell me about it," David said.

Alex slipped the envelope into his jacket pocket. "I have a vivid recollection of my early years when times were so hard. Let's wait until we are on the road, then I will tell you everything I can remember."

"O.K," David said.

Alex backed out of the parking spot, placed the car in forward gear and headed into the busy street.

"How did people actually survive the depression? I would have gone crazy if my son had wanted something and I was unable to get it for him. And how could you go to bed at night knowing your children were cold or hungry? Or that you would not have any money to buy Christmas presents?" Jules said. "I can't imagine it. I never wanted for anything when I was growing up."

"I am sure it broke their hearts. But they found pleasure in simple things. Giving me a ride on the back of the mule while he was plowing was a thrill and my father enjoyed letting me ride. Sometimes when he came home, he would stop the car and give me a ride on the running board. He used to let your Uncle Jed sit in his lap and steer the car for him. Just simple things."

"So people really found happiness?"

"Yes. Mere survival brought happiness. We had none of the conveniences that we have today. It would be hard for you to imagine a home with no electricity, no indoor toilets or running water, central heat or phones and food being cooked on a wood-burning stove. But meals were served three times a day and the whole family gathered to eat food that was grown on the farm. Making conversation and showing that we cared for each other is what made us happy."

"We'll talk about these things as we go along, but right now let's get started on our trip. Have we forgotten anything?"

"I cleared everything off my desk," Jules said. "At least the things that needed my personal attention. I left instructions for our girls in the office to contact us every day. They know they can reach me on my cell phone."

Alex pulled into the circular driveway in front of his house and stopped near the front door. He entered the house alone, leaving Jules and David in the car. Everything was quiet. The only sound he heard was the ticking of the grandfather clock in the entrance hall. Stepping into the living room, he looked around at the familiar surroundings, noting that everything was in perfect order. He walked through the living room, checking to be sure the windows were locked, and drew the drapes tightly against the bright sunlight.

Feeling satisfied that those details had been attended to; Alex hurried down the hall to the master bedroom. He found that the drapes in the bedroom had not been drawn and he quickly pulled the cord, glancing outside at his wife's lovely rose garden. The gardener was working among the roses.

Alex felt comfortable knowing that Jesus Hernandez and his wife, Maria, would be here to take care of the place while he was away. Jesus and Maria occupied a suite of rooms built especially for them over the garage. They were good helpers and had been invaluable to him during Mary's illness and death.

Before closing his suitcase, he put the money in a secret pocket. As Alex picked up his suitcase and started out of the room, he heard his grandson calling. "Is anything wrong, Grandpa? We're waiting."

Alex knew how anxious David was to get started, but he wanted to say goodbye to Jesus and Maria. It would take only a few minutes. He found Maria on the patio arranging a bouquet of flowers. He smiled and set his suitcase down. He gave her a hug. Tears were in his eyes as he said goodbye, remembering that this was supposed to be the trip he had promised Mary for so many years. Maria hugged him back, brushing the tears from her own eyes with the back of her hand.

"Don't worry about a thing, Mr. Presswood," she said. "We will take good care of everything just as if you were here." He knew that she would.

Alex picked up his suitcase again and started around the house where he had seen Jesus working. At that moment, Jesus appeared from around the corner. Alex shook his hand, said goodbye, and hurried to the car where his son and impatient grandson were waiting.

"O.K. Let's hit the road." Alex smiled.

It was quiet for a while. Each of them was absorbed in his own thoughts about going away. Jules was not altogether happy about leaving Agnes alone, but she insisted that he go with his father. She knew this would be an emotionally trying time for Alex because he had not returned to Alabama since before the war. He had, however, kept in close touch with his family and they had visited him during the years. Agnes planned to join them later in Alabama.

A lump formed in David's throat as they drove past his school. He saw his best friend, Freddie, playing catch with a boy he did not know. David waved to them, but they did not see him. He thought about the swim meet that he would miss and the hike to the mountains that his scout group had planned. He had to convince himself again that he was going to have more fun on the trip than he would have had at home.

Alex tried hard to concentrate on his driving and dismiss thoughts of remorse. The thought of going through life without Mary made him sad. He would have to make a new life for himself.

"I love your car, Dad," Jules broke the silence. "It has a comfortable ride."

"I like it too. It just seems to drive itself."

"Grandpa, did they have cars when you were a little boy?" David asked.

"Of course we did. There is a lot of difference between cars now and then, but they would take you where you wanted to go, and bring you back. That was what mattered.

"Roads were different also. I can remember when even the main roads connecting important cities were not paved. They were covered with gravel that would sometimes fly up and break the windows if you were going too fast. They were narrow; two lanes at the most.

"The worst thing about the roads was that they were bumpy and dusty in dry weather. But when it rained, they were muddy and slippery. And the tires made deep ruts that were difficult to get out of. Big holes were sometimes washed out. One night my father got stuck in the mud. He had to wait until morning to get a farmer to pull him out with his team of oxen. Since we didn't have a telephone, there was no way to let my mother know what the trouble was. She worried, but she understood."

"I would have worried, Grandpa."

"My father, your great-grandfather was an insurance salesman (seems to run in the family). He needed a car to make a living. The first car I remember was a little Chevy coupe. And then he traded every few years.

They reached the expressway and Alex waited for a Greyhound bus to pass. They followed along behind the silver and blue bus with the sleek racing dog painted on the side. "We seldom traveled on buses in those days, but the Greyhound bus played a very important roll in our lives."

"How?" David asked.

"Well, you see, we did not own a clock. Mother was able to tell the time of day by the bus. The bus that passed our house at six o'clock in the morning meant it was time to get up. The 7:00 bus meant the school bus would be along soon. There were buses that told her it was time for lunch, time to put the sweet potatoes in the oven for our after-school snack, suppertime, and time for bed. Of course the buses were going in both directions."

David could picture a Greyhound dog running around the face of a clock, ticking off the hours and minutes of a day. There was a clock in every room at his house so it was hard for him to imagine a house with out even one clock.

"Tell me about my great-grandmother. Is she still living, Grandpa?" David asked.

"No, she passed away just about the time you were born. She died in her sleep one night. I had just taken your grandmother to the hospital for an operation and I could not leave her. I had to miss my mother's funeral. At first my sisters did not understand, but when they realized how sick Mary was, they forgave me.

"Your grandmother was wonderful. Everyday tasks that women do today with the help of machines had to be done by hand when I was growing up. Life was hard.

"After my father died Mama bought a house in town, where

she lived the rest of her life."

Alex stopped talking for a long while. He looked over at Jules. "Have you been sleeping?" he asked. "You were so quiet."

"I think I did nod off."

"Aren't you going to tell any more stories?" David asked.

"Sure. I didn't know you were still listening. I'll tell you about something I longed for all of my boyhood days."

David leaned forward on the front seat, getting as close as he could to his grandfather. "I'm listening," he said.

"Do you have your seatbelt fastened?" Alex asked.

"Stop the car and I'll move to the back seat," Jules said. "David, you can sit up front with your Grandpa."

After they were settled in, Alex started his story.

"I always wanted a bicycle. I was about eight years old when Bill Simmons, a neighborhood kid, got one. It was blue, with a white line running down the middle of the frame. White stars were on the front and rear fenders. How badly I wanted one like it!

"I had been told that my father could not afford to buy me a bicycle, but when I asked him, he half way promised that he would get one for me. I spent hours fantasizing about the bike I would someday have. As time went by, I reminded my dad about the bike. I told him I could use it for running errands or get a paper route make money for all of us. But I never did get a bicycle. I always wondered why I was led to believe it might someday be a reality. Now, I think that my daddy was trying to teach me to hold on to my dream even though it appeared to be beyond my reach."

"Why didn't you get a job and save up for a bike?" David asked.

"Oh, I was willing to work for it. I did all sorts of jobs for my father and neighbors, but I never came close to making enough to buy a bike. I have never owned a bicycle in my life."

Jules laughed, "Pop, I will buy you a bicycle as soon as we get back home."

"Good, I am going to hold you to that."

"Do you know how to ride a bike Grandpa?" David asked.

"Sure. I learned on Bill's bike. He would let me borrow it."

Jules asked, "Would you like me to drive for a while, Dad?" He had noticed that every time his father was telling an episode he slowed down and he knew they had planned to drive at least three hundred miles today.

"That would be nice."

After they changed drivers, Alex continued. "It has now been fifty years since we lived on that little farm in Alabama. When you look back that far you get a different perspective. At one time I was embarrassed. I wanted to forget about how poor we were and how hard we worked. I couldn't admit that some of my clothes were made from feed sacks or that we didn't have a set of dishes or silverware. That all four of us kids had to sleep in one bed for years.

"Perhaps this was one reason I stayed on the west coast after the war. I could not have left Mary. I loved her from the minute I laid eyes on her. So I was willing to stay here rather than insist that we return east after our marriage. The hardships that my family endured when we were growing up gave me a sense of urgency, a feeling that I had to be successful to make up for all the deprivation. Fighting for dollars that would put distance between me and the life I knew as a child became an obsession."

There was another reason Alex had not returned to Alabama after the war: Jeannie. He had managed to put her out of his life in California, but he could not face returning after the war knowing she had married someone else.

"I think I am ready for a rest stop," Alex said.

"I think I see an Exxon station up ahead." Jules said.

Jules slowed down and exited. "We may as well fill her up as long as we are here." He opened the door.

"I must have fallen asleep," David said. He stretched his legs and looked around for the bathroom.

"Are we still in California?" David asked as they all returned to the car.

"Yes," answered Jules. "Just outside Barstow."

"We haven't gone very far," David said.

Alex looked at his watch. "Maria packed some sandwiches and fruit. Up ahead there is a little park with picnic tables beside the Mojave River. We could stop there for lunch. Mary and I used to go through here on the way to visit friends in Bakersfield. We often stopped here to eat our lunch."

Jules slowed down and pulled into the park. He found a table in the shade and parked next to it. David hopped out to look for rocks to throw into the water. He ran down to the water's edge and began pitching them in. He was exploring a large boulder when his father called him back.

"Grandpa has lunch ready."

*DAVID MARSHALL*

Several cars were parked near them and a van was farther up. A man and a woman were outside the van preparing lunch and a boy about David's age was walking his dog along the riverbank. He saw David and came up to their table to speak to him.

"Live around here?" he asked.

"We live in San Diego." David reached down to pet the dog. "Nice dog. What kind is he?"

"He is part collie and part beagle, I think. I call him Plunder because he is always plundering around where he has no business."

"That's a great name. We are going to Alabama. Where are you headed?"

"New Orleans. But we're spending the night in Needles."

"So are we. Maybe we will see you there."

"What is your name?" the boy asked.

When David told him his name, the boy laughed. "That's my name too. David...David Marshall."

"All right!" The boys slapped hands.

"DAVID!" called the boy's mother. "Come on, lunch is ready." David Marshall said, "See you later." He hurried to his van.

"We may see him again. We are headed the same direction," Jules said.

They heard the dog barking from down beside the river near the boulder, where David had been before. David Marshall and his mother and father ran down to see what Plunder was barking at.

"It's a turtle just sitting on a little ledge under that boulder." David's mother said. "Call Plunder. He will disturb the turtle."

"COME BACK PLUNDER! Come back now."

Several picnickers stood watching near the water's edge. The turtle slowly slipped into the water and swam away.

I didn't know turtles could swim," David said. "I thought they'd drown in water."

"They can swim. Many turtles live in the water." Alex said. He walked back to the table, picked up the picnic things, and took them to the car. "I think we'd better get started again."

"Would you like to sit in the back seat for a while?" Jules asked his father. "You could take a nap while I drive."

Driving had made Alex a bit sleepy, so he welcomed the opportunity to relax for a while.

David sat in the front seat with his dad. He waved to his new friend as they passed. Alex sat up until they got to Route 40 and started across the desert. Mountains loomed in the background. He settled back on the pillow and closed his eyes.

"Do you think you will always live in California?" David asked his father.

"I've never really thought of living anywhere else. I was born in Santee."

"In school, we talked about the fault lines. Wouldn't it be safer in another part of the country?"

"Well there are dangers wherever you live. In other places there are snowstorms, hurricanes, and floods. It takes hearty people to live in New England and Minnesota, where temperatures of twenty and thirty below zero are common. We have warm beaches, incredible scenery and not too many bad storms. How do you feel about where we live?

"I might want to live somewhere else when I grow up," David admitted.

This surprised Jules. He looked forward to his son coming into the business with him.

"It's just that there would be no way to escape a really bad earthquake," David said. "Everything you own could be destroyed in a few minutes. Everyone you know could be killed."

"I didn't realize you were concerned about earthquakes. I suppose a lot of people think it isn't going to happen. Of course many buildings are supposed to be earthquake proof. I wouldn't worry if I were you." They were quiet for a while.

"How much further to Needles?" David asked wearily.

"Less than a hundred miles. Are you getting tired?"

"I was too excited to sleep last night. Can I take a short nap?" David asked.

"Go right ahead." Jules said.

Jules reached over to tune the radio. He fiddled with the knobs for a minute and pressed the scan button. He found a Las Vegas station with excellent reception. He smiled. *Pop sure got a powerful radio with his new car.*

Jules thought about the conversation with his son. He couldn't remember how long it had been since he and David had talked like this. David was growing up and he was missing it because he hadn't taken the time to talk.

Yet, it wasn't entirely his fault. David was always on the go. After dinner he watched TV or played computer games. Then he did his homework. On Saturdays, he watched cartoons after breakfast and ran out to play when they were over. Sometimes on Sundays the family went out together, but even then David asked a friend to go along.

Jules missed Agnes. He was thankful for a second chance with a wonderful woman. They allowed each other to pursue their own career and the time that they had together was precious. Being away from her for a month was going to be the only thing that would mar this trip. She was flying over to be with them on the return trip.

The scenery was tedious, mile after mile of sand and dried grass and cactus, and an occasional clump of mesquite trees. Mountains they drove over were bare and uninteresting. A sign on the roadside said forty-two more miles to Needles.

Jules glanced into the rear-view mirror and noticed a van with a California license plates approaching. He reached over and shook David gently. David sat up and rubbed his eyes.

"What is it?" he asked. "Where are we?"

"Look behind us," Jules said. David turned around and smiled. He watched as the van overtook them and waved as they passed. They followed the van for several miles until it signaled that it was turning off the highway. It pulled into a gas station. Jules decided to stop, too. It had been a long time since lunch and he wanted something to drink.

David Marshall was already out of the van and was walking toward their car. "We are going to a campsite near Needles," he said. "Where are you going to spend the night?"

"We have reservations at a motel in Needles," David said, "The Sunset Motel." The boys stood talking while their fathers filled their gas tanks. David Marshall had Plunder on a leash and they played with him.

David Presswood walked around with his friend and talked about the trip. Alex woke up. He smiled when he saw the van and the two boys walking together. They went over to a fence to check out the farm animals penned behind the station. They had drinks and potato chips and were laughing at the animals.

## *AN OLD FRIEND*

Alex stepped out of the car and stretched. "Riding makes an old man stiffen up," he said to Jules.

"Younger men get kind of stiff too," Jules laughed. "Did you enjoy your nap?"

"Sure did. Where are we?"

"Not far from Needles."

Alex headed for the restroom, and then stepped into the station. He noted the name on a shingle over the door. William Walker. Alex looked at it again. That name sounds familiar somehow. William Walker, Bill Walker.

"Bill Walker, is that you?" he asked the man.

"Sure is," Bill answered.

"I might know you," Alex said when he heard the voice. "I'm Alex Presswood."

"Yes, you do." he waited for Alex to place him. Alex smiled.

"You don't look like anyone I know, but your name and your voice. . ."

"We were neighbors in Los Angeles thirty, maybe forty years ago. My wife is Julie and my son is Steve."

Bill walked around the counter to face Alex. "Bill Walker!"

The two men embraced. "What a surprise to find you here!"

"I retired from Western Electric a few years ago. Julie's family lives in this area, so we came back here. Come over to the house. Julie would be so happy to see you.

"Where is Mary?"

"Mary passed on. Jules and his son, David, are going on a trip to Alabama with me."

Bill expressed condolences. "Let me call Julie. She can be down here in a couple of minutes. Don't leave until she gets here." He reached for the phone.

Julie was delighted to see Alex and Jules. The young boy she had cared for in her home many years ago had grown into a handsome man with a son of his own. She hugged Jules and kissed David's cheek.

"Come over to the house," Julie said. "Spend the night. We have so much to talk about."

"Thank you," Alex said, "but we must go ahead. We have reservations at the Sunset in Needles and we'd better push on." Alex knew that Jules and David would be more comfortable in a motel.

"Nice place," Julie said, "but I wish you would stay with us." Alex insisted that they go on after exchanging addresses and promising to get in touch when he returned from Alabama. Alex, Jules, and David resumed their travel, hoping to reach Needles in time for a swim at the motel before dinner.

Alex told Jules and David about the Walker family. He told them about the accident that almost cost Steve his life. "They had three more children after they left L.A.," Alex said. He remembered how much Mary had loved their little girl and wanted one just like her, but that never happened.

"You never know where you will meet someone," Jules said. "How fortunate that you noticed the name over the door."

"Incredible," Alex said. "Bill and Julie were wonderful. Julie took care of you while your mother worked. And she was there for us when Mom lost the baby."

"Friends are important when there are problems. I could not have made it through my divorce if I hadn't had good friends to lean on."

"That is so true," Alex said under his breath. Both men were silent as they thought about times in their lives when grief brought them to their knees and held them there until little by little, time smoothed over the wounds and gave them strength to resume their normal lives. Strong and loving friends had stood by them and helped to ease the pain.

*TRAVELERS IN NEED*

"What is this?" Alex said as their car drove past a man and woman with three children walking beside the road, each carrying a bundle or suitcase. Their faces looked grim and tired, their shoulders bent over, and their steps faltering. "They look like refugees from a foreign country."

They were approaching their destination, Needles, California, and Jules had his eyes peeled for the Sunset Motel where they planned to spend the night. "I'm ready for a hot bath and a nice soft bed," he said. "I'd like to rest a while before dinner." Alex spotted the motel at the edge of the town.

It was daylight now and would continue to be light for at least an hour, giving them time for a quick walk into town and a swim in the pool before dark. It took only a few minutes to check in and find their room.

Since Jules wanted to lie down, Alex and David went into the town by themselves. David looked into the shop windows. He kept a sharp eye out for his new friend, David Marshall, and his dog Plunder. Alex inquired about the campgrounds and was directed to a trailer park east of town. Behind the trailers were sites for mobile homes and a few tents.

"I expect your friends will be pitching a tent," Alex said. "Their van didn't seem large enough for beds and tables."

"I think it was big enough for three people to sleep in," David said.

"You are probably right," Alex said. "They should be here already because they left the gas station ahead of us."

"They may have stopped to eat somewhere," David said. "Maybe we should ask in the office. We know their van and the license number.

Alex laughed, "You'll make a fine detective, David. "That is a lot to go on."

When they found the office, several people were in the room waiting to be helped. Standing at the counter was a man, a woman, and three children. Alex recognized them at once as the group he had seen walking beside the highway a few miles back. He realized that there was a problem when he heard the clerk say that he would have to call the manager. The man asked for a place to pitch his tent for the night. He said that he had no car. The clerk didn't know if he could rent space if there was no automobile license number. The manager said they could pitch their tent for twelve dollars, but they would have to pay extra for the use of the bathhouse. It was obvious that the family was in trouble. Alex saw the manager shake his head and turn them away when they could not pay. He followed them out the door and introduced himself as a fellow traveler.

"You seem to be having a bit of bad luck," Alex said.

"You can't imagine it," the man said. "I am having trouble grasping what has happened to us."

"It is late and you don't seem to have a place to pitch your tent," Alex said. "I might be able to help you if you care to tell me why you are traveling on foot and can't pay twelve dollars for a night's lodging."

"We have had a streak of bad luck." He seemed reluctant to talk about it. "Until three months ago, I had a good-paying job. My wife had a job. I got laid off one day and she got it the next. I had worked in the warehouse for Pacific Northwest for seventeen years, but along with 120 other employees, I was told that I was no longer needed. My wife was a waitress at a small sandwich shop nearby that closed its doors at the same time. We had hospital bills that we could not pay. Our mortgage company foreclosed, and our car was repossessed.

"I thought I was set for life. We had a nice home, a nice car, and everything we needed. Then the bottom fell out. I didn't know that something like this could happen so quickly. I have spent every day since the day I was laid off looking for a job. There just aren't any jobs to be found."

"Where are you going now?" Alex asked. "My wife's family

lives in Albuquerque. I am hoping to find a job here in Needles or in a town farther along the way to make enough money to pay for bus tickets to Albuquerque. We didn't tell our relatives just how desperate we really are, but it looks like we are going to have to ask for help. My family could have stayed with friends until I found work, but they all insisted on coming with me."

Was he telling the truth? Alex had heard stories about freeloaders traveling across the country living off other people, telling pitiful tales of woe. But these people seemed genuine. He had heard of the downsizing at Pacific Northwest. He knew how bad luck snowballs once it gets started. The wife stood respectfully beside her husband. The children sat quietly on the ground nearby. Alex thought that one night's lodging would be no sacrifice for him. He gave generously to charitable organizations, but seldom had the opportunity to help an individual. His mother had offered food to anyone who came to her door, never doubting them, and always feeling good after she did it.

"It seems that you have had enough bad luck for today. Wait here. I will pay for your lodging tonight." After making arrangements, Alex said, "Go ahead set up your tent for the night. Then come on over to the restaurant at the *Sunset Motel*. I would like to have you as my guests for dinner. We'll be ready to eat in about an hour."

"Thank you. I will find a way to repay you for your kindness. My name is Joseph Fullerton. My wife is Rachael, and our children are John, Betty, and Linda."

"I'm Alex Presswood and my grandson is David."

Alex and David went back to the motel. Jules was waiting for them. He had showered and dressed, and was cleaning out the car. Alex told him about the family he had helped. He expected Jules to admonish him for being taken, but Jules said very little.

"I suppose a night's lodging and a hot meal won't break you," Jules said. "Even if they do turn out to be fakers."

"I know you take a chance when you try to help a stranger," Alex said, "but I find it hard to turn my back on a hungry family."

At the restaurant, they sat at a table near the door. After ten minutes a couple and a young boy came through the door. David jumped up and rushed to meet his friend.

"We looked for you over at the campgrounds," David said. "Where were you?"

"My dad wanted to get his tires rotated. We had to drive five miles out of town to find someone to do it" David Marshall explained.

"Sit with us," Alex invited.

The Marshalls were looking at the menu when the Fullerton family arrived. Alex introduced everybody. The Marshalls were cordial. They talked about the weather, the long day's ride, and things they had seen along the way. Everyone seemed comfortable. Alex quietly told Mr. Fullerton to order anything they would like to have.

As the meal progressed, Mr. Fullerton talked more about his being laid off and the foreclosure.

"Do you have furniture?" Mrs. Marshall asked.

"Yes. It was all paid for, thank goodness. Instead of selling it we put it in storage until we can get another house. I couldn't bear to part with our beautiful pieces. I know we will get back on our feet. My husband has a good education. He'll find a job, somewhere." Rachael Fullerton had not spoken before, but after relaxing and eating, she felt better. She seemed more confident.

"I am hoping I can find a job. I will do anything to make enough to pay for bus fare to Albuquerque. I just can't believe how fast all of this happened. We had a little money in the bank, but that disappeared in the weeks we had no income. We spent most of what was left putting the furniture into storage. Unfortunately, most of our friends were in the same boat we were. They all left for friends and relatives in different parts of the country."

Shirley Marshall said, "I have a suggestion. We are going right through Albuquerque. We will be there tomorrow. We would have to rearrange a few things in our van, but we could probably make room for all of you." Turning to her husband, she asked, "What do you think?"

"I have been thinking along those lines myself, but I am not sure all of us could fit. He asked Joseph Fullerton, "Would you mind being crowded? It would be for only one day, less than a day, actually."

"That would be a huge imposition on you. We can't ask you to make such a sacrifice."

"We will be happy to do it," Stan Marshall said. "I think it is a good idea."

"It stinks." David cried.

"David!" his mother said.

"I mean it. It stinks. I won't be able to lie down or play with Plunder."

"We will make do. It will be just fine." Stan said. "We will wait for you tomorrow morning. I hope to get started about six o'clock, if you think you can be ready by then." He took David by the arm and led him to the men's room for a man-to-man talk.

In a few minutes, David and his father returned. David walked up to Mr. and Mrs. Fullerton and said, "I am sorry. I will be happy to have you travel with us."

"We appreciate your apology, David. We are sorry to impose. It will mean a lot to have my family off the road and safe," Joseph Fullerton said.

Alex paid for his and the Fullertons' dinner and began walking toward his room. "We'll see you in the morning," he said. "We want to get an early start too. Good-night."

The next morning they all met at the restaurant for breakfast before starting their day's travels. Jules wasn't surprised to see his father slip a hundred dollar bill into Joseph's hand.

"The best of luck to you," he said.

"Thank you" Joseph said quietly.

## *A SNAKE IN THE DESERT*

"Dad, are we going to Albuquerque?" asked David.

"Yes, I believe we are," Jules said.

David turned to his grandfather. "Grandpa, could we let David ride with us to Albuquerque? It would give them more room in the van."

Alex looked at Jules. "Why not?" Jules said. David Marshall ran to ask his parents permission.

"Where can we meet you?" Stan Marshall asked. "I don't know a thing about Albuquerque."

"Let's look at our road maps," Alex said. "There is a small

town just west of Albuquerque called Jaquna. We can meet there."

"Perfect," Stan said. "How long do you suppose it will take us to get there?"

Alex looked at the map and thought for a few seconds. "I think we should make it by three or three-thirty if there are no delays."

"We'll probably see you along the way. We'll watch for you."

"O.K. See you later." Alex drove as they started out of town.

"Maybe we should fill our gas tank," Jules said. "There might not be any stations along the way."

"Good idea. I always like to start the day with a full tank."

They filled the tank at a MOBIL Station at the edge of town, and were on the road again in a matter of minutes.

The boys settled down in the back seat. "Let's count animals," David Presswood suggested and David Marshall quickly agreed.

At first they enjoyed the scenery, but soon the occasional tree became non-existent. They could see for miles across the dry Arizona wasteland of sky and grass. There were hills and in the distance, tall bare mountains rose on the horizon. Desert flowers and shrubs caught their attention at first, but after mile after mile of sameness, the travelers became weary of the sand and tumbleweeds blowing on the desert floor. They changed drivers often and slept when they weren't driving.

The boys played games. They talked about their favorite teams, and exchanged a few jokes they had heard. Both of them fell asleep.

Most of the time the van was within their view. When they came to a tiny village in the desert, Alex slowed down and turned off. The van followed.

"I thought we might be able to get a bite to eat here." Alex got out and stretched. Jules and the two Davids woke up and got out of the car. David Marshall ran over to greet his parents as they climbed out of the van.

David called to Plunder and he began to bark. He put Plunder's leash on and began walking him along the road. Before David's mother could call a warning to him about rattlesnakes, one had lunged at Plunder and hit him in the neck. David jerked the leash and began dragging Plunder to the car, crying and screaming to his dad to help him. The snake slithered away into the brown grass. In a matter of minutes the dog was dead. They poured water on the shivering animal, but it was too late.

David's mother was holding her sobbing little boy and saying over and over, "It could have been you." She led him to the van and sat with him on the seat, hugging him and trying to comfort him. Everyone stood around, not knowing what to say.

A man came out of the building, which was a combination gas station, restaurant, truck stop, and grocery store. He offered to take the dog and bury it in back of the building. He said he had lost his dog the same way when he was a boy and he knew how it felt. He picked Plunder up and carried him gently around to the rear of the store. Mr. Marshall followed him and helped him find a box the right size. They put the dog in the box and covered him with a blanket that Rachael Fullerton found among her things. She had tears in her eyes as she watched the man dig a hole and place the box in it. David was still in the car being comforted by his mother who was trying desperately to distract David by talking about getting him another dog as soon as they got back home. She did not want David to see what the men were doing with the dog.

"I don't feel like eating now," Alex said. "I think I will buy something that we can eat in the car and some drinks. I'd better fill the gas tank, too, in case we don't come to another gas station before we run out."

"I suppose it is better to be safe than sorry," Jules said although he thought they had enough gas for several more hours.

"I am very sorry about the little dog," he added, "but I think I had better eat something while we are here. It has been a long time since breakfast." He went in and ordered a sandwich and a salad.

"I can't eat right now," David said. "I am still too upset. It really could have been David who was bitten by that snake." He walked over to the van to see how David Marshall was getting along, watching every step he made.

"There will never be another dog like Plunder," David Marshall said. "I've had him since he was three weeks old and I loved him so much. He was like a brother, since I don't have a brother."

"We'll get you another dog," Shirley Marshall said again. "I know it can't take Plunder's place, but you will learn to love another dog just as much as you loved Plunder."

At last Alex said, "I suppose we had better get going. We do want to get to Albuquerque before dark."

"Do you want to continue riding with us?" Jules asked David Marshall, "or do you want to be with your parents?"

"I'll go on with you," David said. "I am enjoying riding in your car."

They all returned to their vehicles and started on the next leg of their journey. Everybody shared David's grief, but were thankful that the boy had not been hurt.

It took eight hours to travel from Needles to Jaquna. Jules stopped at the cafe at the edge of town and waited until the van arrived. The boys, who had talked excitedly and played travel games, had become good friends. They had enjoyed each other's company and promised to call when they got back home.

Joseph Fullerton shook Alex's hand and thanked him for all he had done. "We are in familiar territory now," he said, "at least for my wife. I have a good feeling about coming here. I want you to know that I appreciate your kindness."

Alex handed Joseph one of his business cards. "We will be back in Santee in a few weeks. If I can be of further help, feel free to call. I may be able to help you find a job if you are unsuccessful in locating one in Albuquerque. They shook hands again and said good-bye.

"Do you think we will ever see the Marshalls or the Fullertons again?" David asked.

"It's hard to say. We could meet the Marshalls somewhere up the road; maybe stop at the same restaurant or motel. We are following the same route until they drop down to New Orleans," Jules said.

"How much farther is it to Atmore?" David asked.

Jules looked at the map. "Over a thousand miles. We've planned a good three or four days continual driving," Jules said. "Longer if we decide to do some sightseeing. You aren't getting tired of riding, are you?"

"I was just asking," David said.

Jules studied the map. "I think we can get to Oklahoma City by noon tomorrow and in Dallas by tomorrow night."

"Dallas!" David exclaimed. "Can we go downtown and see where President Kennedy was assassinated?"

"Yes," Alex said. "I'd like to see it. When I heard that Kennedy was shot, I was having coffee in San Carlos. Walter Chronkite made the announcement on TV. Everybody bolted out the door. I did too. Everyone wanted to get home and turn on his own TV to see if it was really true. We all went back the next day to pay our bills. During the whole week that followed, it was the only thing on television. We saw lines of people, filing past the closed casket to pay their respects. We saw the cortege as it made its way to Arlington Cemetery."

David was listening, but he was having shortness of breath. "Did you pack my inhaler?" David asked.

"Sure did," Jules said. "Do you need it?"

"I'm starting to have a little trouble breathing," David said.

"The air out here is thinner," Jules said. "I'll get your inhaler when we stop."

At last they came to a restaurant that looked inviting. Alex drove in and stopped the car. David looked to see if the Marshall's van was parked there, but he didn't see it. Alex caught the glance. "They probably won't stop until they have made arrangements to meet Rachael Fullerton's sister."

David laughed, "How did you know what I was thinking?"

"I guess I was kind of wondering, too."

Jules opened the trunk and unzipped a suitcase. He pulled out a little bag that contained an inhaler. David took one puff on the inhaler and handed it back to his dad. "I'll be all right now."

After dinner and a cup of coffee, Jules felt wide awake. "I'll drive and you can rest," he said to Alex, who accepted the offer.

"I'll have a nap then," Alex said. "David, would you like to sit in front?"

Jules stayed behind the wheel for the next two hours, having a wonderful conversation with his son. David talked about his friends, his schoolwork, and some things he liked to do. Jules was thrilled to have this time alone with David while his father slept in the back seat.

He began thinking about a place to spend the night. A road sign mentioned the Holiday Inn in Santa Rosa, New Mexico. It was forty miles ahead. "We can probably make it to Santa Rosa in thirty-five or forty minutes," he said to David. "We can stop there."

After checking in and finding their room, David and Jules decided to cool off in the pool. A few other guests were also in the pool area, swimming or sitting around resting and talking.

Alex was fast asleep when Jules and David came into the room. They got up early the next morning and pushed on toward Dallas. Driving steadily, they reached Dallas by 4:00. They found a motel on the outskirts of Dallas and checked in before going into the city.

"Can we see South Fork?" Jules asked. He admitted that he had watched almost every episode of the TV program Dallas with Agnes.

"We'll make a point of it," Alex said.

"I have an idea," Jules said. "Let's drive downtown and hop on a tour bus. It will be a lot easier than trying to find our way around. We will see more than going on our own."

"One of your better ideas," Alex agreed. "We will be much better off on a tour bus."

"When are we going to eat?" David asked. "I am hungry."

"Let's check on the tours first, and then we'll plan our meal. O.K.?" Jules said. "Our tour guide will be able to direct us to a nice place to eat. I think there is a pack of cheese crackers in the glove compartment. You may have it."

"O.K." David said.

The tour lasted four hours. It included the spot at the corner of Houston and Main Streets where Kennedy was assassinated, the John F. Kennedy Plaza, and the Sixth Floor Exhibit. They examined the displays of artifacts depicting the life, death, and legacy of the thirty-fifth President of the United States. The tour guide recommended a restaurant where they enjoyed Texas T-bone steak with all the trimmings.

Then the three tired travelers made their way back to their motel for a good night's rest. They had received directions to South Fork and planned to drive past it on their way out of the city. They hoped to have a tour of the beautiful home.

"I'd like to spend a whole vacation in Dallas," Jules said. "There is so much to see here. And I would like another Texas T-bone."

*ON TO ATMORE*

Before they went to bed, David asked for his inhaler again. He coughed for a minute or two. Jules handed David his inhaler and watched to make sure he felt better. David inhaled deeply, and then lay down on the bed. He had to be reminded to brush his teeth and put on his pajamas before he fell asleep.

"I am glad we have just two more days of driving," Alex said. "I am getting a little bone-weary."

"Do you think you will recognize any of your old friends?" asked Jules.

"I doubt it. I don't resemble my high school yearbook picture at all. I expect everyone else will have changed too." Alex thought about Horace Bailey and Jim Masters and Bill Simmons. He hadn't heard from any of his friends since graduation. Everybody had scattered so quickly.

He sighed when he thought of Jeannie. He went to sleep thinking of her and wondering why she had suddenly married someone else when they had planned their future so carefully. Maybe she would be at the reunion and they could talk.

Jules asked if they could sleep a little longer the next morning. "Yesterday's activities knocked me out. I had a good time, but I am still tired." When they got into the car later, he said, "I picked up a couple of tapes for us to listen to today. Maybe they will make the time go faster. Agnes and I listen to tapes when we go on trips."

The trip went smoothly that day. They found a motel in Jackson, Mississippi. David used his inhaler again and they all had a good night's rest.

When they got up the next morning, Alex said, "Well, we should be in Atmore by this evening."

When they walked out of their door, David shouted, "Look! There is the Marshall's van." He ran around the van to check the license plate.

"I don't believe this," Jules said. "Of all of the places they could have stopped, they chose the same motel we did. Unbelievable!"

"Let's go to the office and see if we can find out which room they are in," Alex said.

David urged his grandfather to hurry up. He pulled him along in his haste to inquire about his friend. His grandfather gently admonished him.

"I am sorry, Grandpa. I just want to see David again."

"I am sure you are, but be patient. We'll be there in a minute."

As they approached the door to the office, David saw a boy with a little white puppy on a leash. His back was turned toward David, but David knew at once who it was. He ran up to David and hugged him.

"Where did you come from?" David Marshall cried.

"We spent the night here. We saw your van when we came out of our room. Where did you get the puppy?"

"We stopped in Oklahoma City and went to a pet shop. My mother bought him for me. "

"He is beautiful."

"I missed Plunder so much that they let me have another dog even before we got back home."

Alex and Jules had gone on into the office. Breakfast was being served. The Marshall's were eating. Mr. Marshall jumped up and shook their hands when he saw them.

"I am so glad to see you," Stan Marshall said. "We had no problem finding the Fullertons sister's house. It was only a couple of blocks out of our way, so we took them right to the door. Her sister insisted that we stay for dinner which she had ready when we got there. She thought they could find a job for Joseph in a day or two. Rachael's sister works for an employment agency. She says there are many job openings in the area."

"That is great," Alex said.

"And we got David a dog," Stan said. "I couldn't stand to see that sad face any longer, so we stopped in Oklahoma City and bought him another puppy."

"I think what happened taught us all a lesson. I will certainly be more careful about where I walk in the desert. You never know where one of those horrible creatures might be hiding."

"It happened so quickly. I didn't even see David put the leash on the dog. Poor kid. He acted like he had lost the only friend he had. Now he has a new pet and he is happy."

Jules and Alex had toast and coffee in the motel lobby.

The two Davids came in, both of them holding onto the puppy's leash. They showed the puppy to Alex and Jules.

"I think we'd better hit the road," Stan Marshall said.

"We expect to be in New Orleans by noon." He shook Alex's hand. "I'm glad we happened to meet again. We have shared in a very satisfying experience. I just hope the Fullertons will have better luck from now on."

"So do I. Nobody needs that kind of luck."

On the way to the car, David said, "What did you name your puppy?"

"Barker. He barks at everything," David Marshall jumped into the van. Everybody waved as the van pulled out of the parking space. Alex followed them out. David talked non-stop about the puppy as they rode along. It wasn't long before he asked for his inhaler.

"You have been using that inhaler quite a bit lately," his father said. "Do you suppose you might be allergic to dogs?"

"Oh, no," David said. "I'm sure it isn't the dog."

"Well, we can't be too careful. We don't want you to have a serious attack."

"I'm O.K., Dad." But Jules was concerned.

"There's a sign for Mobile, only fifty miles away." Alex said. He was getting edgy as they got closer.

"Dad, I think my inhaler is used up."

"Let me see it." Jules examined the inhaler. He squeezed it and nothing came out. "How do you feel?"

"I'm alright now. I think I will be O.K. if I just lie still. I'll try to sleep."

"Do you want to stop and look for an inhaler?" Alex asked.

"Since we are only a couple of hours from Atmore, let's go ahead rather than try to find one here. Most druggists need a doctor's prescription to sell one. We can find a doctor to help us in Atmore." Jules replied.

"Don't worry. I'm fine." David continued to lie on his back as they drove along.

"This is a nice highway," Alex said as they speeded along Route 65. When I was a boy it took a long time to go from Atmore to Mobile. We drove on narrow two-lane roads and some areas weren't even paved." They approached the bridge across the Tombigbee River. "Now that is impressive," Jules said. "Do you suppose ships go up this river?"

"The Tombigbee and the Alabama Rivers join somewhere along

here. There may be large vessels using this waterway." They rode through a wooded area for about fifteen minutes then Jules said, "Looks like our trip is almost over."

Alex said, "The next Exit is for Atmore. And there is our Motel, *The Best Western*. But it doesn't look right." he said. "I see no evidence of a town."

"We'll find out." Jules pulled up to the motel office. "Atmore is about five miles south of here," said the motel clerk. Route 65 bypasses Atmore by about that distance."

"Oh, I see," Alex said. "So the interstate didn't follow the old Highway 31?"

"No. Highway 31 is still a main highway going from Montgomery to Mobile, straight through Atmore. Most people use the Interstate though because it faster."

"I can't wait to see the old town," Alex said.

"Here are two keys. Room number 117. Drive around to the back. You'll find parking in the rear of the building. Have a pleasant evening. We stay open all night. And the restaurant is open until eleven."

David coughed and began gasping for breath. They would have to drive into Atmore to try to get an inhaler for him.

"There were three drug stores in Atmore when I lived here," Alex said.

"You'd better hurry," the motel clerk said. "The Escambia Drug Store is the only drug store in town now, just over the railroad tracks. But it closes soon."

At the Escambia Drug Store, Jules was told that he should take David to the hospital for treatment.

That is where they met Dr. Daniel Anderson and his mother, Jeannie Carlson Anderson. Alex now knew that Daniel Anderson was his son and that Jeannie had kept his existence a secret for fifty years.

## *THE REUNION*
## BACK TO REALITY

Alex sat in the auditorium of the old Escambia County High School, which was now the headquarters for the Atmore Chamber of Commerce, thinking, remembering. It had been a long time since he had sat in this room with his classmates. His childhood hopes and dreams had all faded away. Yet, there was hope for the future.

Life would have been different if his country had not been engaged in a war; one that took him from his family, his friends, and his life. Most of his family members had passed away: his father, in an automobile accident, Jed in the Korean War, and his mother, old age and finally cancer. His sisters were still living. He'd see them soon.

Alex stood up and walked quickly back to the car where Jules and David were waiting. He would stop at the drug store for an inhaler for David. Then they would drive back to the Best Western. There would be time for a swim after lunch before keeping his two o'clock appointment with Jeannie. He could hardly contain himself.

### *JEANNIE AND ALEX TALK*

Alex was waiting in the driveway when Jeannie came home from the hospital. Daniel had arranged for her transportation and he sent a nurse along to help her. It did not surprise Alex that Daniel was a doctor since he had wanted so much to be a doctor when he was young. It seemed natural for his son to be led in that direction.

Alex opened the door for Jeannie and helped her out of the car. He kissed her cheek and offered his arm for her to lean on.

"Thank you, Alex, but I really don't need help. My doctors treat me like a baby." She reached for his hands instead and stood looking at him. She dismissed the nurse and sent the ambulance away.

Mrs. Baker, Jeannie's housekeeper, met them at the door. She hugged Jeannie. "Do you want to lie down?" Mrs. Baker asked.

"I am a little out of breath. I probably need to be near my oxygen tank in case I need it."

Mrs. Baker settled Jeannie in her bed while Alex looked around. This was the same living room where he and Jeannie played Bridge with her parents. Some things had changed, but it was still recognizable. In a few minutes, he was asked to join Jeannie. He pulled up a chair and sat down.

"I feel fine, really I do." Jeannie smiled. "I get panicky sometimes when I am left alone, and call my doctor. When I called Thursday night, he insisted that I check into the hospital just to be sure that I was all right. He wanted me to stay until Daniel returned from Montgomery. He takes good care of me. I plan to go to the reunion dinner tonight. I just have to rest for a while. They fuss over me too much."

"How long have you had emphysema?"

"I was diagnosed about eight months ago. I have been in the hospital several times and I have this oxygen tank here in case I need it. I have an inhaler that I carry with me when I go out."

"I am so sorry, Jeannie. I feel so responsible for this happening to you."

"I am sure I would have started smoking in college if we hadn't decided to try it when we did. Do you still smoke?"

"I gave up long ago. My wife didn't smoke and that made it easy for me to quit."

"I am glad you did. I enjoyed it and I continued the habit until I got sick."

"Let's talk about what you have been doing." Alex reached for her hand. He had not noticed the diamond ring Jeannie wore until that moment. Alex caught his breath.

"Jeannie," he whispered, "don't tell me I have come too late. Oh, God, Jeannie."

"Your showing up now certainly gives me something to think about."

"Bill Simmons?" Alex stared at the ring.

"Yes," she whispered. "He is my doctor."

"Bill Simmons! The doctor who saw my grandson? I didn't recognize him."

"Bill and his wife were divorced several years ago. We have been dating for nearly a year."

"I have loved you for a long time, Jeannie. Forever. I had no real expectations when I decided to come to this reunion, but I was hoping that I would see you and we would be able to talk. I wanted to know what happened. Why you dropped me and married another. I think I have pieced together some details now that I have met Daniel, but I would like you to tell me."

"Alex, when I realized that I was pregnant and that you were so far away, I had to do something to save my reputation and my family's reputation as well as that of my unborn child. There were fewer options open for me then than there are for girls today. I took the first solution that presented itself. I didn't even tell my husband that I was pregnant when we were married. We met. We dated a few times. He proposed, and I accepted."

"What happened when he found out you were pregnant?"

"I faked that at first. I told him that the baby wasn't due for nine months, but he found out about that too. Instead of kicking me out, he accepted the baby as his own if I would promise to stay married and to build a life with him. That is when I wrote you and accepted the fact that you and I could never be together."

Alex couldn't move. He finally knew. It had been his fault. He had never guessed.

"I was awfully dumb not to have guessed. You should have told me."

"Your letter said that you were being shipped out. You couldn't tell me where you were going or when you would be back. I was scared. I did the first thing that came to me." Jeannie sobbed.

Alex held her in his arms and cried. "You went through so much alone. I am so sorry."

"After Daniel was born, Walter accepted him as his own and everyone else did too."

"Did Daniel know?"

"I did not think so, but he told me this morning that Walter had told him. I was relieved."

"Tell me about your life."

"Walter was a wonderful husband and father. We had a good life until he died. He was a lawyer and I taught school. After Walter died, I made enough teaching to see me through and I retired with enough to live on."

"You haven't told me anything about yourself, Alex. You were obviously married. You mentioned your son. Tell me about your wife."

"Yes, I was married to a wonderful girl. I met her in San Diego after my leave from boot camp. We had one son, Jules, who came with me on this trip and a grandson, David. We had a happy life, but Mary passed away about a year ago.

"I was never able to come back to Atmore in all of those years. I wanted desperately to come to Jed's funeral. He was killed in Korea. But I was in the hospital when his body was returned. We planned a trip nearly every year, but something always happened to prevent it. After a while, Mama started coming to California every summer and sometimes Marge came with her. Mary was in the hospital when Mama died and I couldn't leave her."

"I am so sorry about Jed. Your mother told me about that."

"You saw my mother? You talked with her?" Alex was surprised.

"Yes, I saw your mother every time I came home. I made a point of visiting her and letting her see Danny."

"When I moved back to Atmore after Walter died, I taught in the same school your mother did. We became good friends."

"She never told me."

"When he was older, Danny would go over to your mother's house by himself. She loved Danny, but she never told him that she was his grandmother. She never told anyone. It was our secret."

"She didn't tell me."

"I am sure she felt it was better that you didn't know about Daniel. We had our own lives. Knowing about him might have upset your family. Walter knew your mother and I were friends, but I never told him the relationship.

"Then one day I ran into Bill Simmons at the Post Office. We talked. He said he had practiced medicine in Brewton most of his life. He has changed, Alex. You would like him."

"No, I wouldn't, especially now that you are involved with him. He has always been my enemy. I cannot make myself believe that this is possible. I'll do anything, Jeannie. I'll move to Atmore or take you to California or to any place you might want to go. This should never have happened to us. We loved each other and we should have been together. The war did this to us. The war changed our lives. Let's change it back."

"Alex, we lived through the situations that changed our lives. My love for you had to die. I had to love the man who accepted my son as his own. I could not allow myself to think of you."

"Jeannie, I had to accept that you had married someone else. It never entered my mind that you were pregnant, never. There is nothing I could have done if I had known. But now we are both single. We could, even now, have some time together. I want to marry you." Looking at the ring he said, "I hope I can convince you to change your mind."

"I am not sure of my feelings. I had no doubts about marrying Bill. But now...I will think about your proposal. I can't make a decision yet. Bill is my doctor and I rely on him."

"There are other doctors."

"I know."

"You need rest before the dinner tonight. I will see you at school." Alex held Jeannie in his arms and felt her melt into his embrace. He caught his breath. "I love you, Jeannie." They kissed. He left.

Jeannie felt assured that Alex would not cause a scene about Bill's taking her to the reunion. Bill would pick her up at six, as planned.

As Alex was leaving Jeannie's house, he passed Bill's car in her driveway. Neither acknowledged the other.

*I suppose I have lost her again.* Alex thought. *But I won't give up. Bill Simmons hasn't won yet.*

Later Alex visited the graves of his mother, father, and Jed. He was overcome with grief.

### *JEANNIE AND BILL TALK*

Bill let himself in the side door. He knocked quietly on Jeannie's bedroom door and greeted her with a kiss.

# Reunion

"Jeannie, let's get married this afternoon. We've had our license for three weeks. Let's go ahead and tie the knot."

"But we are going to the reunion tonight. I want to see all of my old friends and catch up."

"We can get married before we go. Announce our marriage at the reunion. Surprise everyone."

Jeannie had been excited about being engaged to Bill. She loved the beautiful ring he had given her. And she might even be excited about getting married this afternoon if Alex had not shown up. But now she was having second thoughts. Life with Bill would be comfortable. He had been a very good doctor. She would be able to travel first class, drive any car she wanted, and have anything that money could buy. Bill had been kind to Jeannie. He understood her illness and he made sure she had the best of care. When she had to go to the hospital, she got the very best treatment. She knew he would be at her side when she needed him.

Jeannie liked Bill. She knew he had his faults, but everyone had faults. His habit of calling attention to himself and his accomplishments annoyed her. But he had always been that way. Even in school, he tried to put others down, especially Alex. They were never good friends and she understood why.

Jeannie looked at her ring. She had never owned anything so spectacular. Several smaller diamonds surrounded its one-karat diamond. Bill always brought her gifts when he went away on trips. He was good to her.

"This is so sudden. This afternoon? Before the reunion?"

"Please. I want this so much. You know I love you. You will make me a happy man if you will only say 'yes' today."

"I can't marry you today," Jeannie said. She wanted to say, "I can never marry you because I love Alex," but she wasn't sure. She wanted to be sure about Alex first. "I'm not ready."

"Not ready? It's so simple. We'll go to the church and have a short ceremony, and then it will be over. People do it all of the time."

"Give me a little more time. Just a week, or two. I want to regain my strength."

"You will never regain your strength, Darling. You have emphysema. I will be with you to help you through the months ahead.

I will do everything for you, Sweetheart. I will be your strength. I will be there for you to lean on forever."

"Bill, you are so sweet. I know I will be in good hands married to my doctor, but I just don't want it to happen today." She was running out of excuses, but she had another proposal to consider. Besides, Jeannie had not told Bill about Daniel. It simply never occurred to her to explain about her son. She had covered up the circumstances surrounding his birth so completely that no one knew that Alex was the biological father. Now, she knew she could not marry Bill without telling him and she didn't feel up to it at this moment.

"Jeannie, this is something I want very much. I am not asking you to do something you haven't already agreed to; it's just the date. How exciting it will be to tell everyone that you are my wife!"

"We can set a date after the reunion, but it won't be today."

"I want everybody in our class to know that we are married. It would give me so much pleasure."

Jeannie had been dating Bill for a year. She had accepted his proposal. Everything was working out just fine until Alex showed up this morning. She hadn't seen Alex for fifty years. How dare he come back and expect to pick up where it broke off fifty years ago? She was about to give in to Bill when the telephone rang.

"Hi, Jeannie, it's Lucy. Is Bill there? I want to check on his list of responses for the dinner tonight."

Jeannie handed the phone to Bill. Lucy said, "Do you have your list for tonight?"

"Sure, I have it here in my pocket."

"Read it to me," Lucy said. "I want to be sure we have name tags for everyone."

Bill began reading, "Frank Sellers, Otis Helton, Brooks Jones, Ben Haley, Alex Presswood, Dallas Rhodes- - - -." Bill read the rest of the names and hung up.

"You knew Alex was coming and you never mentioned it to me? Jeannie said. "Why didn't you tell me?"

"I guess it just skipped my mind. I didn't think you would be interested." Quickly, he said, "Now where were we? What do you think about getting married just before dinner, say about four o'clock.

Then we go to the reunion as Mr. and Mrs. William Alfred Simmons." Bill could tell by the expression on her face that he had lost ground.

"No, Bill, I will not marry you today. I am going to the reunion as Jeannie Carlson Anderson and have the time of my life."

"I'll pick you up at six then." Bill hurried out the door.

Jeannie lay back on her pillow. She had a decision to make. Bill had deliberately refrained from telling her about Alex. His scheme for them to get married before she saw Alex just didn't quite work out; though a few hours earlier, it might have. She shuddered. He lost out by procrastinating. She would have married him last weekend. How long had Bill known that Alex was coming to the reunion? Her guess was that Bill had bought the ring after he had heard that Alex was coming. He was satisfied to just date her before Alex came into the picture again.

Should she give Bill his ring back? Should she accept Alex's proposal? What did she really know about Alex? After all, it had been fifty years since she had seen him. He looked good. Was she sure that she still loved Alex? He might have changed.

Did she love Bill enough to go ahead with her plans to marry him? She had felt good about it until this morning. She wanted the comfortable life Bill could give her, but she wasn't sure she could give up Alex again.

"I have to talk to Danny," she said out loud.

### *JEANNIE AND DANIEL TALK*

Jeannie looked at her watch. The time was three o'clock. She reached for the telephone and dialled Daniel's number. "Can you come over and talk to me? I know you are busy, but I really do need to talk." She was glad to find him in his office instead of trying to relay a message through his secretary or his answering machine.

"I'll be right there." Daniel knew there was much that he and his mother needed to discuss. As he drove, he thought about his father.

Walter was the only father he had ever known. He was the greatest man in the world. While teaching Daniel to ride a bicycle, Walter had fallen when he tripped over a rock. That was the first time Danny had realized that Walter had an artificial leg. Walter had taught him to play softball and kickball. He had taught him to toss a football and had taken him fishing. He had been a Boy Scout leader, had taken him to Sunday school, gone to his school plays, his baseball and football games. He had been a perfect father, listening to his troubles, advising him, and laughing with him.

One day in his senior year in high school. Daniel was walking home from school with his friends. A neighbor's car stopped beside him. She rolled down the window and beckoned to him.

"Danny, come with me," she had said. "Come quickly." Daniel ran around to the passenger side of the car and jumped in.

"Is something wrong?" he asked. Mrs. Shirley, his neighbor hesitated. "I have something to tell you."

"What happened?" A million thoughts flew through his head. *What have I done*? he thought.

"Danny, it is your dad. He got sick at work and was taken to the hospital. Your mother is with him and she asked me to pick you up and bring you there."

"What is wrong with him?"

"A heart attack maybe. But the doctor isn't sure yet."

Danny caught his breath. "He isn't going to die is he?"

"Oh. I am sure he won't die. This is his first attack. People can have several heart attacks. Of course it could be serious. Hopefully he will just have to rest for a few days." She was talking fast as she hurried toward the hospital.

Mrs. Shirley found a parking place right away. As they walked toward the door, Danny clung to her.

"I have never been to the hospital to see anyone. I had my tonsils out, but that's not like this."

Mrs. Shirley put her arm around his shoulder." I will stay with you."

A receptionist directed them to the cardiac wing of the hospital. "Someone will meet you and tell you where to go."

In the elevator, Danny began to shake. His hands felt cold and clammy. "Danny," Mrs. Shirley cried, "Lean against the wall. We'll be there in a minute."

# Reunion

Mrs. Shirley helped Danny out of the elevator and to a chair. A nurse came to assist. "Lean over. Put your head between your legs. You'll feel better in a couple of minutes," she said.

"What happened?" the nurse asked Mrs. Shirley.

When Mrs. Shirley said that he had just found out that his father had had a heart attack, the nurse spoke harshly.

"You told him?"

"Yes. His mother asked me to bring him here. I had to tell him what had happened."

"You should have left that for the doctor. You didn't know what to say to him."

Danny raised his head. "I am glad she told me. I wanted to know why we were coming to the hospital and she told me." Danny asked to see his father.

"Not now. He can't have visitors." Danny looked at her through teary eyes. "Could you tell my mother I am here?"

"Wait here. I'll see what I can do." Danny sat quietly beside Mrs. Shirley. He held his head in his hands and cried softly.

In about ten minutes, Jeannie came out and sat down beside Danny. She put her arm around his shoulder and hugged him close.

"How is he?" Danny asked without looking at his mother.

"Daddy had a heart attack at work about an hour and a half ago. It was a bad one, but he is resting now."

"Is he going to be all right?"

"I sure hope so."

"Mom, we cannot live without Dad. He has to be all right," Danny sobbed.

Mrs. Shirley stayed with them, sitting quietly while mother and son cried together. "He has to be all right," Jeannie whispered.

A nurse came and spoke quietly to Jeannie and Danny. She said that Walter was resting and that they could go into the room one at a time. They dried their tears and walked behind the nurse. Jeannie went in first. She bent over and kissed him. She reached for his hand and squeezed it. She felt a weak squeeze in response. Walter's breathing was quick and shallow. A nurse came in and felt his pulse. His heart was beating fast, but steadily.

The nurse motioned for Jeannie to follow her into the corridor.

"The doctor wants to speak with you," she said.

"We have to try and slow his heart beat," the doctor said. "And get his temperature down. There has been a little improvement since he has been here, but not enough to give us much hope."

"What are you saying?" Jeannie cried.

"I am saying that Mr. Anderson is a very sick man. We will do everything we possibly can to help him, but I am not promising anything at this time."

Jeannie sat down.

"You have to do something. He has to get better."

"We will do all we can," the doctor said. "Prayer will help, not only for him, but for yourself as well. I am a Christian, Mrs. Anderson and I rely on help from above. So pray for me, too, and we will get through this together."

Jeannie went back into the room. "I love you," she whispered. "We will be with you every minute."

Danny appeared at the door. She motioned for him to come in. She walked on shaky legs out of the room. Danny stood beside the bed. He listened to his Dad's breathing and watched for any sign of consciousness. He leaned over and kissed his father's forehead and brushed his lips across his cheek. His face felt hot. It frightened him to see tubes taped to his father's wrist.

"We are giving him his medicine intravenously." Dr. Albert had slipped into the room. "Nurses are monitoring his heartbeat. Come outside and I will talk to you and your mother together."

"Mr. Anderson has had a serious heart attack," he said. "His secretary saw him fall over and called the hospital. We sent an ambulance and someone was working on him within minutes. Because we got to him so fast, he may have a chance of pulling through."

"Are you saying that there is a chance that he won't get over this?" Danny said.

"There is always that possibility," Dr. Albert said as kindly as he could. "We will do everything that we can do to get him back on his feet in as short a time as possible. But a lot of things are up to the Lord."

When Dr. Albert left, Jeannie said, "We'll take turns staying at his bedside in case he wakes up and wants to talk to us. There is nothing we can do but wait."

Jeannie went back into the room and sat beside Walter's bed. Danny walked around to the waiting room, got a drink of water, and picked up a magazine. He absentmindedly flipped through the pages and then laid it down.

Mrs. Shirley appeared with Danny's books. "I started to go home, but I noticed your books in the car. I thought you might want to start on your homework."

"Oh, thank you. And thank you for all you have done for us."

"Have you heard anything?"

"We talked with the doctor. He said that it is very serious, but he thinks he has a good chance of pulling through."

"Everybody will be praying for him," Mrs. Shirley said. She left.

After a long time, Danny walked down to his dad's room. He thought he would relieve his mother for a while. She was sitting quietly with her eyes closed. She heard him enter and opened her eyes. She tried to smile, but the worried look on her face remained. "How is he?" Danny asked.

"No change. He hasn't moved, but his breathing seems to be a little slower and deeper."

"Take a break." Danny sat beside the bed. His father made no sound except for inhaling and exhaling. At last Danny closed his eyes and drifted off to sleep.

"Danny," he heard his named called. He looked at his father and saw that his eyes were open.

Danny jumped up and leaned over his father. He kissed him on the forehead. "I love you, Dad."

"I love you, Son," Walter whispered haltingly. "Where is your mom?"

"She's outside in the hall, I'll get her."

"Mom, Mom," he called in a loud whisper. Jeannie came running. "He's awake. He asked for you."

Jeannie said nothing to Danny, but rushed into the room. She crept quietly to his bed and touched his arm. "Hi," she whispered.

He tried to smile. "Hi." Jeannie bent down and kissed his lips. "I love you," she said.

"I love you," he answered.

"How do you feel?" Jeannie asked.

"Not good, weak."

"Lie still and rest," Jeannie said. "We will be right here if you need us. We won't leave you for a second."

Walter went back to sleep. Jeannie sat holding his hand. Danny stood beside the chair.

"Danny, you should go try to find something to eat." Jeannie looked in her purse for money. She handed Danny a five-dollar bill.

"I'm not hungry."

"Go eat something to keep up your strength."

"O.K." Danny went to the nurse's station and asked directions to the cafeteria.

When Danny returned, his mother said that Walter had been awake and asked for him. Walter had gone back to sleep and was resting quietly now. They stood there and watched him. Jeannie smoothed the sheet and rubbed his back.

"I'll get something to eat now," Jeannie said. Danny gave her directions to the cafeteria.

"I'll call my principal, too, and tell him I won't be able to work for the rest of the week."

Danny walked to the window and looked out over the parking lot. He was able to spot his mother's car. Cars were moving slowly in and out of the parking places. He sat down beside the bed.

"Danny," he heard his father whisper. "I have to tell you something." Danny moved closer. Walter continued. "Your mother would never tell you, but I think you should know."

Danny had difficulty hearing Walter speak. He put his ear near his mouth to be sure he did not miss anything. He heard his father say, "I am not your real father, your biological father. Your mother and I were married before you were born, so I have loved you as my own son from the moment you were born. I thought I should tell you so your mother would not have to. Your mother is a wonderful woman. She loved another man before we met. Your biological father was in the Navy and was shipped out during the war before she knew that she was going to have a baby. She married me and never told anyone. I love you and I love your mother." Walter looked at his son through half closed eyes. There were no tears.

"Dad, I love you. You are the best father a boy could ever have. I am glad you told me but I will never tell anyone else. You will get better, Dad. You have to."

Danny held his father's arm. He had trouble comprehending what he had just heard. The fact that Walter was not his real father had no effect on the way he felt about him. He loved Walter and always would. His only concern was that he get better soon and continue living his life. Danny prayed.

Walter went to sleep. He never spoke again. He stayed in a coma for the next four days, waking enough to open his eyes and blink, but he did not speak.

Danny and Jeannie took turns sitting beside him. Soon the room was full of flowers and cards. Friends sent messages and offers of assistance, but no one was allowed to go into the room except his wife and son. They were both with him when he died.

That memory flashed through Danny's mind as he drove to his mother's house. He had thought about it after the funeral, but he couldn't speak to his mother about it while she was grieving. He thought that some day she might want to tell him, but it had never been mentioned until today.

Jeannie was waiting for Danny in the living room.

"I am ready to have that talk." He came into the room. "Tell me what you know and I will fill in the details."

"I know very little. Dad told me just before he died that he was not my real father. It came as a shock, but things happened so quickly after that that I didn't have time to think about it. He said that my father was in the service and was shipped out to the war zone. What happened? Who is this Alex whom I met this morning? Should I be angry with him for deserting you?"

Jeannie repeated the story. "Alex didn't know that I was pregnant. I wrote him a 'Dear John' and told him I had married someone else. I never heard from him again." Jeannie looked at her hands the whole time she was talking.

"That was awful, Mother," Danny said.

"I had no choice. I wouldn't have considered an abortion. I couldn't bear to have a baby out of wedlock. Alex was being shipped out, I supposed to the war zone. There was a war going on. Things were completely out of our control."

"And nobody ever knew?" Danny asked.

"I told one person. Alex's mother, Mrs. Presswood. She promised not to tell. She took my secret to the grave."

Danny thought a second. "Do you mean that Mrs. Presswood was my grandmother? She was so good to me. I had no idea. If only I had known." Danny shook his head in disbelief.

"She knew that too many lives would have been disrupted if she had told. She never spoke to Alex about me and she never told him about you. She was a very wise woman."

"What did Alex say to you?" Danny asked.

"He said that he was sorry. He felt responsible for all that had happened, even for my emphysema since we had had our first cigarette together. And he asked me to marry him."

"Mother, you are engaged to Bill Simmons. You will have a wonderful life with Bill. I can't believe you would dump him for someone you haven't seen for fifty years. Bill will take such good care of you. And you have given him your word. Don't do anything foolish. Go ahead with your plans."

"I was hoping you would be more sympathetic toward your father, Danny."

"My father died over thirty years ago in a hospital in Monroeville, Alabama. This man, Alex, is not my father."

"He could have been."

"Could have been doesn't count. He could have been if he hadn't knocked you up and then gone away and left you."

"It wasn't Alex's fault. He loved me." Jeannie cried. "And don't talk to me like that."

"It came as a shock when I found out that I was a bastard. I have not married all of these years because I did not know who I was. It seems to me that you made the wrong decision then and are about to make the wrong decision again."

"I don't think we should be having this conversation. It is getting out of hand," Jeannie said.

"It seems to me that we should have had it many years ago."

"Danny, you are nearly fifty years old. You are a successful doctor.

You have had a good life. Walter and I did everything we could to make yours a normal, happy life because we loved you. It isn't fair of you to blame me for your decision to remain single." Jeannie had carried the guilt of her mistake for fifty years, but she was not willing to take the responsibility for Danny's misplaced judgment.

Danny waited a moment. "Let me retract that statement. I am single because I haven't found anyone I wanted to marry. The few girls I have been interested in just didn't have the same interest in me.

"Actually, I haven't spent much time worrying about who my biological father was. I shouldn't have said that. I am sorry. And I have drawn you from the subject you really wanted to talk about, haven't I?"

"I wanted to explain who Alex was and to tell you what happened. And I wanted to tell you that Bill wants me to marry him this afternoon at the church before the reunion."

Danny looked relieved. "Are you going to do it?"

"I was close to saying 'yes' when I found out that Bill knew that Alex was coming and seemed anxious for us to get married before I saw him."

"That certainly would eliminate the possibility of losing you to an old flame," Danny said. "A rather clever move, I would say."

"For Bill, yes. And it might have worked if I hadn't seen Alex this morning. Now I want to have a chance to talk to Alex. And I would like for you to get to know him."

"I think you are making a mistake. But I don't know what is in your heart. You made a tremendous sacrifice when you married a man you couldn't have loved to save a lifetime of humiliation. To marry Bill would be a sacrifice if you didn't feel deep love for him. Wait until you know for sure. Bill gets my vote at this time, but I don't know Alex. I will go along with whatever decision you make."

"Danny, you have said all of the right things. My head tells me to marry Bill at once, but my heart tells me to wait. I will wait until my head and my heart agree.

"Are you satisfied with the answers I have given you concerning Alex?"

"Yes. I really am glad you have explained it to me. Thank you." He kissed his mother on the cheek and gave her a hug.

"Have a great time at the reunion tonight," Danny went down the steps. "I'll see you soon."

*JEANNIE'S QUANDARY*

Bill had been devious about not telling her that Alex would be there for the reunion. As she talked with Alex this morning, the thrill of fifty years ago was still there. She wanted to be with Alex. She wanted to touch him, to kiss him, to melt in his arms as she had done when she was young. She wanted Alex to know their son and to love him as she did.

Where had the years gone? It seemed like yesterday when she had made the decision to give herself to Alex. It had not been done in a moment of passion. She had thought about it. She had dreamed about it. She had wanted it. She had encouraged Alex to take her so he would have the memory of their blissful moment to cherish in the months they would be apart.

She had loved Alex then, and now the memory of their young love, a memory that she had suppressed those many years was making its way back into her consciousness.

Alex was still handsome. His dark brown hair had turn to a soft silver grey. His expressive dark brown eyes were bright and clear. His smile was warm. His thin, firm lips pressed against hers sent shock waves through her body.

Bill arrived at Jeannie's door at a quarter to five, corsage in hand. He was dressed in a dark blue suit. He was shorter and thinner than Alex. In high school Bill had been bigger than Alex, but now Alex was a little taller, heavier, and much more handsome.

"We still have time to stop by the preacher's house and tie the knot before going to dinner," he said when Jeannie opened the door. He kissed her and held her at arm's length.

Jeannie was dressed in a pink silk pants suit. She wore an oval pendant that Bill had bought for her. "You look lovely. You will make a gorgeous bride, my darling."

"We have just enough time to get to the school house," Jeannie said, brushing aside his final attempt to get her to the alter.

This last refusal hit Bill between the eyes. He was about to lose Jeannie to the one person he hated most in the world.

"I can't believe you are doing this to me. I am offering you a chance to live a comfortable life with me, your physician, standing by to attend to your every need. You need me, Jeannie. And I need you. I love you,"

"Bill, I saw Alex this morning. I have to talk with him before I take this step with you. I know it has been a long time. Half a century. But I have some things to straighten out with Alex."

"About your bastard son? I figured that out as soon as I saw the two of them together. There is no mistaking the fact that your son and Alex's son are brothers. They look like twins. I figured it out. Everybody else will too."

"Bill!" How dare you speak of my son like that?" The anger masked her fear that what he said was true. Everyone would know.

"Oh, Jeannie, I am sorry. I just don't want to lose you. I love your son. We work well together. Please forgive me."

Jeannie turned away. "I'll drive myself to the dinner."

"Let me take you, Jeannie. We have planned this for so long. Please."

"I will go with you. But I will talk with Alex and everybody else." Then she added in a quiet, almost tender voice, "I haven't said I won't marry you. I just want some time. The fact that you now know my secret will make it easier for me to make a decision. You will have to be patient."

"We can be happy together. I know we can." Bill pinned the corsage on her shoulder and they walked to the car.

*THE REUNION*

They entered the second story room in which the reunion was being held. The room had been the library when the class of 1944 had attended school here. It had been renovated into an elegant social hall. There were tables and chairs at one end and a comfortable living room at the other. That is where the members of the class of 1944 and their spouses had gathered.

The senior citizens who had assembled looked at each other's nametags. Could these old people be the same ones they had known when they went to school here? Jeannie recognized no one except a few who still lived in Atmore. She heard her name being called and saw a little old lady approaching with outstretched arms. "Jeannie!" The shocked Jeannie had to read the nametag. "Dorothy!" she shouted. "You recognized me!"

"I was watching for you," Dorothy said. "Come sit down. Let's talk. Where have you been all of these years? Where do you live now?"

Jeannie answered her questions, and then asked the same ones. Her head whirled as stranger after stranger introduced themselves and asked questions about what she had been doing in the fifty years they had been apart. Everyone talked about their spouses, their children, and their grandchildren. They all laughed as the names and faces were matched up. Nobody looked the same. Skinny friends were now fat, fat ones were now skinny. Hair was grey or dyed, or in the case of many of the men, nonexistent.

They were requested to find seats in the dining area so that the servers could begin taking orders for their meals. Bill found Jeannie and they decided on a table near the center of the room. Bill wanted everybody to see him and Jeannie together. Each table was set up for eight. Two couples and two single ladies joined them. Jeannie was happy to be with old friends again.

Jeannie glanced around the room, trying to locate Alex. She finally spotted him across the room. She waved when she caught his eye.

Alex walked over to Jeannie's table. He kissed her on the cheek and acknowledged the others sitting with them. Then he found himself standing beside Bill Simmons. They shook hands warmly. After all, it had been fifty years. They exchanged greetings, but made no mention of Jeannie. Before he returned to his own table, he whispered to Jeannie, "Am I going to get to see you tonight?" He saw that the diamond was still on her finger.

"Yes, of course. As soon as possible."

"What was that all about?" Bill asked.

"What do you mean?" Jeannie asked.

"You know what I mean. Why did he have to come over and

act so innocent?"

"I thought he was very friendly, coming over and greeting all of us. Do you object to that?"

"Well, it is a reunion. But you came with me. You are my date this time. Not like in high school when you couldn't see anyone else but Alex Presswood."

"Bill, I told you I wanted to talk with Alex. I want to talk with everybody here. I am anxious to know what my friends have been doing all of these years. Don't you?"

"I don't care about any of them. You are the only person I care about, the only one I want to talk to."

Jeannie felt suffocated. She began to gasp for breath. She searched in her purse for the inhaler that she used when she felt the need for more air. She couldn't find it. *Calm down. Take slow, deep breaths. Stay in control.* She looked down with her hands folded in her lap. Bill noticed that she was pacing her breath deliberately and asked if she was all right.

"I left my inhaler in the car, on the seat. Would you get it for me?"

"I told you to keep that inhaler with you at all times," Bill scolded. "You never know when you will need it. I will get it for you." He hurried out to the car.

Alex saw Bill leave. He saw Jeannie sitting quietly at her table and knew there was a problem. He hurried over to her. "Can I help?" he asked.

"Alex, I felt so overwhelmed. I have trouble breathing sometimes, but I can control it if I just sit quietly and breathe slowly. I will be all right in a minute or two. Bill has gone to get my inhaler."

"OK. If you are sure you are all right. When can I see you, Jeannie?"

"Pick me up at ten o'clock tomorrow. We'll talk. Go back to your table now. Bill will be jealous if he sees us talking."

"Tomorrow at ten." Alex walked back to his table. He saw Bill come back in.

"Did you miss me?" Bill sat down.

Jeannie started to say "yes" just to be polite, but she knew she would be lying. In fact, she was glad he had been gone. She felt uncomfortable being here with Bill. She looked at him. She had accepted his proposal because it seemed right. She had needed him as her doctor and her friend. But did she really want to spend the rest of her life with this man? Jeannie did not answer his question. She asked if he had found her inhaler.

"It was on the seat. You should be more careful."

Jeannie took the inhaler and asked to be excused. She would use it in the restroom.

"I'll go with you," Bill said.

"I can go alone, thank you."

"I don't want you walking all over the place alone. You have just gotten out of the hospital. I'll walk with you."

"If you insist."

Jeannie stepped into a stall and began using her inhaler. She put the cover down and sat down for a few minutes to regain her composure.

"Did you see that silly Bill Simmons?" she heard a voice say. "He won't even let Jeannie go to the bathroom alone. I guess he is afraid she will speak to someone else." Jeannie tried to make out who was talking, but she didn't recognize the voice.

"He said he was her doctor," a second voice said. "Can you imagine Bill Simmons a doctor?"

"He's the last person I would have expected to become a doctor."

"Well, he was kind of smart in school."

"Not as smart as Alex Presswood. I wonder why Alex and Jeannie broke up."

"She met someone else in college."

"I saw Alex. He is gorgeous. If I were Jeannie, I'd drop Bill in a minute and make a beeline for that beautiful hunk."

"Did you see the diamond ring she is wearing? It would be hard to give that up."

"Not if she knew what a rough time he gave his first wife. My cousin lived next door to them in Brewton. She said Bill ran around on her and paid no attention to her or the children. He claimed he was too busy working. Sure, that is a nice ring, but she will probably end up paying for it. He's a compulsive gambler, you know. He goes all over the country hitting casinos and racetracks. He gambles on anything. I heard he won that Mercedes he drives in a Poker game."

"I'll bet Jeannie doesn't know that."

"Somebody ought to tell her, but not me. I don't want to get mixed up in other people's business."

They quit talking when someone else came in. Jeannie waited until she heard the door slam several times before she came out of the stall. She stopped in front of the mirror to check her hair and lipstick.

She met Bill outside the restroom door. He was talking with some people Jeannie didn't know. When he saw Jeannie, he walked over and grabbed her hand.

"Come on. Our food is getting cold. I paid good money for this dinner and I don't like to eat cold food."

"You are hurting my arm."

"Oh am I? I'm sorry." Bill continued to lead her to their table.

Jeannie felt threatened again. She sat down and tried to catch her breath. She didn't want Bill to know she was having difficulty so she sat still and took quick, short breaths. Conversation was loud. She listened to the squeals of joy that erupted when long-ago friends came face to face with each other again. Jeannie knew that Bill would insist on taking her home or to the hospital and hooking her up to a respirator if he knew how she felt. She didn't want to miss a minute of the excitement, so she sat there willing herself to get over the attack.

A few moments passed before she felt well enough to begin eating her meal. She picked at her food just enough to assure Bill that she was eating. Bill had been looking around the room. He knew a few of his classmates because he ran into them from time to time, but he did not consider engaging anyone in conversation.

"Do you know any of these people?" Bill asked.

"I have met three or four whom I recognized, but most of them have changed so much. I guess we have changed too. You don't notice it as much when you look at the same face in the mirror each day.

"I once saw an artist take a blob of clay and fashion the face of a young boy. Then he changed the face just a little and the boy was clearly a teenager. He changed it again to a young adult, then an older adult, and finally to a very old man. It was amazing how just a pinch here or a squeeze there could make the face reflect aging."

Bill was looking around. "Some of the girls are more attractive now than they were in high school. And most of the girls have kept their weight down. I expected to see more stout ladies, didn't you?" He chuckled.

"The ladies have done a good job, but I have seen lots of pot bellies on the men."

"So have I," Bill laughed. He was comparing other men with his slim, well-preserved physique.

"Keeping in shape is not an easy job," Jeannie said.

"It is for me. I know how much to eat and I never eat more than I should."

"You do a nice job with your weight." Jeannie disliked the way Bill gloated.

"I wonder how many doctors we have in this group." Bill was beaming. "I don't suppose Alex Presswood made it to medical school."

"Why do you say that?"

"I didn't hear anyone calling him Dr. Presswood, did you? His name was listed as Mr. Presswood in the register."

"I didn't notice that. I wonder what he did become."

"You didn't ask him?"

"No. I just thought that he had become a doctor like he always planned."

"I don't think so," Bill said sarcastically. "Why don't you ask him?"

"I'll do just that." But Bill didn't move. "I didn't notice that he drove up in a Mercedes Benz either."

"What did he drive?"

"He had a Lincoln Continental."

"Not a bad car."

"Just doesn't compare with a Mercedes."

"Where did you get that car, Bill?"

Bill squirmed. "In Memphis."

"Where?"

"Well I was playing Poker with this guy. I got everything he had,"

Bill laughed. "He bet me his new Mercedes that he could beat me. He had a full house, but I had four Aces. Nothing beats four Aces."

"And you took his car?"

"I won that car fair and square."

"You are a gambler," she cried.

"I am a doctor. You know that. So I play a little Poker on the side. It's fun. Poker is a challenge. It keeps you sharp."

"Suppose the other guy had won? What did you wager?"

"I bet my summer place in Gulf Shores. But I knew I was going to win. I only bet on a sure thing."

"You were betting that I wouldn't see Alex before the dinner, weren't you? You were betting that I would marry you before I knew he was coming. You knew he was coming and you didn't tell me."

"Sure, I knew he was coming and, yes, I wanted to marry you before he had a chance to break us up."

"I can't marry you under these circumstances. Take your ring back. It is beautiful, but the stakes are too high. Don't worry about seeing me home. I can make it on my own. I can find another doctor, too." She took off the ring and placed it in his hand. "There," she said.

"I haven't paid for it yet anyway. I'll just take it back to the store." Jeannie got up and walked over to Alex. "May I sit with you?"

"Certainly. What happened?"

"I just want to be with you, Alex. Can we talk?"

"Come over, sit with me. Tell me what is bothering you."

"Alex, I can't marry Bill. The moment I saw you in the hospital, I knew I wanted to be with you. I found out some things tonight about Bill that would make marrying him impossible. I want to spend time with you so that we both know that our love is genuine, not just an infatuation because of the excitement of seeing each other again. Getting back together would mean serious changes in our lives."

"I meant what I said to you earlier. I love you. I don't know how I was able to put you out of my mind for so many years. It is as if that part of my life is blanked out. Loving you is so easy, so right. Do you have the same feelings?"

"Just this morning I was planning to marry another man. I thought I loved him. But I was substituting security for love. What a mistake that would have been."

## *EPILOGUE*

It took Jeannie and Alex only a few hours together to know that they wanted to spend their remaining years together. Jeannie made the decision before she knew that Alex was a wealthy man. She thought she was giving up a comfortable future for the man she loved, only to find that the man she loved could provide everything her heart desired.

Alex drove Jeannie home after the reunion. They stayed in each other's arms until the golden rays of the morning sun began to creep through the windows and chase away the shadows that lay in the dimly lit living room. They would be together from this day forward.

Jules and David stayed in Atmore for the wedding. How could anyone doubt that the two men standing up with their parents were brothers? They looked like twins. Jules stood with his father, Daniel with his mother. Liz and Marge came to the wedding with their husbands, and Agnes flew in from California. Jeannie's sister and brother were there. The ceremony took place following the Sunday morning service and the congregation was invited to attend.

Classmates from the class of 1944 were invited and many attended. They witnessed the union of their two friends who would have been married fifty years earlier if the war had not interfered. Alex found a contractor to build Jeannie's dream house on land he had inherited from his parents. He and Jeannie traveled first to New Orleans, then to California via the Panama Canal. In California, he made the same arrangements with Jules that Mr. Yardley had made with him when he took over his agency in 1951. Jules would give his father 10% of his net profit, assuring him of an income for the rest of his life. Jules moved into his father's home and Jesus and Maria remained as caretaker and housekeeper.

David visited his grandfather often when Alex moved back to Alabama. Later, he decided he wanted to attend the University of Alabama.

Alex was interested in Daniel's profession because it was the one he had wanted to pursue. After he and Jeannie returned home from a honeymoon trip to England, a trip he had promised himself fifty years earlier, he went back to school and became a medical assistant. His health was good, his state of mind was excellent, and he did not wish to remain idle. Daniel encouraged him to follow his dream and he let Alex assist him when it was feasible. The father and son relationship was equal to the relationship he enjoyed with Jules.

Jules and Daniel became friends. Daniel liked the climate in California and flew out for vacations every chance he got. Daniel fell in love with a nurse who worked with him and they were married. He adopted her three teen-aged daughters.

Jeannie learned to control her breathing by keeping calm and by taking short, shallow breaths when she became excited. The previously incurable disease, emphysema, was found to respond to a derivative of Vitamin A and was arrested by the use of Retinic Acid. She was able to live a normal life with infrequent stays in the hospital.

Bill Simmons moved to Gulf Shores while Jeannie and Alex were on their honeymoon. He married a young waitress he met in a bar.

# About the Author

Elizabeth Ann Scott wrote her first poem at age eight and continued writing poetry and stories during her school years. Some poems were published in her school's newspaper, the ESCOHI.

Encouraged by her family to focus on making a living during hard times, Elizabeth attended a teachers college for two years. She started teaching at nineteen. During the next five years she taught school and continued her education in the summer. She received her B.S. Degree in Education and taught school for forty years.

Elizabeth often wrote stories, plays, and poetry for her students. While working toward a Masters Degree, she wrote a book for her Children's Literature class. She has also written biographies of her mother and for William Marvin Bass, the person for whom the school she taught in was named.

Her poem, *RELIEF THAT THE ORDEAL IS OVER* (Iran hostages release) was published in *THE LYNCHBURG NEWS AND ADVANCE*.

*REUNION* had been on Elizabeth's mind for a long time. When she retired she worked hard to complete it. Writing is Elizabeth's hobby. She also loves to travel. She and her husband visited every state in the U.S. except Hawaii and Alaska and also traveled in Canada and Mexico. Elizabeth's three sons encourage her to continue writing.